THE
NIGHT
CROSSING

ALSO BY ROBERT MASELLO

FICTION

The Jekyll Revelation
The Einstein Prophecy
The Romanov Cross
The Medusa Amulet
Blood and Ice
Vigil
Bestiary
Black Horizon
Private Demons
The Spirit Wood

NONFICTION

Robert's Rules of Writing
Writer Tells All
A Friend in the Business
The Things Your Father Never Taught You
What Do Men Want from Women?
Fallen Angels and Spirits of the Dark
Raising Hell: A Concise History of the Black Arts

THE
NIGHT
CROSSING

ROBERT MASELLO

47N⬥RTH

Published by 47North, Seattle

www.apub.com

Amazon, the Amazon logo, and 47North are trademarks of Amazon.com, Inc., or its affiliates.

ISBN-13: 9781503904101 (hardcover)
ISBN-10: 1503904105 (hardcover)
ISBN-13: 9781503904118 (paperback)
ISBN-10: 1503904113 (paperback)

Cover design by Kirk DouPonce, DogEared Design

Printed in the United States of America

First edition

For Mary Joan,
with love and unbounded admiration

The centurion banged the hilt of his sword against the blacksmith's door, and when the blacksmith answered, the centurion said, "Nails! We need nails."

But the blacksmith, seeing the commotion in the road, said, "The only nails I have are for horseshoes. They're not the kind you need."

The centurion then went to the wheelwright's house, and the wheelwright said, "Mine are all in wagon wheels. I don't have any left."

At the tinker's house, the man who answered the door said, "Nails? Yes, I can sell you some."

"And a hammer, too."

The centurion threw some silver coins to the ground, and the tinker gave him the hammer and the nails.

That night, a terrible storm broke out, destroying the tinker's house and everything in it. But when he went to the other houses for help, the doors were all closed against him.

The next morning, with only the clothes on their backs, the tinker and his wife walked down the road, beneath the shadow of the three crosses, and into other lands . . . where they, and all who ever descended from them, are condemned to walk unto Judgment Day . . .

1895

CHAPTER ONE

The Carpathian Mountains
Romania
October 31

"Hurry!" she said, consulting her pocket watch yet again. "There isn't much time!" Dusk was fast approaching.

Cezar, the oldest and thus the lead porter, grunted, and the two men behind him muttered something to each other that she couldn't make out over the rising wind. It wasn't hard to guess its tenor, however; they didn't like taking orders from a young woman, much less one of Romany ancestry. If she hadn't offered them more money than they'd make in a year of goat herding, she'd have had to make this climb alone, toting her tripod and camera along with all her provisions and her tent.

Glancing to the east, she saw a bank of turbulent dark clouds racing toward them like a legion of demons rushing to protect their lord; that lord reigned, if she had plotted her course correctly, no more than a few hundred yards farther up the craggy mountainside.

It had taken her weeks to reach this remote stretch of the Carpathian mountain range, and a steady climb all day to get where she was going now. If legend had it right, then she had to be there, camera set up and ready, at the precise moment when the sun set on this, All Hallows'

Eve, the night that witches flew through the skies and evil held sway over the world.

But she was running late.

The ascent had begun in flower-filled meadows and densely forested valleys, and her heart had been light. The air was cool, but not yet cold, and rich with the scent of evergreen and pine. Red hawks had circled overhead; fat black bears had swatted fish from the rushing streams; deer had peered fearfully from the trees. Apart from the three bearers she had hired in Sinaia, she had not seen a human in many days. It was a primeval place, with nothing of the modern world—no glaring gas lamps, sputtering electricity, or clanging trolley cars—to disturb the natural quiet, and she had hiked on, head down under her wide-brimmed hat, rapt in her own thoughts and observations, searching the ground for any errant clue or geological anomaly.

"You'll never need spectacles," her father had often proclaimed. "You see more than an owl." That's why he'd named her Minerva—Mina, for short—after the wise goddess who kept a pet owl and saw everything.

But making her way up the steep mountainside now, she'd have been glad of a bright lantern. She had to be careful not to trip over the jagged stones, or set a cascade of loose scree skittering down onto Cezar, Anton, and Radu. The trees and brush had given way far below, and up here—roughly eight thousand feet above sea level—it was nothing but bald, wind-scoured rock and barren earth, pockmarked by caves as black as they were forbidding.

"They're coming," she heard Radu say to Cezar, nodding toward the oncoming clouds.

"We should turn around," Anton threw in.

Cezar, the grizzled veteran, barked at them to shut their mouths. "What, are you afraid of fairy tales?"

Mina pretended not to hear, keeping her eyes on the uneven ground and plowing ahead. What would she do, she wondered, if a full-blown mutiny erupted?

And then, even as the sun passed below the trio of surrounding gray peaks—called the Old Women because of their fearsome, hunched-over shapes—she saw in the gathering gloom a flat plateau, the size of a town square. But where a town square might be laid out before a church or city hall, this one was dominated by something else entirely—a massive brooding figure cut from the stone, easily thirty feet high and nearly half as broad. The sight of it stopped her in her tracks, and Cezar, who had been watching the ground himself, bumped into her.

Then he stopped, too, and looked up.

The figure was a sphinx, the mythical monster from Middle Eastern legend and lore—the great half-human, half-lion beast, resting on its haunches, whose baleful stare had gazed out over the Saharan desert for millennia, whose headdress—the iconic *nemes*—echoed the Egyptian pharaohs' own.

But to find it here, of all places, thousands of miles from the delta of the Nile or the Valley of the Kings, atop a nearly inaccessible Carpathian mountain peak, its huge empty eye sockets looking west toward the pale sun setting over the cliffs and treetops of neighboring Transylvania, was unnerving. Mina thought she had been prepared for it—she had heard the stories; she had seen the original monument squatting on the desert sands—but she had not been as prepared as she thought. Not for this. Her mouth fell open in wonder.

"Mother of God, protect us," Radu said, dropping to his knees and crossing himself three times.

"How long do we have to be here?" Anton asked anxiously. "We've seen it—now let's go!"

"Not until we've done what we came here to do," Mina ordered, throwing him a coiled rope marked with a knot every three yards. "The sooner you help, the sooner we can be gone."

"What am I supposed to do with this?"

"Measure the depth and width of the plateau, and put it down in the log."

She tossed him that, too.

"And me?" Radu asked.

"You've got your chisel and bag?"

"Yes."

"Take samples of each kind of rock you see." A quick survey, even in this dull light, showed striations of everything from granite to shale. Of these, too, she would need to take photographs—the layering of the various strata would tell her, after careful analysis, what the age of this megalithic sculpture might be. But that would have to wait until tomorrow; they'd spend the night down the slope, wherever they could find a spot sheltered enough to pitch their tents, and then come back with the morning light.

For now, she estimated that she had only half an hour or so before the last rays of the setting sun were directly focused on the face of the sphinx—even less if the storm clouds picked up speed. "Cezar, help me find a flat spot for the tripod."

Together, they paced back and forth across the plateau, the smooth rock almost imperceptibly swelling and undulating, until Cezar called out, "Here," stamping his walking stick on the ground. "This is a good place."

He was right. Glancing at the sculpture, she shouldn't have been surprised—the flat area was smack in front of its face, at a distance of ten or twelve yards. The exact spot where a supplicant, or ancient priest conducting some long-forgotten ritual, might have stood.

"Yes, set it up." While Cezar used the edge of his boot to sweep the rock free of grit and wrestled the legs of the tripod apart and into place, she opened her canvas satchel and removed the camera and plates. It was a field view model, heavy and unwieldy, but the accuracy and depth of its photographs, captured by the precision Zeiss lenses, were unrivaled. She hadn't let any of the others carry it for even a moment; it was too critical to her mission.

Resting its bulk now atop the tripod and securing it in place, she removed the velvet lens cap and bent her head to the eyepiece. The sculpture, though much eroded by wind and weather, was startlingly powerful—perhaps even more so than when it had been carved ages ago. Its broad face had vacant eye sockets—the size of carriage wheels—sunken beneath a protuberant brow and low forehead. The nose was wide and flat, the cheeks hollow. But it was the lips that gave the thing much of its effect—long and thin, they suggested an utter indifference to life.

If this had indeed been a god, it had not been a benevolent one.

"You'd better take that picture now," Cezar warned. "The storm is coming."

She could feel its effects, the ends of her long black hair escaping her hat and whipping around her shoulders. Her trousers fluttered around her legs, and she was buffeted by one gust of wind and then another, forcing her to adjust her stance and use both hands to hold the creaking armature in place.

"What difference will a few minutes make?" Cezar asked, and Anton and Radu, back from their tasks, seconded him.

"Let's go," Radu said, "before it's too late!"

"It's already too late," Anton, ever the pessimist, chimed in. "She's going to get us all killed!"

But Mina was determined to wait. By her watch, the one her father had given her when they had explored the globe together, it should only be another minute or two before the official sunset. Even now, the last rays of light were slanting past the neighboring peaks, as if seeking out the sphinx, to lend their blessing, or their curse.

She lowered her head to the camera, making fine calibrations to the shutter and lens. But she had never had so much trouble bringing an image into focus. It was as if the stone itself deliberately resisted her.

And then, as she watched, tendrils of pale orange light touched its face. The eyes, a moment ago so black, blazed as if rudely awakened from an ancient slumber. The nostrils seemed to flare, and the lips . . . the lips, dispassionate and firm a second before, seemed to take on a slight tilt at the ends, lending the visage a tinge of cruelty. And was there even a hint, heretofore imperceptible, of fangs?

"Take the picture!" Radu shouted.

"Yes," even the gray-haired Cezar implored. "There's something evil here. We have to go!"

So astonished had she been, she had momentarily forgotten to depress the lever and snap the photograph. She did so now, and in the nick of time—a moment later, an icy blast of wind and rain extinguished the animation of the face like a candle being snuffed out. The tripod toppled as if by an invisible hand. If she had not had a firm grip on the camera, it, too, would have crashed to the ground. As it was, she was barely able to save it by landing on her side, with the camera cradled against her abdomen and her face upturned to the pelting rain. A lightning bolt split the black clouds churning above her. Blinking to clear her eyes, she turned her gaze and once again saw the sleeping, impassive face of the monster hewn from the rock . . . though now, and of this she had no doubt, it had seen her, too.

CHAPTER TWO

LONDON

Mephistopheles, clad in scarlet from the tip of his curling tail to the cock feather sticking up from his pointed cap, emerged from a cleft in the rock, Faust clinging to his leg in abject terror. Lightning flashed in the sky, thunder rolled, and scores of tortured souls writhed in agony, wailing and rending their tattered clothes.

Watching from the wings of the Lyceum Theatre, Bram Stoker signaled a stagehand to turn on the limelight that was aimed at the *Book of the Damned* held by the devil, the book that the philosopher Faust had signed in his own blood. The light hit the book squarely, and the audience gasped—they always did—at the power of the effect. This scene—atop the Brocken on Walpurgisnacht, at the opening of act 4—was not only the pièce de résistance of the show, but the most impressive spectacle anyone had ever mounted on the London stage. There were four hundred ropes and pulleys overhead, and every one of them had a unique function and even a name. Stoker knew them all by heart, and could direct the stage crew to raise or lower anything from a flying angel to a witch on a broomstick, to open a trapdoor and send someone straight to hell, or to release another cannonball down the boilerplate to simulate a thunderclap. It had taken months of planning, and inordinate expense, to present this terrifying tableau—not to mention the hiring of throngs of young men and women to impersonate the souls of the damned and the demons that tormented them—but it had all been worth it. The play had taken London by storm. The only bad notice they had received was from that overly fastidious American author Henry James, who called it "a horror cheaply conceived, and executed with more zeal than discretion." Fortunately, Stoker knew enough about publicity to know that even a review like that would sell tickets. Every performance had been sold out, even up in "the gods," as the cheapest balcony seats were commonly known. Stoker couldn't see up there now—the stage lights were too bright—but on his earlier tour of the house, he had counted every seat filled, and dozens of more people milling about in the standing-room-only area.

Henry Irving, the owner of the theater and presently engaged on stage in the role of Mephistopheles himself, would be very pleased with the results of his costly gamble.

"But what of Margaret?" Faust cried out from center stage. "Surely God shall spare a soul so pure and repentant as that?"

The devil, drawing himself up to his full height and waving the book aloft, said, "I see not her name among the damned. No signature in blood to cast her among the doomed."

"Christ Jesus I thank for that," Faust declared. "Mercy yet reigns on high."

"But not here!" Mephistopheles replied, pointing a long, crooked nail at Faust. "Here, I rule alone."

Stoker waved his hand from the wings, and another cannonball went thundering down the chute.

The audience was rapt, and there were even those who claimed, after each performance, that Irving had levitated during this scene. Although Stoker knew better—there were no ropes attached to hoist him—he understood that the power of the performance was so great as to create that impression. Henry Irving was, in Stoker's estimation, the greatest actor Britain had ever produced, and he was proud to serve as his general factotum and manager of his theater.

After the curtain fell—and Irving and Ellen Terry, in the role of Margaret, had taken half a dozen bows—Stoker retreated to his office to tally the night's receipts. He was nearly done when Irving, his long face still raw from scrubbing off all the rouge, appeared in the doorway and said, "Full house again?"

"To bursting," Stoker replied. "Shall we toast to the evening's take?"

"You need never ask me that twice," he said, folding his lean frame into the chair on the opposite side of the desk.

Stoker took the bottle of Scotch from a drawer, poured a generous portion into two glasses, and with a finger slid one of them between the piles of pound notes and loose coins that littered the desktop.

"To Faust!" Irving said, raising his glass.

"To the devil!" Stoker replied with a laugh.

They drank, then discussed the same things they usually did—ways in which the show could be even more effective, programs and autographed items that could be sold in the lobby at intermission, general finances. Irving had little grasp of monetary issues, but he liked to give the impression that he was as wise a businessman as he was an actor. It was up to Stoker to keep the place running at a decent profit, which, despite the rich returns, wasn't easy—the expenses, too, were staggering.

Irving was always more reluctant than Stoker to end these colloquies—he was a man who feared silence and solitude—but eventually, he left Stoker to finish the books, lock up, and make his own way home.

Even at this late hour, the streets were never entirely deserted. It was one of the many things Stoker appreciated about the city and his late-night walks. He had his inner demons to attend to, not to mention a wife at home whose bedroom door had been closed to him, more often than not, since the birth of their son. Florence Balcombe had been a celebrated beauty in her day—wooed by none other than Oscar Wilde, among countless others—and Stoker had considered it a coup when she had consented to marry him seventeen years before. He was not unattractive—burly, bearded, with deep-set blue eyes and an innate Irish charm—but back then he was not exactly a catch. He'd been scratching out a living as a clerk at Dublin Castle—a job his father, who had worked there for decades, had procured for him—while trying to make some name for himself writing journalism and the occasional gory Gothic tale. But despite his mathematics degree from Trinity College, he had not securely established himself in any profession.

Which was when Fortune struck quite out of the blue.

A laudatory review of *Hamlet* that he had written in the *Dublin Evening Mail* caught the eye of its principal performer, and Henry Irving had invited him to dinner in thanks. Over whiskey and cigars at the Shelbourne Hotel, overlooking St. Stephen's Green, they had discovered that they agreed on a great many things, most notably the urgent need for a renaissance of the English theater. By daybreak, when Stoker finally staggered out of the hotel, he was in the actor's employ.

A night wind carried the unmistakable scent of the Thames—mud and brine, sea and sewage—his way. He liked to take his leisurely stroll home along the esplanade, smoking a cigar and watching the boats unload at the West India docks. It was not an altogether safe place at this hour, but a bobby could usually be relied upon to pass by with his whistle and lantern every quarter hour or so. Tonight, the moon was nearly full, and Stoker sauntered past a parked carriage, its horse munching on a tuft of grass and weeds while the driver snored soundly, slumped atop his box. Up ahead, in the flickering glow of a gas lamp, he spied a lone figure leaning against the iron railing, her gaze turned toward the black water churning below.

It was an unlikely spot for a lady of the evening to be prospecting for customers—they generally hung about the pubs and busier thoroughfares. There was only one reason she was likely to be here at all, and she wouldn't be the first.

He tossed his cigar over the railing and, coughing so as not to startle her, walked slowly in her direction. She did not acknowledge his approach—indeed, he had no way of knowing if she was even aware of it—but when he got closer, he swore he had seen her before. That very night, as it happened, in the gods, standing behind the last row of seats, waiting for the curtain to rise.

Thus providing him with the perfect opening.

"Pardon the intrusion," he said, doffing his beaver-skin top hat while maintaining his distance, "but I believe you attended the Lyceum tonight."

She made no answer.

"Allow me to introduce myself. I'm Bram Stoker, the theater manager. May I ask if the performance lived up to your expectations?"

Though she remained silent, her head turned slightly. She had pale eyes but ruddy skin, especially on one side of her face, where he noted that her mouth looked swollen.

"We are always keen to know what our audience thinks," Stoker went on, simply to keep her distracted. "And by all means you may speak frankly."

"It was . . ." she said, in a soft, slurred voice, "terrible."

Not what he was expecting. "Terrible, in what sense? As in badly done? Or, as in frightening to behold?"

"Both."

Her eyes finally came up to meet his, and if he'd had any doubt about her intentions, he didn't now. There was a bottomless despair in them.

"Well then, I guess we've done our job too well and not well enough. Our aim was to create a vision like nothing you'd ever seen before, but to carry it off with style. What didn't you like?"

"You ought not to do that to people."

"Do what precisely?"

"Show them hell."

"It's a part of the story that we couldn't very well avoid. Faust does indeed sell his soul to the devil."

"But hell is so much worse than even you made it. Yours is all trickery. Hell is real."

"And how would someone so young as you know that?"

"Because I am going there."

"Oh, I doubt that," he said. "I doubt that very strongly. Come along now, why don't we walk a bit," he said, hoping to cajole her away from the rail, "and you can tell me more. I'm quite interested in what you have to say."

But she was having none of it. Her fingers gripped the railing.

He was failing in his mission. He pretended to shiver and rubbed his hands together briskly to warm them. "It's getting colder by the minute, don't you think? Why don't we see if we can find someplace warm? Perhaps I can treat you to something to eat or drink. Hot tea? A brandy?"

"I am not one of . . . those women," she said, turning away. "Please leave me be."

"My apologies," he said, backing off. "I meant no offense."

There was nothing more he could do but walk on, and from a short distance keep watch until a constable happened by on his rounds. He took up his vigil in the shadow of an elm, and when at last he did hear an approaching footfall and saw the swinging of a bull's-eye lantern, he stepped out.

But the girl must have noted it, too, and decided to take action before it was too late. As carefully as one might mount a stepladder to dust the library shelves, she hoisted her skirt and coat and clambered over the iron railing.

"Stop!" Stoker cried out, racing toward her. "Stop!"

She hesitated on the brink for just a second before she leaped forward over the brushy bank, splashing into the water.

Stoker threw off his coat and hat and swung himself over the railing.

"What's going on?" the constable shouted. "You there, stop where you are!"

But Stoker shouted back, "A girl's gone over!" Then he dove into the river.

He landed with a mighty splash and went several feet under. The water was black and frigid, and he put his hands out blindly in all directions, hoping to find her. Bobbing to the surface, he took a breath, then submerged again, already carried a yard or two downstream. He could see nothing, but suddenly felt the fabric of her coat and clenched it with all the strength in his fingers. She was sinking, but he was able to arrest her descent and drag her up.

Once her head was above water, he wrapped an arm around her shoulders and kicked for the riverbank. He felt her hands on his chest, but instead of holding onto him, she was struggling to break free.

"Stop that!" he sputtered, hauling her toward the muddy fringe of the river.

"Let me go."

"Not till you're safe."

With his free hand, he snagged a broken piling. His feet found the riverbed, and he was able to straighten up just enough to lift her out of the water. She was far heavier than he would have imagined, which he attributed to the weight of her soaked clothes. It was only after he had wrestled her out of her overcoat that he saw the broken bricks tumble from its pockets. Plainly, she had not wanted to float.

The policeman had made his way down, and with his hand under one of her arms and Stoker's under the other, they got her back up the slope and over the railing. She had stopped fighting but moved like a sleepwalker. They laid her on a bench, and the policeman blew his whistle for help.

"You're a mighty lucky young lady," the constable said to her. "Pulling a stunt like that and living to tell the tale. You'll be spending the night under lock and key, I can guarantee you that."

Remonstrating with her, Stoker knew, would do little good, and he feared that as soon as she was at liberty, she would try it again, perhaps with more success. But what could have convinced such a young woman to end her life? As a fellow human being, he wanted to know, but as an occasional writer of morbid tales, he had a professional curiosity as well.

Picking up his coat from the ground, Stoker drew it over her. "You'll be all right now," he assured her. "Everything will come right. You'll see."

She looked up at him and between her chattering teeth, whispered something.

"What was that?" he said, lowering his ear.

"God may forgive you," she said. "But I never will."

He drew back in horror. The constable asked the girl for her name, her address, her occupation, but she made no reply. Then he took down Stoker's name and information, "for the official record."

Within minutes, another policeman arrived, commandeered the coach, whose driver had been awakened by the whistle, and the girl with no name was taken off.

"Will she go to jail?" Stoker asked.

"Not tonight, she won't," the constable replied. "There's a lockdown ward at St. Thomas's Hospital. That's where the suicides are sent."

Suicides. It was an odd word, but Stoker was relieved to hear that she would receive medical care rather than a cold cell, and resolved to follow up on the case to see that she made a full recovery.

"You're a bit of a hero, you are," the policeman said. "Once I turn in my report and the papers get a hold of it, don't be surprised if you get a free round at your pub."

It was the last thing on Stoker's mind, and now that the excitement of the event was wearing off, along with the adrenaline, he began to feel his exposure to the night, coatless and drenched. Only his beaver-skin hat was dry.

"Can you make it home all right?"

"Yes," Stoker said. "It's not that far, and I travel fast."

"Well then, good night to you. Get into a hot bath, mind you, or you'll catch your death."

"I shall."

"You've done a good deed tonight, Mr."—he referred to his notepad—"Stoker."

But had he? Was the girl suffering from some malady that would take her life anyway, but only after prolonged suffering? Or was it just a case of a broken heart she was unable to bear? But if that were true, why would she believe she was going to hell? Had she committed some heinous crime—it seemed unthinkable—or, more likely, some trivial offense that had grown to monstrous proportion in her mind? He could not credit any of it. Nor, all the way home, where he entered quietly by the side door and shrugged off his wet clothes, could he fathom her final reproof:

"God may forgive you, but I never will."

CHAPTER THREE

As soon as the sun had fully set over the Carpathians, the temperature plummeted, too, and the cold rain turned to hailstones that drummed down so hard Mina feared not only for the safety of herself and her crew, but also for the integrity of the camera. She had come so far, and at such cost, she did not want to lose the photograph to an ice storm— especially one which, irrational as it was, seemed to have been conjured by the sphinx itself.

Getting down the mountain in the dark would have been a feat, but to do so in the teeth of this storm was well-nigh impossible. Cezar led the way, swinging his lantern to and fro to guide them down the rocky slope, until the lantern stopped, and the old man shouted, "It's too dangerous! We can't go on."

"We can't pitch the tents here," Radu hollered back.

"They won't stand for five minutes!" Anton added.

"The caves!" Cezar cried out over the howling wind. "We have to use a cave."

Mina knew that the very prospect would strike terror into the hearts of her porters, and she had hoped to avoid it. The entire mountain was considered sacred, though more in a superstitious sense than a reverential one. The caves were considered the tombs of a people so ancient as to defy belief—the survivors of the Great Flood that Noah had weathered in his ark. But there was no avoiding it now—the hail was turning to a swirl of wet snow that made the ground too slick even to stand on, much less descend.

Waving his lantern at a black hole in the mountain and pointing his walking stick, Cezar said, "There!"

Mina immediately made for the cave, sheltering the camera in her arms like a baby, and ducking her head at the entrance. Inside, the slashing of the snow and ice instantly stopped, the screaming of the wind in her ears abated, and she was surrounded by a silence that seemed as old as time. Cezar came in a moment later, the others following like sheep at his heels, shaking off the snow, dropping their drenched rucksacks, and looking around with wide and fearful eyes.

The ceiling of the cave was low and punctuated with sharp spikes pointing down like the bottom of a portcullis gate. The damp walls reflected the lantern's light, though only for a yard or two—beyond that was an impenetrable blackness. Perhaps to keep his men from focusing on that empty void, Cezar ordered them to unload the supplies and start a fire.

"And burn what?" Radu sneered.

Cezar stuck his stick in the ground at an angle, then stomped on the shaft three times until it snapped. He tossed the pieces at them.

"Soak them in the kerosene, and they'll burn long enough to melt some snow and heat some of the sausage."

Mina took a spot along one wall, not far from the entrance, and lovingly dried the outer camera case. She was soaked to the skin—they all were—and a fire of any kind would be welcome. Cezar plopped down on the opposite side, fished inside his sheepskin coat, and produced a short briar pipe. Apparently, he'd also kept his matches dry because a few moments later the smell of tobacco wafted around the cave, and he chucked the box of matches at Anton.

"Get it done the first time," he said. "Don't waste them."

They ate their rations in silence, huddled around the tiny fire as the storm raged outside. What would they do, Mina wondered, if it did not let up by morning? Or for days? They'd freeze to death if they couldn't get down the mountainside.

When the last of the stick had burned, augmented by several pencils and the unused pages of the log, they retired to their chosen spots and curled into balls to preserve whatever warmth their own bodies could provide. Anton and Radu stuck close together, and before she fell asleep with the camera nestled beside her cheek, Mina could hear them muttering in the dark.

Her dreams were muddled, and, as was so often the case with her kind, they seemed to portend things to come. Her people were reputedly blessed—or cursed—with the gift of second sight, with the ability to grasp what others could not, to access a realm invisible to anyone other than the Romanies. Her ancestors, unlike those of the others in the cave that night, had come from far distant lands, over centuries of time. It was what had drawn her to the sphinx—the quest to fathom ancient mysteries, in the hope that they would shed some light on the darkness from which she had descended.

There was a faint light—gray and gauzy—filtering into the cave when she was awakened, her cheek against the camera case. It wasn't the sun that awoke her, but the sound of a footfall. Through half-open eyelids, she saw Radu's boot stepping over her, and then the back of Anton's coat. They were leaving the cave. Cezar's snoring was uninterrupted. She thought of springing up to stop them, but something—that inner voice—told her to lie still and let them go.

They disappeared, and after waiting a minute or two, she sat up, rubbed her eyes, and looked around. What confused her was that they'd only been given half their wages. The other half was due them when they got back to the village. Why would they have given that up?

Brushing the grit off her leather trousers, stiff as boards from the soaking the night before, she stood up, lit the lantern, and used it to survey the ground. She could see the flat spot where the two men had been lying, and then a dusty footprint or two leading toward the back of the cave.

Had they summoned their nerve and explored it?

Following the tracks, and keeping her head low enough not to crack it on the sloping roof, she inched her way back. In the lantern's light, the walls, smooth at the entrance, changed—there were scratch marks here, deliberate marks, as if something had been recorded or counted. A few yards further in, there were crude drawings— outlines of animals. Wolves prancing with upturned tails. Bats with outspread wings. Crocodiles.

This last one puzzled her. How could people in this area, thousands of years ago, have ever seen a crocodile?

Or, for that matter, a hyena—unless of course, it was simply a badly drawn dog. Its snout was raised in a snarl, and above it, a robed figure was depicted sitting on a throne, wearing a helmet with horns curved like a bull's.

She lowered the lantern, and saw the yellowed remains of a skeleton, most of it withered to dust, but a few scraps of animal hide, adorned with faded beads, still clung to the upper torso. The hands had been crossed across its chest, but they looked as if they had been pried back. The finger bones were disarticulated. Had it been holding something close to its breast? A child? A memento? A sacred object of some sort?

"Where is everyone?" Cezar's voice boomed from the front of the cave. "What's going on?"

"I'm back here!" she called. In the hard earth around the bones, she saw a few crude but empty vessels.

"Where?"

"Here." There was a shallow wooden bowl, a cracked clay urn. The bowl had probably once contained food of some sort to sustain the soul on its voyage to the afterworld. The urn, however, put her in mind of Egyptian Canopic jars, used to hold the body's vital organs after evisceration.

Cezar found his way back, his hands feeling along the walls, until he came within the glow of the lantern. "Where are Anton and Radu?"

"Gone."

He grunted. "Good. Now you won't have to pay them."

Then he took in the sight of the bones and crossed himself. "So, it's true."

"Something is," she said, solemnly. "But I'm not sure what."

"We shouldn't be here. He should be left in peace."

But this creature's peace had already been disturbed. Unless she'd missed her guess, its most prized possession had been stolen, and even now Anton and Radu were hustling down the mountainside with some secret treasure in their possession. But what?

CHAPTER FOUR

"Hail, the conquering hero!"
 "Savior of fair maids!"
 "The man of the hour!"
 It was just as Stoker had feared. The story of his adventure the night before had made the afternoon editions of the London papers and, depending upon the publication, had been rendered in a variety of styles—in a restrained and authoritative fashion in the *Times*, and suitably embellished in the less scrupulous sources. In the pictorial accompaniment to the *Illustrated London News*, he was seen bare-chested, his braces dangling, as he dove in perfect style off what looked more like the heights of London Bridge than a humble embankment. The *Pall Mall Gazette* described him as the "muscular and athletic manager of the city's finest theater," and said that he was carried downstream a hundred yards before he was able to grapple the forlorn young woman and carry her in his arms to safety. The *East London Observer* added that she had kissed him on the forehead and blessed him for his mercy and courage, twice, before fainting away from the shock and the cold.

None, of course, recorded that she had whispered she would never forgive him.

As he entered the hallowed precincts of the Beefsteak Club, a richly adorned and wainscoted room tucked away behind the stage of the

Lyceum, the dozen or so men gathered around the long trestle table raised their glasses to him with a chorus of huzzahs. Henry Irving leaped to his feet with a pewter goblet in hand—all the utensils, as custom dictated, were of dull and strictly utilitarian pewter—and in the stentorian tones that carried all the way to the back of the house, proposed a toast.

"To Bram! They say that no actor is a hero to his house manager"—there was a ripple of laughter, as most of the other guests were also men of the theater—"but how often is the manager a hero to his actor?"

W. S. Gilbert, usually more self-contained, clanked his mug against the side of his metal plate in approbation.

"To Bram!" Arthur Conan Doyle seconded the toast, and they all drank deeply of the club's port.

Stoker, loitering bashfully in the doorway, acknowledged them all with a brisk nod, then handed his hat and second-best coat (the first one had gone off to St. Thomas's Hospital wrapped around the girl) to the steward named Charles; for the sake of simplicity, all servants of the Beefsteak were simply called Charles. Then he took a seat reserved for him at Irving's right hand. ("Like unto Jesus, at the side of God," as Willie Wilde, Oscar's brother, had once remarked, "though of a suspiciously Hibernian cast.")

For several minutes, the ribbing went on, and Stoker knew it was best to let it run its course; Irving would step in soon enough. No actor worth his salt could stand to be out of the limelight for more than a short time.

"But why so late?" Conan Doyle asked from across the table. "Were you checking in on your new charge?"

"I did send a message to the hospital—"

"Which one?"

"St. Thomas's, to inquire about her recovery today."

"And what did they say?" Doyle asked. As a writer himself, he never failed to follow up one question with another until a topic was exhausted.

"I have not heard back." A waiter placed a plate of bloody beef and boiled potatoes, garnished with a layer of onions, in front of him, and Stoker, famished, snapped open his napkin to begin work on it. "I suspect they seldom get such odd inquiries."

"And I suspect they get more than you know. This is a city where desperation and untold wealth live cheek by jowl. Most of us have learned not to see the evidence right before our eyes."

Perhaps to keep the conversation from turning in a dark direction, Irving cut in to compliment Gilbert and Sullivan's new show, *Utopia, Limited*, which had just opened at the Savoy. Notoriously incapable of attending performances of his own work, Gilbert often loitered among the Gothic trappings of the Beefsteak Club until the show was nearly over, returning to the theater only to accept a curtain call.

Even over his plate, Stoker could not fail to notice that the club had a new guest tonight, no doubt brought there by Doyle, who was bending his ear to attend to him. He was an older man, plainly of Eastern European ancestry, with a high and intellectual forehead and drooping moustache. Stoker also noted, hooked to the back of his chair, an elegantly tooled and lacquered zebrawood cane, its handle the golden head of a wolf.

"No, no. I won't hear a word against Gladstone," Irving boomed from the throne he occupied at the head of the table. "The man has been a welcome guest of the Beefsteak." Whig in its general inclination, the club could turn Tory for a night if Gladstone was in attendance.

As the debate swirled around him, Stoker drank his port and sawed through his meat; it was the first real meal he'd had all day. By the time he'd arisen that morning, Florence was already at her desk attending to her correspondence; Mary, the housemaid, was sweeping the carpet stair; and the cook, Mrs. O'Toole, was wondering if he would like a late breakfast or an early lunch. Given the subtle, or overt, English prejudice against the Irish, Stoker always made it a point to hire his countrymen whenever possible.

Florence did not share his view on that—having eradicated any trace of her Irish accent—or for that matter, on many other things besides. Her bedroom door was firmly closed by the time he had stripped off his wet clothes the night before, and not even a glimmer of light peeked out from under the jamb. Just as well. They had lost the ability to communicate, too, in all but the most perfunctory manner. When he married her, she had been the most beautiful girl in Dublin, one of six daughters of a highly decorated army officer. But beautiful as she still was, there was a brittleness to her, born, Stoker believed, of a secret frustration. As he had become more and more immersed in the theater world, she had found her own ambitions in that direction unfulfilled. Unseemly as it would have been to pursue a career upon the stage—most actresses came from less distinguished backgrounds—she had been complimented on her tall, slender figure, long neck, blonde hair, and fair complexion for so long that she hankered for an even greater audience. Irving had cast her as a supernumerary—a vestal virgin yet—in a production of Tennyson's *The Cup*, but she had displayed no particular stage presence and after the birth of their son, Noel, now sixteen, the subject had been quietly dropped. She had since found other popular pastimes—mesmerism and the like were just then becoming the fad—in which to immerse herself.

It was only on the way out, as Stoker wrapped his scarf around his throat, that Doyle and his guest made their way toward the door and a proper introduction was made. Doyle had to repeat the man's name—Arminius Vambéry—before Stoker could catch it, and shake the man's hand.

"Professor Vambéry hails from Hungary, where he has codified their language in their first dictionary," Doyle said, "though developments on that continent have, to our own good fortune, persuaded him to take sanctuary here."

All of which, Stoker instantly understood, was a polite way of saying the man was a Jew fleeing the rampant anti-Semitism presently sweeping that part of the globe in especially virulent fashion. Not that England was immune; here, the sentiment was simply played in a lower key. Stoker himself felt no particular prejudice toward the Hebrew race, and had found that, despite the common slurs, in business dealings they were no better or worse than their Christian counterparts; the banker Alfred de Rothschild, for one, had dealt with the Lyceum's occasional need for loans in an entirely forthright, even generous, manner.

"I am honored to be included in such a notable gathering," Vambéry said, in his heavily accented English, "and to make the acquaintance of so many illustrious men, skilled in so many different fields."

"And what work are you engaged in now?" Stoker asked.

"This and that. Some private commissions."

"I'm putting in a word for him at the Foreign Office," Conan Doyle interjected.

"The Foreign Office?" Stoker asked. It seemed unlikely that a man so recently arrived should be entrusted with delicate matters of state.

"No one knows the politics and intrigue of the Continent, or the East, better than the professor. He has traveled from Helsinki to Budapest, Mecca to Medina, and much of the latter disguised as a pilgrim of the Moslem faith. You two must talk sometime, Bram—he's got enough stories to fill a volume."

"Aren't you putting them to use for Sherlock Holmes and Watson?"

"Plenty to go round," he replied. "Plenty."

"My friend is being too kind," Vambéry said.

But Stoker's interest had indeed been piqued—he was always on the lookout for material that he might turn into one of his short stories, or even a novel, and he favored those that had an element of the exotic or bizarre. Surrounded by so many men of great accomplishment and fame, he secretly longed to rank among them, to appear as something more than an accessory to Henry Irving and the Lyceum.

The exit from the Beefsteak led into the stage alleyway, and Vambéry leaned heavily on his cane as he made his way down the steps and over the rough cobblestones toward the front of the theater. In front of the grand columned portico, Doyle hailed a passing carriage and offered to drop off Stoker at his home in Chelsea.

"No, but thanks," Stoker said, putting up the collar of his coat against the autumnal chill. "I'm in the mood for a walk."

"Not along the embankment again. I think it might be considered showy if you were to rescue another fair damsel in distress."

Stoker laughed, and although he assured him he would be taking a different route—"The damsels will have to fend for themselves tonight"—his feet decided otherwise, and before long he had come to the very spot where the girl had jumped. He knew it from the bits of broken brick littering the ground. What a difference a night could make. He had most definitely altered the course of one young woman's life, but had he, he wondered, thinking of her strange words to him, also altered his own in some way? Confronted with despair greater than he had ever himself experienced, he felt his own sense of empathy increased, his imaginative horizons expanded. What might such an expansion offer to his art? How might it aid him in his own struggle to create something of lasting importance? No, he could not allow this story to end on an ambiguity. Tomorrow, he would see things through—he would find the girl, again.

CHAPTER FIVE

"We should have stolen the camera, too," Radu grumbled, as he picked his way around a rocky outcrop.

"She was sleeping on it," Anton said. "Anyway, this will be worth a hundred times what the camera was." He had made sure to keep the treasure in his own rucksack as they navigated the treacherous slope. He didn't trust Radu any more than he had trusted that girl.

"But how will we find out what it's worth, or what it even is?"

"The old Gypsy will tell us."

"He'll just steal it."

"He won't have the chance. He'll tell us what he knows, and we'll take it all the way to Vienna if we have to before we sell."

Anton was careful to say "we," though it had already struck him that that was unfair. Whose idea had it been to explore the back of the cave? His. Who had found the skeleton and the empty vessels scattered around it? He had. And who had had the guts to pry the gold box from the bony fingers that clutched it tight? He had. And now Radu thought he was due an equal share of the spoils? It gnawed at Anton like a rat.

All day long they hiked down the mountain, then into the woods, making sure to put enough distance between themselves and Mina and Cezar before setting up camp beside a stream. Radu wanted to make a fire, but Anton insisted they lie low. "You never know with Cezar. He could track a white rabbit through a snowstorm."

They ate cold sausages, washed them down with frigid water from the brook, and made beds out of boughs cut from the evergreen trees. Anton cradled his rucksack against his cheek, but he couldn't sleep. His mind was filled with questions—why couldn't he open the box? What could be in it?—and visions of what he would do once he was rich. A big house, with a beautiful young wife, herds of sheep and goats and cows. Wine and beer flowing like water. The only thing that kept muddying his dream was that useless Radu making off with half the riches. Nestling his head against the sack, he could feel the sharp edges of the golden box. It was as if the box itself were whispering to him, like a snake in his ear, *It's not right.*

Rolling onto his side, he looked toward the thick bundle of leaves and branches Radu was sleeping under. Radu was the village idiot. He couldn't have hatched this plan if he'd had his whole life to do it. Even if he had the money, he wouldn't know what to do with it—he'd just lose it to some swindler. And how unjust would that be? All the gold that Anton had discovered, winding up in the hands of some passing crook?

It would indeed be unjust, the sack hissed.

Beside his hand lay a rock. Anton reached out and picked it up. It was heavy and jagged. But if necessary, it would do the trick.

It is necessary, he heard in his head.

He grasped the rock tightly and with his other hand brushed aside the branches and leaves he had used to cover himself. He rose slowly, waiting for a cloud to pass in front of the moon and obscure their little camp. Then he crept toward the sleeping Radu.

As quietly as he could, he knelt down beside the body and raised the rock. When a glimmer of moonlight fell where the fool's head should be lying, he smashed the stone down as hard as he could. But all he felt was loose dirt and dead leaves. Damn! He slammed the rock down again, a little to one side—and then to the other. Where was he?

A twig snapped behind him, and when Anton turned his head, the branch hit him full in the face. He tumbled onto his back, and then the stick hit him again. Before he could scramble away, knees thumped onto his chest, blowing the breath out of his lungs, and hands grappled at his throat, preventing air from coming back in again. What was happening? He groped for the rock, but couldn't find it. Radu's face, looming above him, was filled with purpose, his arms as firm as posts. Anton wanted to beg for his life, but he couldn't draw a breath, much less speak. His vision narrowed, grew darker. As his final moments of consciousness ebbed, and his heart sputtered to a stop in his chest, he saw the moon, through the trees, first inflate like a bellows, and then swiftly diminish, until it became no bigger than a coin, a crumb, a pinprick, and then . . . nothing at all.

CHAPTER SIX

After the embankment, Stoker did indeed take another route home—he had been in the papers quite enough already—soon leaving the electrified lighting of the West End behind, and meandering through the narrow, winding streets, where the light from the gas lamps threw flickering shadows that danced around the pavement like imps cavorting before him. Not so many years before, Jack the Ripper had haunted the streets of the city, and though his depredations had all been confined to the East End, even the better neighborhoods had felt the effects—the Lyceum had been exhibiting a play based on Robert Louis Stevenson's sensational novel *The Strange Case of Dr. Jekyll and Mr. Hyde*, and attendance had plummeted; no one had wanted to go out at night nor revel in fictional evil when such a real menace lurked. To this day, the murderer had never been caught, and Stoker had considered writing something—a story, or maybe a full-scale novel—in which he might advance some theory about the killer's identity. All he needed was a theory.

By the time he arrived at his home on Cheyne Walk, it was late, but the lights were still on inside. That could only mean one thing. Florence must have been hosting one of her events—a meeting of some psychical research group, or even perhaps a séance. Not wanting to intrude, or for that matter have to make idle conversation with one of the members, Stoker lit a cigar and loitered on the opposite curb. The townhouse was a distinguished one, four stories of red brick at the end of the row, and a leasehold rather than a rental. Frankly, it was beyond his means—even Irving lived on only three floors maintained above a luggage shop—but Florence had wanted it, and brave as he was when it came to other feats, Stoker acquiesced in the face of most of his wife's demands. He so wanted to please her, to recapture the passion and romance of their courtship. What good was it to have bested Oscar Wilde and all those other suitors for her affections if the prize proved so hollow? Was it inevitable, he wondered, that the passion died in any marriage? On many a night, as he hung his coat and hat on the rack in the vestibule, he felt that rather than coming home, he was checking into a small, elegant, but cold hotel.

As he watched, the front door opened, and voices came to him on the night wind. Florence was bidding her guests good night, and as the women tucked their scarves around their necks and the men settled their top hats with a tug on the brim, Stoker receded farther into the shadows.

"On the fourteenth, then," an ungainly woman in bright green boots was saying, "at nine o'clock sharp." It was, unmistakably, Lady Jane Wilde, Oscar's mother.

"Yes, I will be there."

"And Madame Zukoff herself will be leading it," the woman's companion put in. Stoker recognized him as William Stead, notorious crusader for social reform, as well as the editor of *Borderland*, the most eccentric journal of the day, mixing everything from ghosts to graphology.

Madame Zukoff was the most famous medium in London, and Stoker had already met her, once, at a Theosophy lecture that Florence had succeeded in dragging him to—though what his wife hoped to learn was beyond him. Both of her parents were still alive—no need for contacting the next world there—and if she wondered what her son was up to, she had only to write him a letter at his boarding school, a job that invariably fell to Stoker's hand. A copious letter writer—as many as fifty a day went out from his desk at the Lyceum—Stoker was only too happy to remain in touch with Noel. The boy was the best thing to have come from his marriage.

As the last guest descended the steps, Florence was framed in the lighted doorway—a tall and regal figure, her hair still blonde (and so long as the House of Maurice was in business, it would remain so), in a long blue dress of silk brocade, nipped as tightly as she could make it at the waist. The vanity of the day declared that women's waists were to be no more than the circumference of a piecrust, and Stoker knew that Florence had been much troubled, after the birth of their child, that she could not get it back to where it had been before motherhood. In his eyes, it made little difference; she was still an attractive partner, and one with whom he was invariably proud to be seen.

Just as she was closing the door against the night chill, Stoker emerged from the shadows, but she did not see him. How could she? She needed glasses, but seldom if ever wore them in public.

"Hold on," he called out.

"Who's there?"

"Who's there?" he repeated. "Your husband."

"Oh, I just didn't hear you very distinctly."

"You'd think you'd know my voice by now," he said, climbing the steps. "The ushers can hear me all the way up in the balconies."

"It's been a very busy evening," she said, turning inside before he could give her a kiss on the cheek.

"It appears so," he said, glancing into the parlor where Mary was piling a tray with used cups and saucers and wine glasses. Stead would no doubt have helped himself liberally to the decanter of Scotch. "What was the occasion?"

"A lecture."

"On?"

"You know you don't really care, Bram. Why do you ask?"

"I do care."

"Only to make fun—or to make something from it into one of your ghastly stories."

On that last score, she had a point. He had been fascinated by the occult and the otherworldly ever since he was a boy, addicted to the tales of banshees and ghouls and trolls that his mother and the nursemaids told him, and they had never wanted for an opportunity to do so. For the first seven years of his life, he had been afflicted by a malady that to this day had never been adequately diagnosed or defined. It had kept him confined to his bed—nearly unable to walk—in the old house on Clontarf Road in Dublin, listening to the happy cries of other children playing in the garden or chasing each other down the street. The tales had given him a delicious thrill, one which he still sought, but he had never—and there, Florence's point was well taken—been a convert. He was too much the skeptic, the mathematician, the man of business, to treat the invisible world with anything but detached bemusement.

"I suppose you were the toast of the Beefsteak Club tonight," Florence said, lifting the hem of her skirt to go up to her bedroom. "My guests had all read the late papers."

"By tomorrow, it will all blow over."

"We can only hope."

"Did any letter come from the hospital?"

"No, why should it have?"

"I sent an inquiry as to the girl's welfare."

"Oh, so she was pretty, was she?"

"What's that got to do with it?" No matter what he said, he always seemed to be putting a foot wrong with his wife.

"Nothing came." She turned left at the landing. "Good night, Bram."

He watched as she entered her room, her dress rustling as she drew it in, and closed the door.

The grandfather clock began to chime the hour.

In his own room, he went straight to the sideboard and poured himself a generous glass of whiskey—the stuff so good he did not leave it downstairs where the likes of Snead could filch it—and plopped into the easy chair by the window. It was there he sat, many a night, searching for ideas for his stories or novels—something that would finally and forever make his name—or, failing to come up with any, editing scripts for the Lyceum. Irving had certain favorites in his repertory on which the theater could always rely—*Faust, Hamlet, The Bells*—but it was also necessary to come up with new productions, fresh plays, to draw in patrons and keep the Lyceum current.

Tonight, he picked up from the stack of scripts on the floor a rough version of a new play by his old friend Hall Caine, but whether it was the play, or his mental state, he could not focus on it long enough to remember what had happened from one page to the next. He was exhausted, and though he wouldn't mention it to anyone, he still felt a chill in his bones from the plunge into the Thames the night before. He reached for the decanter and filled his glass again. The whiskey went down with a slow, warm burn, and he willed it to enter his bones. His feet were a bit numb, too, from standing in one place on the hard sidewalk across from his front door, with the damp of the river rising up behind him. He unlaced his boots and kicked them off, one flying off so precipitously it struck the bedpost. No mind—there was no one in the bed, nor would there be, excepting himself.

In his breast, a tide of resentment rose—how long could a man live like this?—and a surge of something else, too, fueled in part by the momentary glow of celebrity. He had done something laudatory, without a second's thought or hesitation, and been acclaimed for it everywhere but in his own home, and by everyone but his own wife. Shouldn't she be the most impressed and congratulatory? Shouldn't whatever walls had been erected between them have suffered some breach by this?

He undressed quickly, leaving his shirt and trousers where they fell, wrapped himself in his long woolen dressing gown, and even dabbed on his throat a touch of the fragrant shaving balm W. S. Gilbert had once brought him from Paris. In his bare feet, he padded along on the Oriental runner that ran from his door all the way to his wife's boudoir. Her light was still on, and he could hear the whisk, whisk, whisk of the brush running through her hair. One hundred strokes every night. At one time, she had let him administer them.

Softly, he knocked on the door, but there was no reply. He knocked again, a little more loudly, and now the brushing stopped.

"What is it, Bram?"

How did one answer that? Wasn't it plain? Instead, he turned the handle of the door—at least it wasn't locked—and put his head inside. She was sitting, as usual, at her dressing table covered with perfumes and creams, hand mirrors, and other small articles whose purpose he could never even guess. She was wearing the yellow chiffon sleeping gown he had given her on their recent anniversary.

"I see that the gown suits you admirably."

"Yes," she said, returning to her hair, "it's quite comfortable."

Not wanting to ask for any further permission, especially as he knew it might not be forthcoming, he slipped into the room and closed the door behind him. He felt as if he had just surmounted a major obstacle and took a few seconds to secure his gain.

"I'm very tired," she said. "Is there something you wanted?"

He felt like an oaf. When they had first courted, she had made him feel like a protective giant, a burly brute to keep her safe from the vicissitudes of life, but now, he just felt clumsy and unwanted.

"I sent Noel a ten-pound note today," he said. "I don't want him borrowing from friends at school."

"That was wise. But the boy has no sense of money—he'll squander it in a fortnight."

Now what? He moved toward her, and reached out to take the brush from her hand. "Would you like me to do that for you?"

"No, thank you. I'm nearly done," she said, giving it one more stroke and then conspicuously laying the brush, with its mother-of-pearl handle, down. The brush, too, had been a gift.

She swiveled on the stool and said, "Is that all?"

Surely she knew it wasn't; no grown woman could be so obtuse. Through the chiffon he could easily make out the definition of her breasts—which had grown fuller than she liked after the childbirth—and below that her long straight legs. Her hair, glossy from all the brushing, lapped like waves around her smooth and narrow shoulders. It wasn't the whiskey that was burning inside him now, and when he put his hands on her arms and raised her for a kiss, she didn't resist him.

Nor did she welcome him.

He pressed his lips to hers—they were slick with some unguent she must have just applied as part of her nocturnal beauty regimen—but her lips stayed sealed, and her body did not bend as he clung to her more closely.

"May I stay with you tonight?"

"You know I can't sleep with you in the bed, Bram. You snore."

"I won't tonight. I'll sleep like a baby," he said, though sleep was the furthest thing from his mind.

She knew that, too, and as if it were all in play, she pushed him away. "Do you want me to wake Mary and have her fix you some warm milk and biscuits to help you sleep?"

"It's not Mary I need," he said, more gruffly than he had meant to. "It's you."

With his declaration hanging in the air, she stepped away from the vanity and said, "I'm going to bed now. I've been up since five thirty this morning. I can barely keep my eyes open."

Turning her back to him, she pulled down the coverlet and plumped the pillows as if she were already alone—which, in a sense, she was. Although Bram was physically present, his spirit had already left the room in shame and frustration. He watched as she extinguished the bedside lamp and slipped beneath the sheets, the moonlight slanting through the curtains and touching the tips of her hair.

Then he knotted the belt of his robe, which had come loose, turned around, and left. The light was still spilling from his bedroom door, but it looked less beckoning than forlorn.

CHAPTER SEVEN

By the time Radu reached the Gypsy encampment, he was exhausted, and his boots were barely holding together. Before giving himself away, he crouched behind some bushes to get the lay of the land.

The wagons, their roofs shaped like barrels, were drawn into a circle, with a big smoldering campfire carved out in the center. Horses and goats were tethered to stakes driven into the hard ground. A couple of old women with kerchiefs on their heads were scrubbing clothes in a bucket of soapy water. A younger one was stitching up a vest on the steps of a wagon with a striped awning. That was the one where the old Gypsy lived. Radu had seen him driving it at the head of the caravan when it had passed through the town.

Radu had certainly met his share of Gypsies before, but it had always been in town, where they came to look for jobs as tinkers and the like, or the girls danced for coins in the market square. Other men had told him the girls did other things, too, whatever you wanted, but that you had to be careful not to get robbed. "You're a pigeon, Radu," the mayor had told him. "They'll pluck you clean, and you won't even know it."

But Radu knew better. He knew he wasn't as dumb as they all thought. After all, he'd outsmarted Anton, hadn't he?

When the young woman got up to hold out the vest and look over her work, he stepped into the clearing. She looked at him with a steady gaze, placed one hand on her hip. She had long black hair draped over one shoulder, and several bright bracelets dangled from her wrists.

"Your fortune told?" she finally said. "Is that what you want?"

"No."

She laid the vest down and sashayed toward him. "Maybe you want a love potion," she said in a lower voice, "something to make someone fall in love with you?" Her eyebrows were arched, and the corners of her mouth were tilted upward in an inviting smile. No woman had ever looked at him quite like that. "So, who's the lucky girl?"

"There is no girl."

"Oh, I can't believe that. A handsome young fellow like you." She linked her arm through his and drew him farther into the clearing. "My name's Nadya. What's yours?"

"Radu."

"That's a good strong name, for a good strong man." Her eyes dropped to the bundle tucked tightly under his other arm. "What have you got there?"

"Something."

She laughed, as if that were the cleverest thing she had ever heard. "Is it *something* I can see?"

"I want to show it to the old man."

"Oh, the old man. You mean Tobar?"

"If he's the one who drives the caravan."

"He's my father."

The old women had stopped their scrubbing to watch. Two barefoot boys in ragged clothes ran past, trying to get a kite to lift into the air, but they abandoned it, pausing when they saw Radu.

"I will take you to him. Wait here for just a minute," Nadya said, climbing the wooden steps into the wagon with the striped top.

Radu felt like an object of great curiosity as he waited in the clearing. Even the goats seemed to be staring at him. He cradled the bundle in his arms, high up against his chest. Dusk was falling, and he hoped to be well away from the camp before it grew so dark he couldn't follow the rest of the road into town.

Nadya's head poked out of the back of the wagon, and she waved at him to come.

She held back the canvas flap as he ducked inside. It was like that story he had once been told, about Ali Baba and the forty thieves. There were candles burning on brass saucers, throwing flickering yellow light around the interior; rich red cloths and faded tapestries hung from the curved wooden ribs of the roof, forming a tent. The floor was thickly matted with Persian carpets, and at the end of the tent sat the old man—Tobar—cross-legged on a crimson cushion, sucking on a long-handled ivory pipe. A black cat, with a white blaze on his forehead, lay curled up beside him.

After exhaling a long plume of smoke, he gestured at the cushion opposite, and Radu sat down. Without asking, the girl poured tea into two cups and gave one to each of them. Radu was reluctant to take even one hand off the precious treasure, but now he had to.

The old man didn't say a word, just sat there with the pipe in one hand and the teacup in the other. He had only one good eye, Radu noticed—the other looked like a broken egg. How could this old thing have fathered a daughter so young and pretty? It didn't bear thinking about.

"Well, go ahead," Nadya urged, her face so close, he could feel her warm breath on his cheek. Something stirred in him, but he tried to ignore it. "Show my father what you've got."

Slowly, Radu unwrapped the bundle and took out the box, the size of his palm and only a couple inches deep. In the candlelight, its surface gleamed a bright gold, and the tiny black figure of a man with a snout, etched deeply into the metal, stood out more plainly than ever. He was standing sideways, wore a headdress rather like the one on the mountain sphinx, and his hands were positioned above and below a gold latch at the very center. Radu had tried to move it, but it was stuck, and he hadn't wanted to force it. Maybe the Gypsy would know how.

After another long pull on his pipe, the old man put it to one side, along with the cup, and leaned forward to pick up the box.

"Drink your tea," Nadya said, "before it gets cold."

Radu didn't want it, but he took a sip anyway; it was heavily sweetened. The honey lay like a blanket on his tongue.

Tobar was turning the box over in his hands, gauging its weight, and when he noticed the latch, he, too, tried to budge it.

"You've opened this already?"

"No, I thought you could. I don't want to break it."

The old man's good eye flicked toward his daughter, and she quickly produced a leather sleeve, which the old man unrolled, revealing several tinker's tools and a vial of what looked like oil. He squirted a drop onto the latch and rubbed it in with the tip of one gnarled finger. Then he tried to pry the latch open, but the tool was too blunt.

"Let me try," Nadya said.

Tobar let her take it, and she tried to slip a long, painted fingernail under the latch. After a second or two, she said, "Damn!" and shook her hand. "I broke the nail."

Tobar laughed, and took the box back. He put it to his ear and shook it. Radu had already done that, too. He hadn't heard anything rolling around inside, and Tobar apparently didn't hear anything, either. After one more shake, he tossed it back to Radu. "It's empty, anyway," he said, draining his teacup.

"But even if it is," Radu said, "it's gold! Look at it! How much do you think I can get for it?"

"From me?" The old man shrugged. "Nothing. It's just gold paint."

Radu was stumped. How could that be? Anton had been sure it was gold; if it wasn't, he wouldn't have stolen it and lost half the money he was going to get from Mina for taking her up to the sphinx. And its weight . . . it weighed like gold.

"You're wrong," Radu insisted.

"If you say so."

"I'm going to take it to Vienna! I bet someone there will pay me for it." He took another gulp of the tea, but under all the honey it had a bitter aftertaste.

Tobar picked up his pipe and tamped fresh tobacco into the bowl. "Do what you like." The black cat raised its head to look at Radu, then, as if it, too, were dismissing him, laid it back down again.

Radu started hastily wrapping the box back up, but Nadya suddenly clutched his elbow to stop him, and said to her father, "Oh, but I like it, even if it is just a piece of painted wood."

She thinks so, too?

"It's pretty." She put a finger under Radu's chin and turned his face toward hers. Her teeth were as white as snow, and her eyes sparkled in the candlelight. "Won't you sell it to us, Radu?"

He was getting so confused. He thought they didn't want it.

She put her lips against his ear, and breathed deeply. "Won't you let me have it?" Her tongue flicked against his earlobe. "I like it almost as much as I like you."

"Stop that!" her father ordered, but Nadya squeezed Radu's arm. "I said that's enough."

She drew back, pouting at the old man. Then she reached for the teapot, filled Radu's cup again, and held it to his lips. He drank, hoping it would clear his mind a bit.

"Please?" she said to the old man. "I don't care if it's worthless. Can't you give him something for it?"

He shook his head slowly from side to side, then, once she'd pleaded again, he smiled through his broken and yellowed teeth. "You like it that much?"

"I do."

He sighed. "What do I not do for you?" Looking at Radu, he said, "Never have a daughter. They can make you do anything they want."

Why did his eye look like a broken egg yolk? Radu wondered.

Reaching into his vest pocket, Tobar pulled out a little velvet pouch, dipped his fingers in, and withdrew two silver coins. Then, after deliberating further, withdrew another.

"You're making a fool of me," he said, tossing them into Radu's lap. "But if it makes her happy . . ."

Radu studied the three silver coins. It was far less than he'd have earned if he'd stuck with that English woman and done the rest of the job, but at least it was something. And though he'd insisted he was going to take the box to Vienna, he'd only been parroting what Anton had said. He had no idea where Vienna was, or how in the world to get there.

"Thank you," Nadya whispered in his ear, as if the deal were already agreed to. "I am so grateful to you." She scooped up the coins from his lap, and snaked them down into his pants pocket, her fingers lingering longer than they needed to. Then she plucked the box from his hands and pressed it against her cheek, beaming. Slipping her arm under his to raise him from the cushion, she said, "I want to walk with you, in the moonlight."

As Radu stood unsteadily and turned toward the canvas flap, she surreptitiously flipped the box to her father, who, despite having only one good eye, caught it in midair and slipped it under his cushion. Radu stumbled down the steps, the honeyed tea still warming his tongue, and saw that it was dark out now. Following the road all the way back to town wouldn't be so easy. There were orange flames licking at a pile of dead wood in the fire pit, and several old women and some scruffy children were gathered around it, peeling potatoes, throwing things into an iron pot, or just warming their hands. As Nadya steered him around the fire and out of the camp, he heard a couple of them say something and laugh.

Once into the forest, Nadya kept up a line of chatter that made Radu's head spin—what was she saying? Was she talking about him? No woman had ever said things like this to him—much less while squeezing his arm against her breasts, and once or twice pecking him on the cheek with her wet, red lips. Despite the moonlight, the woods were dark and dense, and he felt as if his boots were filled with lead. He could barely keep walking, and by the time they had emerged at the crossroads, he was half-asleep on his feet. He started to go the wrong way, but Nadya pulled him to the left and said, "Sinaia's this way. Not far. Not far."

She patted him on the back and drew away from him. He wavered on his feet. An owl hooted in the tree branches above him. A troubled look appeared on Nadya's face, and she crossed herself.

Radu didn't understand why she was leaving him—his feet might be numb, but other parts of him were quite alive—and he tried to protest, but his words were slurred.

Her white teeth shone in the moonlight as she smiled and said, "You're as bold as you are handsome. Now go on home."

"But I want . . ." He could not complete the thought.

"I can see you do," she said with a laugh. "Don't you worry. I will come to town and find you there."

She gently turned him in the right direction again, and gave him a playful shove to get him started. "Stick to the road."

The owl hooted again.

"And don't stop until you see the lights."

Then she turned and walked back into the woods, where he instantly lost sight of her. He was alone at the crossroads—where criminals were commonly hanged from the branches of the great standing oak there, and a length of rope still hung from a bough—with a couple of coins in his pocket and a thousand feelings all jumbled up in his chest. He walked no more than a few yards before he saw by the side of the road the remains of a broken-down hayrick. To him, it looked like the softest bed in the best house in town, and he crawled up into it—there was even some leftover straw to stuff in his coat and cover himself with— and fell fast asleep, with the old noose swinging in the breeze above him.

CHAPTER EIGHT

Although the original St. Thomas's Hospital was founded in 1550, it had been moved to, and built anew, at its present location in 1868. Queen Victoria herself had laid the foundation stone on a plot of land reclaimed from the Thames during the construction of the Albert Embankment. The architect, Henry Currey, was an acquaintance of Stoker's—that list included almost anyone of substance or achievement in the city—but the real design for it lay with its presiding spirit, Florence Nightingale. It was she who had learned, from tending to the wounded in the Crimean War, that such things as cleanliness, proper ventilation, nourishing food, and boiled linen, were as essential to the health and recovery of her patients as any surgeon's blade.

In keeping with her dicta, the hospital had been laid out in seven separate pavilions, all of them set 125 feet apart, and at right angles to the river frontage, so as to access the greatest amount of fresh air and sunlight and at the same time to segregate patients with infectious diseases from those who suffered from some other ailment or injury. Connecting the turreted pavilions were low, covered corridors, and even after entering the grounds from the Lambeth Palace Road, it took Stoker several attempts before he found the treasurer's house, where the administrative offices were located and he could inquire about the welfare of the young woman he had saved from drowning.

The chief superintendent of the wards, Mrs. Croft, had his letter on her desk and said that she was just about to reply to it when he arrived. "I am perpetually pressed for time," she said, "and missives like yours are not as uncommon as you might think. Replying to such letters, given the nature of the offense, is an especially delicate matter."

He could certainly see why. Even now, even here, he noticed that she had called it an "offense" and avoided using the word "suicide." It was not a subject easily addressed. As far back as his student days at Trinity, he remembered that the topic had been chosen for an annual dinner of the debate society. He had presented the position espoused by the philosopher David Hume, over a hundred years earlier, in his *Essays on Suicide and the Immortality of the Soul*, arguing that the act should not be considered a crime, as it affected no one but the perpetrator, who was under no obligation to prolong a life he considered miserable and purposeless; his opponent, on the other hand, had sided with the likes of Aquinas, Kant, and John Stuart Mill, the champion of liberty who believed no action should be taken that kept a person from making other autonomous decisions in the future. Stoker had carried the day, less by the force of his arguments, perhaps, than his booming voice and authoritative delivery. It was something he had relied upon in many situations since.

"What is it precisely you wish to know?" Mrs. Croft asked, her eyes as steely gray as her hair.

"First of all, is she well?"

"As well as can be expected."

"She is still here then?"

"Yes, in the ward we keep for women who might pose a danger to themselves."

There it was again, another circumlocution.

"Would it be possible for me to see her?"

"Are you a relative?" Mrs. Croft said, her gaze shifting to the letter. "If I recall correctly, you are not."

"No, I am not, but I am also more than some disinterested party. It was I who fished her out of the Thames, after all."

"Ah, then it is your overcoat in which she arrived here?"

"I suppose it is."

Going to a cabinet, she opened it to reveal a jumble of odd garments, most notably his overcoat on a hanger. When she handed it to him, it was still damp and smelled of the river.

Draping it over his arm, he said, "I am rather pressed for time, so if it would be possible to take me to her?"

Mrs. Croft appeared to be undergoing her own internal debate, and it was several seconds before she said, "I was just about to make my daily rounds, and if you wish to accompany me, I suppose you may."

Whether it was by design or routine, Stoker quickly discovered that her daily rounds took her through virtually every pavilion of the hospital before coming to the one he wanted. And while the other wards had been much alike—great barracks-like rooms with lofty ceilings, tall windows, and long tables, sometimes adorned with flowers, running down the center of the room—this one was much smaller, more isolated, and hushed. It was also behind a pair of locked iron gates, and the windows, too, were barred. A nurse in a white cap and apron sat at a desk squarely in the center of the ward, with a dozen narrow cots on either side.

Every one of them, to Stoker's dismay, was occupied, some by girls no more than thirteen or fourteen years old—what dreadful circumstances had driven them to such despair so soon in life?—and others by elderly women with sunken cheeks and clouded eyes who lay as still as stones.

"Is it always so full?" Stoker asked sotto voce.

"Always."

But a quick survey of the room did not reveal the girl he was looking for. It was only when she rose from the last cot in the row and went to stare blankly out the barred window that he recognized her. Touching

Mrs. Croft on the shoulder to draw her attention, he said, "You haven't yet told me her name."

"How could I? She hasn't told us."

"You still don't know who she is?"

"That's why I decided to let you come along. We know nothing about her. We can't keep her here indefinitely, especially if she refuses to cooperate. Perhaps you will have better luck."

Stoker had little hope of that. He'd told no one of the girl's last words to him—*"God may forgive you, but I never will"*—and he saw no reason to believe she'd change her mind. There was a good chance he'd come on a fool's errand.

"I have work to do in the office," Mrs. Croft said, turning to go. "If you learn anything, come and tell me. The nurse will unlock the gate when you wish to leave."

Stoker hardly knew how to approach the girl, though it dawned on him that the situation was much as it had been the first time on the embankment. Her back was to him, and her thoughts were undoubtedly miles away. The light coming through the window was pale and cold. She wore a drab striped dress, hospital-issue, with a loose sash tied at the waist, and black stockings with no shoes on her feet.

"I hope you don't mind," he said, awkwardly holding the damp overcoat before him, "but I thought I'd look in on you and see how you were doing."

He expected no reply and was not disappointed.

"I'm not sure if you remember, but my name is Bram Stoker. May I ask yours?"

He waited, and was about to plunge ahead with another question, when she surprised him by saying, "What does anyone care? Why do they keep asking me that?" Her voice was low and petulant.

But Stoker was encouraged; it was progress of a kind. "We ask because we are concerned for your welfare."

And the girl laughed. Not a merry laugh, but a bitter one. "If I'd known that killing yourself was the ticket to a clean bed and hot stew, I'd have done it sooner."

"I'm glad you did not succeed."

"You're the one from the theater," she said, finally turning to face him. "I saw you that night, too—up in the balcony."

"Yes, you might well have done."

In the late afternoon sunlight streaming through the window, he could see just how young and fragile she truly was. She could not be more than eighteen or nineteen years old, and one side of her face was red and raw, the corner of the mouth inflamed. It was commonly known as "phossy jaw," a painful affliction suffered by match girls whose prolonged exposure to phosphorus caused necrosis of the tissue and teeth.

"You're as big as I remember," she said. "All those bricks in my coat, and you still managed to get me out of the river."

"Well, you certainly didn't make it any easier."

"No, I didn't," she said, in a tone less peevish than before. "Didn't want to."

The woman in the neighboring bed turned onto her other side in irritation, yanking the thin blanket up to her chin.

"You can call me . . . Lucinda."

"A pretty name."

"It's all I have that is," she said.

"Lucinda what?"

"Watts."

"And where do you live, Lucinda Watts?"

"Here."

"I mean before."

She paused before saying, "I missed curfew."

"Where?"

"The Thorne Mission House. I got locked out."

Bad enough to be a resident of the Thorne—or any of the work-houses or poorhouses that dotted the East End of the city—but to be locked out for the night was even worse. No one went to these institutions unless driven to them by the utmost necessity, and to be turned away left no further prospect but the streets and alleyways. On any given night, thousands of the most destitute and lost citizens of the city huddled in the darkened doorways, under the bridges and closed arcades, hiding from the policemen who would only roust them from one spot until they found another. Dawn brought little relief, either. No wonder she had filled her pockets with broken bricks.

"And what do you do there?" All the occupants had jobs of some kind, not only to force them to better themselves with work, but to bring in funds for the maintenance of the establishment.

Touching her jaw, she said, "You can't tell?"

"I think it's time you found another line of work."

"Easier said than done."

Stoker found himself moved—who would not be?—by her plight. It was so simple to walk by the anonymous figures warming their hands over an ash-can fire, but when confronted by an individual case—a Lucinda Watts, for instance—it became a good deal harder.

"How long will they let me stay here?"

"I'm not sure. I suspect it was until they could figure out who you were, and where you belonged."

"I thought so, too."

So she'd had motive for her silence, after all.

"And," he ventured carefully, "until they can determine why you did what you did."

At this, her face went blank. "It's a long story."

"I would like to hear it."

"I wouldn't like to tell it." She averted her eyes, looking back out the barred window grate.

He knew that now was not the time to press the issue. It was enough that he'd learned what he had.

"But once you tell them my name and such," she said, "they'll be sure to pitch me out. It'll be back to the mission house, if they'll even have me."

She looked him squarely in the eye for several seconds, before he said, "Should you wish to do so, you can always find me at the Lyceum."

On the way out, the nurse gave him an inquisitive look and asked, "What were you two talking about?" Stoker shrugged, saying, "This unusual weather we're having."

"But did she tell you who she was?" she said, opening a ledger and poising her pencil above it. "Or where she belongs?"

"Not a word. The girl remains a mystery."

CHAPTER NINE

"You hear that?" Cezar said, stopping in his tracks.

She did.

"It's the Gypsies."

Mina knew that, too. Their music was distinctive.

She and Cezar had been tracking Anton and Radu for a couple of days, and as the grizzled old shepherd had told her, "They're dumb as stumps," leaving clues of their passing everywhere they went. Tracks in the dirt, broken branches, beds of leaves, and even a spot where birds of prey were circling lazily in the sky. On the ground directly beneath them, Cezar found a short path into the brush, where Anton's body lay. The hawks and other animals had already taken some of its parts, but it was still plainly Anton.

Mina was surprised by that. If she'd had to guess who would get the better of whom, she'd have expected to find the dim-witted Radu lying dead and Anton well on his way to town with whatever treasure he had stolen from the cave.

"We have to bury him," she said, but Cezar shrugged.

"He made this bed," he said. "Let him lie in it." He started back toward the trail. Mina lingered to say a few words, and picking some pale withered wildflowers, laid them on Anton's chest, where she crossed his hands—just as the skeleton's hands had been crossed. His face was the hardest thing to bear, with its hollow sockets—like the monumental sculpture atop the mountain—and she took the scarf from around her neck and shrouded his head in it before leaving.

"Maybe we should skirt round the Gyps," Cezar suggested, but Mina said, "No, they might be able to tell us where Radu has gone—they know everything that goes on wherever they are."

"But they're just a bunch of—" And then he stopped, remembering himself. What he was thinking was as clear to Mina as if he'd bellowed it out loud. *You're one of them.*

It wasn't something she announced to the world, but it was something the world could generally surmise. Her raven-black hair and ebony eyes, her less than porcelain skin, and high cheekbones. Even the slim cut of her waist and hips—a figure most often seen in a Gypsy girl dancing and banging her tambourine in the marketplace. What confused people was that she sometimes wore reading glasses, dressed in ordinary attire, and spoke English as if she'd been to the manner born—which her father, in fact, had been. The very model of the intrepid English explorer, he had been excavating a site in the Nile delta—a prime spot for British archaeologists and adventurers—when her mother had come to the camp one night, offering to sell divining rods for finding the riches buried under the sand. As the story was told, her father's companions had laughed, and one had even set the dogs on her, but Sebastian Harcourt the fourth had called them off. Whether it was her mother's beauty or her salesmanship, Mina never knew—but her father did indeed buy the rod, and within a week he had discovered the tomb of a priest of Khepri. The mummy had been buried with his household utensils, some jewelry, and his mummified cat. At auction in London, the cat went for more than most of the bronze bracelets.

But the attachment between her father and the Gypsy girl—Mirela—became much more than a mercantile exchange. He had come to believe in her, and she had come to trust him as she had never trusted any Englishman. They had fallen in love. While they'd lived and traveled in the Middle East, it had not been a problem; white men had commonly dallied with native girls, and the union was observed by her father's compatriots with a wink and a leer. It was not so, however, when they had moved to England.

Though she'd only been a toddler, Mina had memories of cold, bleak flats, and arguments in the air. Later, she would understand that her father's family had disowned him, and he had to make his way himself, buoyed at first by the spoils of his Egyptian discovery, and later by his wits alone; he hired them out to other would-be explorers and on returning from one long voyage of several months, he found that Mina had been deposited at a foundling home. Her mother, lost and despondent since the day she had first disembarked at Southampton, had presumably returned to her own nomadic people. Sebastian had tried to trace her, but to find one of the Romany people, especially one who wished to disappear, was well-nigh impossible. Even the retired Scotland Yard detective he had set on her trail had abandoned the chase in Liverpool. "Dozens of 'em stowed away, legal or not, in the hold of every ship coming in or out of the harbor. No names—at least none that we can understand. Won't so much as look a policeman in the eye, much less talk."

Mina had never pursued it; if she wasn't wanted, she would not go begging to be. And when, years later, she received word of her father's death from an exotic contagion, on a privately funded expedition she had begged to join him on—the backers, as was not uncommon, chose to remain anonymous—the whole business became too painful to contemplate. The sealed coffin, which came with a dire warning against opening it and spreading the disease, went into the Harcourt family crypt—dead, his family was willing to take him back into the fold—and she was left utterly deserted, and alone, in the world.

"Sounds like a festival or something," Cezar said as they drew closer to the camp, and the ragged sounds of a fiddle and a guitar joined the groan of a hurdy-gurdy. A bonfire was burning, and Mina could smell everything from leather to wool to rubber being consumed. She knew what that meant, and her suspicion was confirmed when she saw the canopy outside the wagon, and the body of an old man lying under it.

"They're not going to burn him, are they?" Cezar asked under his breath.

"No, they'll bury him. But for now they have to burn everything he owned. If they touch those things, they risk becoming contaminated. It's called *marimé*."

A young woman in a red dress—they were all wearing red articles of clothing, meant to symbolize blood and its vitality—spotted them, and when the others saw them, too, the music died down, and the only sounds were the crackling of the fire and the mewling of an infant in one of the wagons.

"Sounds like they were happy to see him go," Cezar said, leaning close to Mina, but again she corrected him. "Not at all. This is a proper send-off to the next world—a festival, not a funeral. If you don't do it right, the spirit can come back as a *muló*—an undead—to haunt you."

"What do you want here?" the girl in the red dress said, scowling and coming toward them.

"We mean no disrespect," Mina assured her, and when the girl got close enough to get a better look at Mina, she appeared confused. The clothing and the speech were English, but . . .

"We are simply looking for someone."

"Everyone is looking for someone, that's nothing new."

"True enough," Mina said. From the corner of her eye, she could now see that a black cat was also lying on the funeral pyre, half-burned. It must have belonged to the old man. Nothing was spared.

"His name is Radu—a young man."

The girl said nothing, but her face betrayed her. "Why?"

"Have you seen him?"

"What do you want with him?"

"He's a thief," Cezar said. "He stole something from us."

"This thing he stole, it belonged to you?" she said pointedly. "Or to her?"

"To me," Mina replied.

The girl whipped around and ran to the edge of the pyre. There she knelt down, and shielding her fingers with the wadded-up end of her scarf, she pulled something from it, kicked it around in the dust to let it cool off, then picked it up again, making sure the cloth kept her fingers from actually touching it.

"Is this it?" she said, showing it to Mina.

Was it? Mina wondered. Even scorched and dusty, she could see that it was a gold box, with some kind of elaborate design carved into its lid. It could certainly have been enough to convince Anton and Radu to steal it and flee.

"Well? Is it?"

"Yes."

"My father bought it from him." She nodded at the body under the canopy. "And now, look, he is dead."

"I am very sorry," Mina said.

"No, I mean what I say—I want you to *look* at him," the girl repeated, dragging Mina by the arm toward the funeral bier. What she saw was a very old man, a man so desiccated he looked almost like a mummy. A red cloth was tied under his chin to keep his jaws from falling open. "Yesterday he was well. Yesterday he was alive. But by this morning, this," she said, gesturing at the body with a look of dread in her dark eyes. "He is like an empty husk."

Cezar instinctively crossed himself and took a step back.

"And all because of this," the girl said, holding out the box like it was a heap of dung.

Reaching for the money purse in her pocket, Mina said, "Let me buy it back from you then." She held out four silver coins, hoping it would be enough but knowing that Gypsies liked to drive a hard bargain.

"My father paid three."

"Then this should be enough, yes?"

"No," the girl said, taking only two from Mina's palm. "Now it is yours."

Cezar looked surprised by the bargain, but Mina instantly understood what had just happened. The girl believed the thing was cursed, and to free herself from its malignant influence, she had done the best thing possible—she had sold it back to the original owner, for less than she had paid. The onus was transferred to Mina.

"Now take it and go!" the girl said, almost spitting her words, and when the others heard her raised voice, their looks of puzzlement turned to something more antagonistic. The fiddler put his instrument down and reached for something inside his vest. Mina did not want to wait around to see what it was.

"We won't disturb you any further," she said, touching Cezar on the sleeve to signal that they should turn and leave. "Blessings on your father," and then, in the Romany tongue, she offered the traditional Gypsy prayer, "May his journey be swift and paradise await."

CHAPTER TEN

The reprieve was a short one. The next day, Lucinda was rudely awakened by the ward supervisor, Mrs. Croft, who informed her that her time was up.

"We can no longer accommodate you here," she said, "or waste the funds of our generous benefactors on a recalcitrant patient. Whoever you are, and wherever you belong, you must now go there."

In a matter of minutes, Lucinda Watts found herself back outside the gates of St. Thomas's Hospital, in her old clothes and shabby overcoat. A stiff November wind was blowing, and she plunged her hands into her pockets to warm them. For a moment, she was puzzled by the grit and sand she found at the bottom, before remembering the bricks she had stashed there. Directly across the river, she saw the pennants whipping in the wind above the Houses of Parliament.

With nowhere else to go, she found herself trudging back, head down, eyes watering in the cold, toward the bleak prospect of the only home she had in London—the Thorne Mission House. She felt like a prisoner begging to be put back in jail, but behind its high stone walls and iron gates were her meager belongings, the few people she could call her friends, and the only mementos of her young son. The mission was, in a way, the last place in the world she wanted to go, but to remain outside its walls would be to freeze to death on the streets, or be arrested for vagrancy and clapped in one of the poorhouses far worse than the Thorne. If the days at the hospital had done anything, they'd done just enough to restore her strength and her will to go on living. A clean bed and hot food could do that, but her resolve was fragile at best.

And it was tested the moment she arrived at the porter's lodge.

"Watts— that you?" Cullen said, leaning on his broom on the other side of the high gates. "Never thought I'd see you here again."

"Neither did I."

"Where you been?"

She realized that her name could not have appeared in any news story, as she had refused to give it out. No one at the mission house would know where she had been. "My mother wasn't well. I had to go to the country to tend to her."

For a second, he seemed to accept that, then put his head back, opened his toothless jaws, and let out a guffaw that echoed all around the vast stone court behind him. "Your mother, eh? Didn't you once tell me you was an orphan?"

She was, though she did not remember telling him that.

"Well," he said, shaking his head as his mirth subsided, "I do hope she is feeling better now." Putting the broom against the door of his lodge, he said, "So you'll be wanting to see the Matron then?"

"I suppose I'll have to."

"Right after you've done right by me."

"I don't have any money, Cullen."

"You got somethin' more precious than that," he said, undoing the padlock, and opening the gates just wide enough to put his head through and pat his stubbly cheek. Lucinda had endured this little ordeal before—all the girls had—and she pecked his cheek with her lips while his hand made a rapid slide down her shoulder and onto her waist.

"Good to have you back," he said, squeezing her hip as she slid past him. One day, God willing, she'd have a hatpin to stick him with.

"You remember the way up to the Matron's, don't you?"

"Yes." How could she forget?

Her chambers were on the top floor of the Thorne, which was built like a great *H*, with two long wings extending back from the street. The wing to her left housed the men, the one to her right the women. Each side had its own vast chambers for the able-bodied of each sex, along with infirmaries and dining halls and airing grounds. In the center were clustered the workrooms and the laundry, the kitchen and nursery and match-making annex. Lucinda had been told there were as many as a thousand poor souls housed there at any one time, and as the Matron had warned when Lucinda had first arrived, "a thousand more banging at the gates for the privilege of entering."

Crossing the court, she saw some boys and girls at play—not one of them wearing a warm coat or decent shoes—and she suddenly felt as if her heart were being squeezed by a great fist. She averted her eyes, and proceeded to the main hall and the winding staircase that would take her up and up to the receiving room. She dreaded each step she took, trying to distract herself with the stained-glass windows that adorned each landing—every one of them displaying a parable of charity or forgiveness, though it had often struck Lucinda that there was little enough of that in the mission itself—before coming to the top, where a great oaken door bore a brass plaque that read "Miss Winifred Thorne, Matron & Benefactress."

She knocked furtively, and on hearing a shout of "Come!" went inside.

Miss Rogers, a former schoolteacher who had fallen on hard times, had been appointed secretary by virtue of her fine handwriting skills. She looked astonished at the sight of Lucinda.

"We thought you'd died, too," she said, before putting her fingers to her lower lip, regretting having referred to Lucinda's poor dead boy. "Oh, I'm sorry to have said that." She came around the side of the desk and embraced her. "We were all so worried about you."

Miss Rogers might have been, but it was doubtful many others were. It was a dog-eat-dog world in the Thorne—a perfect mirror, in Lucinda's estimation, of the city outside—and she prayed that the Matron might not have noticed her absence on the residence records submitted every afternoon.

"I don't suppose I can just take my old place back," Lucinda said, "and my work, without anyone being the wiser?"

"The Matron knows. You'll need to do an interview." She looked sympathetic. "Wait here," she said, "and I'll see what I can do. Have you eaten anything today?"

Lucinda was about to say that she'd had toast and a bowl of porridge at St. Thomas's Hospital, but then she thought better of it. Why bring it up unless she had to? "Yes, I'm all right."

Miss Rogers slipped into the Matron's private chambers, and Lucinda went to the window and looked down into the yards. It was a view she could never fully fathom, the whole vast edifice, a little city unto itself, with gray stone walls dotted with endless rows of narrow windows, and cramped areas where the residents could sit on the hard-packed earth or the single stone bench to smoke or stretch or simply look up at a patch of sky, usually as dull and gray as the walls. And then there was the match-making factory, a ramshackle annex with an orange glow spilling from its doorway and pungent smoke perpetually spewing from its stovepipe chimneys.

When the door opened, Miss Rogers held it so, and announced, "The Matron will see you now," whispering "Good luck" as Lucinda passed by.

Although she had seen this sumptuous flat before—Bartholomew Thorne, the Matron's older brother and the man who had endowed the institution, had escorted her there more often than she cared, or dared, to recall—it was a revelation each time. It was as if she had passed from a dungeon into a palace. Where the halls below were cold and drab, with nothing but lines of cots or workbenches, stone floors and dirty windows, here was light and air and beauty. There were rich red rugs with elaborate patterns and tassels, and wainscoting along all the walls, its varnish gleaming from the gaslight chandeliers and sconces. The rooms were decorated with lots of foreign-looking things—trunks and candelabras and tapestries that had strange human figures on them, some with the heads of dogs or birds marching sideways in profile. They gave Lucinda a shiver, and she wondered why anyone would want to look at them. Raised a Catholic, she had the vague feeling that they were unholy.

"Well?" she heard from the salon down the hall. "Have you become lost?"

It was the voice that brought fear to the hearts of every man, woman, and child in the place.

Miss Thorne was sitting in a wheelchair at the keyboard of a pianoforte, her hair swept into a blonde funnel atop her head—a miracle, Lucinda knew, of the hairdresser's art—that only emphasized her height. A full six feet tall, she wore a severe but elegant black gown, offset with a necklace of beaten gold. No one, least of all Lucinda, could ever guess just how old Miss Thorne really was—there were times she looked a young woman, and others when she appeared a crone, just as there were times when she was seen in the rattan wheelchair, and others when she was walking about the mission grounds, haltingly but erect.

"No, ma'am, I'm right here," Lucinda said, curtseying as if she were being ushered into the presence of the queen.

Her hands still poised on the piano keys, Miss Thorne studied her as if looking for clues. "You're all in one piece, I see."

"Yes, ma'am."

"You may thank God for that."

"I do."

"Do you?" she said sternly, before turning back to the sheet music and striking a chord. For a minute or two, she continued to play while

Lucinda stood awkwardly, waiting for whatever might come next. Miss Thorne's hands, she thought, looked like talons as they swept back and forth across the keyboard, and she wondered how such a thing as complicated as playing a piano could ever be learned.

When the last chord was struck, and Miss Thorne waited for the last reverberation to die down, she said, without even glancing Lucinda's way, "What have we not done for you here?"

Lucinda did not know how to answer. What she wanted to say, she did not dare, though a pang in her inflamed gums reminded her.

"Have we not put a roof above your head? Have we not given you a bed to sleep in? And work to do so that you might earn the daily bread we feed you, ungrudgingly? You, and your son?"

The mention of little Davey, dead no more than a week, brought tears to Lucinda's eyes.

"Yes, I see I have cut you to the quick. That's just as well. God gives us trials, so that he may see how we deal with them. You have dealt with yours by running away, by showing ingratitude to those who have helped you, by reverting to whatever wanton behavior brought you to your calamitous state in the first place."

How she could say that was what most astounded Lucinda. Miss Thorne knew perfectly well how she had come to this pass.

"And now—you don't even need to say it—you have come back to beg for your bed, and your job, and a place at the table. A place that a thousand other girls—more worthy girls—would give their eyeteeth to have."

A tear was rolling down Lucinda's cheek, and she hastily brushed it away with the back of her hand. Grit from the bricks stuck to her skin.

"Am I right?"

Lucinda nodded, but it wasn't enough.

"Well? Am I?"

"You are."

Miss Thorne snorted in triumph. "I am of too generous a nature. My brother is forever telling me so. But I know he would want me to extend leniency in this particular instance."

Was that a confession of sorts? Did she know what had transpired between Bartholomew and Lucinda?

"Tell the guardian that I said you may have whatever bed is free, and if none is, you may sleep on the floor until one becomes available."

"And my work?"

Lucinda saw the Matron's eyes flit to her reddened jaw. "No more dipping. You can work on the boxes and bundling."

"Thank you, ma'am."

"As well you should," she said, turning back to the music and studying the sheet she was about to play.

But there was one thing more that Lucinda could not resist asking. "Excuse me, ma'am, but about my boy—"

"Enough!" the Matron said, slamming her hands on the keyboard. The dissonant chord echoed around the room. "One more word, and I'll regret my benevolence."

Lucinda quickly turned around and on her way out, heard a light and frolicsome melody being played. She was glad of the reprieve—a night of sleeping rough on the street would have been hard—but she wouldn't be able to rest easy anywhere until she had resolved what had truly happened to her son, and where he now lay at rest.

CHAPTER ELEVEN

At Conan Doyle's request, Stoker had reserved the best box seat in the house for Professor Arminius Vambéry.

"Despite his voluminous knowledge of all things past," Doyle had said, "he has an equally strong desire to know what is happening in the present, especially in respect to the theater. He is convinced that your man Henry Irving has been touched with genius."

Any man of that opinion was, indisputably in Stoker's view, a discerning, even kindred, soul. Tonight's performance was a production of a melodrama called *The Bells*, the play that had years before truly made Irving's name. He had toured the provinces with one show after another—Shakespeare, Marlowe, Molière—but it was his role as a tormented burgomaster named Mathias that had catapulted him to fame. In the play, Mathias, a murder suspect, is placed under hypnosis, a novel technique and popular pastime of the day, and breaks down; he confesses to hearing, every night, the jingling of the bells that hung from the sleigh of the Polish Jew, whose murder he has otherwise successfully concealed. It was an eerie tale of ghostly revenge and psychological torture, and Irving, in the confessional scene where he imagines himself being hanged for his crime, routinely brought his audiences to tears and hysterics.

With the exception, Stoker had personally been told, of Irving's own wife. On the night when he had first performed the role, he had been riding home in a hansom cab, filled with joy and triumph, and said to her, "One day soon we will have a carriage of our own." And she, looking at him with what Irving had described as "glacial disdain," had said, "Are you going to keep making a fool of yourself like this for the rest of your life?" Irving had rapped for the coach to stop, and gotten out—at the very corner of Hyde Park where he had proposed to her. Though they remained married, he had never lived with, or even spoken to, her since.

It was one of the things that Stoker thought bound the two men together. Both had made unhappy marriages and lived with the consequences every day.

Tonight, the show had gone as well as ever, and the mood in the Beefsteak Club was high. Stoker had taken the trouble to seat Vambéry on one side of Irving, and himself on the other, so that they could have their own little colloquy at the head of the table. But he wondered, given certain aspects of the play, how Vambéry would react. After all, the victim, murdered with an axe on Christmas Eve and thrown into a lime pit, was a wealthy Jewish seed merchant.

But Vambéry appeared able to overlook, or ignore, any of the prejudicial aspects, and congratulated Irving heartily on his remarkable performance. "I think what added to the power of the performance, was the effect of the bells—heard by the audience and the burgomaster, but apparently inaudible to the other players on stage. It made a very strong impression on the spectators."

"Always does," Conan Doyle put in from Vambéry's other elbow. "That's why my friend here," he said, nodding at Irving, still aglow from the applause, "trots out this old warhorse every few months or so."

Irving laughed and raised his pewter goblet. "Long may the old nag run."

The receipts that night had gladdened Stoker's heart. He was the only one who ever knew exactly what the fiscal state of the Lyceum was, and he was convinced it was best to keep it that way. If Irving ever knew how closely they skated to disaster at times, it might affect his ability to perform.

"The play is, of course, based on *Le Juif polonais*," Vambéry said, "a venerable work created by Erckmann-Chatrian and transformed into an opera by Camille Erlanger. The first time I saw it—the opera—was at the Théâtre de Cluny in Paris, many years ago, and the last time was in Krakow, where, as you can imagine, it is hugely popular. Have you ever taken your production on tour there?"

"Not so far," Irving said. "But if you think it would be profitable . . ."

"Oh, most decidedly. Its story is well known throughout Poland and Ukraine, Romania and Transylvania."

Stoker's ears pricked up at the mention of those lands. It was a romantic region, which, although he had never actually explored it, strongly appealed to his imagination. He had long thought of setting one of his Gothic tales there.

"The planning and expense would be immense, but our man Bram can manage anything, can't you?" Irving said, waving a cigar in his direction.

"Yes, I suppose it could be done," Stoker conceded. The logistics would be daunting, but he was already feeling a tingle of excitement at the prospect of seeing those countries for himself.

"If you have not been there," Vambéry said, "let me say you have missed some of the most dramatic scenery in the world. The towering cliffs capped by the ruined castles of the Romanian voivodes, the deep forests—Transylvania, I need hardly explain to this company, means 'through the forests'—the cathedrals of Krakow, the blue of the Moldau, and the Bucegi Sphinx that has brooded on its mountaintop forever."

"A sphinx?" Stoker asked.

"Yes," Vambéry said. "Distinctly Egyptian in its cast. Venerated by the Gypsies, feared by all."

"But the Gypsies," Conan Doyle asked, "weren't they Egyptian in origin? Why, the name alone . . ."

Vambéry wagged his head back and forth, his eyes alive with intelligence. "It is, I think, a common misconception. The Roma—or Gypsies, as they are better known—hail from many places, but in my travels, where I have studied the peoples of that region linguistically and in many other ways, I have come to another conclusion."

"Which is?" Stoker asked, almost ready to take out the little moleskin notepad he kept in his pocket for jotting down his ideas.

"The Indian subcontinent."

"India?" Conan Doyle said.

The professor nodded his bald head solemnly. "It can be detected in everything from their taste for colorful garb, colors not seen in the more sober countries of the West, to their customs and habits."

"And now that you say it," Irving put in, "just take a look at those dark eyes and tawny skin."

"There is that, too," Vambéry said. "The Roma are just one of the distinct tribes and ethnic strains that mix and mingle in the horseshoe of the Carpathians. Sometimes I believe that all the superstitions in the world have been swept together there, too, making it a great, swirling maelstrom of supernatural beliefs."

It was all Stoker could do not to write down every word Vambéry was saying, but he knew that if he took out the pad, he'd be roundly jeered by the others at the table. For now, he just made mental notes.

But once the dinner was over and the clocks had long since struck midnight, he accompanied Doyle and the professor outside, where a cold fog had wrapped itself around the columns and portico of the theater. Doyle, much the worse for wear, said, "Stoker, would you mind taking the professor with you? He is staying over your way, and I'm in quite the opposite direction."

"Not at all," Stoker said, secretly as surprised as he was delighted; he'd assumed Vambéry was Doyle's guest in London.

"I thank you," Vambéry said, leaning heavily on his walking stick as he ascended into the first cab to answer their call. Once inside, Vambéry offered the street address—in an impressive neighborhood—to which he was bound, and Stoker said, "Oh yes, it's not more than a quarter mile from my own place."

"I'm glad."

"Your conversation tonight was as enthralling as Doyle had predicted. I am so very pleased to know you, and I look forward to many more evenings like this." He knew that he was gushing—a tendency he had had all his life—and he tried now to rein it in lest he unnerve the professor. "You are always welcome at the Beefsteak Club—of that I can assure you," he said, sitting back and willing himself to be quiet.

Vambéry thanked him—Stoker had the impression he was used to such fawning—and straightened his gloves; his hands rested atop the gold-headed cane. "I am a great admirer of the English," he said, hastily adding, "and the Irish, too. You have done so much to advance the cause of civilization in the world, particularly in the East where there must be a check to the Russian bear."

Ah yes, politics—hadn't Doyle implied that there would be work for Vambéry to do at the Foreign Office? Now Stoker could see why.

"Is that why you are here then?" he asked. "To consult with the government on political issues?"

"I may do so," he replied, "but I am chiefly here on a private matter."

"Oh, I didn't mean to pry."

"Do not trouble yourself. I am simply here to offer my assessment of some exotic materials."

This left Stoker baffled and more curious than ever, but he let the issue drop, and for the rest of the ride they discussed the play that night and other trivial business. When the coachman pulled back on the reins, and the clip-clopping of the horse's hooves on the empty street slowed, Stoker glanced out the window and saw two unmistakable stone columns—obelisks, smaller than, but similar to, Cleopatra's Needle that stood upon the Thames Embankment—and between them a pair of towering iron gates, elaborately filigreed with what looked like hawks in flight. There was no question now of whose house they had come to.

"But isn't this . . . ?" Stoker got out, before Vambéry said, "Yes, it is the home of Mr. Bartholomew Thorne. Do you know him?"

"Only by reputation."

"A most interesting, and generous, man. Very charitable, I am told."

"Yes," Stoker said numbly, "or so it's said." All he could think of was Lucinda Watts, her face disfigured from working in his match factory.

"Good night then," the professor said, carefully descending from the coach, his walking stick before him.

"Good night," Stoker replied, as a watchman unlocked the gates, and the professor hobbled across the stone court. The house loomed black as a tomb, apart from a single green light in an attic dormer. Before the coach went on, Stoker thought he glimpsed the figure of a man, large and formidable, parting the curtains to peer out at the coach. And then the driver cracked his whip, and the carriage lurched onward.

CHAPTER TWELVE

The HMS *Demeter* was three days out of Bremen and bound for Liverpool before Mina was invited to dine at the captain's table. When booking her first-class cabin, she had used her full name, Minerva Harcourt, and even so was subjected to unusual scrutiny when boarding. She had given it out that her mother was a Romanian countess, and made sure to wear the faux emerald earrings that her mother had once sported. She was in no way ashamed of her true heritage, but she also had no wish to be thrown among the hundreds of desperate folk crammed belowdecks into steerage—especially with the golden box in her possession. She kept it close, or well concealed, at all times.

To her knowledge, there was only one other box quite like it—and she had only seen it once, in a photograph taken of Sir William Wilde, the eye surgeon and amateur Egyptologist who had single-handedly led the campaign to bring over to London the massive obelisk known as Cleopatra's Needle. Though the doctor was dead, his widow, Lady Jane Wilde, lived in London, and might still have the original box, or her late husband's notes about it. Mina was anxious to study one, or both.

Plush as her cabin was, with red velvet curtains at the portholes, satinwood paneling, and a private bath, it was nothing compared to the public rooms of the immense ocean liner. The main dining saloon, where she was sitting now, had a fifty-foot ceiling of coffered oak and inlaid ivory, around a huge skylight through which, when the electric lights were turned off (as they were for dancing or dessert), it was possible to see the moon and stars.

"More champagne, miss?" the steward asked, but Mina—or Minerva as she had to keep reminding herself in order to remain more acceptably upper crust—declined.

"You won't get a no from me," the gentleman to her left said, leaning unnecessarily close, and his glass was duly filled again. By Mina's estimation, he had drunk at least an entire bottle on his own, and the effects were showing. He had introduced himself as János Szabó, a Hungarian aristocrat, and spoken at great length of his family's castle and lands. He had also contrived to brush Mina's hand or arm frequently, attributing his clumsiness to the swaying of the boat, which was at best negligible.

"Are we making good time?" the elderly Mrs. Hathaway asked Captain Dunbar, a crisply uniformed veteran of the Royal Navy. "The seas have seemed quite calm so far."

"Yes, we've been lucky," the captain said. "This time of year, the passage can be rough."

Mr. Hathaway, at his wife's side, was quick to remind everyone, yet again, that he, too, had served in the Royal Navy as a youth—"The youngest on board, I daresay!"—and was familiar with rough seas. "On the way to the Crimea, we lost half the horses aboard, just from their panic and the constant rolling of the boat."

"Ah, but that wasn't an ocean liner back then," Mr. Rutledge put in. "Those schooners were unstable to begin with. How many ballast chambers do you have on this ship, Captain?"

"Four, and we can easily take on enough water, when necessary, to slow the ship's roll and even things out in heavy seas."

"And the engines?" Hathaway asked. "How much horsepower can they muster?"

"We have two engines," the captain replied, "each one capable of generating fourteen thousand horsepower to the screws. We have two of them as well."

He was expatiating on the mechanics of the ship when Szabó, bored, leaned in again, and said to Mina, "Pardon me, Miss Harcourt, but where was it exactly that you said your mother's family was from?"

"I didn't say."

Szabó laughed and clapped his traveling companion, a younger man named Ludvig, on the shoulder. "You see, I was right! She never said exactly."

"So you mentioned," Ludvig replied. He had yet to speak one word directly to Mina, and almost none to anyone else. Nor did he meet anyone's eye.

Turning his attention back to her, Szabó said, "I know Romania well. Took long hunting trips in the Carpathians with my uncles. Lots of big game and beautiful country."

"Yes, it is."

"And where *was* your home there?"

She couldn't duck it again. "Near Brasov," she said, deliberately choosing an out-of-the-way place.

But instead, Szabó perked up and said, "There's an old hunting lodge there, at the foot of the valley, by a stream. I stayed in it for several weeks."

Mina smiled. Damn, she had chosen wrong.

"The Boar's Den," Szabó said, snapping his fingers. "That's what it was called. But this was many years ago. Is it still there, do you think?"

"To the best of my knowledge," Mina said, hoping to change the subject. Captain Dunbar was just then offering to conduct, if anyone wished, a tour of the engines and boiler rooms.

"Mind you, it's a long way from these surroundings," the captain explained, "and not fit, I think, for gentle and feminine eyes, but a wonder to behold, nonetheless."

The two other ladies at the table obligingly demurred, but Mina said, "My eyes are quite prepared to take the risk. May I come?"

Mrs. Hathaway and Mrs. Rutledge looked askance at her, but when the last of the dessert—gooseberry soufflés with lemon cream—was cleared, and everyone rose from their seats, the captain offered to lead the way. Mina followed, with Szabó's hand—in a monogrammed white glove—at the small of her back. She wanted to swat it away, but antagonizing him would only make the remaining days of the voyage that much harder.

The captain had not overstated the case. After a brief detour onto the main deck, where the cold wind blew right through the blue cashmere shawl around Mina's shoulders, they passed through a steel door marked "Crew Only" and into a maze of winding stairs and twisting corridors, all the while going down and down into the very bowels of the ship. The noise grew louder as they descended, a low growl putting Mina in mind of a minotaur lurking in his labyrinth, until they passed through several more closed doors and hatchways and into what suddenly looked less like a maze, dreadful as that might have been, and more like a full-blown vision of hell itself.

Their little band was standing on a narrow iron catwalk and below them—a full twenty or thirty feet down—was an inferno of orange flames and piles of glistening black coal, bare-chested men gleaming with sweat and dust, shoveling coal at a prodigious rate onto conveyor belts of iron chains nestled in chutes that led to the wide-open doors of the furnaces. The fire inside was almost too bright to look at, and the heat, even at this height, was nearly unbearable. Mina let the shawl slip off her shoulders.

Captain Dunbar, leaning close to the group and shouting so as to be heard over the clamor below, said, "They're called the 'black gang,' and you can undoubtedly see why."

Mina most certainly could—the men were so soiled as to appear African, and if they were aware of the onlookers overhead, they made no sign of it. Their heads were kept low, their backs bent.

"The trimmers are the fellows shifting the coal inside the bunkers," Dunbar shouted. "The passers are the ones pushing the wheelbarrows toward the boilers."

Hathaway and Rutledge nodded, and moved on a bit to catch a better view.

"The firemen are the chaps who stoke the belt and the furnaces."

"And how much can they shovel?" Szabó asked while resting a plump and surprisingly proprietorial hand on Mina's bare shoulder.

"The stokers shovel anywhere from eight hundred to a thousand tons of coal per day," the captain replied. "That's if we want to keep up a pace of sixteen knots or so."

Ludvig was leaning perilously far over the railing, transfixed by the sight below, and the captain gently pulled him back by the tail of his dinner jacket. "We don't want any accidents down here."

Noticing something below, or perhaps just wishing to put in an appearance for the morale of the workers, Dunbar said, "Will you excuse me for a minute?" He then moved on a few yards to a connecting spiral staircase leading to the boiler room floor.

As the group spread out along the catwalk, each seeking the best vantage point, Mina found herself alone with Szabó, who put his lips to her ear and said, "Is it too much for you?"

"Not at all," she replied, taking a step away.

But he took an extra step, too.

"You might want to go up to the main saloon with me, and take in a view of the night sky," he said. "So much lovelier."

Mina didn't answer, but pretended to be absorbed in the rattling spectacle of the conveyor belt below, from under which a stoker was raking out cinder and uncombusted lumps of coal. The captain was making himself known, strolling amidst the seeming chaos in his immaculate uniform and cap and hailing the firemen tending the furnaces.

"By the way," Szabó said, in an altered tone of voice, "did you know that I am a man of rare talents?"

Mina could imagine that he had several, none of which she cared to know.

"Yes," he went on, "I can knock the eye out of a buck at a hundred yards. One shot and it's done."

"Remarkable."

"I can guess the carats in a diamond at one glance."

"You should be a jeweler."

"Perhaps I should." He smirked, pretending to be amused. "Because I can spot a fake from a mile away."

At this, Mina paused, her hands on the railing, not daring to turn around to look him in the face.

"I've been to Brasov, that much is true, but there is no hunting lodge called The Boar's Den."

"I may have been mistaken. I have not been back there in years."

"When? Was it when your caravan stopped there to steal some goats and sell some potions?"

And now she did turn around. His porcine face wore a knowing leer.

"You think I can't spot a Gypsy when I see one?" he said, slipping an arm around her waist to draw her close. "Or a pair of paste earrings? All that puzzles me is how you stole enough money to pay for a first-class cabin."

"Let go of me," she said, casting an eye around to see if anyone else from their group was close by. Only the shifty Ludvig, Szabó's confederate, was close enough to be of any conceivable use, and even he had his back to her.

"Come now," Szabó said, "business is business. Let's discuss it in my cabin."

He tightened his grip and planted a kiss, wet with the taste of champagne, on her lips. Squirming to get out of his drunken embrace, she pushed him away, but he caught at her drooping shawl and spun her around to face him again.

"I'll make it worth your while," he said, and before he could lean in for another kiss, she tried to push him away. In the flickering light of the roaring boilers, she saw him laugh and felt his white glove pawing at the small of her back. "No more of that," he said, his voice harder than ever.

He tried to crush her against his chest, but this time she put her hands to his shoulders and pushed with all her strength. His hands slipped off her body, and suddenly it appeared as if a shadow, blacker than those already caroming around the engine room, had enveloped him in its embrace. He was backpedaling on the catwalk, but far faster than her shove would have warranted. His eyes were opened wide, his arms were wildly windmilling. Mina blinked as an errant ash lodged in her eye, and when she looked again, through a clouded perspective, she saw Szabó struggling, as if with some unseen assailant.

"Let me go!" he shouted at the empty air, before tripping over his feet, losing his balance, then screaming as he toppled over the iron rail. The scream ended abruptly as he crashed onto the chute below, so hard that his body jounced from the impact of his back hitting the iron chains of the conveyor belt.

Two of the stokers raised their heads in astonishment, unable to grasp what had just occurred, and the captain whipped around at the sound of the fall.

But the belt didn't stop its relentless motion.

One of the stokers ran to a great iron wheel, the same one Dunbar was running toward, but it was already too late. The flames of the furnace licked out at the bed of coal on top of which Szabó's stunned body was lying; and as Mina watched in horror, he stirred, his head rising a few inches from the chains and his hands in their white gloves groping for the blazing hot sides of the iron chute. His feet in slick patent leather scrabbled at the mounds of loose coal all around him, but escape was impossible, and, as his mouth opened in a cry that was swallowed by the roar of the furnaces, the conveyor belt fed him headfirst into the gaping maw. There was a sudden belch of fire and a gust of purple smoke, as if the furnace especially relished this unusual morsel, but by the time someone had turned the wheel and the belt had ground to a juddering halt, it was all over and done. The captain and the other members of the black gang stood in silent, impotent horror as whatever remained of János Szabó—nothing but ash and powder—billowed up the smokestack of HMS *Demeter* and drifted off over the dark waters of the deep.

CHAPTER THIRTEEN

Although Lucinda wasn't working in the dipping room anymore, her teeth ached nonetheless. She had already had two teeth removed from her lower jaw, and agonizing as that experience had been, she knew she might need to have two more taken out if she didn't want the infection to spread. She had seen match girls who had waited too long; they had lost their entire lower jaw, and their faces looked like crumpled paper bags.

She stuck as close to the one small window as she could, and when an especially strong odor of the white phosphorus wafted her way from the next room, she tried to hold her breath until the smell dissipated. Above the mixing bowls, stirred by one child or another, a fine mist often arose, a mist that carried a cold and almost refreshing tingle, but breathe enough of it and the consequences, as all who worked there knew, were dire. The tips of the matches had to be dipped before being dried and tied into bundles, and then packaged in cardboard boxes with a sandpaper strip at one end for striking. The wood to make them, Lucinda had been told, came all the way from Norway. It was deal, and of the finest and straightest grain. Sometimes, falling into a stupor over the dipping vats, she had dreamt of going to Norway—a place she imagined as nothing but snowy mountaintops and reindeer with bells around their necks.

The night before, however, she had not dreamt of anything so pleasant. Her usual cot was already taken by another occupant—a burly, brawling woman who worked in the mission house infirmary, from which, rumor had it, no one ever returned. Lucinda knew of two or three people who had been taken there—one a young man who had merely broken an ankle in the yard—never to be seen again on the mission grounds. As there was little chance of dislodging the woman from her cot, Lucinda gathered a pile of straw and rags together, and when she asked after her son's effects—a wooden top, painted red; a pair of scuffed shoes; a couple of old shirts and pants—the infirmary worker said, "The clothes went to the rag bin. Ain't seen no toy."

Lucinda had slept fitfully, dreaming of little Davey so realistically that she could hear his voice prattling in her ear. Then she would awaken, see the rows of beds stretching through the vast barracks, hear the snoring and scratching and occasional cry from someone else caught in the coils of a nightmare, and wonder what had become of him. Had he had a proper burial, or had he simply been thrown into the anonymous mass grave for paupers who died under the tender auspices of the workhouse? Thank God she'd had him baptized—at least he would be spared the sadness of purgatory—but it troubled her terribly, not knowing for certain.

She had been at work since eight o'clock that morning, cutting and gluing the boxes together, when Annie, the bedraggled girl working beside her, nudged her in the ribs and tilted her head toward the outside door.

"Knock me over with a feather," she said.

Mr. Bartholomew Thorne—in a burgundy wool coat with a fur collar—and his sister strode into the room, followed close behind by a scrawny man in a blue uniform and cap, scribbling notes in a pad.

"It's an inspection, that's what that is," Annie said. "Be sure now to smile or the Matron'll have it out of your hide when it's done."

"Good afternoon, ladies," Mr. Thorne announced in a booming voice meant to carry over the clatter of the manufacturing; in one hand he held his bowler hat, while the other rested on the silver watch chain that hung over his substantial belly. "We do not wish to disturb you—"

"Or cause any delay in your work," Miss Thorne put in sharply.

"But this gentleman comes to us, quite unexpectedly, from the Women's and Children's Employment Commission. He is making a report, to Parliament no less, on working conditions in the match-making trade." He looked about with a broad smile, as if he were surveying a beautifully appointed drawing room. "And in that capacity, I'm sure we'll all make him welcome."

Thorne applauded, though the sound was muffled by the kid gloves he wore. The workers put down their sticks and splints and clapped along dispiritedly.

"Better hide them teeth of yours," Annie whispered. "Keep your mouth shut."

The inspector looked around, no doubt noting the low ceiling, the single window, the dim interconnecting rooms where the various parts of the task were done.

"You there," he said to Lucinda, who happened to be standing closest by. "Take me through."

"Oh, surely, you want a more regular worker," Miss Thorne remonstrated, moving quickly to grab another of the women—one who had worked there only a month or two, and had no visible injuries as a result—but the inspector would have none of it.

"This one'll do," he said, his eyes flicking to her swollen cheek. "What's your name?"

Lucinda answered softly, hoping to conceal her teeth.

"How long working here?" he asked, pencil poised.

She was stumped. How long had it been? She'd come to the mission house at sixteen, so far as she knew—who had ever celebrated her birthday?—and after working in the rag room for a time, had been assigned to the match-making trade.

"She's been away to see her mother, in the countryside," Miss Thorne interjected, "and only back a few days now. Isn't that true, dear?"

Lucinda nodded, and the inspector pointed with the blunt end of his pencil toward the next room. Lucinda glanced at the Thornes—what was she to do?—but Mr. Thorne gave a warm smile from under his thick brown moustache and nodded at her to go along.

Brushing the grit from her hands, Lucinda led the inspector into the next room; he would be going through the whole process backward. He had started in the last room, where the matches were stuffed into the boxes, one hundred into each, all labeled "Thorne's Own Lucifers—Bringing Light out of Darkness." The room they entered now was the most repugnant of them all—filled with vats of bubbling sulfur, kept over low flames and stirred by several children anywhere from seven to ten years old, whose faces were as white as the chemical stew, their eyes red and hands chafed. The inspector stepped to one wall, then putting one foot in front of the other, toe to heel, he measured the dimensions of the room, this way and that, and counted its occupants.

"Where's the water bucket?" he asked, and Lucinda pointed to a pail in the corner. Empty.

"No windows?" he said, twisting his neck around.

"No, sir."

The odor in the room—a vile mix of sweat and sawdust and phosphorous fumes—was suffocating, and after surveying the drying tables, and making some notes, he started for the next door, but not without stopping to study it, on both sides. "There is no iron plating on this door," he said, "or the walls."

Lucinda didn't know there should have been.

"What's to keep a fire from starting in here and spreading through the whole annex?"

"I'm sure I don't know, sir."

"I'm sure you don't."

The next chamber was, by comparison, a paradise, much larger and filled with long blocks of fresh wood, which were laid on flat iron plates and cut, with astonishing precision and speed, by circular saws; these were operated only by men, three of whom stood mutely behind their machines, silent for now, waiting for the order to get back to work. Beyond that, a double door stood open to a courtyard where additional timbers were stacked ten feet high.

The inspector stuck his nose outside, then, sniffing, made more notes in his pad before heading back through the rooms he had just traversed. Lucinda followed him, eyes downcast, wondering what if anything she should have done or said, something that might have put her back in to the good graces of the Thornes. As they passed through the dipping room, little Timmy Conway, Davey's only playmate, put down the lead paddle that stirred the phosphorus and tugged at her sleeve. With his head down in shame, he held something out toward her.

"I'm sorry," he said, "I shouldn't have, but I . . ."

It was the red wooden top.

A sob rose in Lucinda's throat, and her hand went to her ruined mouth.

"It's just that, well . . ." he stammered.

A cry of "You're dismissed, miss" came from the inspector as he moved on. "The commission thanks you for your services."

Timmy was crying, which made his pale-blue eyes even more bloodshot and swollen than they were from the work.

Lucinda knelt down and hugged him as tightly as if he were her Davey. "You keep it," she said. "You keep it always. Davey would have wanted that."

"But it was only fun when we did it together."

"You'll find someone else to play with."

Miss Thorne clapped her hands together in the doorway and said, "The inspection is over, everyone. Work begins again, right now."

Lucinda rose, and when she got back into the boxing room, she saw the Matron and the inspector leaving, but Bartholomew Thorne lingered behind. If she had any doubt why, it was soon resolved.

"Miss Watts, a word, if I may."

Annie gave her a knowing look as Lucinda was ushered out into the side yard. Damp and foul as the air was here—the whole vast edifice of the mission house seemed its own gloomy clime—it was better than any found indoors. Lucinda could smell the scent of bay rum from Thorne's neck and chin. It was one of the many things that had once enchanted her.

"You did well in there," he said.

"I didn't do anything, really."

"You kept your wits and held your tongue. Under the circumstances, that cannot have been easy."

If by "circumstances," he meant what she thought he meant, then it had been a miracle. Little Timmy Conway and the top had nearly done her in.

"If I may, I'd like to say something of young David."

Although it was only afternoon, the lights were on in the windows of the mission that surrounded them, and Lucinda felt that there was a pair of eyes behind every dirty pane.

"I'm very sorry, of course, about what happened. It was quite sad indeed."

"But was he . . . treated right?" was all she could get out.

"Do you mean, did he receive a proper burial?"

She nodded, almost afraid to know the answer.

"No, he did not."

The wind went out of her, and she started to collapse, but Thorne put a strong arm around her waist—ah, how she remembered the first time he had done that, too—and said, "Wait, you miss my meaning."

But what else could it be?

"He has not been buried at all because we did not know what had become of you. He lies in the mortuary."

"Still?" It had been days and days now.

"And the body is uncorrupted."

Her mind was spinning. Lucinda had seen death before—you didn't grow up in the East End and not see all manner of horrible things—but what Thorne was saying made no sense.

"We have taken certain precautions, ancient ones, long utilized, while awaiting word of your fate."

Precautions? His words were simple enough, but she had no idea what he was trying to tell her. "You haven't got a way, have you, to bring him back to life?" She was so befuddled, it seemed he might be suggesting that, and she clutched at that hope like a life rope.

A strange smile floated across his lips. "This life isn't the only one," he said, sounding a bit like the priest, not so many years ago, who'd grudgingly performed the baptism only after separating Lucinda and her illegitimate baby from two respectably married women who had come to the church for the same purpose; he had scowled at her, and even at her newborn, while sprinkling the holy water.

"You can see him again," Thorne confided, "if you wish."

She could hardly believe her ears. "Now?"

"Soon."

"How soon? Oh please, sir—"

"I will send for you when it's time."

Lucinda was confused. *Time for what? With each passing day . . .*

"If the Matron hears of any of this, she will have my head."

Although it was he, and his fortune, that had established the mission, he liked to pretend that it was his sister who ruled the roost. Lucinda had always had to play along.

"I can't bear it," she said. "I need to see my Davey, even if it is only to say goodbye again."

He nodded, and she saw his gray eyes pass to her swollen cheek, but not as if he felt pity, or even revulsion . . . no, baffling though it was, it seemed almost as if it aroused his desire.

CHAPTER FOURTEEN

Although Bram usually left his wife to attend her spiritualism events on her own—either he was busy at the theater, or he simply had no interest in listening to another endless lecture on Swedenborg's levels of heaven—tonight's event he would not have missed for the world.

Lady Jane Wilde's salons were always interesting, and tonight Madame Zukoff, the most famous medium in all of London, would be conducting a séance. Stoker himself was a strange mix—a skeptic who longed to believe, a practical man who was fascinated by tales of the supernatural and occult—and if nothing else, the evening's entertainment would provide him with grist for the mill. Perhaps he'd alight on that single great story idea, the one he was forever in search of, and which seemed always just out of reach.

By the time they entered 146 Oakley Street, a Chelsea address not far from their own, most of the other guests had already arrived. But in the gloom it was never easy to tell. Lady Wilde had grown larger, and more eccentric, with each passing year, and her salon was like entering the devil's own antechamber. The gas jets were hooded with scarlet shades, the French doors were concealed by long red damask curtains, dusty mirrors reflected a hundred wax tapers flickering on end tables and bookcases, which were in turn adorned with rare and ornate objets d'art. Many of the artifacts were Middle Eastern in origin, as her late husband had been an avid collector—Canopic jars, candlesticks shaped like minarets, beaten boxes decorated with hieroglyphs. And, standing fully three feet high atop the mantelpiece, the grisly pièce de résistance—a mummified dwarf that Sir Wilde had dug up outside Memphis in Lower Egypt.

"How she can live with that there," Florence whispered—her lips concealed by the Japanese fan W. S. Gilbert had given her as a birthday present, from the chorus line of *The Mikado*—"is beyond me."

But that, Stoker knew, was precisely the point. Épater le bourgeois— and everyone else besides. Flanked on either side by copper braziers, in which almond-scented pastilles were burning, the dwarf showed only a narrow band of its face—shuttered eyes, a nose reduced to a brown beak, lips stitched shut—between its tattered bandages. The top of its head grazed the ceiling.

Passing under its malign influence, the Stokers approached their hostess, whose eyesight was growing worse by the day, and were only a few feet away before she saluted them warmly and came forward with both hands extended. Lady Wilde, a fierce nationalist who had written violent screeds in favor of independence, was always more effusive in greeting her fellow Irish.

"I'm so pleased you've come," she said, embracing Florence before firmly shaking hands with Stoker, "so very pleased. And I believe you know everyone else already," she added, sweeping an arm around the dim interior. Stoker nodded to several of the others huddled over cups of weak tea or dry cakes (Lady Wilde was known to buy day-old, as her finances were forever precarious), including Conan Doyle and Professor Vambéry; it was no surprise that Doyle, an outspoken spiritualist, was there, or, for that matter, the ubiquitous William Stead. Conan Doyle, unless Stoker missed his guess, was a devoted subscriber of Stead's odd magazine *Borderland*, packed with occultist twaddle.

There was only one figure Stoker did not recognize, sitting quietly, observantly, in a great wingback chair in the corner. She was a fleshy woman, in a black silk dress with a fur stole around her neck, the fox's head with its black beady eyes and tiny claws still attached. Her own eyes were perfectly concealed behind tiny round glasses with tinted lenses.

"Allow me to introduce Madame Zukoff," Lady Wilde said, and as the formalities were conducted, Stoker sensed that though the woman's expression remained flat and affectless, she was taking in everything. Was she, he wondered, gathering clues for the reading? Trying to pick up on items or verbal cues that might improve her performance? For a performance was what he thought it would be—nothing more. He wore his cynicism like armor.

Madame Zukoff extended a languid and liver-spotted hand, and Stoker thought, *If she thinks I'm about to bend down and kiss it, she has another think coming.* He shook it—the skin was cold and doughy—and said he had looked forward to this evening.

Zukoff nodded, barely acknowledging him, and said to Florence, standing beside him, "He is a needy man, your husband."

Florence gave a nervous laugh—"Aren't they all?" she said—and Stoker, taken aback, did not know what to say.

"Some more than others," Madame Zukoff replied, in a thick Russian accent. "Let him come to you at night."

This was positively shocking, and Lady Wilde let out a whoop of joy. This was just the kind of frisson she liked her evenings to provide.

"Let him brush your hair," the medium added.

And now it was Stoker's turn to be rocked back on his heels. His first reaction was to wonder how on earth she could know that—but his rational mind quickly stepped in to offer an explanation. Surely she must have noticed something in their respective postures—his own and his wife's—to indicate a lack of physical intimacy, and his wife's long blonde hair would of course require many strokes of the brush every night. It could all have been easily surmised, in the way that Conan Doyle's Sherlock Holmes arrived at his startling, but intuitive, conclusions.

Still, if it was her goal to unsettle him, she had done so. And Florence, too, who looked mortified; he quickly escorted her away, to a clutch of guests listening to Professor Vambéry expounding on the peculiar similarities between various Indo-European languages; he was reputed to speak over twenty different tongues. Doyle, his sponsor as it were, looked on like a proud father.

But as the evening wore on, most of the other guests departed, and soon it was down to just the few who were to join the medium for the séance. As if the room were not dim enough already, Madame Zukoff ordered the gas lamps extinguished, and after a large round table had been cleared of bric-a-brac, Stoker and his wife sat down along with Doyle and Vambéry, Stead, Lady Wilde, and Madame Zukoff, whose back was to a hastily erected Japanese screen.

"She doesn't like the spirits sneaking up on her," Lady Wilde confided, but Stoker thought it was more likely that she used it to hide a confederate. How she could see anything through the tinted glasses she wore remained a puzzle.

"You will touch hands," Zukoff said, and they all placed their hands on the green baize table cover, lightly touching their neighbors'. Stoker was seated almost directly across from the medium. No sooner had he followed her instructions than he was overcome by an urge to scratch his nose, and then to shift in his seat, and finally to clear his throat. The medium waited patiently, as the others, too, settled down to business.

Which seemed to require nothing but silence and stillness, for some time. Stoker listened to the distant tick-tock of a clock in the foyer, and wondered what his fellow participants were doing to occupy their minds. Doyle and Stead, true believers, had their eyes closed, as if in prayer. Zukoff's head was lowered, almost as if she'd fallen asleep, but her lips were moving, mumbling something quite unintelligible. Vambéry, Stoker noted, was paying special attention.

Judging from her ramrod posture and distracted air, Florence, he suspected, was still smarting from the implication that she was wanting in marital devotion.

Gradually, the mumbling grew louder, and the medium's head came up, until she said to the empty air, "I am here to serve you."

To whom was she talking?

"Yes, you may come," she went on, as if in conversation with an invisible guest. "Here you will find nothing but friends."

There was a pause, presumably while the guest—or ghost?—debated the issue.

"Can you let everyone here know, by some sign, that you are present?"

Again, a pause. Then, there was a gentle, but distinct, rap on the table. Even Stoker was startled.

Lady Wilde, herself the author of a compendium of Irish superstitions, let out a satisfied sigh.

"Thank you," Madame Zukoff said. "Will you knock once for yes, and twice for no, so that we may communicate?"

Another rap, and Stoker was damned if he could see how it was done.

"Have you come far?"

A rap.

"Have you recently passed over?"

Two raps.

"Ah, you are then an older spirit?"

One rap.

"Very old? Ancient?"

One rap again.

All seemed to be going according to plan. The spirit was proving very amenable and answered several leading questions about the afterlife—whether it was pleasant or painful, what was done to occupy the time, how the souls of the departed comported themselves among each other—and at one point Stoker became aware of a delicate sound, like a reedy flute, playing not far off. If there was a melody, it was an eerie, and stuttering, one at best.

Though the almond scent lingered, the pastilles on the mantel had burned out, and the mummy between them was nothing but a dusky silhouette.

"Is there someone here to whom you would wish to communicate a message?" Zukoff asked.

A single rap.

"May I ask each of you to speak your name in turn," Zukoff said to her tablemates, "starting with Lady Wilde?"

The hostess announced herself, her voice eager with anticipation, but the spirit knocked twice, and then twice again for Professor Vambéry, Doyle, Stead, and even Florence, whose dread, and then relief at being passed over, Stoker could sense.

Which left to his astonishment, only one possibility. Had the medium, guessing him to be a cynic, singled him out?

Or had some spirit actually done it?

"As you are an ancient soul, you cannot have been acquainted with Mr. Stoker in this lifetime," Zukoff said. "Did you know him in some previous life?"

Two hard raps. A definitive no.

"Ah. Then you are acting on behalf of some other?"

One rap.

"May I be so bold as to ask for whom?" Stoker inquired of both the medium and the spirit at once. If he had broken with some protocol, he didn't care.

Two raps.

"Please speak with greater respect," Zukoff cautioned.

Stoker didn't know if he was playing along, or if he believed he was actually in conversation with the dead.

"May I ask then," he said, "what you wish to tell me?"

There was a little draft in the air, the way it felt when he was standing in the wings of the Lyceum and the curtain swung closed; he noticed that the medium herself looked toward the French doors, which were still shut tight.

"Is it about the past?" he asked.

No.

"The future then?"

Yes.

Although he couldn't tell if the current had passed from right to left, or left to right, a current did seem to pass through his fingers, and judging from the reaction of the others, they felt it, too, as it went round the circle. Doyle muttered, "By Jove!"

Zukoff had tilted her chin down, her tinted spectacles slipping down her nose, as if to better assess this phenomenon.

"Is it a benediction, or is it instead a warning of some kind?"

"The spirit cannot answer a question so phrased," Zukoff interjected.

Did he detect a trace of fear in her voice?

"A blessing?" he ventured.

Two raps.

"A curse?"

Nothing. Silence. They all waited, holding their breath. The flute music had died, the almond aroma dissipated. Instead, there was now a dry and oddly desertlike scent in the air.

And then, as if she were shocked at the words coming from her mouth, the medium spoke in a voice utterly unlike her own—masculine in timbre and unintelligible. Still, in whatever tongue it was—the only word that Stoker thought he could make out was that of a figure from Greek mythology—it conveyed an unmistakable note of urgency. The glasses fell from her face, and even in the gloom Stoker could see the terror in her wide eyes.

Something had gone beyond her control.

"Am I in some danger?" Stoker asked.

Again, a torrent of incomprehensible words spilled from the startled medium's mouth.

"It's an Egyptian dialect," Vambéry whispered, in response to Stoker's puzzled glance. "An ancient one."

"Quiet, everyone," Lady Wilde cautioned. "You cannot disturb a medium in trance!"

But Stoker's curiosity could not be contained. "Is something coming?" he asked Madame Zukoff.

The words were hardly out before the French doors exploded open, the curtains flapping wildly in the wind. He felt his face pelted by a thousand tiny grains of grit and sand. Florence screamed as the Japanese screen collapsed—was that a girl crouching behind it, a wooden instrument in her hand?—and the last candles blew out. By only the light of a streetlamp outside, Stoker saw the others push themselves away from the table—Vambéry struggled to his feet; Stead, shielding his eyes from the storm, backed into the fireplace, knocking over the pokers and setting the dwarf rocking in place on the mantelpiece.

But the little mummy had been transformed. Its eyes were open, and its mouth stretched wide in the rictus of a grin. It rocked harder than even the wind could explain, and stopped only after Doyle had slammed the French doors shut and Lady Wilde had stumbled her way to a gas jet and lit it. The scarlet shade had blown off, and the light glared white and harsh. A sprinkling of russet-colored sand—in Chelsea?—dusted the furniture and floor.

Madame Zukoff, slumped in her chair, was pale as a ghost, blinking her undisguised eyes, her fingers grazing her lips as if they were foreign to her touch. "Blimey," she muttered, her accent entirely forgotten, the fox stole drooping from her shoulders, "what in God's name was that?"

But even as Florence clutched him by the arm and begged him to go, Stoker stood, awestruck and staring in wonder at the silent sentinel atop the mantelpiece. Was it the mummy's voice that he had heard? If only he had been able to prolong the séance for just a few more moments, long enough to ask this bundle of bones and rags, what, precisely, was coming . . . and when.

CHAPTER FIFTEEN

Mina had never been happier to get off a boat than she was when the *Demeter* docked in Liverpool and she was able to descend the ramp and put behind her the glowering looks of her fellow passengers, and even the crew. Word of the catastrophe in the engine room had circulated around the boat, despite the captain's best efforts to quash it, and she knew the sailors considered her a bad luck omen.

Mr. Rutledge and Mr. Hathaway had done what they could to offer her support. "An accident, of course, how could you possibly have foreseen it?" Rutledge said. "The man was plainly too drunk to stand," Hathaway offered. But their disapproving wives quickly shut them down, and for the rest of the voyage, Mina dined alone, often in her cabin—though even there she had the strange sensation of being watched.

The first thing she had done after the "accident" had been to bathe in the cramped half tub and put on a nightgown unsoiled by Szabó's gloved hand. If only she could have shed the images from her mind as easily as she had her clothes; she knew full well that she would never be able to forget the sight of the conveyor belt feeding him into the furnace or the blast of smoke as he was consumed. She certainly had not wished him well, but neither had she wished him a fate so terrible as that.

When she had finished with her bath and dried her hair, she had opened the wall safe to check on the security of the gold box.

It was nestled safely right where she had left it, along with the photograph she'd had developed and her notebooks containing the record of her journey to the Carpathian Sphinx. But before she closed the safe again, one thing caught her eye, and she took out the box to confirm it: the tiny latch on the box, the one she had never been able to budge, was open. The aperture it had concealed was shaped like a sliver of the new moon, and she held the box up to the electric light, tilting it this way and that. But she could not detect anything inside. Nor did she hear anything rattling around. What, then, could have been the box's original purpose? And how had it sprung open?

Even more puzzling than that, however, was how it had come to reseal itself. The next day, it was again closed as tightly as it had ever been. It was a mystery for some antiquarian to solve. Right now, as she took her seat in the compartment of the London and North Western Railway train to London, the box was tucked safely and securely into the buttoned pocket of her overcoat. After consulting the current issue of Bradshaw's railway guide, she saw that it would be six hours before she arrived at Euston Station, and her fare would be twenty-nine shillings. That was high, but she planned to go to the Bank of England once she arrived in London and withdraw some money from the account left there by her late father.

Before the train had even pulled away from the station, a gentleman in a beaver top hat had started to enter her compartment, and she had glanced up at him with an anodyne smile, but something made him hesitate all the same. Upon ascertaining that she was traveling alone, he doffed his hat and bowed out again.

A seasoned traveler, she knew what had just happened.

There were attractive, and conniving, young women who rode the trains unaccompanied, only to complain to a conductor that they had been "interfered with." In the kerfuffle that inevitably followed, the gentlemen were often encouraged to make monetary amends on the spot in order to avoid any further embarrassment or the involvement of the constabulary at the next station.

When a noisy family joined her, busy with their own affairs, it was a relief, and she was able to keep to herself and gaze out the window at the ever-changing landscape as the train rumbled through mill towns and farm fields, past dairies and factories, sprawling slums and green hillsides dotted with white sheep. Over the past decade, the railroads had proliferated mightily, cutting a swath in every direction, through towns and countryside, willy-nilly, belching their black smoke and blasting their whistles and rattling toward Manchester or Bristol, Birmingham or Newcastle, at a breakneck pace. Every time Mina had returned, she had seen more railroad tracks, crisscrossing each other at a thousand junctures, until she had come to picture the whole of England as one vast spiderweb, with London sitting squarely, smugly, at its core.

For the last hour or two of the trip, she had fallen asleep, her head cradled between the back of the upholstered seat and the shuddering windowpane. The conductor woke her when they pulled into Euston.

"Shall I send a porter for your bags?" he asked, but Mina declined. Her father had taught her to travel light, and she had packed everything she needed into a single, slightly bulging Gladstone bag.

Stepping out onto the platform—a solid concrete that neither rolled beneath her feet like the ship, nor rumbled like the railway carriage—was a relief. Though it was late in the day, the sun was still shining, its autumnal light pouring down through the vaulted glass and iron ceiling of the great hall and onto the surrounding train platforms—by Mina's estimate, there were at least a dozen or more—congested with porters hauling luggage, passengers hurrying to get on board in time, conductors blowing whistles, newsboys hawking the late edition papers. The contrast between this hurly-burly and the wildernesses in which she had spent so much of her life—lonely deserts, forest glens, mountain peaks—could not have been more extreme, and she could well imagine her father noting the habits and attire of these Londoners, the commotion, and yes, the architecture (as she passed beneath the ponderous Euston Arch) of the city, with the same objective, dispassionate eye he applied to geologic strata or potsherds found on the floor of an Arabian cave.

"And what's the proper name for that arch?" he might have asked her.

"A propylaeum."

"And the columns that support it—which of the five classical orders are they?"

Noting the circular capital, plain architrave, triglyph, and guttae, "Doric," she'd have replied, all to win his smile and the gentle hand on her head that felt like a benediction.

"My little Britannica," he called her at times like that, though nearly all the knowledge she contained he had put there. How she missed him now, how she had missed him for years.

Perhaps that was why she had decided to stay at the costly Brown's Hotel; whenever they had happened to be in London on her birthday, he had taken her there for afternoon tea. She could still taste the raspberry jam and warm scones.

But booking a room there, as a single female traveling alone, could still raise an eyebrow at the lobby desk, and it was fortunate that the elderly clerk remembered her father well.

"And how is Mr. Harcourt?" he asked, and when she told him that he had passed away, he looked genuinely sorry to hear it.

"Always felt a bit like I was talking to Charles Darwin," he said, proffering a key to one of the rooms on the fourth floor. "You know that Mr. Darwin was often here at the hotel?"

"I do." Her father had told her all about the elite X-Club, which had first convened at the hotel decades before in support of Darwin's *The Origin of Species*. It was the chief reason, she thought, her father liked to frequent the place.

Her room was spacious and looked out on Albemarle Street, where hansom cabs rattled over the cobblestones and businessmen hurried to and fro, but by the time she had unpacked her bag and settled in, it was too late to pay a visit on the Bank of England. It would have to wait until the next morning.

Passing by the front desk again, on her way into the dining room—she hadn't eaten since dawn on the boat—the clerk called to her, waving a small envelope.

"Your friend left a note."

"My friend?" No one even knew she was here.

"Yes, miss. He asked if you had checked in yet, and when I said it was hotel policy to reveal nothing about our guests' coming and goings, he said he would simply leave a message for you."

Opening the envelope, she found a sheet of hotel stationery, with one line hastily scrawled on it. It was an old Romanian saying, but in English, with one misspelling. "The dead travell fast." She turned it over, looking for any other words or a signature, but there was nothing.

"Did he leave his name with you?"

"No. Didn't he sign the note?"

"What did he look like?"

The old clerk scratched his forehead. "Ordinary-looking fellow. Dark hair, long, parted down the middle. About thirty? But a foreigner."

"How did you know?"

"Accent. German maybe?"

Another client rang the bell at the far end of the desk, and the clerk held up his index finger to signal he was coming. "If you want to leave a reply," he said to Mina, "I'll give it to him if he comes back."

But what sort of reply could such a message warrant? "No, that's all right."

All through dinner, Mina puzzled over the note. Though she had a few acquaintances in London—most notably, Mr. Cruikshank, the curator of Middle Eastern antiquities at the British Museum, on whom she planned to call—none of them answered the cursory description the clerk had given her—and none would have left such a cryptic greeting. Indeed, the only person she could think of who might have done so was the odious young man, Ludvig something, who had been traveling with János Szabó on the *Demeter*.

But if that were true, it would mean he had been tracking her since Liverpool—and why?

Before she went to bed that night, she left word at the desk that she was not to be disturbed by anyone, for any reason, then double-bolted the door to her room. Apart from a shoeblack in a ragged navy jacket, huddled in a doorway, there was no one on the street now. She pulled the curtains closed, and before going to bed, she took the gold box, in its worn valise, from its hiding place beneath the washbasin. She had learned not to be surprised any longer by the latch of the box being open. As best she could determine, it was almost as regular as a clock, opening at sunset, closed by sunrise. It was a question she hoped the papers of Sir William Wilde might hold an answer to. For now, she placed it under her pillow, and with no rocking of a boat or rumbling of an engine to disturb her, fell asleep so quickly, and so deeply, she didn't even hear the doorknob being tried.

CHAPTER SIXTEEN

The days following Thorne's promise to let her see the body of her son one last time were an agony for Lucinda. She had received one message, in a fancy envelope embossed with a Chelsea address, and torn it open eagerly, hoping it would contain word of when and where the viewing might finally happen. But instead it had simply been a well-meaning, but ultimately disappointing, note from Mr. Stoker inquiring after her welfare and recovery. "I remain a concerned friend," he wrote, "whom you may feel free to call upon at any time." She had stuck the note in the pocket of her dress along with a worn set of rosary beads.

When the message from Thorne did arrive, it came in the form of little Timmy Conway pulling on her sleeve in the boxing room. "Mr. Thorne told me to tell you it's tonight," he said, concentrating so hard he bit his lip.

"Where?"

"The underground gate."

As far as Lucinda, or anyone, knew, the underground gate was permanently chained shut. It led to nothing but an abandoned tunnel excavation for the electrified trains that ran beneath the city streets.

"At what time?"

"Eleven o'clock."

"So late?"

"Eleven o'clock."

Though the main gates to the mission house were locked tight at ten, it would not pose an insurmountable problem—the underground gate was located within the workhouse walls, and all she would have to do was absent herself from her makeshift bed and hope that the night watchman did not spot her loitering in the yard after curfew.

At ten minutes before the hour that night, she rose from her pallet and tiptoed out of the vast, cold barracks, down the back steps leading to the infirmary and laundry rooms, and out the side door that opened into the women's airing ground. Bleak as the yard was during the day, it was far worse at night. In her pocket, she had a packet of Thorne's Own Lucifers, but she didn't dare light one for fear of discovery. Gathering the collar of her coat tighter at her throat and keeping close to the shadow of the walls, she made her way to the underground gate. The padlock was still in place, the rusty chain hanging down, and she huddled under the little roof that the gate provided.

When she heard whistling, she crouched to make herself even less noticeable, and watched as Cullen, the lecherous porter, passed by, swinging a lantern. He was almost out of sight, and she was about to breathe again, when she heard him call out, "You there—wot you think you're doin' out here this time o' night?"

The breath froze in her lungs, and against all hope, she stayed low.

"Answer me!"

The jig was up, and she rose slowly to her feet. But what could she say? To implicate Mr. Thorne in her conduct, in any way at all, seemed unwise, and yet . . .

"Well?"

But oddly, Cullen had his back to her and she saw that he was holding up the lantern in the opposite direction.

"At ease, Cullen," she heard from the darkness just before she was about to speak. All she could see was a tiny orange flame approaching, the end of a lit cigar. "It's me."

"Mr. Thorne, sir?"

"None other. Go about your rounds. All's well."

"As you say, sir, as you say," Cullen gushed, trotting off with the lantern banging against his knee.

Lucinda breathed a sigh of relief and, once Cullen was safely around the corner, stepped out into plain sight in front of the gate.

"Close call," Thorne said, though Lucinda wondered what danger he thought *he* could ever have been in. Thorne was the master here, and most anywhere else she could imagine.

Taking a key ring from the pocket of his long overcoat, he unfastened the padlock, put his shoulder against the steel door, and shoved it open, the bottom screeching against the landing of the cement staircase. A black hole yawned below.

"After you," he said, but Lucinda didn't dare take a step inside.

Thorne chuckled, and reaching past her shoulder, threw a switch on the wall.

"Courtesy of the Albion Amalgamated Transit Company," he said, as a feeble light crackled into life along the steps. "They installed everything from ventilation to electric current before going bankrupt."

It was a steep descent, and Lucinda hesitated.

"Come along," Thorne said, leading the way down the narrow stairs. "Just watch you don't step on any of the rats."

At the bottom of the stairs, there was an iron accordion gate, but this one wasn't locked, and Thorne brushed past it with a firm step. Lucinda kept close behind, as there were blind tunnels leading this way and that, many unilluminated by the tin fixtures. There was a foul and moldy odor in the air, and the cement floor was occasionally obstructed by an old pickaxe or dented helmet or rubber boots, as if the workers had simply dropped their gear on the spot and left, never to return.

Here, the familiar scent of Thorne's cigar was especially welcome, as was his booming voice telling her that it was just a little bit farther on. "But I must warn you, you will have to brace yourself. It won't be an easy sight for you."

She knew that; she had been both dreading it, and aching for it, ever since he had told her Davey was still unburied. The day he died, he had been under the Matron's care. Suffering from a fever brought on by the cold and damp of the workhouse, the meager rations, and other deprivations, he had been transferred to her quarters, for which Lucinda had been grateful. At least it would be warm there. But the next thing she knew, she'd been told he was dead, and the corpse placed in quarantine until the medical examiner could be summoned. She'd been blocked at the door, turned away, and had wandered out of the mission in a daze. Stumbling into the shelter of the Lyceum, she had seen on its stage a vision of the hell she feared she so richly deserved. A better woman would never have had a child out of wedlock, nor allowed him to live out his short life in such a brutal place. She'd left the theater with only one destination in mind—the Thames. The broken bricks, she had found near the embankment, and after loading them into her coat, she had stepped over the railing, and . . .

"We're almost there," Thorne said, turning a sharp corner. The light suddenly became brighter. It wasn't the soft glow of gas lamps, but the harsh white glare of the electric arc lights gradually taking their place around the city.

The chamber was unexpectedly large, but narrow, and she soon saw why. It was a train platform, the tracks leading into darkness at both ends. The overhead lights, hanging from a thick wire, revealed a vaulted ceiling, wooden stools, and several tables covered with cloths in the space where passengers were once intended to stand.

It was the table in the center of the lighted area, however, that her eyes were drawn to.

Could it be?

It was raised, like a bier, and resting on a layer of sand was the shape of a body under a white sheet. A small body. Guarded, it seemed, by a pair of alley cats.

"Here you go," Thorne said, pulling from his pocket a tin of sardines, opening it, and laying it on the concrete. The cats leaped for the treat, snarling and hissing at each other. "Now, now," Thorne said, "share and share alike."

"Well, what do you think of my little laboratory?" he said to Lucinda, who was transfixed. "Nothing fancy, but all that is required." Whisking a cloth off a neighboring table, he displayed a host of strange stone jars with ornate lids, and surgical utensils, their silver blades gleaming. It looked like a cross between an operating theater and an apothecary's shop.

But Lucinda gave it all only a momentary glance. As if in a trance, she moved to the raised table, where the sheet was wrapped around what had to be Davey's little body. The reddish sand had spilled onto the floor all around it.

"That sand came all the way from Saqqara," Thorne said. "It has sacred properties."

She didn't know what he was talking about.

There was a strange odor about the table, too. She had smelled something like it once when she attended an Arabian exhibition at the Crystal Palace. Sweet and fragrant.

"It was my last expedition there, and as dangerous as it could be. Thieves and grave robbers, scorpions and sandstorms. Had to scrape our way out of a fallen tomb with nothing but knives and a spade with a broken handle."

She was used to his stories. Soon after her arrival at the mission house, he had put them to good use, seducing her, not that he'd had to. For a young girl like her, starving and without hope, the scent of his cologne, the soft fur of his coat collar, the lavish meal he could put before her with a snap of his fingers, were enough to overcome any resistance. It was only later, after her belly began to grow large, that he rapidly lost interest, and she could see that she was just one of a string of unfortunate girls who were used, and then cast aside like yesterday's newspaper.

"The other chap, poor fellow, never made it back. Too much of that sand in his lungs."

She was paying no attention. Untucking a corner of the sheet, she noted that the sweet smell grew stronger, and under it the salty scent of the open sea.

"That's natron you're smelling now," he said, changing tack. "A natural salt and wonderful preservative. You'll see."

What she saw was a mound of linen bandages, wound and wound around a body like a cocoon. She could barely make out the arms, bound together, with something stuck between the sad little clasped hands.

Hovering right behind her, Thorne said, "It's genuine papyrus." Then, to explain: "A kind of paper. Very ancient."

But where was Davey? Where was her son in all this? The head was also wrapped in a veil of gauze, and as she began to pluck at it, Thorne interposed himself and said, "That's delicate work—better leave it to me."

As Lucinda stood by the table, Thorne, his cigar still stuck between his teeth, used one hand to cradle the back of the head, lifting it up from its bed of sand, and the other to expertly unravel the long strip of fabric concealing it. Gradually, the lineaments came into relief—she could see the slight protuberance of the nose, the brow, the chin. But the face was still hidden.

Thorne paused. "Now before I go any further," he said, round the lit cigar, "you must understand that this is all for the best. Do you understand?"

"Yes." What else could she say?

"And I can't have you swooning. You asked for this privilege, remember?"

She nodded; he grunted and went on. The last strip of bandage was pulled away, and finally she could look at the face of her little boy—though all she felt was shock.

His blond hair was twisted into a knot at the top of his head, his mouth gaped open with what looked like a snowball wedged into it, and his eyes—his eyes were closed but painted open. The lids looked glued down, and over them had been drawn big blue circles with black pupils staring straight ahead. He had been turned into a mask, a goblin, and her first thought was, how would Saint Peter recognize him at the gates of heaven?

"Before you ask, there's a reason for everything," Thorne said, blowing a cloud of smoke into the air. "That paint, for instance—"

Lucinda screamed, so loudly it echoed off the walls of the tunnel and the length of the platform. Thorne grabbed her and shook her, but she wouldn't stop. Her fists hammered at his broad chest. He flicked his cigar onto the tracks and slapped her.

"I was afraid of this," he said. "No good deed . . ."

She tried to push him away, but he slapped her again, this time on the injured side of her face, igniting a blaze of pain. She didn't care. He hit her again, harder, and when she tried to retaliate, he shoved her away. She went backward, banging into the foot of the bier, and then, as he came after her, head lowered, a wicked but playful look in his eye—she remembered well the kind of games he liked—she turned to run, but there was nowhere to go but down the platform.

Nevertheless, she ran, and once she had gone beyond the pool of light above Thorne's monstrous scene, she collided with something tall and thick, something that rocked on its base like a hobbyhorse, and then with another obstacle much the same. She felt like she was surrounded by a pack of giant bowling pins, one of which suddenly toppled forward, knocking her off the platform and onto the tracks below.

She hit with a thud, and she could hear Thorne raging at her. "Get back here! Right now! Where the hell are you?"

She realized her only salvation was the inky blackness where she lay, and as he paced up and down the platform, she remained perfectly still. When she heard his voice moving in the other direction, she got on all fours and crept down the tracks, farther into the tunnel. All around her, she could hear the squeaking of the rats.

"Lucinda, I'm warning you! If you don't come back here, I shall leave you down here to rot!"

She kept going, staying between the rails to keep her bearings.

"I'm not going to tell you again! Come back, right now, or I will turn off the lights and leave you here till kingdom come!"

She shuddered at the thought, but nothing could persuade her to go back. Not to Thorne, and not—without some means of rescuing him—to the desecrated body of her boy.

"Have it your way then, Lucinda! Have it your way!" Thorne shouted into the darkness. "This is your last chance!"

She had taken that already, she thought. There was no going back now.

After a few seconds, "May you rot in peace!" he hollered.

She must have been twenty or thirty yards away by now. In the distance she could hear his boots clomping on the cement platform, and a moment later she saw whatever faint trace of the lights that had spilled onto the tracks suddenly disappear.

She was alone in the pitch black of the abandoned tunnel. And even if she could find her way back again, up onto the platform and then through those underground corridors and up the stairs, she knew full well that he would have closed the accordion gate behind him and locked the door that led to the airing ground. She'd be trapped, for sure.

There was nothing to do but go forward—the tracks must have a terminus somewhere—and after she had taken a breath, it occurred to her that, if they had not been lost in the fall, she might still have the box of matches in her pocket. Fumbling in her coat, she found an envelope—the one from that Stoker—and under it, thank God, the matchbox. Probably a box that she had made with her own hands.

She struck one, and the blue light flared. In its glow, she saw the glittering eyes of rats, squatting on all sides, no doubt wondering who had had the gall to invade their realm.

"Scat!" she said. "Get out of my way!"

But they didn't budge, and rather than waste the duration of the flame on them, she simply brushed the dirt from her knees, stood up, and stumbled on. She hadn't gone more than ten or fifteen paces before the match burned out, but she knew she had a good supply. One hundred to the box. She lit another.

She kept going, past railway switches and rusted tracks, occasionally spotting metal signs affixed to the tunnel walls with the names of the streets and crossings that must run above them. At least in that way, she could chart her progress.

Slowly, carefully, stepping over one wooden tie after another, she went farther and farther down the track, until a couple of dozen matches had been used up, and she had to stop. The pain in her jaw was excruciating. One of Thorne's slaps had rocked a tooth loose, and she could taste blood. The rats, she feared, could smell it. They were following her like that Pied Piper she'd once seen in a panto.

She stuck a finger in her mouth and found the bad tooth wobbling in its socket. A painful jolt shot through her jaw, but she knew it would only get worse, and so she yanked on it. The tooth came away instantly, and she tossed it as far behind her as she could, spitting a wad of blood in the same direction. She heard a mad scuttling in the dark as the rats went after it.

Looking ahead, she saw another metal sign, but beside this one was an iron ladder fixed to the wall. Above it was a grate, and through it she could see the faintest but most welcome glow of a streetlamp. Forcing herself not to run, she crossed to it. The sign was so dirty that all she could make out was the word "Station," but now she could actually look up and see feet—in boots and shoes—passing over it. She could barely contain her joy as she climbed the rungs and pushed up on the grate.

Which didn't move an inch.

She tried again, but she could only use one hand at a time without risking a fall off the ladder, and after several useless attempts, she saw no other course but to stick her fingers up through the mesh and wriggle them. Several times they were nearly crushed before she saw one pair of soles stop dead.

"Can you help me?" she called up.

"What?"

"Can you help me?"

Of all people, a bobby in uniform bent down, and she saw the badge on his helmet shine.

"Who are you?"

"What difference does that make? Can you get me out?"

"Well, how did you get in?"

"I don't know."

"You don't know?"

She was almost out of breath from clinging to the rungs and trying to ignore the galloping pain in her gums, but she said, "Can you lift this grate?"

A couple of other people must have stopped, as she could hear some muttering and see a pair of hobnailed boots.

"Hold on then," the policeman said impatiently. "We'll have to see about this."

Several hands went to work, and after much groaning and heaving, the grate was pried loose and slid to one side. The constable put his hand down, and Lucinda took it and climbed up onto the pavement, dusting off her coat and brushing the hair back behind her ears. A sign in the window of a milliner's shop announced the latest Paris fashions.

"Now, do you want to tell me just what you were doing down there?" he asked.

"Sightseein'," Lucinda blustered, as the other man laughed and said, "Plucky one, ain't she?"

Thanking them for their time, she walked on, as calmly as if she were taking a stroll in the park, not daring to look back, and all the while suppressing the urge to cradle her aching jaw and flee as fast as her tired legs would carry her.

But where?

CHAPTER SEVENTEEN

Stoker had no use for churches, but he did feel the need to worship. To satisfy it, he went to one place only—the Reading Room of the British Museum.

Under its vast dome, second only to Saint Paul's, a million books were arranged on sturdy iron shelves encircling the main floor where the desks and chairs—hundreds of them—were located. Since the museum's founding in 1753, many of the greatest names in English history had bent their heads in study and reflection here, creating some of the most notable and enduring works in the British canon.

It was Stoker's greatest desire to be numbered among such men, to create something—one thing—of lasting value. Something to assure him of the only immortality any man can truly achieve.

Inside himself, he felt a seed, still buried, that would one day flower . . . but with each passing day—and he was forty-eight now—he could hear the clock ticking and sense his frustration mounting.

Professor Vambéry was already at the desk, waiting, with his cane hooked to the back of his chair and a pile of books spread before him. Some were Arabic dictionaries, some were atlases open to northern Africa, others were travelogues and accounts of archaeological expeditions to the Holy Land.

"Ah, you are here," the professor said, sweeping some of the books to one side to make room for Stoker to sit down. "I have been making headway."

"So I see."

"It all fits rather neatly."

Still shuffling the coat off his shoulders, Stoker said, "What does?"

"The elements, if we shall call them that, of the séance."

Ever since that night, Stoker had not been able to shake off a vague sense of dread. To be told—and by a mummified dwarf no less—that something is coming for you was not easily forgotten; to paraphrase Dr. Johnson's famous dictum about a man to be hanged in a fortnight, it had a tendency to concentrate the mind wonderfully. Stoker was walking more deliberately, coming around corners more slowly, checking both ways before crossing a street, and looking up whenever passing under a crane or ladder.

Tapping a foreign dictionary, the professor said, "I was correct in my first surmise. The dialect she was speaking, or transmitting, as it were, originated around the ancient Egyptian capital of Memphis. Her pronunciation was, of course, muddled"—Stoker remembered how suddenly her Russian pretense, too, had been dropped, and her native English had come bursting through—"but the words were relatively clear."

"The only one I thought I could make out was Demeter," Stoker said, "the goddess whose daughter was kidnapped by the lord of the underworld."

Vambéry nodded. "Yes. But that was not what it alluded to."

"To what then?"

"A ship of that same name. She said *Demeter* was traveling fast across a great sea."

"Something is coming here by boat?

"Indeed, it might already have done so."

Stoker sat back in his chair in shock.

"Yes, my friend, I have consulted the latest editions of the maritime guides—this library is nothing if not thorough—and it appears a ship by that name, sailing from Bremen, arrived in Liverpool on Wednesday."

Stoker remained nonplussed.

"And do you remember that wind, the one that turned Lady Wilde's parlor into a sandstorm?"

"I could hardly forget it."

"To anyone who has ever experienced it, who has felt its dry fingers raking his hair, cracking his lips, or clawing at the back of his throat, it is unmistakable. It is the sirocco."

Stoker had certainly heard tell of it, but no more.

"I was caught in it once, on an expedition in southern Italy. It starts in the Sahara and carries red sand and dust from the coast of northern Africa all the way across the Mediterranean region. The Italians call it the 'blood rain.'"

But how, Stoker wondered, could it have fallen in London?

"When it struck, my horse choked to death under me," Vambéry continued, "and I had to take refuge under an overturned rowboat for three days."

It was hard for Stoker to reconcile this man of such limited mobility with an adventurer of the first water. But so, apparently, he had once been, and Doyle had assured him the tales were all true.

After another hour or two of mutual study—during which Stoker did his level best to peruse an old copy of the *Dublin University Magazine*, in which Sir William Wilde had first advocated for the transfer of an Egyptian obelisk to London—he suggested they take a tour of the museum's unrivaled antiquities collection. He was still struggling to absorb the chilling news he had received. But the professor, to his disappointment, demurred.

"Normally, I would take you up on it—I long to see again the fragment from the Great Sphinx of Giza—but I'm afraid I have an appointment with Mr. Thorne," he said, providing Stoker with an opportunity he had been waiting for.

"May I ask what you are doing for Mr. Thorne?"

The professor paused, as if deliberating how much he might divulge, before he said, "Are you familiar with the German word *Schatzkammer*?"

"Treasure house."

"Precisely. Mr. Thorne has accumulated a very great treasure house—artifacts from all over the world—but does not always know what he has. I am here to offer him my assistance. Nothing more."

Stoker wasn't surprised to hear this. Thorne was a man of great mystery, who had returned from expeditions to the Middle East and Africa with a fortune in his pocket, and had a reputation for louche behavior. The latter he had done his best to amend with eleemosynary gestures such as the mission house, but no one, least of all Stoker, was especially fooled. Even that workhouse had been turned to Thorne's profit, with match making and other services. The girl Lucinda crossed his mind; he hoped she had received his note.

"You will tell me if anyone, or anything, from the *Demeter* should enter your life?" Vambéry asked.

"I can let you know tomorrow afternoon, if you stop at Lady Wilde's. I have to return to fetch my wife's fan. In her alarm, she rushed from the room without it."

"We were all rather perturbed."

Under the stately front portico of the museum, its mighty columns towering above them, the two men parted, and Stoker, checking his pocket watch, set out for the Lyceum where *The Bells* was again being performed that night.

When he got there, he was distressed to have Samuel, the aged stage-door guard, confide, "Mr. Irving, he don't look well, nor sound it neither."

"Where is he now?

"Dressing room."

Stoker had been through it all before. Irving's health was always precarious. As commanding, and even robust, as he could appear on stage, he was a man of questionable constitution—a long and angular frame, beset by aches and pains and, when on stage, a curious affectation in which he often dragged his left leg behind him like an afterthought. Stoker knocked on the door gently, announced himself, and heard a feeble "Come."

He was not alone. Ellen Terry, his leading lady, was seated beside the divan on which he lay, his left arm hanging to the floor, dramatically, like the dead poet Chatterton. His lean face was pale, his gray locks draped limply over his shoulders. A balled-up handkerchief was clutched in his hand.

"When did this come on?" Stoker asked, closing the door behind him and leaning against it. The room was small and the air stale with the odor of sweaty costumes and makeup jars.

"Last night," Ellen answered for him, refreshing a cold compress in a bowl of water she held in her lap. It was Ellen Terry, not his wife, who was Irving's true soul mate and paramour. "I don't think he should go on tonight. The role is too taxing."

"They're all taxing," Irving croaked.

"Do you feel up to it?" Stoker asked.

"When does the fire horse fail to respond to the alarm?"

"Never."

It was what Stoker had expected to hear. Irving would perform that night, no matter the cost to his health.

Leaving him to Ellen's tender ministrations, Stoker went about the usual business of opening the box office, checking the traps and stage arrangements, totaling the day's early receipts, paying the most pressing bills. And when the curtain rose that night, Irving was center stage. Miraculously, the man was always able to rise to the occasion. He was like a vampire, feeding on the energy of the audience, absorbing the heat of the stage lights, soaking up the applause. Although he might have to be carried from the stage once the final curtain closed, he would stand there so long as there was breath in his body or a living soul to holler "Bravo!"

But he did not appear at the Beefsteak Club after the performance—and this indeed was rare. Stoker had to manage in his place, and reassure W. S. Gilbert, Conan Doyle, and several others that Irving was simply recuperating from a cold.

"In Miss Terry's company, no doubt," one of the wags observed.

"I'd gladly contract pneumonia if I could be promised that nurse," another said.

"Gentlemen," Stoker remonstrated, with a glance at the oil portrait of the actress that held pride of place on the walls, and the ribaldry subsided.

Closing up after the last guests had gone, Stoker was on his way to leave by the stage door when he heard Samuel saying, "He's not here, miss—long gone, and there's no use your hangin' about any longer."

Stoker assumed it was an admirer of Irving's—he had many of them—but was surprised when he got closer and saw that the woman at the door, shivering in a threadbare coat, was Lucinda Watts.

She looked as bad, if not worse, than she had when he had first dragged her from the river.

"It's all right, Samuel, I know this young lady."

Samuel stepped back, and Stoker said, "Come in, come in, let me look at you."

Timidly, she stepped into the shelter of the backstage doorway, and he could see that her jaw was inflamed, there was dried blood on her chin, and her eyes were sunken and bewildered.

"My God, what has happened to you?" he said, ushering her toward the back staircase and the dressing rooms downstairs.

She started to reply, but her teeth were chattering, and he could only make out a few words here and there. He heard "my boy, my boy Davey," and "nowhere to go but the street." She certainly looked as if she had been sleeping rough, and it was all he could do to sit her down in Ellen Terry's empty dressing room to use the washbasin there to cleanse her face and offer her some salicin pills for the obvious pain in her jaw.

"Have you eaten today?"

She shook her head, and Stoker went to the foot of the staircase and hollered up to Samuel. "Go to the kitchen and see what you can rustle up for a dinner."

Then he returned and wrapped a shawl—the one Ellen wore in the play—around Lucinda's frail shoulders. This was someone, he thought ruefully, who needed a good deal of saving.

When Samuel came back with a tin plate of mutton and peas, Stoker urged her to eat, but he could see that the meat gave her too much trouble.

"Here," he said, shredding it with his fingers, "try it in little bites and chew only on the right."

"Beggin' your pardon, Mr. Stoker," Samuel said, "but should I fetch a bit of rum? Might warm her up a bit." Now that he could see which way the wind was blowing, Samuel wanted to make up for his earlier rudeness at the door.

"Yes, good idea." And off Samuel went again. "Can you tell me what's happened to you? Why you're not at the mission house tonight?"

Gradually, the story came out, a morbid one at first—had Thorne truly hung on to the body of her dead son?—but one which became increasingly fantastical as it continued. Underground gates, dank corridors, painted corpses. She had drunk the rum, and Samuel had been enjoined to return to his post while Stoker listened to the broken and confusing narrative.

"When did this all happen?" he asked, beginning to wonder if she had not simply lost her mind again.

"Night before last. I had your note, with the address, so I went there first."

"You did?"

She nodded. "Went to the back door, but a cook shooed me away, said she'd call the police on me if I showed my face there again."

"So you came here?"

"I didn't know where else to go. Who'd believe me?" she said, lifting eyes wet with tears. "And who could help me get my Davey back? He can't be left down there, not in that tunnel. God can't find him there."

Stoker did not dispute her.

"Nor recognize him," she went on, "not with those painted eyes, and lyin' on that bed of red sand like some fish on a slab."

Stoker slumped back in his chair. "Red sand?"

"Yes. Thorne went on about it, too, said it was from someplace with a name I never heard of."

No doubt it was an Egyptian name.

"And I can't go to the police. It'd be his word against mine, and who am I? A match girl who's already had to be dragged from the river and stuck in the mad ward of St. Thomas's Hospital. They'd stick me there again."

"The police would listen to *me*."

She grabbed his hands in her cold and fragile ones, and said, "No, I don't want that neither. He's a rich man, he'll say it's all a lie, and then you'll be in it up to your neck, too. And all you've done is be good to me."

"What, then, do you want me to do?" he said.

She paused, apparently aware of the magnitude of what she was about to ask. "I want to get my boy back," she said, solemnly. "I want him to have a proper Christian burial."

Even in her ravaged face, Stoker saw fierce determination, and in his breast he felt the first stirrings of righteous anger. Should he permit such a monstrous deed to stand? Could he live with himself if he did? As the firebrand Lady Wilde had often observed, a single Irishman aroused by injustice was the equal of a hundred English cannons.

CHAPTER EIGHTEEN

In any tally of the magnificent and imposing buildings in the city of London, the Bank of England, on Threadneedle Street, could not be included. The first time Mina's father had taken her there, she was eight or nine years old, and she'd balked on the curb because she thought they were entering a prison.

"It's just a bank," her father had assured her. "It's where they keep our money safe."

An old, low-slung building with blank walls, into which blind windows and useless niches had been intruded, even its iron gate was less ornamental than strictly utilitarian. It wasn't until they had entered the forecourt and a friendly red-coated porter directed them to the office of Mr. Jacobs that her fears had been allayed, though even now, so many years later, she still felt a residual twinge of apprehension—abetted, perhaps, by the mysterious note left for her at the hotel.

In the main saloon, there were long rows of clerks sitting behind a well-polished mahogany bar, counting and collecting gold and silver coins, notes and bills and bonds, with an alacrity and assurance that astounded her. The customers, jostling for position, barked and begged and argued, demanding undivided attention and prompt service for whatever they were there to do. Nothing much, she reflected, had changed, with the exception of Mr. Jacobs.

When she was ushered into his private office, she thought at first there had been a mistake. He had aged so much. Still in his black tail-coat and white cravat, he was a throwback to another era, but his head had settled into his shoulders, his wispy hair was white, and his hand, when he shook hers, trembled ever so slightly.

"I would hardly have recognized you, Miss Harcourt," he said, echoing her own unspoken but reciprocal sentiment. "But I can see your late father—may he rest in peace—in your eyes."

Although Mina felt her dark looks much more closely resembled her Roma mother, she accepted the compliment with grace and took a seat in one of the two worn leather chairs in front of his desk. The walls were lined from floor to ceiling with weighty, leather-bound ledgers, their spines stamped in gold with letters and dates, and although they looked so heavy she thought the elderly banker might topple over while removing one of them from an upper shelf, he managed to plunk it down on the desk with a resounding thump before easing himself into his own chair.

"And where are you coming to us from this time?" he said with a genial look. "Mesopotamia, the Amazon basin, the mountains of the moon?"

"Nothing so exotic as that," she said. "Romania."

"Oh, that will do, that will do fine," he said, his fingers deftly rif-fling through the pages of the immense ledger, looking up the Harcourt accounts. "Were you on an archaeological expedition?"

"Of sorts."

"Did you find what you were looking for?"

Instinctively touching the gold box buttoned into her overcoat pocket, she said, "Not what I was looking for, but something that I found, nonetheless." Or had it, she had come to wonder more than once, found her?

"I am glad to hear it," he said, alighting on the proper page and smoothing the paper with the flat of his hand. Adjusting his bifocals, he studied it for several seconds, his brow furrowing.

Mina did not like the look of that. "I have not requested my monthly stipend since September," she said.

"Yes, I know," he said, not looking up. "We had not heard from you, and we did not know where to send it."

"So there should be a bit of a backlog due me."

He did not reply, but turned to the next page and read what looked to Mina, even upside down, to be a legal missive of some kind.

"What is it?"

"A memorandum from the Harcourt family's barrister."

The Harcourt family had disinherited Sebastian on his marriage to Mina's mother, and she had never had any dealings with them herself.

"One of the clerks must have entered this into the ledger in my absence." Glancing up, he said, "Brighton—I took a week's holiday there, with my brother-in-law. Good to get out of London now and then."

Mina nodded, waiting.

"It appears," he said, "that this account has been closed."

"Closed? How could they do that? It was money left to me by my father."

Still studying the letter, he said, "They contend that the proper arrangements had not been made and notarized in his existing will, and as there had been no codicil either, the money therefore reverted to the family's control upon his death—"

"But that was years ago now."

"You are correct, and the letter in fact states that you are in arrears regarding the reimbursement to their estate." He handed the letter across to her. "It's from Swain and Leggett, of Lincoln's Inn."

"Which means?"

"That you would be in for the fight of your life, I'm afraid. They are a very powerful firm with connections all the way to Whitehall."

"But I'll have to fight. It's rightfully mine."

Taking off his bifocals and wiping the lenses on a linen handkerchief, Jacobs said in a rueful tone, "That alone will cost you a good deal. Have you ready money on hand?"

"No, almost none at all."

"I'm sure they are relying upon that."

Mina's head was spinning. Suddenly, she had washed up in London, and at Brown's Hotel no less, with nothing to show in her bank account.

Mr. Jacobs looked sympathetic, and fitting his glasses back onto the bridge of his nose, he bent his head to the previous page of the ledger.

"There may be something I can do," he said, and her heart momentarily lifted.

"What's the date of that letter again?"

She told him, and he again focused on the ledger entries.

"This is entirely unorthodox, and I must swear you to secrecy now and forever—"

"Consider me sworn."

"—but there is space enough at the bottom of this page for me to enter one additional payment as having already been made before the letter arrived. Where were you based in Romania?"

"Sinaia among other places."

"No, too insignificant for us to have wired there." Mr. Jacobs was the expert on foreign currencies and conversions, which was why her father, an international traveler, had been steered to him as a client. "Where else were you?"

"Bucharest."

She saw his hand beginning to write it in. "According to the bank records now, you were duly wired the monthly stipend for August." He completed the entry, then made out a receipt. "You may give this to any of the clerks in the counting room, and they will pay you the money now."

She looked at the slip for fifteen pounds. She was grateful to have it, but how long would it last in a place as expensive as London? A month? Two? And what would she do once it was gone?

"Where are you staying?" he said, and when she told him, he sat back in his chair, his fingers steepled under his chin. "For someone in your situation," he said, in a not unkindly manner, "it may be difficult to find suitable lodgings."

By "someone in your situation," she understood him to mean everything from her straitened circumstances to her Gypsy looks and unmarried status. Most West End lodgings would cost too much, and many of the respectable landladies would refuse her.

He took a business card from a drawer of his desk and scrawled a name and address on the back of it, followed by a couple more lines.

"I warn you, it is less than you deserve and in a less than desirable location, but you have only to show this card and you will find clean and reasonable quarters."

She read the back of the card, addressed to a Mr. Eli Strauss at 12 Raven Row, in Spitalfields—the Jewish quarter of the infamous East End. The rest of the message was a mystery to her, as it was written in Hebrew.

CHAPTER NINETEEN

Once she happened upon a synagogue on Brick Lane, Mina knew she was in the correct neighborhood. And with her dark complexion, she did not stand out so much among the Jews who populated the area. They had immigrated from every quarter of the Continent—Russia and Poland, Holland and Germany—with nothing but the clothes on their backs and a book in their pockets, and settled in the tenements of Spitalfields. Noble houses that had belonged in a previous century to wealthy Huguenot silk merchants had now been broken up into dozens of dilapidated apartments swarming with families, all living on top of manufacturing businesses, making everything from shoes to chandeliers, waistcoats to wardrobes.

As she consulted the paper Mr. Jacobs had given her, her bag between her feet, an old woman with a scarf tied over her hair said, "Are you lost?"

"I'm looking for Mr. Strauss, at 12 Raven Row."

"You're not far wrong then," the old woman said, pointing to the corner. "Turn there, and you'll see a sign in the window. 'Furniture Finishing and Upholstery.' That's him."

"Thank you."

She shrugged. "He won't waste your time. I'll say that for him."

She made it sound like that was *all* she could say for him.

Mina heard the store before she saw it—hammers were banging, handsaws whining, oaths ringing out. A leaflet announcing a union meeting was tacked to the front door. She stood before the smudged windows for at least a minute before a man came out, brushing sawdust from his sleeves, and said rather brusquely, "How can I help you? What do you need?"

"Are you Mr. Strauss?"

"Yes, yes. Are you here to buy or sell?" His accent was Austrian.

"I have this," Mina said, handing him the card from the bank. "I need a place to live."

Strauss, built like a bulldog, read the front of the card, then turned it over, and after a second laughed.

"He still thinks he can tell me what to do."

"Who does? Mr. Jacobs?"

"He thinks he's English. The English think he's a Jew."

Not knowing what to make of that, Mina said, "He thought you might have a room to let. Cheaply."

"That's what he wrote here," Strauss said, smacking the card with the back of his hand. "Said if I charged you more than four shillings a week, I was a thief."

"I had no idea it said that."

Strauss stood back and looked her over from head to foot. "Where are you from? You're Sephardic?"

"My mother was from Romania; my father was English."

"Romania, huh?" he said, thinking. "You don't fool me. You've got Gypsy blood in you."

"I do." She had hated the masquerade on the boat, and was glad to abandon it now.

"What's your name?"

"Minerva—Mina—Harcourt."

He glanced up at a fourth-story window, where a woman in a kerchief was leaning out over the sill to hear what was going on.

"Is that room clean yet?" he called up to her.

"No."

"Then make it clean." Turning to Mina, he said, "Four shillings a week. And you can tell that to my brother-in-law."

"Was it you he went to Brighton with?"

"He told you that?"

"My father did business with him for many years."

"Like I said, he thinks he's English."

The hallway reeked of furniture varnish and linseed oil, and though the room was small and low ceilinged, the window onto Raven Row allowed in a lot of light. When Mina entered, the woman was sweeping the floor and said, "It'll be ready soon."

"That's fine. I have an errand to run, and I won't be back for several hours."

The woman nodded and continued about her business. Leaving her bag, but holding onto the valise that contained the gold box and the photograph of the Carpathian Sphinx, Mina went out again and boarded one of the underground trains at Liverpool Station. It was a miracle of the age, she thought, this ability to travel so rapidly beneath the congested thoroughfares of London, to start out in the sorry streets of Spitalfields and emerge a short time later into the late afternoon sunshine of Chelsea. Persephone escaping the underworld.

She had read about the eccentric Lady Wilde's salons in, among other places, the magazine *Borderland*, but she had not expected to arrive at her house during one of her "at homes." That, however, turned out to be just what she had done—she had no sooner raised her hand to lift the knocker than the door opened and a couple exited, the man tipping his hat. He looked suspiciously like the painter James Whistler. The maid held the door open, and Mina simply entered, as if expected.

She was ushered into a double drawing room, where a round table held a silver samovar, a collection of mismatched china teacups, and the remnants of various cakes and biscuits. The event must have been drawing to its close, and indeed, there were only two men still remaining with Lady Wilde herself, who squinted up at Mina from under a lace mantilla.

"Good afternoon, my dear," she said, "I'm so glad you could come."

As if she had expected her all along.

She was wearing an old-fashioned lavender gown over a crinoline, tied with a bright green sash to match the ropes of green glass beads draped around her neck and bosom. Mina did not know what to make of it all, and Lady Wilde did not help when she suggested, perhaps to disguise her own confusion, that she introduce herself to the other guests.

"Yes, of course, Lady Wilde, and thank you for your hospitality."

"It's nothing. My house is open to anyone of interesting aspect and amusing conversation. You certainly have the first, and I have every confidence that you shall prove to be adept at the latter."

Mina could see where Oscar got his famously aphoristic way of speaking.

The two men, meanwhile, had stood up—one of them a burly fellow, inexplicably holding a Japanese fan, and the other a bookish, balding sort.

"Professor Arminius Vambéry," the bookish one said, bowing from the waist. "A pleasure."

"Bram Stoker," said the second, extending a hand as big as a bear's paw. Noticing that she had glanced at the fan, he laughed and said, "My wife's—she left it here the other night and sent me back to fetch it."

"I haven't been back to London for several years," she said, "but I doubted that fashion had changed so much in my absence."

"It hasn't. And you are?"

"Minerva Harcourt."

"Did you say Harcourt?" the professor asked. "Is your father named Sebastian, by any chance?"

"Yes, he was," she said, much surprised, "but he passed on several years ago."

"Ah, my condolences."

"Did you know him?"

"Only by reputation. He contributed some splendid pieces to the *Times* on archaeological subjects of interest to me."

"Please, take off your coat—you must be toasting in it," Lady Wilde said, "and pour yourself a cup of tea. It should still be hot."

It wasn't, but Mina was glad to have it, nonetheless. It had been a long day, and now that she found herself installed in Lady Wilde's drawing room, she realized that she had failed to think through her approach. How was she to broach the subject of the gold box? Or inquire into the late Sir William Wilde's papers and journals? Her father had often accused her of being too impetuous for her own good, and this was one of those occasions that proved him right.

"You say you have been away from London," Vambéry said, coming to her rescue. "May I ask where you have been?"

"Many places," she said, "but most recently the Carpathians. Romania and Transylvania."

"*Such* beautiful country," the professor said, with genuine passion. "I am Hungarian myself, but like you, a world traveler," and at that, he began to reel off a long list of exotic places and foreign sites.

The other gentleman, meanwhile, would only glance up at her, shyly, before returning his gaze to his empty teacup or to the fan he batted absentmindedly against his knee.

Around the room, dimly lit by the waning afternoon sun, Mina noticed half a dozen objects germane to her quest—a framed papyrus, an inkwell made to look like an oasis, and on the mantelpiece a perfectly hideous mummy standing no more than three feet high.

"The Blue Mosque in Constantinople—are not its six hundred stained-glass windows the equal of any in the world?" Vambéry was saying, though it was plainly a rhetorical question. "The light, reflected on the blue tiles of the interior—"

"Undoubtedly very fine, very fine indeed," Lady Wilde interrupted, revealing her impatience to know more about her mysterious young guest. "But what has brought you back to London now, Miss Harcourt?"

"You," she blurted. Her father would have blushed for her.

But Lady Wilde laughed with delight. "I only wish Oscar were here to hear that. He thinks the world revolves around him, and here a winsome young woman has traveled a thousand miles to see his old mother. I knew I was right about you!"

"I was recently on an expedition in the Bucegi Massif of the southern range—"

"An impressive perspective from that vantage point," the professor threw in, but before he could go on, Mina continued.

"—where I went to see for myself the monumental figure carved into the mountain peak."

"What figure would that be?" Stoker asked.

"It is sometimes referred to as the Carpathian Sphinx."

Stoker's ears all but visibly pricked up, and Vambéry took the chance to say, "Ah yes, many legends adhere to that particular megalith."

"I am eager to hear them," Stoker said, his hand moving to his coat pocket and removing a small leather-bound notebook and pen.

Mina suddenly felt as if she were at a lectern, and it made her uncomfortable. She had never imagined this interview to be anything but a private dialogue between herself and Lady Wilde.

"Is not one of the legends that it was created by a race of humans, long extinct, who had fled there to escape the Great Flood?"

"That is one," Mina concurred.

"Or, alternatively, that it was built thousands of years ago by a lost tribe of Israel? The same Hebrew slaves who constructed the pyramids?"

"That is another." Would there be any subject, she began to wonder, on which this professor would not prove an authority? And volubly so?

"But what were you hoping to discover?" Stoker said.

"On a certain night of the year—All Hallows' Eve—at the moment the last rays of the sun touch the stone, the face of the sphinx is reputed to change—to come alive, as it were."

Stoker's pen scratched a few words on the page, and without looking up, he said, "And did it?"

"You may be the judge."

He looked up, his brow raised. "And how would I do that?"

Her fingers undid the clasp on the valise. Lady Wilde appeared entranced; if Mina hoped to gain permission to see Sir Wilde's unedited notes on his fieldwork, much less his own gold box, this was the best way to go about it. She carefully slid out the photograph, covered with glass and backed by a thin panel of board. When she had first developed it, in a borrowed darkroom in Hamburg, she could hardly believe her luck; it had come out perfectly. But the light in the room now was insufficient to properly assess it, and Vambéry took the liberty of stepping to the windows and yanking the half-closed curtains open before returning to his chair.

As the late-day sun penetrated the parlor, Mina held out the photograph, angling it slightly to catch the light, and she could hear the intake of breath from all three of her spectators.

The sphinx's hollow eye sockets glowered, its thin lips sneered; the entire expression was one of vitality wedded to malevolence.

"And you took this picture yourself?" Lady Wilde asked, with unconcealed enthusiasm.

"I did."

Even Vambéry for once, was silent. Stoker's pencil, too, held still.

"It is remarkable," her hostess said. "Quite remarkable. But forgive me, I have yet to understand what has brought you, however fortuitously, to my door. Why show this to me?"

Mina waved a hand around the room, encompassing the various artifacts, most notably the dwarf atop the mantel. "Your late husband brought back many things from his expeditions."

"That he did."

"But there is one thing I have seen in a photograph that I should very much like to see. For purposes of comparison."

"Comparison to what, dear?"

No going back now. She let the photograph rest in Lady Wilde's ample lap, and with the same caution she had displayed before, she removed the gold box, swaddled in a protective layer of velvet. The moment the box, with its black silhouette atop the lid, was revealed, Lady Wilde recoiled in her chair.

"It is the very duplicate."

Mina rejoiced; she had been right.

"But you shan't see its twin here," Lady Wilde said.

"You do still have it?"

"Under lock and key I do."

"To keep it safe?"

"To keep *us* safe."

Stoker looked beside himself with anticipation, and the professor leaned forward in his chair, hand extended, and asked if he might hold it.

Mina allowed him to do so, and he examined it closely. "It is undoubtedly of an Egyptian character—the black silhouette, with the head of a dog. But you say it was found in the Carpathians?"

"It was held in the arms of a skeleton, in one of the ancient caves below the sphinx."

"And this latch?" he said. "Have you opened it?"

"It only opens of its own accord."

"What did you say?" Stoker asked, but Lady Wilde, eyes closed, nodded sagely.

"Sir William unearthed a similar box in the tomb of a priest of Isis," she said. "He brought it back to Dublin, where we were living at the time, and where it caught the fancy of one of his nieces who had come for a visit. He gave it to her as a present, to commemorate her coming out into society."

"A commendable gesture," Vambéry put in. "He was known for his generosity."

"But the consequences in this instance were dreadful. At the ball, in County Monaghan, a candle fell to the floor and set the train of her dress on fire. She was not able to wriggle out of it in time. She was rolled, screaming, down the hill and into a snow bank as quickly as possible, but the burns were already too great. She lingered for a week, in agony, before mercifully passing on."

Stoker, out of deference, had not written a word of it, but Mina could see that he had made a mental note of the tale, nonetheless.

"At the funeral, her father would not speak to us—we did not know why, but assumed it was simply from an excess of grief—but when we returned home and unpacked our bags, we found that the box had been inserted into my jewelry case."

Mina was reminded of the haste with which the Gypsy girl had snatched this one from the funeral pyre and sold it back to her. "So you did regain possession of it?" she asked urgently. "And retained it?"

"That I did. We had kept the box in my husband's office at the hospital, but after he passed away and I moved here—Oscar was making quite a name for himself in London—I thought to display it again, among the many treasures Sir William had recovered. From the day I did, my cat would not enter the room anymore—she would stand at the threshold and hiss—and the housemaids would barely stay long enough to dust the furniture or draw the curtains. One of them said that there was always one too many shadows in the room than she could rightly account for—I remember her saying it, as I used it in one of my essays on Irish superstition."

Mina's thoughts flashed back to the engine room of the *Demeter* . . . and the strange shadow that eclipsed János Szabó just before he plunged to his death.

"Where is it now?" Vambéry inquired.

"In a trunk, hidden in the attic of an old house in Sligo. There, it is wrapped in rosary beads and a crucifix blessed by the pope."

"Why did you simply not sell it off and be rid of it?" Stoker asked.

"What, and have that on my conscience? If it's cursed, I won't pass it on, nor leave it for some other poor fool to find it."

The clock struck the hour, and the last light of the sun was extinguished. A maid slipped into the room, lit a pair of gas lamps shielded by crimson shades, and slipped out again just as unobtrusively.

There was a tiny clicking sound, and all eyes went to the lid of the box still held in Vambéry's hands.

The latch was open.

CHAPTER TWENTY

As he left the gloomy confines of Lady Wilde's, his wife's fan tucked into his coat pocket, Stoker's head felt as if it had been stuffed with more than it could rightly hold.

No sooner had he been told Lucinda's horrific tale of the underground travesty—and provided her with a room at the Lyceum—than this new visitor, Mina Harcourt, of the flashing eyes and jet-black hair, had appeared with a story equally fantastical. One which he hoped to explore further with her the next day, at the British Museum.

Even more bizarre was the fact that the tales seemed entangled in some way. A sphinx in one, a mummy in another. And a sinister prediction at a séance, to boot. He could not yet figure out the puzzle or pattern, but it seemed unlikely to have all come about by chance. He felt like he was caught up in some greater narrative; he was a character being driven from pillar to post without yet knowing why or to what end. There was only one thing he did know, and it had been gnawing at him, preying on his mind, all through the day.

Not another night must pass before he had retrieved the mortal remains of little Davey Watts. Such an abomination must not be allowed to stand.

Lucinda had slept the night on the divan in Ellen Terry's dressing room, and Stoker had left word with the stage-door man to move her somewhere else in the theater the next day.

"She's in the props," Samuel confided when Stoker arrived. "I made up a nice little spot for her in back."

Stoker found her fretting among, of all things, the papier-mâché boulders that made up part of the hellish scene from *Faust*. Crumbs of toast and cheese littered a tin plate beside a water jug.

"Here you are," Stoker said. "I see Samuel kept you fed."

"What are we going to do?" she said, looking as if she were ready to jump out of her own skin. "I can't bear it—me here, and him lyin' there in the dark, with his eyes painted shut and all wrapped up like something you'd see in a museum."

"Tell me, where exactly was this grate you came up out of?" he asked with as measured a voice as he could.

"Where exactly? I don't know that I can describe it, but I can show it to you right enough."

He was afraid of that. He would need her to come with him at least that far.

"Then I will need you to do that," he said, "as soon as the show is over tonight."

"And then we can go down there and fetch him?" she said, so eagerly she clutched his hands.

"Then I can follow the tracks and if the body is still there"—one more reason for haste—"I will carry it out again."

"*You* will carry it out?" she protested. "What about me?"

"Your health is still fragile," he replied, "and if I follow the train tracks, I will no doubt get where I need to go on my own."

"I'm his mother, and it's me he'll expect to see."

Stoker did not dare to argue such a point, however misguided, but simply pointed out the horrors she had already endured and that he hoped to spare her revisiting.

Lucinda would have none of it. "I failed my boy once. I'll not fail him again."

Stoker could see she would follow him through the gates of hell itself sooner than be left behind. And so, instead of lingering at the Beefsteak Club once the performance was over—and the pale Irving had been returned to his sick bed—Stoker collected Lucinda from her lair in the properties room and, hailing a carriage from the alleyway, set out, carrying with him a crowbar and a lantern. The coachman looked askance at him, but said nothing, even when he was ordered to go up one street and down another, while Lucinda, her head out the window, tried to ascertain precisely where she had emerged from the subterranean world. It was only when they had passed a milliner's shop for the second time that she spotted a sign for Paris fashions and said, "There—I remember that!"

Alighting from the carriage, Stoker saw an iron grate that was not properly positioned. He would hardly need the crowbar to remove it. Even so, they had to wait for several minutes, lurking in the doorway of the millinery, before the sidewalk was untenanted, and Stoker whispered, "Now."

Removing the loose grate was easy work, and once Lucinda had gone down the iron rungs, and he had handed her the lantern and bar, Stoker followed, lingering only long enough to drag the grate most of the way back into place. He deliberately left it slightly askew, enough that they could quickly manage to push it to one side in the event of a hurried escape.

The air below was stale and dank, and the barrel roof of the tunnel not as high as Stoker would have expected. The lantern light reflected off the walls, exaggerating their shadows as they made their way along the tracks. That Lucinda had made this journey herself, armed with only a matchbox, astounded him and served as a reminder that for all her frailty, there was a core of steel in her that he might yet have to call upon.

The rats were everywhere—this was plainly their kingdom—and he was glad he had issued Lucinda a pair of lace-up boots from the costumes closet. But as if in some strange deference to the interlopers, the rodents kept their distance, scuttling out of the way, or silently watching from their perches, whiskers twitching, their tiny eyes gleaming red in the lantern's glow.

Stoker made note of the grimy street and station signs affixed to the walls, but he would hardly need them to renavigate the way out; apart from a swerve or two, the tracks led in only one direction, and after no more than ten or fifteen minutes, Lucinda raised a finger to her lips and said, "Shhh. It's not far on from here."

With the lantern held low in case Thorne happened to be in his private mortuary, Stoker advanced along the tracks with Lucinda close behind. Just ahead, he could see the tunnel widening to accommodate the platform, and on it he glimpsed what at first he took to be bundles of rags, some of them standing on end, others lying on the cement. Lucinda tugged at his elbow, and pointed up at them.

"I ran into those," she whispered.

It was only when they got closer, and it was clear they were alone, that Stoker climbed up onto the platform and helped Lucinda up. The bundles were all around them, and when Stoker raised the lantern and opened the aperture to allow for more light, he saw that he had stepped into a virtual necropolis.

Several of the tightly wrapped figures were ancient—mummies still swaddled in the winding sheets of ancient Egypt, their empty eyes and whittled brown features familiar from displays in the British Museum. But it was when Lucinda took in the others that she cried out, quickly covering her ruined mouth with her hand.

These were no ancient remains—these were the faces, some painted, some not, of ordinary people, men and women of all ages, their bodies bound tight in linen bandages.

"You know them, don't you?"

Lucinda nodded vigorously, and pointing to the body right in front of her, a young man with his eyes closed and his lips stitched shut, she said, "A broken ankle—he had a broken ankle. That's all."

And yet he had wound up here. There must have been fifteen or twenty of them in all. Stoker felt that he had stumbled upon something even greater, and more malevolent, than he had already imagined.

He lifted the lantern above his head and caught sight of the funeral bier farther along the platform—and the small body that still lay beneath a sheet.

Lucinda was already hurrying toward it, ripping the sheet away, and clutching the body in her arms. Standing in place, she rocked back and forth on her heels, the boy's head cradled against her bosom.

"It's me, Davey, it's me. I wouldn't leave you down here, not like this, not where no one can find you."

Stoker looked around at the tables covered with tarps and cloths, and lifting them saw everything from surgical instruments to stone jars with handles shaped like birds and bulls. He was not unfamiliar with ancient Egyptian practices, and knew that these were meant to contain the visceral organs of the deceased.

"Come on," he said to Lucinda, placing the lantern and crowbar on the edge of the table. "We've got what we came for."

She remained in place for several more seconds, until he gently interposed himself, removing the body from her grasp and gathering it up into his own. The boy couldn't have weighed more than three stone. Good Lord, he thought with horror, had the boy been eviscerated, too?

Lucinda picked up the lantern and bar, and as they turned away, Stoker heard the crunch of footsteps on gritty concrete, approaching from the opposite direction, and then voices—a man's and a woman's.

"Hurry," he whispered, leaping dexterously onto the tracks. He may have been past his prime, but he was still the renowned rugby player of Trinity College, Dublin. Lucinda scrambled after him, the crowbar clanging on the edge of the platform.

The footsteps paused, then resumed in a flurry.

Stoker didn't look back, but moved down the tracks into the enveloping darkness.

"Who's there?" he heard a man's voice, presumably Bartholomew Thorne's, calling out. "Lucinda, is that you? Have you learned your lesson?"

"Where are you, girl?" a woman's voice demanded. "Come out here right now!"

"The Matron," Lucinda murmured.

"Goddamnit!" Thorne exclaimed, no doubt having discovered that Davey was gone. "Bring it back—you don't know what you're doing!"

"She was always a bad one," his sister said. "You should never have taken up with her in the first place."

"Stifle yourself."

"How dare you speak to me like that?"

"If you don't, I'll never get this done in time!"

Get what done? Stoker wondered.

The words that carried down the tunnel were no longer decipherable, though to Stoker's ear the cadence and accents sounded like something he might have imagined issuing from a minaret. He crept on, the boy cradled in his arms, making sure not to trip over the railroad ties. Lucinda held the lantern aloft, and could no more resist looking back, every few seconds, than Orpheus could with Eurydice. Stoker had the feeling she believed, in some small corner of her being, that once she had brought the body above ground again, scoured off the awful paint and unwound the bandages, ripped the papyrus still wedged in his hands into a thousand pieces, that the curse would be magically undone and he would once more spring to life.

That much, he knew, would not happen.

"This way, this way," Lucinda urged, as Stoker shifted the body to lie over his shoulder, in the manner a father might carry a child up to bed. Many were the evenings he had done so for Noel after reading him to sleep in an armchair with tales of the Arabian nights. But where Noel had been soft and pliant, Davey was stiff and hard, the linens having been coated in some sort of aromatic resin. It was more like carrying a life-size marionette than what had once been a living, breathing boy.

"What was that?" Lucinda whispered, turning round again and looking back down the tunnel.

"I didn't hear anything."

"Listen again."

And now, having stopped in his tracks, he realized that the rustling of the linens in his ear had masked the other sound—a distant shuffling, like something slouching along in the dark. They had just come around a swerve in the track, so there was no chance of seeing someone's lantern, if there was one, following their trail. But the sound was unmistakably there.

"Hurry!" Lucinda said under her breath, and Stoker picked up the pace, taking long steps over two or three of the wooden ties at a time.

A street sign on the wall showed him they were nearly back to the ladder and grate.

But damn if whoever, or whatever, was pursuing them didn't seem to be drawing closer.

It had to be Thorne—who else *could* it be? But what struck Stoker was that the man might not be alone. The sounds seemed to come from more than one source, stopping, starting, bobbing, and weaving, like a pack of dogs finding, and then losing, a vagrant scent. He wouldn't have been surprised to hear the baying of hounds.

"Run!" he said to Lucinda, and tightening his grip on the boy, he hurtled along the tracks, staying just within reach of the lantern light. Lucinda let the crowbar slip from her hand, banging on the iron rail, and they had to stop to grope around for it again. When they found it, Stoker grabbed it with his free hand and with the other conveyed Davey to his mother.

"Give me the lantern, and go on ahead, as quick as you can—just keep one foot against the inside of the rail and you won't go astray."

"What are you going to do?"

"Just go! I'll catch up."

Much as he'd have liked to give her the lantern, she would not have been able to carry it along with her son—and he would need it to see his adversary . . . for adversary he knew it would be. But how would this enemy be armed? He weighed the crowbar in his hand—fine in a brawl but useless against a pistol.

He held the lantern up above his shoulder, and swung it back and forth to throw its light around the tunnel. At first, all he could see were the ropy tails of rats running for cover, but then something else came into view, scuttling along, head lowered, arms dangling down like an ape's.

What the hell is this? he wondered.

He backed up slowly, and no sooner had the thing disappeared into the shadows than another, on the other side of the chamber, slouched into the glow of the lantern. This one was slightly more upright, lumbering along like a drunk reeling out of a pub, its sleeves hanging loose, its trousers flapping around its skinny legs.

Neither one was Thorne—and neither one was quite human. Not anymore.

His breath froze in his throat, but his hand clenched the bar tighter than ever. Taking a wide stance in the middle of the tracks, he was determined to make sure neither of these abominations would get past him.

Nor did they try. The first one came scurrying out of the dark and went straight for him, rushing hard and low like an enraged boar. Stoker was able to crack it on the skull, but not before it had smacked into his legs so forcefully he had to stagger backward, the lantern waving wildly. In its crazy orbits he saw an upturned face—brown and wizened—and a mouth whose lips and teeth had been eroded by centuries of desert wind and sand. Bony hands clawed at the hem of his coat, and he had to back up again, just in time for the other creature to lurch out of the shadows and, arms outstretched, snatch at the light. Its eyes were open now, and the sundered stitches hung from its lips, but Stoker recognized him: the lad with the broken ankle.

The lantern was batted from his hand and crashed to the ground, rolling between the tracks and casting a mad glow on the withered limbs of the bandaged creatures grasping at his arms and legs. Swinging the crowbar backward and forward to keep them at bay, he grabbed the lantern again, then continued to back out of the tunnel. Every second that he could delay them meant another second for Lucinda to reach the ladder and drag her son up with her.

But how much farther was it?

He gave a quick glance behind him, even waving the lantern in that direction to see if he could catch sight of Lucinda, but there was nothing. That was good. She must almost be there by now.

But how he would get up it himself with these monsters clawing at his limbs?

At some point, he would have to make a break for it. And when he saw, in the distance, a third shadow racing along like some immense black insect, plainly there to join the attack, he knew the time had come. Instead of retreating, he stepped forward and dealt a smashing blow, and then another, to the spindly frame of the hunched creature, which let out the sound of a teakettle screaming on the boil. The other, the lad, tried to stumble past him, but Stoker wheeled around and struck it on the back of the head so hard it sprawled forward, and when it turned to rise, chittering like a monkey, he split its skull in two with the crowbar. The eyes stayed open, blank, but it exhaled a breath, foul as a sewer, as he wrenched the bar loose again.

And then Stoker ran, the lantern light sputtering, the shadows fleeing along beside him, his boots clattering on the ties. Ahead, he could see a shape moving on the wall—Lucinda struggling to climb the ladder, the body slung over one of her narrow shoulders.

He could hear something gaining on him, something that sounded as if it were running on as many legs as a spider.

"Keep going!" he shouted to Lucinda. "You can manage it!"

He had heard of mothers performing feats of superhuman strength when it was needed—and even once had seen a woman shift a fallen dray horse off the body of her pinioned child in Piccadilly Circus—and he prayed that Lucinda would be able to do the same.

He glanced behind him and saw something as black as a scarab but big as a goat, skittering across the tracks.

"Climb!" he hollered. "Climb!" And by the time he got to the bottom of the ladder, she was on the uppermost rung and pushing the grate aside. As soon as she had made it out, he dropped the lantern and crowbar and started up himself, only to feel something snag his boot and try to drag him down. He kicked out, felt his heel connect with something brittle, heard what sounded like the chirp of the biggest cricket the world had ever known. All he could see, as he shook his leg loose and clambered up the rungs, was something black and shiny, with tiny wet teeth and spindly arms waving like broken branches. It hopped up, jaws snapping, but he was already out of reach, and once above ground, he slammed the iron grate back into place.

A twisted pincer stuck up through the slats, waving wildly, but Stoker stamped on it—the wet splat reminding him of crushing a snail underfoot—and it slithered back below.

Lucinda had hauled herself into the entryway of the milliner's shop, where she was holding Davey across her lap like the Virgin Mary holding her son in the Pietà. Stoker scrambled after her, said, "Are you all right?" And she nodded gravely. He slumped beside her, back against the door, taking deep breaths. She was stroking Davey's brow, and even in the dim recess of the doorway Stoker could see that the boy's eyelids had come unglued—his vacant stare directed at his mother's tear-stained face—and the papyrus drooped from his bandaged hands. For several minutes, they remained that way, until a lamplighter came by and saw them there. Taking them for a family of vagrants, he said, not unsympathetically, "Best move along sharp now"—cocking his head—"the copper's coming."

CHAPTER TWENTY-ONE

Mina was no longer sure if the room she had rented was located above a furniture shop or a revolutionary cell dedicated to the overthrow of capitalism. On the first night, after the fortuitous interview at Lady Wilde's, she had returned to her room, her head filled with plans to comb over Sir William Wilde's published and unpublished materials, and she had found everything in her new quarters neat and tidy, awaiting her arrival. Several leaflets, left on the dresser, advocated the end of workhouses, improvements in working conditions, more sanitary housing for the poor. All that morning, she had heard, mixed in with the clamor of the tools, voices raised in argument about employees' rights, union rules, and meeting times. The debate carried up the stairs and out into the courtyard behind the building, where wagons came and went with desks and armoires, tables and chairs, hat racks and banisters.

On her way out, Strauss himself accosted her to ask if she would be attending that night's lecture on socialism at the Hebrew International Workingmen's Association.

"But I'm not a working man," she said, nonplussed.

"That's just a name on the door."

"And I'm not of the Hebrew faith."

"You're splitting hairs again! That's what they'd like us to do. Squabble among ourselves."

"As you yourself pointed out, I have Gypsy blood." For once in her life, she *hoped* it would disqualify her for something.

"Exactly. Jews and Gypsies have plenty in common, if you take the time to give it a second's thought. Who else is driven to the outskirts of every town we're in? Where you get a field, we get a ghetto. Who else is more discriminated against by those oh-so-pious Christians? We call them goy— you call them *gadjo*. What's the difference?"

She almost had to laugh at his tenacity.

"And who else is blamed for the crucifixion of Christ? If it's not the Pharisees, it's the Gypsies who supposedly supplied the hammer and nails. The Wandering Jew, the Gypsy in his wagon—we're all condemned, persecuted for crimes we didn't commit, then sentenced without a trial!"

He was at once argumentative and beguiling, his eyes sparkling with both fervor and challenge.

"I'll try."

"Eli, where's the trim for the settee?" someone called out from the workshop.

"Or the tortoiseshell," someone else cried, "for the boulle table?"

"I'm coming!" he hollered back, already rolling up his sleeves and returning to work. "Do I have to do everything around here?"

It was a cold, crisp morning, with a brisk wind to dispel the fog that often clung to the streets of the city, and Mina, her valise tucked under her arm, set out with a determined step for the British Museum, where Lady Wilde had donated Sir William's journals and notes.

"He would have wanted me to do that," the Lady had confided when Mina had finally found an opportunity to ask for them. "He wanted the knowledge to be shared with other scholars of antiquity." Stoker, within earshot, had not only praised his hostess's generosity, but on the street outside, he'd given Mina his business card and confessed that he would like to hear about anything she might discover there.

"Can you tell me why it is of such interest?" she'd said.

"A certain medium told me, and in Lady Wilde's parlor as it happens, that something was coming for me."

"And you think it's got something to do with this gold box?" she'd replied, patting the precious cargo under her arm. Lady Wilde had, in no uncertain terms, forbade her twin box from being retrieved or revealed.

"It might," he said, with a shrug. "Or it might not. Madame Zukoff was shouting gibberish—"

"Mediums often do that, I'm told."

"—and the only word of it that I could quite make out was the name of a Greek goddess."

"Really? Which one in particular?"

"Demeter."

She had paused, before saying, "Well, isn't that an odd coincidence?"

"How so?"

"The boat I came here on was called the *Demeter*."

Stoker did not look amused, but had suddenly regarded her with the most intense interest. "May I meet you at the museum?" he said with a note of urgency. "It may be more pertinent than we know."

She had agreed, in part because two heads were better than one, as her father had often said on their explorations, but also because there was something in the man's earnest and intelligent manner to which she naturally responded.

As she crossed Great Russell Street and approached the imposing front portico of the museum, with its towering columns and wings extending on either side, she scanned the faces of the many passersby. Dozens of people were ascending or descending the steps, which were flanked with newsboys waving the day's papers, flower girls with baskets slung on their arms, and shoeblacks, one of whom was just then laying out his rags and battered footstool.

Heading straight for the great Reading Room, where they had agreed to rendezvous, Mina was reminded of the first time she had entered it, her father's hand resting lightly atop her head. He had tilted her gaze upward to take in the vast domed ceiling and the seemingly endless bookcases, packed to the gunwales with leather-bound volumes.

"Everything man has discovered and recorded, up until now, is in here somewhere. You just have to know where to look for it."

"Everything I'd ever want to know?" she'd asked, incredulous.

"I didn't say that. There might be things you want to know that no one has discovered yet."

"Oh."

"But then you might be the one to do it!" It wasn't until she had grown a bit older that Mina began to grasp how much her father's views on women's abilities departed from the conventional wisdom. Maybe she *should* go to the Hebrew International Workingmen's meeting that night—women's suffrage, a subject close to her heart, might come up.

The Reading Room itself had always reminded her of a gigantic wheel—round, with a central hub where a battery of librarians was stationed to assist with requests and questions, and radiating out from it, like spokes, long wooden desks, partitioned every few feet to allow for privacy, with patrons seated on both sides. It was considered impolite to speak to the person sitting opposite, or even acknowledge his presence. Her father had taught her that, too, when she had tried to share her bag of sweets with a grumpy gent deep in his studies.

Stoker was already at the main desk, his arms filled with bound books and dusty boxes of papers. "I took the liberty of getting started," he said, "as I am well known here."

"It looks like we have plenty to start with," Mina said. "Shall I find us a good spot?"

"I've already staked out my usual. Follow me," he said, leading her to the far end of a spoke; he seemed to be walking with a slight limp, which she had not noticed when she met him at Lady Wilde's. Papers and pens were already laid out; it was plain he had his methods and routines. But as she sat down in the second chair he had drawn up, she had to smile at the incongruity. Here was a man who had struck her at first as a bit of a bear, a burly athlete, the kind to whom she seldom had much to say, fastidiously polishing a pair of reading glasses and spreading library materials out under the shade of the conical reading lamp with all the glee of a child on Christmas morning.

"How do you think we should go about this?" he said. "Bound books first, papers later?"

Glancing at the spines of the books with their variegated titles, she said, "Yes, let's dispense with the published books first so we can clear the decks."

"Done. And the first one to come across any mention of dwarves, mummies, or gold boxes, wins."

"What's the prize?"

"The knowledge, of course!"

It was just the kind of thing her father might have said. And like him, Sir William Wilde was nothing if not a polymath. A renowned physician, he'd written books ranging from *Practical Observations on Aural Surgery and the Nature and Treatment of Diseases of the Ear* to a travel diary entitled *The Narrative of a Voyage to Madeira, Teneriffe, and along the Shores of the Mediterranean*. On all subjects, from the anatomy of the porpoise to the beauties of the Boyne and the Blackwater, he wrote with facility, but Mina detected a special fervor in the descriptions of his voyages to the Holy Land and the discoveries he had made there.

By law, a copy of every book published in England had to be deposited in the library of the British Museum, so with their heads down for a couple of hours, she and Stoker skimmed through each of Sir William's books; once they were done with those, to no avail, they then returned them, and bent their efforts to the private files.

Lady Wilde had collected virtually every word Sir William had written—and these included numerous articles for the *Dublin Journal of Medical Science*, letters to the editors of dozens of newspapers, lecture notes, public addresses, encomia to colleagues, and conclusions on the Irish census from 1841. It was Stoker who scored the first hit, of sorts.

Passing her a yellowed piece from the *Dublin University Magazine*, he said, "Egypt! At last!"

A fellow on the opposite side of the desk frowned, and Stoker apologized for his outburst.

It was an article arguing that one of the Egyptian obelisks—or Cleopatra's Needles, as they were commonly known—be transported to England and erected in some suitably public place. In 1878, the argument had been won, and the needle raised on the Thames Embankment.

"I've won," Stoker said, smiling.

"Oh, I've already passed by many references to Egypt in the books I surveyed," Mina said softly.

"You did?"

"But the rules of the game are more specific, aren't they?"

Feigning disgruntlement, Stoker said, "Oh, all right, have it your way."

And back they went in to the musty papers.

It was funny, Mina thought, that such a dry endeavor should foster such a sense of kinship. There weren't many men who would derive the same enjoyment that she did from digging through piles of old papers and journal entries. If it had been a scavenger hunt, she'd have congratulated herself on landing the perfect teammate.

It was only when she loosened the string on a folder holding a batch of unpublished handwritten notes that she felt a current of excitement coursing through her veins. The fact that a few grains of reddish sand clung to the pages only increased the sensation. These were dated 1839, from a place called Saqqara, and had plainly been composed on the spot. She had no sooner read the first few crabbed but legible lines than she gripped Stoker's forearm.

"Listen to this," she whispered:

My surmise was correct. I seem to possess an infallible talent for discovery. At first light, we descended again into the valley under a sun already hot as a branding iron. The sandstorm had swept the dunes into new configurations, and the outline of a doorway was suggested. The workers had lifted their axes and were prepared to chop down the door, when I intervened in time to stop them. The door still bore its mud seal, into the clay of which the image of a scarab had been impressed. This told me that I was to enter an unmolested tomb sacred to the god Khepri, and lest we lose such an artifact, I had them remove the hinges of the doorframe and keep it whole. Given their eagerness to reveal more precious treasures that might lie inside, there was much grumbling, but they did as they were told.

"Khepri?" Stoker said. "I took several courses in orientalism at Trinity—in fact, I still own my much-annotated copy of Petrie's *Egyptian Tales Translated from the Papyri*—but that's not a god I recall."

"The Egyptians had so many deities," she said, "it's no surprise. My father gave me a scarab amulet, sacred to Khepri, when I was a child, and when I told him I didn't want to wear it—what little girl wants to wear a horrible beetle with sharp pincers around her neck?—he explained to me that according to one version of their ancient theology, the sun rose and was pushed across the sky each day by a gigantic dung beetle."

A look crossed Stoker's face that she would have been hard pressed to identify. But his eyes had dropped to his left boot, where she saw deep grooves and scratches.

"What?" she whispered, playfully. "Did a beetle eat your shoe?"

Again, he did not look amused—it was the same expression he wore when she'd told him she had traveled on a ship called Demeter.

"Go on," he said simply.

She returned to the page, reading softly:

> *Once entered, the tomb proved to be less of a treasure cham-*
> *ber than a charnel house. Bones were scattered everywhere—*
> *and this disarray I found most unnatural, especially as the*
> *sanctum had remained inviolate—among sacred vessels, also*
> *still sealed. Presiding over it all and in a vertical posture,*
> *which I again found unusual, was a mummy no more than*
> *three or four feet high. This was no pharaoh's tomb, with its*
> *golden masks and elaborate wall paintings, but the tomb of a*
> *religious functionary of some kind. A priest, or prophet. The*
> *workers, who had, against my strict orders, preceded me into*
> *the tomb, were much disappointed, but as my aims were not*
> *material but historical, I was as pleased as if I'd uncovered*
> *the riches of Araby.*

"What about the gold box?" Stoker said. "So he didn't find it there?"

"Wait, wait," she said, quickly scanning down the page, and on to the next. Miraculously, the arid smell of the desert still lingered on them, taking her back to her own expeditions there. "He lists the contents of every jar and vessel he opened," she said, continuing to read, "but here he has drawn an underline."

The reader opposite harrumphed at their disturbance, and they bent their heads closer together and conferred even more softly than before.

"It is the next morning, and he writes":

> *Upon awakening, I found one of the workers on his knees,*
> *weeping before my tent and offering me a small gilded box,*
> *and when I asked him where it had come from, he confessed*
> *that he had taken it from the hands of the mummy before I*
> *could see it. Now he wanted me to have it, and thereby remove*

the curse. Although I admonished him severely for his theft, I assured him that he had incurred no curse. He shook his head most vigorously, and told me that in the night his son was bitten by a snake and died. It was a sad enough story, I suppose, but as it had brought the box to me, not without its saving grace.

"Not a man known for his compassion," Stoker said.

"No, I wouldn't say so." But she was inevitably reminded of the old Gypsy in whose possession the box had been and what had happened to him. If indeed the box carried some malign influence, how was it that she had so far escaped unscathed?

After quickly perusing the rest of the file and making notes on their discoveries, Mina replaced the papers, bound them again with the frail string, and returned them to the librarians, to be deposited somewhere in the bowels of the vast institution. It was Stoker who suggested that they stretch their legs, but as a heavy rain was beating against the windows, Mina said, "Why don't we take a trip down the Nile?"

It took him just a second to grasp her intent, and together they went to the north gallery of the museum and, passing under the rubric of "Semitic Inscriptions," into the six large rooms devoted exclusively to the wonders of Egypt. Back when she had first come there, and been transfixed by the red granite statue of Amenhotep, her father had told her the collection contained over twelve thousand objects. But in recent years, as Egyptomania had swept the nation, its size had easily quadrupled. The only place that rivaled it was the Musée du Louvre, which had snatched from the British consul Henry Salt anything that the British Museum failed to acquire.

She had, truth be told, another and more private reason for visiting the galleries. Among the colossal bust of Ramesses II and casing stones from the Great Pyramids of Giza, there were countless vitrines displaying more delicate and everyday artifacts, everything from flint knives with ivory handles to sandals from Abydos. It was here that she hoped to find, and soon did, a selection of items with a slim brass plaque announcing their donor.

She waited until Stoker's eye had, of its own accord, alighted on it, before blushing with pride. "Donation of Sebastian and Minerva Harcourt," the plaque read, and Stoker looked at her with undisguised pleasure and surprise.

"I was only a child," she said. "It was my father who made the find and was kind enough to include me."

"I bet it was more than that," he said, and though she felt that she had already overstepped the bounds of modesty, he was right. She had been playing with a Bedouin boy when she tripped over a thick stone buried in the sand. Brushing the sand aside, she had detected the faintest of figures etched into the stone. It was a stela, a limestone slab, and from under the ground all around it, her father had excavated a site containing myriad household objects, many of which were now in this and other cases.

When a pair of other patrons sauntered over to look into the glass, she and Stoker moved aside, and she watched with a profound sense of satisfaction as they commented to each other on the simple utensils and vessels on view. If only her father could have been there beside her . . .

"I'd have liked to know your dad," Stoker said. "I believe he'd have been a man after my own heart."

"That he would have."

Gazing down the length of the gallery, past the many mummies around whom most of the spectators clustered, she saw two gentlemen deep in conversation. One was a big fellow—even bigger than Stoker—in a fur-collared coat, and the other was an elderly man in a black tailcoat, bent over like a waiter carrying a too-heavy tray. With one arm, he gestured at a rear area of the gallery, apparently suggesting how it might be reconfigured. The other man nodded, but looked unconvinced.

"Come with me," Mina said, slipping her arm into Stoker's without even thinking about it. "I've someone I want you to meet."

When they came within earshot, Mina could hear her old friend saying, "But the sarcophagus that's here now can be moved to the next gallery, and that will allow plenty of room for your marvelous donation."

"But I don't like my things being scattered about so. I want a whole section entirely devoted to my contributions—and advertised as such."

The old man looked stymied, and seemed glad at the approach of a couple who might defuse the situation for a moment. He was, however, even more relieved when he saw who it was.

"Miss Mina!" he said, taking her by the shoulders and kissing both her cheeks. "This is such a wonderful surprise! I'd no idea you were in London."

"I only arrived a few days ago. I was meaning to look you up."

"I should hope so! And who is your friend?"

She introduced Stoker, and then, in reciprocation, Mr. Cruikshank, the curator of Middle Eastern antiquities, introduced his companion, Mr. Bartholomew Thorne, who took her hand and held it fixedly.

"Well, with beauty like this in London, it's a shame I've spent so much time abroad."

Mina was not altogether unused to such fulsome compliments, but she did notice that Stoker seemed particularly put off. When it was proffered, he had barely shaken the man's hand, and then stood a couple of feet back, as if expecting to level—or receive?—a blow. She would have to ask him later, and in private, why he appeared so aloof.

"Miss Mina is a great explorer in her own right," Cruikshank explained to Thorne, "and her family has donated any number of invaluable artifacts to our collection."

"Have they now?"

"And Mr. Thorne," Cruikshank then related to Mina and Stoker, "is planning to make a very generous gift of his own to the museum. We are just now trying to decide how and where to do it perfect justice."

"What is it?" Mina asked.

"A trio of green siltstone statues of the goddess Sakhmet."

"When from?"

"About 1400 BC, by my best estimate," Cruikshank said. "And quite imposing."

"Where did you find them?"

"Luxor," Thorne said. "Under water."

"Under water?"

"They had been reused as dock pilings," he said, with a scornful laugh. "The natives have no damn respect for their own heritage. If it weren't for us rescuing these things, they'd be consigned to oblivion, encrusted with coral or wasting away in some desert wasteland."

"'My name is Ozymandias, King of Kings,'" Stoker recited, from the Shelley poem. "'Look on my Works, ye Mighty, and Despair!'"

While Thorne, plainly unfamiliar with the verses, looked at him as if he had just lost his wits, Mina knew full well what point Stoker was making, and added the last lines, "'Round the decay of that colossal Wreck, boundless and bare / The lone and level sands stretch far away.'"

Cruikshank softly applauded, and Mina, turning her attention back to Thorne, asked, "Presumably, you found them on the west bank?"

"I did."

"Close to the necropolis?"

"Quite." He gazed at her with wonder . . . and something more vulpine, too. "I wonder if you wouldn't like to attend a little unrolling party I'm hosting this Saturday night?"

"An unrolling party?" she said quite innocently, though she could guess what he was talking about—the desecration of a mummy by cutting away its bandages and seeing if any treasures—amulets, necklaces, beads—were hidden on the body or in the folds of the winding sheets. Small and insignificant items were distributed as favors among the guests. It was a common practice—though sacrilegious to her mind—among wealthy Londoners.

"It's going to be quite a special occasion," Thorne said. "It's the mummy of Nebetia, a chantress of Amun."

"I wonder what our Mr. Cruikshank thinks," Mina said, turning to the curator, "of such pastimes?"

She knew that she was putting him on the spot, but hoped that he might say something to indicate his disapproval. He was a scholar, after all, and a man of rectitude. But in this instance she proved to be wrong.

"Mr. Thorne understands the gravity, I believe, of the procedure," he stammered.

"Indeed I do."

"And will display all the commensurate respect."

Never expect anything from an official angling for a major donation, she thought.

"Then I accept," she said. "Someone has to be there to observe and ensure the proper decorum."

Which left only one man out.

"And may I bring my friend?" Mina said, indicating Stoker. "He is a great Egyptophile, and I know he will gain much from the experience."

"Certainly," Thorne said, "certainly," though his expression revealed anything but welcome. "Come at seven for a light supper, and the unrolling after. Ten Belgrave Square."

They parted company, and as Mina walked away on Stoker's arm, she leaned her head toward his and said, "Was I mistaken, or do you harbor some strong aversion to Bartholomew Thorne?"

"You were not," he replied, "mistaken in the least."

CHAPTER TWENTY-TWO

Knowing how much it meant to Lucinda, Stoker had not stinted on the various additional funeral expenses. The hearse, black and gold, was filled with flowers visible through its glass sides, and the black horse drawing it had been adorned with a pair of dyed ostrich plumes. In the mourning coach right behind it, Lucinda sat beside him in a somber crepe gown he had purchased for her, with a veil over her face and a handkerchief edged in black clutched in her hand. He himself was wearing a black band around his top hat. Although he was not a great believer in these shows—for that was what they were in his eyes—he knew that the residents of the East End put great store by them, and so he had ordered the coachman to take a roundabout route to the Tower Hamlets Cemetery, where so many from that part of the city found their final resting place.

Though cold out, it was an uncommonly bright day, the sunlight gleaming off the gilding on the hearse, and as the little procession passed by, people stopped to doff their hats or bow their heads. For the poor and downtrodden of London, the funeral was the one and only occasion in their lives when respect was paid to them, when their brief and often brutal sojourn on this earth was acknowledged, and their souls, if such a thing existed, escaped to a better and more peaceful place. He knew that Lucinda, a Catholic, clung to that hope with every fiber in her being.

"Are you all right?" he asked her now, and she nodded.

"Warm enough?" But that she didn't appear to hear. She wore a glazed expression, and barely acknowledged the people on the streets or anything else around them. Stoker glanced at the dilapidated storefronts they were passing, and wondered, not for the first time, how this young woman had not only come into his life, but become in some ways his charge. If he and his wife—to whom he had not dared even mention this event—had had a daughter, she might very well have been about this same age.

Once the hearse turned into the cemetery gates—under a great and Gothic portal, as most London cemeteries displayed—the sounds of the city abruptly dropped off, and all that remained was the huffing of the horse and the creaking of the wheels. Row after row of graves and mausoleums marked the surrounding acres, the headstones conveying some last message of the deceased—the clasped hands on one plot indicating that a husband was now welcoming his wife to the afterworld, an upside-down dove on another representing the eternal life of the winged soul. Lucinda had agonized over what to put on Davey's headstone, and Stoker had suggested a broken bud, signifying a life cut short, but whose flowers were turned toward heaven.

The cemetery, opened only in 1841, was already quite full, with many of the occupants sharing mass graves as much as forty feet deep; the bodies were stacked one upon another like pancakes. Lucinda had had a horror of that, and so Stoker had reserved a private spot, still tiny, in a less tenanted part of the grounds, not far from a duck-filled pond. When they neared the site and the hearse slowed, Lucinda let out a sob, and Stoker wrapped a consoling arm around her shoulders.

"It's a beautiful spot," he said. "You will always be able to come and visit him here."

The grave, already dug, yawned wide, and the two gravediggers now came over to assist in the unloading of the coffin. It was a simple elm box with side handles, and they seemed relieved to see how small and lightweight it was. Touching the brim of their caps in respect, they carted it toward the grave as Stoker helped Lucinda down from the coach.

Unlike some of the other cemeteries, Tower Hamlets was nondenominational, and covered a good deal of acreage, which meant that the official representatives of various faiths were sometimes hard-pressed to get from one burial service to another. Father Cochran was out of breath by the time he reached Davey Watts's grave, where he introduced himself, shook their hands solemnly, and offered Lucinda the most cursory of condolences.

The coffin had been laid across the top of the open plot, suspended on ropes that would be used to lower it once the service was done. The body inside, Stoker knew, had not only been wiped clean of the bizarre paint on its face, but the bandages had been removed and burned, replaced by a white burial gown, something an altar boy might wear. Lucinda had wanted that most particularly. All that Stoker had quietly retained was the papyrus scroll that had been wedged into the boy's folded hands.

As the priest recited the litany of homilies, in a singsong voice that revealed the perfectly perfunctory nature of the ritual, Stoker allowed Lucinda to lean against him, sniffling and staring at the coffin so hard it was as if she needed her gaze to penetrate it. Birds flitted through the bare branches of the sycamore trees, and squirrels scampered around the grounds, looking for their buried nuts. It was only as Cochran was closing his remarks—"Ashes to ashes, dust to dust."—that Stoker was aware of someone calling, "Wait, please wait," and turning, saw a woman with a black cloth tied round the sleeve of her tattered coat, clutching the hand of a child, and hurrying toward the grave.

Lucinda, too, turned to see, and gasped, putting a hand to her perpetually inflamed jaw. "Oh, I didn't think to . . ."

Once the woman saw that they were aware of her, she slowed down, a hand to her heaving chest, and walked the rest of the way.

"Do you know her?" Stoker asked.

"She's Timmy's mother, Maude."

"And that's Timmy?"

"Davey's friend."

"You should have told us sooner," Maude said. "I'm not the only one who'd o' come."

"How did you find out?"

"My cousin Joe, he works for the undertaker." She glanced at Stoker, and Lucinda introduced her.

"It was kind of you to come," he said.

"We wanted to give you my condolences, dear, and tell you that all o' us at the mission house miss you and Davey." Putting her hand on top of her son's head and smoothing down a cowlick, she said, "Timmy here most of all."

He nodded shyly, and Stoker noted that he held something wrapped in paper in his hand.

Lucinda knelt to hug the boy, and he said, "I didn't want him to go with nothin' to play with, so I brung him this." He opened the paper, and Stoker saw a red top and a pair of marbles.

"Oh, but I told you already, Davey would have wanted you to keep that top," she said, but Timmy shook his head. "Don't want it no more. Nor these."

The priest, growing impatient, coughed, and they turned their attention back to his final words. When he was done, but before the coffin was lowered, Timmy was allowed to step forward and place the parcel of toys on its lid. Stoker could not help but be put in mind of the funerary items placed in the tombs of the ancient Egyptians—mundane things, from hairbrushes to honey pots—to ease their transition to the next life. Or of the Canopic jars and face paints employed in the embalmment of young Davey. The fundamental beliefs and superstitions of mankind, however much they lacked in evidence or efficacy, were as universal and timeless as joy or anger.

Once the coffin began its descent—the gravediggers standing on either side of the grave and letting out the ropes a foot or two at a time—the priest mumbled some further words, and Lucinda wept openly, the black-bordered handkerchief pressed to her ravaged mouth. Stoker kept a firm grip on her elbow, less to lend her emotional support than to keep her from impulsively flinging herself into the open pit. Maude stood behind her son, her chapped hands clasped around his breast. A hawk circled in the sky, casting a flitting shadow as it passed back and forth across the cold, bright sunbeams.

Back on the carriage road, Stoker could hear the drivers turning the hearse and mourning coach for the return journey, and he quietly enjoined Maude and her son to ride back with them.

"That's very kind of you, I'm sure," she said, flustered, "but me and Timmy—"

"You and your son will be a great comfort to Lucinda," he interjected. "You must come."

Out of deference, the gravediggers held off on shoveling the pile of dirt into the grave until the coaches had started back, the black ostrich plumes on the horses' heads billowing in the breeze. Passing the still pond, Stoker could tell that Maude was distinctly uncomfortable in such a lavish contraption, but Lucinda did seem to welcome her company, and Timmy's lopsided grin clearly indicated that he relished the novelty of traveling like an aristocrat.

"Have you been in a carriage like this before?" Stoker said, leaning forward.

The boy shook his head, which looked almost too big for his spindly little body.

"You've been a very brave lad today," he continued, but so softly that Maude and Lucinda, consoling each other, would not overhear, "and that's why I want you to have this reward." He drew a gold sovereign from his pocket, and to Timmy's astonishment, placed it in his grubby palm. "Now don't tell your mother until you get home." If the mission house could properly be called home by anyone. "Promise?"

"I promise."

"Good boy."

With the coin clutched tight in his fist, Timmy rode the rest of the way with his head out the window. Stoker had the boy and his mother deposited at the mission gates, where he could see the porter leaning idly on a broom, before instructing the coachman to go on to the Lyceum. He had a great deal of work to attend to, and Lucinda, he surmised, would be relieved, after the strain of the day, to return to the quarters that had been carved out for her at the rear of the properties room at the Lyceum. It was a temporary refuge, just a safe place where he could keep an eye on her until a better plan could be devised. Samuel, the stage-door sentinel, had taken his cue from Stoker, and, genuinely or not, begun to show her civility, and even kindness. *Lord knows she needed it,* Stoker thought, as the carriage wheels bumped along the cobblestone streets toward the West End, past the dismal storefronts and dark barrooms, the crowded tenements and the bleak workhouses of the city. Kindness—such a simple thing—but in such short supply, he reflected, that one would have thought it had to be imported to London from somewhere as far away as the Saharan desert, where Bartholomew Thorne had grasped his fortune and learned his nefarious practices.

Practices, Stoker resolved, that would have to be brought to an end. Both underground, and above it, by any means required.

CHAPTER TWENTY-THREE

Much to Mina's surprise, and relief, she was far from the only woman in attendance at the Hebrew International Workingmen's Association that night. True, the preponderance of the crowd, milling about, elbow to elbow, was made up of working men—mostly Jewish, though not all—in clothing that indicated in one way or another their trade. The butcher's apron, the stevedore's cap, the scholar's skullcap. A nearsighted man standing beside her was studying a copy of the newspaper *Arbeter Fraynd* (*The Worker's Friend*) through a jeweler's loupe suspended from his neck.

The air was thick with smoke and resounded like the Tower of Babel—she heard everything from Yiddish to Portuguese, German to Hungarian, Polish, Dutch, and some she could not even guess. Everyone was arguing, but not in anger. It felt much more like sport, a debate where the object was to score points, impress the others, issue a telling riposte. It only simmered down when one speaker or another ascended to the podium—three packing crates, each atop the other—and launched into a tirade, in heavily accented English, against the ruling class or the sweatshop owners who exploited the match girls, seamstresses, or boot finishers who worked for them.

"An eight-hour day!" a man with a thin goatee was declaring. "No more working our fingers to the bone, for slave wages, from dawn till dusk—"

"Or all night long!" someone hollered.

"No more destruction of our eyesight, trying to see a seam or nail a boot heel by artificial light—"

"Or no light at all!"

"No more breathing of fumes from tanning leather, or dipping matches, or varnishing cabinets without fresh air from open windows and open doors!"

"And open wallets!" an old woman cried out, to cheers and laughter. "A fair wage for fair work!"

A round of clapping began, followed by a song, "The Starving Poor of Old England," sung haltingly by people who could barely carry the tune, much less properly pronounce all the words, but Mina found it affecting nonetheless. It was sung with such fervor. She had traveled the world, and met such people as these in their own native lands, and been welcomed by them.

And now she had seen, from her perch in Eli Strauss's house above the furniture store, exactly how they lived here in England—in cramped quarters above filthy streets, deprived of sunshine and privacy and such common necessities as fresh air and clean running water. She now got her water, as did everyone in the house, from a rusty spigot at the curbside.

She had still been unsure of attending until Strauss himself had banged on her door and said, "The meeting's about to begin! Anyone who's not in the House of Lords is expected to attend!"

She'd laughed and called through the closed door, "I'll be there!"

"Around the corner and on the left side of the street!"

Rather than carry the gold box with her to such a crowded venue, she'd found a secret spot for it behind a loose board beneath the washstand. But the valise she brought with her, with a pad and pencil for taking notes, if she wished, of the proceedings. An old habit, hard to break.

But she hadn't counted on being so squashed among the crowd that she could hardly open it if she tried, a situation that grew even worse when Strauss, plainly a popular speaker, jumped up on the makeshift stage, threw some papers on the crates, and started talking as if he were already in midstream.

"I'm a simple man, and so I'm going to ask a simple question. If one man works all day, straining his eyes, his back, his arms and legs, why should another man, who lives in a fine house and eats fine food and does nothing all day but stroll around St. James Park, profit from it? Why should one man barely have time to see his family, while another man has all the time in the world for climbing on a horse and chasing foxes all day? And does it really take twenty of them riding in a herd with a pack of hounds to catch one little fox?"

"The fox is smarter than they are!" a man in thick glasses called out, then looked around to enjoy the laughter.

"That may be true, my friend! But why does one man grow old before his time, while another is free to enjoy all the years of his life in perfect splendor? No man should be idle, no man should be rich, and no man should be both rich *and* idle!"

There was a general huzzah, and Mina could see that Strauss was a skilled orator, one who could engage the crowd. His gaze darted about the room, meeting people's eyes and making a brief but telling connection. She felt herself jostled by a boy behind her, no doubt aroused by Strauss's words and eager to press closer to the stage. Many were.

Strauss continued in the same vein, though now he began to enumerate more definite demands, from universal education of the young and an end to child labor, to public ownership of banks and railroads and docks. Voting rights should be extended to all persons, twenty-one years of age, male *and* female—she was especially pleased to hear that—and on matters of international importance, a council should be formed, of paid and professional public servants. "No king or queen should be dictating the fate of a nation from a palace on high!"

There was little he said with which Mina could find fault, even as she knew it was almost entirely pie in the sky, notions that would never come to pass, at least not without a prolonged fight. Still, she admired his dedication to the cause, and when the meeting disassembled and everyone squeezed back down the staircase to the street, she was surrounded by people seconding his ideas or, more optimistically, debating how to implement them one day.

It wasn't until she was at the corner that she went to retrieve her notepad from her valise and saw that the buckle had been undone. Quickly, she looked inside, only to see that the pad and her coin purse were missing. Her mind immediately went back to the moment she had felt herself jostled in the crowd but failed to get a good look at the boy's face. How could she be so careless? Thank God she had not had the gold box with her.

But was that what the thief had been looking for? Was she merely the random victim of a pickpocket, or was it someone with more deliberate aims in mind? She hadn't forgotten the cryptic and anonymous note left for her at Brown's Hotel.

Hurrying back to the apartment, she shot up the stairs, holding to the rail as she rounded the top of the banister, and it was only when she thought to fumble for her key, that she realized that it, too, was missing. She tried the handle, and the door was indeed unlocked.

Lighting the gas lamp by the door, she quickly turned, and saw that her worst suspicions had been confirmed.

He was sitting silently, legs crossed, in the chair by the window. Before she could think to stop herself, her eyes darted to the baseboard by the washstand—which looked undisturbed—then back again to her visitor, who took a long drag on his cigarette, blowing the smoke toward the open window. No wonder the room was so frigid.

"What I still can't make out," he said, in an Austrian accent, "is how you did it." He was dressed as a gentleman, but his coat was shiny at the elbows and his trousers needed pressing. Only his shoes gleamed.

"What are you doing here?"

"Mind you, I did not see the whole event in the boiler room, and I do know that my friend János was drunk. He was drunk from the time we got on board the ship. But look at you—you are not strong enough to shove a grown man over a railing, no matter how drunk he is. No, something else entered into it."

It was a question, strangely enough, that she had asked herself. She had given the man a good push, but then . . . something else *had* happened. A shadow had passed across her vision, and the next thing she knew, Szabó had been toppling over the catwalk.

But as for the box, she reminded herself, Ludvig couldn't be here specifically in search of it; he had no way of knowing it even existed.

"Do I have you to thank for rifling my valise at the meeting?"

"I can hardly be in two places at once."

So he had a confederate. A boy. Redheaded, was all she'd made of him. Except . . . there had been something familiar about him.

"Can I get my things back?"

He gestured at the bed, where she saw her purse, her pad, and her door key on the pillow.

"I told him to bring me anything of interest. There was nothing of interest to me."

She looked in the purse and saw that the money, too, was still there.

"It's not the boy's true profession. He's not a thief."

The purse, fawn-colored, had black smudges around the clasp.

The shoeblack, that was it—she'd seen him outside her hotel. And again, at the British Museum.

"What did you expect to find?" she said.

"That is what I am here for you to tell me."

She thought of simply calling for help—the tenement was full, and even Strauss himself might be home by now. But the menace she sensed from Ludvig was not physical. Not yet at least.

"I am thinking that you Gypsies always have some trick up your sleeve. You are a wily lot."

"Of course we are," she said. "That is how I wound up living in one tiny room above a furniture shop in the East End."

"Jews and Gypsies, thick as thieves. But if Mr. Jacobs is your man at the Bank of England, then you do have resources. Why you choose not to spend them is your business."

"But you mean to make it yours?"

"Alas, I am a man in need of some assistance, washed up upon this alien shore. János Szabó was not only my friend, but my benefactor. And now you have done away with him."

"I did no such thing."

He waved away her objection, flinging the butt of the cigarette out the window in the process. "You will have to make up for my loss."

"Or what?"

"Oh, I do not see any reason to cross that bridge until we come to it. Isn't that what you English say?"

"A moment ago I was a Gypsy."

"You are both—and neither is commendable." Brushing ash off his trousers, he rose from the chair and took a step toward the door.

Mina stepped back, her legs bumping against the side of the bed, to let him pass.

"For now, I am at the Langham Hotel. My bill will not be due until the end of the week. By then, I expect you to have left me sufficient funds to pay it."

He opened the door and departed, and she flopped on the bed in relief. But then a thought crossed her mind, and she hurried out onto the landing. He was halfway down the top flight of steps. "Who are you?" she called out. "I don't even know your last name."

"Gerhard," he said, without looking back. "Ludvig Gerhard."

Craning her neck over the banister to monitor his descent, she saw Eli Strauss coming in, and the two men passed each other with a wary glance. Strauss caught her watching from above, and once her visitor was gone, he said, "And who was that?"

"If you ever see him here again, feel free to throw him out."

"With pleasure," he said, glancing back at the door as if the man were still there. "I didn't like him on sight. Capitalist swine."

CHAPTER TWENTY-FOUR

Stoker had never been a good liar, and so he dressed as quickly as possible in his room, and hoped to get out the door before Florence could take note of his more formal attire. But Mary, the housemaid, stopped him in the hall to ask if he could leave her a ticket to the Lyceum on her afternoon off—"Up in the gods is more than good enough for me."—and then the cook wanted to know if he would be dining at home that night. Florence overheard him saying he would not be.

"Where will you be instead?" she said from the parlor, where she was arranging some flowers in a vase. "Your infernal Beefsteak Club, I suppose?"

"Yes."

Glancing over at him, she said, "Aren't you a bit overdressed for that lot?"

"It's the anniversary of the club. A special banquet."

"Just don't make a racket coming home."

And then he was out the door and on his way to Mina's in a closed carriage. In all the years of his marriage, he had remained faithful and proper, and so now, even though he had no untoward intentions, he felt not quite himself. He had never, for instance, engaged a mistress. As the manager of a theatrical company often on the road, he had not wanted for opportunities; Henry Irving made fun of him for squandering them.

"Good old Bram," he'd say, clapping him on the shoulder on his way to some local house of ill repute. "Loyal to the home fires, even when they have been banked for years."

Now, dressed for the unrolling party at Bartholomew Thorne's and traveling to pick up a beautiful young woman, he felt like some illicit lover on his way to a secret assignation. It was not an altogether unpleasant sensation, even if the occasion was a peculiar one indeed.

When the cab drew to a stop before the furniture shop, Stoker consulted the piece of paper in his hand again to make sure this was the right address, then got out, and in the vestibule—if the dingy, dark entryway could be so called—encountered a pugnacious fellow with rolled-up sleeves, who said, "And where do you think you're going?"

"I'm here for Miss Mina Harcourt," Stoker said.

"She's expecting you?"

"What business is that of yours?"

"I'm Strauss. I own this place."

"Oh, in that case, yes. Mina has spoken of you, and well."

"I'm coming right down, Bram," she called from the upper floor.

The two men waited together, somewhat uncomfortably, as a door was locked, and footsteps descended the stairs. Under an open cloth coat, Mina was wearing a simple black frock with a single piece of jewelry—a carnelian ankh, the Egyptian symbol of enduring life—around her neck. When she saw Stoker noticing it, she said, "My father found it, and I loved it. It was one thing he did not donate, or have to sell."

"Very fitting, given where we're going."

"Where *are* you going?" Strauss asked, still behaving like an anxious father.

"An evening at the home of a collector of all things Egyptian," Mina said, circumspectly. Had she told him it was a mummy party, he'd have probably evinced disgust; if she'd told him it was at the home of the plutocrat Mr. Bartholomew Thorne, he'd have been spitting nails.

Stoker half expected him to impose a curfew next, but instead he grunted and went back into his workshop.

As they settled into the cab, Mina said, "He's very protective of his tenants."

"I rather like that."

Smiling, she said, "So do I."

Stoker held his hat on his lap, his fingers nervously twirling it by the brim. He had not counted on feeling quite so . . . awkward. On the two occasions he'd seen Mina before this, it had been among company—at Lady Wilde's parlor and at the library, toiling over the books or strolling through the museum galleries. They had never sat in such close and confined quarters, their shoulders touching, their knees, too, when the coach hit an especially rough patch of road. Mina, he felt, sensed it, too, and kept her eyes averted, looking out at the fogbound streets through the small window, as the neighborhoods changed from dirty and congested to the quieter and more refined sanctuaries of Mayfair and Belgravia.

Even here, however, all was not completely still. Under the feeble glow of the streetlamps, Stoker saw an open pit not more than a block or two from Thorne's manse, with men working feverishly by artificial light to make progress on yet another of the underground lines that were forever being built and extended beneath the streets of the city. By day, the pit would be covered with wide iron plates, to accommodate the normal traffic, but at night, when commerce, particularly in a district such as this, was less prevalent, the work recommenced. Stoker wondered that the residents—the wealthiest and most powerful in London—had not found a way to put a stop to the disturbance.

When the carriage arrived, Stoker helped Mina down, and they turned to see that the front courtyard was ablaze with torches, and that the servants waiting in the entryway to take their hats and coats were liveried in long tunics of an Egyptian cast, and wore sandals on their feet. All the rooms of the house, and there were many, were electrified, and in them the guests moved about freely, mingling and observing the thousand and one objets d'art gathered from around the globe. The plunder was astounding, and most of it from the Middle East. Lady Wilde's collection was put to shame.

"He could furnish an additional gallery at the museum just from the loot in this room," Mina said, as she and Stoker, champagne flutes in hand, circulated among the other guests.

"And he has," a voice said, as Stoker turned to see Professor Vambéry leaning on his walking stick. "I have been cataloging his things for weeks now, and still have much to do." Taking Mina's hand, he said, "Ever since you showed me your striking photograph of the sphinx, it has remained an indelible image in my mind. You should really exhibit it."

"You are too kind."

"Not at all. And has the latch on the Carpathian box continued to open and close in its singular fashion?"

She nodded, though Stoker could tell that this line of questioning made her uncomfortable. She was not one to vaunt her accomplishments, or, for that matter, advertise the discovery of the box.

"Where is our host?" Stoker asked, doing his best to conceal his true opinion of the man.

"Oh, he's about here somewhere—no doubt in the greenhouse with William Stead right now."

"The greenhouse?" Mina said.

"It's where the unrolling will take place. I recommended it myself, as the heat and moisture in the air may make the task easier."

"And Stead you say is with him?" Stoker said.

"Yes, making a chronicle of the event for a feature in his magazine."

Thorne, it was becoming plain, never did anything for motives that were other than mercenary, self-promoting . . . or worse. Stoker had not yet shared with Mina the truly horrendous discoveries he had made with Lucinda in the underground tunnel beneath the mission house; it was all too fantastical, too bizarre . . . and potentially too dangerous for anyone who might possess the knowledge of it. He had no doubt that anything truly incriminating, such as the remains of the workhouse lad with the broken ankle, had been summarily removed, and that the very existence of the place could be explained to the authorities as a laboratory used to investigate and store his various finds. Stoker was more than aware of the influence that power and money could exert—he had seen it done—and he had no doubt that a man of Thorne's depravity would wield that influence ruthlessly.

And as for whatever unholy forces had been unleashed down there . . . how could he begin to explain any of that to Scotland Yard without winding up in the ward where Lucinda had once been constrained? In the light of day, he had begun to doubt some of it himself . . . until he saw the deep grooves in his boot.

A servant with a brass bell was circulating from room to room, announcing that a buffet supper was being served in the dining room, and the other guests migrated in that direction. But Stoker had no interest in it, and Mina had gravitated to a wall of the study, where a dozen sepia-toned photographs were hung between the bookcases; upon closer inspection, he saw that they bore small plaques. One said, "Thebes Expedition, 1881," and showed a younger, and leaner, Thorne surrounded by native workers outside a crumbling tomb. Another was labeled "Abydos, Spring of 1883: Stela of Ahmose I," and displayed Thorne with his elbow resting on a chiseled stone tablet. But it was on the picture just above the mantelpiece that Mina's attention was riveted. Looking at it over her shoulder, Stoker saw four Englishmen in dirty shirtsleeves, standing between the extended paws of the legendary Great Sphinx. The plaque read: "Giza Plateau, December, 1885."

"One of the seven wonders of the world," Stoker observed. "I remember my professor at Trinity telling us that its very name, the sphinx, meant 'the terrifying one.' I always thought I could use that somehow in one of my stories."

But Mina did not reply.

"It must be close to five thousand years old today."

"That man, the one right there, is my father," Mina said softly.

"Which man?"

"The one standing next to Thorne, holding the canteen."

Stoker leaned in. He was tall and thin, wearing wire spectacles and a pale moustache. The only resemblance he could see to Mina was in the aquiline features of his face; her coloring must have come entirely from her mother.

"He worked with Bartholomew Thorne?" Stoker said, in wonder.

"Not to my knowledge," she said, "not until this second. But the men who funded these expeditions often kept a low profile so as not to alert competitors."

Now, taken aback by the revelation that her father had worked with Thorne, he was even more relieved that he had shared nothing of his nightmare in the tunnel; he would need to sort all of this out first.

When Mina turned her gaze from the photograph, she seemed to survey the room with a newfound eye, as if registering all the ancient artifacts on display on the mantel and bookshelves and end tables afresh. He had the sense she was doing some sort of mental inventory, and under her breath she murmured, "Of course . . . of course . . ."

The dinner bell had stopped ringing, and off in another portion of the house he could hear cutlery clanging and voices in conversation, but here there was only the ticking of the clock and the rustle of curtains caught in a draft, throwing strange shadows on the Oriental carpet.

"Why did you say 'of course'?" he asked.

"Because everything is familiar."

"Why wouldn't it be? You, and your late father, have excavated similar sites and recovered similar items."

"They're more than that," she said, but before she could continue, Thorne himself, resplendent in a black silk tailcoat with a diamond-studded crescent moon on one lapel and a ribboned medal on the other, loomed in the doorway.

"I thought I might find you two in here. You're missing a meal fit for a pharaoh."

"You were on an expedition with my father?" Mina said.

"Ah, so you noticed. The sphinx photograph."

"Why didn't you say anything when we were introduced at the museum?"

"I wasn't sure of the response I'd receive, and wanted to spare Cruikshank any embarrassment."

Mina looked more puzzled than ever. "What do you mean, the response you'd receive?"

Now it was Thorne's turn to look uncertain. "That expedition was, as you have surely noted, your father's last."

"I did not know that. I know that it was early in the next year that his body was returned to his family home, in a lead-lined coffin. We were told he had died of a high fever, brought on by some disease."

"By some miracle, he survived the fever."

"Then how did he die?"

"He died much as he lived."

"What is that supposed to mean?" Stoker asked, though he wouldn't necessarily believe a word of the answer.

"Shortly after that picture was taken, Sebastian Harcourt fell from the head of the sphinx."

"Why would he have climbed up there?" Mina said.

"He was of the opinion that the sphinx had once been a polychrome piece of statuary. He had found flecks of paint—red and yellow and blue—on its flanks and wanted to see if he could find further proof on the brow or headdress."

"And did he?" Stoker asked, as Mina seemed nonplussed by the information she had received.

"He did, but it's doubtful the paint could have lasted so many centuries. I am of the opinion that it was left by Napoleon's soldiers, who clambered all over the monuments of Egypt and played all sorts of pranks we would never condone today."

From what he knew of Harcourt, Stoker found the explanation of his death plausible, at least; he was a man accustomed to following his nose, taking risks, doing whatever it took to confirm his theories.

"I must get back to my other guests," Thorne said. "The ceremony will begin shortly." He lumbered from the room like a bear, though trailed by the scent of expensive bay rum.

"Are you all right?" Stoker asked, instinctively laying a consoling hand on Mina's shoulder. She had just absorbed a good deal of information, and if she were a bit in shock, it would not have been surprising.

"Yes," she replied, in an absentminded tone.

"Would you like to sit down, or perhaps go to the dining room and take a glass of wine? Something to eat?"

"No, I'm fine. It's just that he lied."

"Thorne?"

"My father did not fall from the head of the sphinx."

"How would you know that?"

"My father was a brave man, and an intrepid one. He would burrow into caves, dive underwater, crawl on his belly into ancient tombs. But he did have one great fear."

"Of what?"

"Heights. My father was acrophobic. Even if he had wanted to check for paint on the top of the sphinx, he'd have delegated that task to one of the workers." Looking him straight in the eye, she said, "And if Thorne lied about that, what else has he lied about?" Waving her arm around the room, she said, "The provenance of all of these treasures, for instance."

"What are you implying?"

"My father did not do his work for personal gain; what did not go to the British Museum went to the Ashmolean at Oxford, his alma mater, or to other public collections. Thorne explored for money . . .

181

and might not my father have stood in his way? Many of the treasures here are remarkably similar in era and cast to things my father had previously found; but if my father found these, too, and could have laid claim to at least half of them, wouldn't that have come as a costly blow to Thorne? Why divide the spoils when a simple accident, if it could be called that, would double Thorne's take?"

Though Stoker had no way of knowing for sure if her surmise was true, he did not doubt for an instant that Thorne would have been capable of it.

A gong, not a bell, was rung this time, to announce the adjournment to the greenhouse.

"Shall we go?" he said.

Without a word, she took his arm, and after one more prolonged look around the room—he had the sense that she was literally making a mental catalog of everything she saw—she resolutely marched them toward the evening's grim entertainment.

CHAPTER TWENTY-FIVE

"Beg pardon, miss," Samuel said, poking his head into the properties room, "but Mr. Irving asked if you could fix this tail for him."

"What's wrong with it?" Lucinda said, looking up from the lace border she was sewing onto the hem of the gown Ellen Terry wore as Lady Macbeth.

"It's drooping, he said, and the fork at the end is coming loose."

"Leave it on the pile, and I'll get to it quick as I can," she said.

"The devil oughta look perky, Mr. Irving said."

She would just as soon not be reminded of Irving's role as Mephistopheles. She had studiously avoided any subsequent performance of the play, as it could only serve to cast her mind back to the night she had decided to join her dead son in the afterlife. Oh, she knew that suicide was a sin, but if God was all loving, as she had so often been told, she felt confident that he would be able to look into her heart and judge her anguish fairly . . . especially now, given what she had learned about his death, and desecration.

Far from lessening, her obsession had only grown stronger. Just what *had* happened to Davey when he had been taken from the infirmary and placed in the care of the Matron? And how had his body then been transported to that awful underground chamber of horrors, and bound and painted like one of those mummies? Time had begun to hang heavy on her hands now that she was no longer employed at the match works, and she had been only too happy to find something to do with them; she had always been a passable seamstress, and by mending the costumes she felt that she was earning her keep, as it were.

When she finished the hem, she attended to the crimson tail of Irving's costume and a couple of other items, but then could do no more. She had pricked her fingers too many times, and her eyes hurt from the glare of the light. She rested her head on the back of the threadbare chair and closed her eyes, and though she would have welcomed a bit of sleep, her mind would not let her. All she could picture was the cemetery and the little headstone with the broken bud chiseled into it, and she was overcome by the dread feeling that little Davey was all alone there, shivering in the cold ground, wondering why she had abandoned him.

Contrary to his usual habits, Mr. Stoker was not in the theater, bustling about and making sure everything was in order for that night's performance, and consequently she felt even more at loose ends. Gradually, the thought came into her head that she should go out, that it was not too late, that if she hurried, she could get to the graveyard before the gates were closed at eight. Wrapping herself in her shawl, and then throwing over it one of the warmest coats she could find from the back of the costume cabinet, she scurried to the stage door.

"It's a real pea-souper tonight," Samuel said. "You sure you want to go out in that?"

"Yes, I have to," she replied, at which he looked puzzled.

But he was right. The fog was so thick in the alleyway that she had to wave her hands in front of her face several times to clear a path to the street, where the lamps looked as if they were cocooned. The sounds of horses' hooves clip-clopping on the cobblestones were similarly muffled. But knowing the way, she was able to find the stairwell to the Underground, and after a jostling, crowded ride, emerged again close to the gates of the cemetery.

If she had been hoping that the fog would disperse, she was wrong. It clung to the wrought-iron gates like ivy, and blanketed the high brown brick walls. A few other visitants were straggling out as she went in; bearing to the left as she remembered the coach doing, she followed the path by keeping her feet on the pavement and catching glimpses of the gas lamps strung intermittently along the way. How, she wondered, was she going to find the little gravesite itself, as it was off the beaten path and among the trees and thick foliage? The best she could do was gauge the distance, though it seemed quite different on foot than it had been in the carriage, and if it hadn't been for the honking of some ducks, she might have passed it. But the pond allowed her to locate herself, and she turned off the road and onto the soft green turf.

Despite the fog, the moon was full, and in those brief moments when the mist cleared, she peered ahead, navigating carefully among the monuments and headstones; it was those laid flat in the ground that proved most dangerous. Several times she tripped over the edge of one or the other, and once was flung headlong onto the earth. The sound of her cry alarmed the ducks, and an echoing call went up. When it finally subsided, and she had stood, rubbing the knee on which she had landed, she heard something that at first she mistook for the hoot of an owl. Staying quite still, she waited, and then it came again.

But instead of the "Who?" from an owl, it seemed much more like a voice saying, "You."

A little voice. A young voice. A boy's voice.

Should she answer? As any Londoner knew, the fog could play tricks with sound as well as sight, carrying words from one place to another as easily as the gallery in St. Paul's Cathedral.

Taking a deep breath of the cold, damp air, she ventured, "Is someone there?"

A duck replied with a quack.

She must have imagined it. Ever since Davey had passed, her mind had been toying with her.

Resting her hand atop a tombstone, she waited for another break in the rolling fog, and this time glimpsed—or did she?—the shimmering outline of a child, attired in a white burial dress, and holding something in his hands. The mist was too thick to make out his features.

"You . . ." came again, in a quavering voice.

She waited, shivering. Was that . . . his voice?

"—left . . . me."

It was like an arrow shot straight into her heart. "Oh, Davey, my boy, I did not leave you," she uttered, overcome with sobbing. "I would never leave you. Never."

But the fog, like a crashing wave, surged over the ground again, obscuring the specter and swallowing its voice. Lucinda stumbled forward, snaking her way between tombstones teetering so close to each other that her elbows grazed the stone on either side; she felt as if she were slipping through the crowd on an opening night in the Lyceum lobby.

Something scampered across her path, and she drew up short. It was a little gray rabbit, and as it paused, nose twitching, to gauge the safest direction to pursue, there was a sudden flurry in the air, a swooping, darting motion that rocked Lucinda back on her heels, almost toppling her again. The rabbit screamed, a blazing cry of pain and fear, as the owl's talons dug into its body, and then it was borne aloft, up into the trees and the nest, hidden somewhere high among the branches, where it would be torn to pieces and eaten. The screaming died after a few more seconds.

Lucinda shuddered, rubbing her hands together to regain some feeling in her fingers. The cold, damp air was settling into her aching jaw. The grave could not be far off now, and if she listened intently, she could hear a little crackling sound, a whirring, somewhere ahead of her.

"Davey? Is that you?"

But there was no reply.

"Are you there?"

Something coalesced in the mist, then dispersed, floating off like the tops of the dandelions that she'd blown on when she was a little girl . . . a little girl the same age as Davey when he'd died.

"She did it."

The voice startled her. "Who?"

She took a few more steps.

"Who did what? Davey, you must let me see you again."

There was a clattering sound, like pebbles skittering across cement, and she went toward it.

"Matron."

What? Had she heard the word correctly? Even through the fog, she thought she could discern the silhouette of Davey's gravestone, standing straighter than most of the others in the graveyard. A few more steps, and her surmise was confirmed—the tombstone bore her son's name chiseled above a broken bud.

And lying on the brown earth just before it was a red wooden top beside a pair of glass marbles. The burial gifts from little Timmy Conway.

A tide of anguish, so keen it could not even escape her throat, nearly choked her. She dropped to her knees, her head against the cold monument, her fingers splayed across the carved petals stretching toward heaven.

"Oh, Davey, my darling, darling boy, what are you trying to tell me? What did Matron do to you?" Was it the horrors she had seen in the underground tunnel? The painted face, the bandages binding his tiny limbs? She had attributed those atrocities to Bartholomew Thorne. Was she wrong?

The owl hooted in the tree, no doubt digesting his meal.

She picked up the wooden top, with its bit of tangled string. Tears streamed down her face, their warmth coursing across her inflamed cheek. The marbles glistened in a beam of moonlight that penetrated the surrounding fog. "What did she do to you, Davey?"

And then, in a voice so close it felt as if it were whispering in her ear, she heard, "She ate . . . my soul."

CHAPTER TWENTY-SIX

Immense as Thorne's mansion was, the grounds extended to an improbable length behind it. Down a flagstone path, lighted by cast-iron gas lamps, Mina saw what looked like a smaller-scale version of the Crystal Palace. Given the dense fog, however, it was like seeing it through a cloudbank. A golden glow emanated from within the greenhouse's glass walls, and as soon as she and Stoker approached the open doors, they were greeted by a wave of warm and verdant air. It reminded Mina of the Nile Valley during the rains.

The interior, however, was more like a jungle, filled on every side with towering ferns and stunted palms, orchids and tulips, and a host of more exotic blooms. Guests ambled up and down the narrow pathways between rows of potted plants and under the canopy of waxy green leaves, some of the men holding brandy glasses, the ladies fluttering their fans or bending to inhale the aroma from the blossoms. Grated vents in the floor emitted a soothing breeze of heated air, and Mina lingered atop one just to toast the soles of her shoes.

"I see you've come, after all," Cruikshank said, approaching them, "despite the hint of reproach you expressed at the museum."

"You know my feelings about these events."

"And truth be told," he said, leaning in and speaking softly, "I share them."

"Then why not openly oppose them?"

"Because I have to think of the greater gain, not only to the museum, but to the furtherance of human knowledge. This unraveling was going to take place regardless of its morality. Better, in my view, to have present a few of us who feel the full weight of the occasion."

She was relieved to hear it.

"Not to mention," he added, "people who may have a far better understanding of anything that might unfold, or be revealed, in the process."

There was that, too—a feeling that even Mina knew. Like her father, she lived for the sense of discovery.

Thorne's voice rose above the crowd, summoning everyone to the far end of the hothouse, where a platform had been raised, upon which a shrouded table lay. Stoker stiffened at the sight, and Mina had to urge him to the front of the assemblage. Professor Vambéry and Conan Doyle, not surprisingly, were huddled to one side and already in deep confabulation, while William Stead, his pad and pen at the ready, stood directly below Thorne, who strode the stage as if he were Tamburlaine.

"It is my pleasure, and my honor, to welcome you all here this evening," he announced. He had shed his dinner clothes for a long white cotton gown, embroidered in gold thread with an Egyptian motif around the collar and sleeves.

"And are we now to take him for a pharaoh?" Stoker whispered in Mina's ear.

"No, I think he means to be a high priest of Amun." She thought he looked perfectly ridiculous, with his bushy brown moustache and sideburns, attempting such an impersonation.

"A priest? Isn't that a demotion for someone of his self-regard?"

"Not as much as you'd think. The high priests of Amun wielded so much power they were the de facto rulers of Upper Egypt."

"*Ankh! Udja! Seneb!*" Thorne called out now, and before Mina could provide a translation, he did it himself. "Life! Strength! Health!"

Several in the audience raised their glasses, or called back, "Cheers to you, too!" There was a merry mood in the greenhouse, which was exactly what Mina had feared. It was as if a debutante were about to be introduced into polite society, instead of a corpse, thousands of years old, uprooted from its grave, and desecrated purely for entertainment and the few baubles that might be hidden in its wrappings.

And all by a man she now suspected of having murdered her father.

"Tonight, we discover the ancient secrets of the Chantress of Amun."

"Amen!" some drunken wit called out.

"You are, sir, surprisingly on point. That word, with which we end our prayers, is a corruption, drawn down through the ages, of the name of this deity, the veritable king of the gods. Later, when he was identified with the sun itself, he became better known as Amun-Re. Tonight I am to be the god's servant, his *hem-netjer*, at this unveiling, though I shall not serve alone." Swinging one arm wide, the sleeve of his gown hanging low, he welcomed onto the stage—for there was no other way that Mina could accept this spectacle—a tall woman, made even taller by her blonde hair piled high on her head and held in place by tendrils of vine, and similarly garbed. But unlike Thorne, her long, gaunt face had been daubed with yellow ochre—the color, Mina knew, that was used on the features of female mummies. "My cherished sister, Winifred, who works tirelessly on behalf of her many unfortunate wards at the mission house."

Things were growing more offensive and self-aggrandizing by the minute. Mina glanced over at Cruikshank, whose visage was stoically frozen, and even when she caught his eye, he betrayed nothing of any inner turmoil he might feel. Among the rest of the guests, there was a simmering anticipation and excitement. Stead was scrawling furiously in his notebook. Vambéry was leaning forward on his ebony walking stick as Conan Doyle muttered something in his ear. Stoker loomed beside her, providing a sense of protection, for which she was grateful.

But with a showman's true instinct, Thorne did not yet address the mummy, whose slim, straight shape was betrayed by the overhanging cloth tented at the bottom where its feet pointed directly upward.

"Before beginning the procedure," he said, "a few words of explanation may be in order. When we think of ourselves today, we think of a body and of a soul. For the ancient Egyptians, however, things weren't so simple. Yes, there was the body, whose physical parts were collectively called the *haw*. But when it came to the soul, things got stickier."

"Isn't that always the case?" the same wag called out, before his companion batted his elbow with her fan.

"They divided that entity into five pieces," Thorne continued. "First, there was the *jb*, or heart, which they believed was formed at conception, with a single drop of blood from the mother's heart. Then there was the *ren*, the name someone was given at birth and which would live on for as long as the name was spoken or remembered."

"Do we know *her* name?" Stead asked, with a hint of impatience.

"Yes, we do, and I will get to that shortly. Third, there was the *ba*," Thorne resumed, "something akin to our idea of a personality. In other words, everything that makes one person unique—and which the Egyptians believed lived on after someone had died. The *ba* was thought to fly out of the mouth at the moment of death, to be reunited with the *ka*, or vital spark, which also departed at that same moment."

Despite herself, Mina was impressed at Thorne's display of erudition; if she had taken him for a mere adventurer, she had been mistaken. Perhaps he *had* been after more than the gold and other treasures he had so effectively accumulated.

"Finally, there was the *sheut*, or shadow. Because it was always present, they believed it must contain some essence of the person to whom it was inescapably attached."

"There is a certain logic to that," Stoker murmured in her ear, and she nodded.

"It was considered a servant of Anubis," Thorne continued, "the jackal-headed god of death, and was often represented as a small human figure, painted completely black."

Into her mind's eye instantly flashed the black silhouette on the gold box. The man with the animal's head. Could the box have been made to contain . . . a shadow? Before she could further consider the idea, Thorne, with the sort of flourish a magician might use to reveal a trick, whisked away the outer covering that concealed the mummy, and let it fly into his sister's waiting arms. A murmur of appreciation and wonder hummed among the onlookers.

"So much for proper respect and decorum," Stoker said.

"Meet Nebetia, the enchanting chantress, whose physical body has been preserved for three thousand years, as home and refuge for all of those ephemeral elements of which I have just spoken."

The corpse, tightly bound in discolored linen, lay like some sacrificial beast on the trestle table before him. Winifred Thorne, acting as if she were a surgeon's nurse, picked up a pair of garden shears from a cabinet atop the stage and placed them in her brother's open hand.

"You might wonder," Thorne announced, "at the need for these rather than scissors. The cotton strips you see here have not only been tied as tightly as possible, but they have then been coated with a resinous liquid to stick them in place—and a very effective resin, at that."

The outermost bandages crisscrossed across the body, and as Thorne began to snip away at them, his sister grabbed the loose ends, tore them off, and let them flutter to the floor like confetti. A woman at the back of the assemblage let out a little whimper, and Mina saw her mince about in place, glancing at the floor around her. The gentleman with her said, "It's nothing, Edwina. Get a grip on yourself."

Thorne kept cutting, and Mina was close enough that she could smell the antique aroma of the mummy—the tarry bitumen that made up part of the coating, the salty natron that was employed as a preservative, the ancient oils and fragrances that had anointed the body after forty days of drying. The mummification process could be a long and laborious one, especially when done properly. Each limb, each finger and toe, was separately wrapped to maintain the body's integrity. Reversing the process, undoing layer after layer of protective covering, was not an easy task.

"But why," Stead asked from the front, "did they go to all this trouble—especially as they believed, from what you have already said, that the *ba* and the *ka* and whatever else had already departed?"

Without looking up from his work, Thorne said, "Because they also believed that the spirit crossed back and forth between this world and the next, between night and day, the living and the dead. Mummies, like this one, had to represent an easily identifiable home for the returning spirit. Sometimes their names were painted on their shrouds or caskets; this one was housed in a tomb, with her name on the door and inscribed again on the wall she was resting against when we found her."

Who, exactly, was *we*, Mina had to wonder.

"And so we have now done away with the outermost shroud," Thorne declared, straightening, as his sister peeled off the last remaining strips; the layer revealed beneath it was slightly lighter, and in the crossed hands Mina could see the papyrus scroll that accompanied bodies on their spiritual journey.

"What's the letter say?" the same man who had interrupted before called out. "If it's a mummy's curse, leave me out of it."

"It won't be a curse," Thorne said, delicately removing it, "though those were common enough on temple walls." Glancing at its furled shape, he said, "It is undoubtedly instructions of some kind from the Book of the Dead."

"You mean," the man asked, "like a Baedeker to the underworld?"

"In a way."

Mina saw Cruikshank rise on his tiptoes to get a better look, and she suspected he would make off with the papyrus, for further study, before the night was through.

193

"Well, what's it say?" Stead asked.

"Careful, Bartholomew," his sister warned, "it's about to fall apart. Perhaps it should be left unopened."

"No, no," Stead insisted, scenting some lurid tidbit to add to his article.

"Oh, give it a go," Conan Doyle called out. Although Mina might have expected more from such an acclaimed member of the British Society for Psychical Research, she could see that the novelist's natural curiosity had overwhelmed his sense of decorum.

Holding it gingerly with just his fingertips, Thorne acceded, unrolling the fragile parchment and then turning its surface toward his audience. Mina saw the faintest markings densely recorded upon the page.

"If I could beg the assistance of Professor Vambéry, who is best suited to this task . . ." Thorne said, handing the scroll down to him.

Vambéry slipped a pince-nez onto the bridge of his nose, studied the page for a minute or so, before saying, "It is what we call the Declaration of Innocence, made to assure entry into the Field of Reeds, or paradise. It swears that the bearer has not done evil to anyone, has not harmed the offering loaves of the gods, has not stolen from the tombs of the blessed dead. It is what we might call a character reference." Still studying the parchment, he then added, "Though, if I am reading this correctly, there does seem to be one unusual admonition."

"I told you there was a curse!" the wag proudly announced.

"It implores the god that if any impurity still stains her soul, he should dip it into the Lake of Fire to burn it away. Assuming the chantress composed this herself before dying, it sounds as if she might have had some secret offense still weighing on her conscience."

The woman who had exclaimed earlier did so again, this time crying, "It just ran over my foot!"

"What did?" her gentleman asked.

"That did!" she said, pointing a shaky finger at the bottom of a camellia bush. Mina saw only a bobbing leaf.

But from another quarter, another voice arose. "Here, too!"

"Good God," a man said, "it's a whole pack of 'em!"

Several cries came up, and now Mina could see a hasty blur of gray fur and ropy tail, slipping up through a floor vent and disappearing under the vegetation.

Thorne tried to reassure everyone that nothing was amiss, but Winifred stood transfixed, her bewildered eyes made more pronounced by the ochre paint that encircled them, then suddenly looked upward at the vaulted ceiling.

At first Mina could not make out what she was seeing there—it looked like rivulets of rain coursing across the glass panes, but they were traveling in all directions, sideways, up and down, helter-skelter. Tiny pink feet, with claws, were sticking to the roof.

"It's a swarm of rats," Stoker said, gripping her by the elbow.

"That's more than a swarm—that's an army!"

The spectators behind them were rushing for the door.

"But why?" she asked. "Where have they come from?"

"The underground, I'd bet. The construction must have disturbed their nest."

There were screams now, as the guests pushed each other out of the way in their mad rush to escape. But no one seemed to be getting very far; it was as if they had hit a barrier.

Even the Thornes could no longer deny what was happening. Winifred fell back from the mummy as the rats took over the stage, and her brother whirled about, snapping the garden shears at several of them atop the cabinet, cleaving one neatly in two.

Stoker pulled Mina toward the exit, but they, too, bumped up against the crowd, which wasn't budging.

"Move!" Stoker insisted, but a woman turned to him, her face ashen, and said, "Through that?"

Craning her neck, Mina could see the lamps leading back to the house—but the flagstones were all but hidden beneath a seething, squeaking carpet of brown and gray rats.

"Oh, for God's sake," Stoker said, "give me that!" And he grabbed an umbrella from the arm of a man stalled at the threshold.

With one arm around Mina's waist, and the other swinging the furled umbrella like a scythe, Stoker waded into the vermin, knocking them off the stones and clearing a path. Several of the braver souls followed close on their heels. The house was still another hundred yards off, but Mina felt strangely emboldened, not only by Stoker's strong arm, but as if by some invisible presence. With each lamp that they passed, her shadow, and his, passed before them, and by the time they had regained the shelter of the house, where the staff had armed themselves with brooms and pokers and coal shovels, she felt a kind of jubilation. The unveiling of the Chantress of Amun had proved a catastrophe, which was to her mind the only fit conclusion. Nebetia had prevailed! Perhaps there was some truth to those stories of the mummy's revenge, after all.

CHAPTER TWENTY-SEVEN

"I told you, Bartholomew, it was a bad idea, but you never listen to me."

"Shut your mouth."

"That I will not; and how dare you speak to me like that?"

Thorne was slumped in the corner of the carriage, escorting his sister back to the mission house, and all he wanted was to be alone with his thoughts. He was sick to death of Winifred's jabbering and complaints and criticisms. All his life he had cared for her—kept her alive, if it came to that—and now, when things had taken an inconsequential turn for the worse, she could do nothing but add to the problem.

"Haven't we already suffered enough exposure?" she said.

She was adverting, no doubt, to the incursion in the underground tunnel.

"And now, you wanted to throw more fuel on the fire with this ill-advised unrolling party. That nosy bastard Stead will have a field day recounting all this in his magazine."

"I didn't see you shrinking from the stage," he remarked.

"You didn't see me reveling in it, either. I was only there because I knew I would never hear the end of it if I weren't." She rubbed roughly at her cheek. "And this paint is going to do nothing good for my skin."

"It'll come off."

"It had better not take my skin with it."

Thorne had taken the time to change out of his priestly garb and into everyday attire, but Winifred was still wearing the Egyptian gown under her beaver coat. When they pulled up at the gate of the mission house, Cullen hurried out of the porter's alcove, bowing and scraping, and helped her down from the coach.

"Will you be wanting your chair?" he asked Winifred, and she barked, "No."

"Did you have a pleasant evening, sir?" he asked Thorne as he stepped down.

"No, we did not."

Cullen, suitably chastened, shrank back as they entered the gates, traversed the broad forecourt—why was there a lamp burning in one of the windows, Thorne thought with annoyance, after curfew and lights out?—and went up to the Matron's private apartments on the top story. Winifred tossed her coat on a divan, and, finally out of steam, threw herself back into the rattan wheelchair parked by the piano. "You don't have *this* to worry about," she said, gesturing dramatically at the apparatus.

"Don't I?" Sometimes, he thought, she acted as if he had never ventured to the ends of the earth, down into long-lost tombs and vaults, risking his life to discover the ancient papyri and dark rituals that had revealed the secrets that sustained her. "I think I have done as much for you as any brother has ever done. More, if it comes to that."

"Oh, spare me—it wasn't on my behalf you undertook your exploits. You did it for the glory, you did it for the money, you did it for yourself."

"And who has been the chief beneficiary?"

"You have, Bartholomew—you have. Tell me you haven't used the mission, and its poor pathetic crew, for your ends as much as mine? Tell me you haven't bolstered your own constitution with the last sad breath of these creatures? We breed them like sheep, and slaughter them just as readily."

He hated it when she spoke so bluntly, making it seem as if that was all there was to it.

"Not to mention the fact that you have used some of them, the chosen few, as if they were your harem. Why, I once bumped into that one with the phossy jaw—what was her name again? Lucinda something— scarcely dressed after one of your private trysts. I found her stocking under the divan. That was disgraceful, positively disgraceful."

"You didn't find it so disgraceful to put her son to use."

"The boy wasn't going to get any better, anyway. There was no point in letting the spark—"

She always called it the spark.

"—vanish into the ether."

"Much good it did you."

"How was I to know that? He was so young and so small, and the fever, I suspect, did not help. Still, it got me off my back and out of my sickbed, and into this again," she said, smacking the arms of the wheelchair. "If he'd been stronger, I'd have been back on my feet, but I can't say it was a total loss."

Wasn't it? Of all the sacrificial lambs who had passed through the gates of the mission house, the boy—Davey—was the one that most rankled his conscience. By the time he had heard the boy had been taken ill, his sister had already spirited him up to her rooms and virtually finished him off. Thorne had tried to resist her entreaties, but Winifred insisted she was at death's door herself—"I can feel the sweeping of the scythe," she had moaned, "and at the next swipe I shall be gone!"—and so he had gone forward with the ritual.

Claiming exhaustion from the evening's debacle, Winifred asked Thorne to wheel her back to her boudoir. The thick Persian carpets underfoot made pushing the chair harder than ordinary. He had been caring for her since childhood—ever since she had been laid low by rheumatic fever, and then by one debilitating ailment after another— and having him push the chair now was just one of the myriad ways in which she maintained the natural order. Winifred relied upon him for everything, and yet she managed somehow to make him feel forever in her debt. Perhaps that was the way with older sisters. And perhaps, it crossed his mind, that was the reason she had been so quick to dispatch Davey Watts. Had she harbored suspicions that the boy was his son, and as such, a rival for his attention? He remembered how she had reacted to a sweetheart he had acquired when he was a much younger man; he had brought her to dinner one night, and Winifred had baited her all night, until the girl had fled in tears to the vestibule.

"Your sister is a monster!" the girl had cried, snagging her coat from the parlormaid, and even then, Thorne had felt it incumbent on himself to defend her.

"She's not been well," he had said, and the girl had shot back, "In the head!"

He had never seen the girl again, and before long Winifred had convinced him that she was a ninny who had never been worth his time. It was to be the two of them, against the world, forever.

In her bedroom, Thorne drew the curtains and lighted the gas lamps; his sister hated electricity, and though she claimed it was because it was an unnecessary expense, he knew it was really her vanity at play. She didn't like to see herself in the harsh white glare, but preferred the warm glow dispersed by the traditional glass globe.

"Can you undo me?" she said, rising from the chair and turning her back. With one hand, she held up the stray strands of dyed blonde hair that trailed onto the nape of her neck. "I shall have this awful gown turned into rags by morning."

Thorne unfastened the top clasp of the Egyptian robe, then undid the buttons one by one, revealing an incongruous black lace corset underneath. When he stopped halfway down, she said, "All of them— undo them all."

He finished the job, the back of the gown falling open like the petals of a wilted flower, and turned away as she went into her dressing closet. He could hear the sound of her running a hot bath—that was one modern luxury she had insisted he install, at great expense and trouble—but he knew not to leave. She would expect him to be there when she came out. He sat down in an armchair by the window, opening the copy of the *London Times* on the side table.

There was an article about that actor Henry Irving being knighted, the first of his profession ever to be so honored, and a short item about Oscar Wilde being transferred from Pentonville Prison to Reading Gaol to serve out his sentence—the man had been an absolute fool, in Thorne's view, for taking on the Marquess of Queensberry in court. But his mind kept returning to the events of the evening. Even if his sister was content to believe that the invasion of the vermin was coincidental—the butler had floated the theory that it had to do with the verdant odors emanating from the greenhouse—Thorne wasn't so sure. He had been conducting a sacrilegious act, defiling a chantress of the great god Amun no less, and such things often brought consequences. Rats could well be one of them. Vambéry clearly suspected the same, as he had fixed him with a cold, inquisitorial eye after the last guests had scurried off in horror.

Perhaps Winifred was right, too, about his penchant for fame. Thorne had always wanted to cut a fine and imposing figure on the public stage, but he was playing with fire when he delved into the Egyptian mysteries in such an open fashion. Only he, and his sister, knew the true depths to which he had penetrated them, and when he performed a demonstration like the one he had done that night, he skated perilously close to revealing what must always remain secret.

When the bathroom door opened, his sister emerged in a flowing, diaphanous nightgown, her hair combed down now to flow over her shoulders. As she passed him on the way to her canopied bed, he could smell the perfume she had sprayed on her wrists and neck.

"What are you reading about?" she said, as she folded back the coverlet and then slipped between the sheets.

"Henry Irving has been made a knight of the realm."

"It's not possible. An actor?"

"An actor."

"And to think that you, despite your many good works and lavish contributions, have been overlooked. That's a scandal."

Thorne thought so, too. He had hoped that by cultivating Cruikshank at the British Museum, and Vambéry, who had friends in high places at the Foreign Office, he might make some headway in that regard.

"Come and tuck me in."

The ritual was always the same. Thorne put the paper back on the table and went to the bedside, but when he had finished tucking the blankets tight and began to rise, Winifred stopped him.

"Did I get all that dreadful makeup off my face?" she asked.

Thorne studied her features, which had been scrubbed quite clean of the paint, but were now delicately rouged and mascaraed, instead.

"Yes, it's all gone."

Still she held him low.

"Aren't you going to kiss me good-night? I'm not at all mad at you any longer."

"You'd no right to be mad at me at all."

"Oh, let's not start into that again. Let's kiss and make up."

Thorne bent and planted a kiss on her forehead, as her hand went up to caress his cheek. Her eyes were closed, her lips parted.

"Sleep well," he said, rising.

Her head was tilted back on the pillows.

Going to the door, he cast one more look back before extinguishing the gas lamp. Her eyes were open now, staring at him, as hard and black and shiny as obsidian, and even after he'd closed the door, he could feel them boring into him.

No, he thought, it was no accident she had killed Davey Watts—there could be no rival for his affections. Afforded the right opportunity, she'd gladly complete the task his unholy minions had failed to accomplish in the underground tunnel. She'd kill the boy's mother, too.

CHAPTER TWENTY-EIGHT

Even for the Beefsteak Club, the uproar was unusual. Round after round of drinks and toasts were made to the newly minted *Sir* Henry Irving, and not with the usual tankards of stout but with crystal flutes of Piper-Heidsieck champagne. Rumor had it (probably started by Irving himself) that the Prince of Wales had sent a congratulatory telegram, and that when Queen Victoria laid the sword upon Irving's shoulder to knight him, the first of his profession ever to be so honored, she had whispered, "I am very, very pleased." With his ascension, the entire theater world felt ennobled and recognized, the actors and actresses in particular, experiencing an especially keen and long-denied conferral of dignity.

Watching the banquet, Stoker couldn't resist adding up the expense in his head, but even if he had been disposed to cut back on the extravagance, tonight was not the night to do so. Irving, whose health was always precarious, looked strengthened by the personal tributes and printed encomiums that had come his way in droves. His long, gaunt face had some color in it, and his eyes sparkled with the energy of yore. With Ellen Terry sitting by his side at the head of the long table, he basked in the adulation and praise.

W. S. Gilbert recited a singsong verse in his honor; Conan Doyle made a witty speech, conjecturing that now that even actors could be knighted, Sherlock Holmes might be next; and William Stead, ever the reporter, asked for a quote "to mark such a felicitous and unprecedented occasion."

Irving pretended to demur, but Ellen, knowing he could never resist an audience, cajoled him to his feet; his skin was still glowing from having rubbed off the evening's makeup, and the ends of his long gray locks were damp from the washbasin. But with admirably feigned modesty, he thanked the assemblage, conducted a rambling survey of his lengthy career, from recitation contests in Cornwall to stock companies in Scotland, and gave a generous tip of his hat to Stoker, "without whom no production would ever get mounted, no performance ever made, and no bill ever paid." When the laughter subsided, he concluded with Macbeth's banquet toast, "To the general joy o' th' whole table."

Stoker, all the while, had been anxiously waiting for his chance to pounce on Professor Vambéry, and when the merriment had settled down a bit, he drew him away from the table and said, "May I call upon your expertise for a few minutes?"

"Now?" Vambéry said, casting an eye back at the sizzling platters of beef being brought to the table.

"It shouldn't take long."

Ushering him into an alcove under the backstage stairs, Stoker took the shade off the light to provide greater illumination, and withdrew from his vest a folded parchment—the very one he had removed from the mummified remains of Davey Watts. Having learned something of its possible significance at the unrolling party, he needed the professor to tell him if there was anything unusual in it.

"Is it the same sort of character reference, as you called it, as was found on the chantress? Even I can see that it is considerably shorter."

"Indeed it is that," Vambéry said, affixing his pince-nez. "Where did you get this?"

"I'm not really at liberty to say." Had he recognized it? Stoker doubted that Vambéry was complicit in Thorne's sacrilegious practices, but he had decided to chance it, anyway.

"It was found in a mummy's bound hands?"

"Yes."

Vambéry perused it again—unlike most such papyri, this one was relatively smooth and new, and though it had few markings and glyphs, the ink was dark and fresh. "It does not look authentic."

"What does it look like, to your practiced eye?"

"It looks like a weak forgery of an ancient text. But it makes no sense, either."

"It is gibberish?"

"Worse than that. It is an abomination."

"How so?"

"It does not say the name of the deceased, for one thing. Unless the mummy was enclosed in some other casket or tomb, plainly labeled, how could the wandering *ka* know where to return at night? Was it so enclosed?"

Stoker pictured the shrouded table on the abandoned underground platform. "No, it was not."

"I am not surprised. This document," he said, waving it like a scrap of confetti, "expressly instructs the spirit to ignore this unworthy body."

"And go where instead?"

"As best I can make out, it is directed to return to the 'devourer of souls,' in whose bosom it now resides forever." Removing the pince-nez and looking into Stoker's eyes, Vambéry said, "It's not the traditional Declaration of Innocence, or even a commonplace prayer from the Book of the Dead. Whoever wrote this intended something malevolent."

There was a roar of laughter from the dining hall, and Vambéry cast another longing glance back. He stuffed the papyrus into Stoker's hand, and said, "If I were you, I would burn this."

Although he doubted now that he would ever share its contents with Lucinda—why add one more stone to the burden the poor girl carried already?—under no circumstances was Stoker about to destroy it. It was only with Mina, he realized, that he could share what he had learned.

"Let's go and enjoy the supper, shall we? Irving is in great humor tonight, as well he should be."

Leaning on his cane, Vambéry went back to the party as Stoker folded the parchment and slipped it back into his vest pocket. But he'd lost any appetite he might have had. He knew who had forged the paper—it had to be Thorne. Was there no end to the man's evil? Hadn't he already done enough to ruin Lucinda's life, and the lives of so many others incarcerated in his mission house?

Stoker hadn't liked the look of her lately; ever since the funeral, she had worn a distant, distracted expression on her face, as if she were always somewhere else in her mind. He could well imagine where. Glancing at his pocket watch, he decided to check on her once more before making a discreet exit by the stage door. He'd had enough of the gaiety.

Crossing the stage, where a single light—the ghost light—kept the stage alive, he descended a rickety staircase into the bowels of the theater, where the sets were stored, the wardrobes hung, the props assembled and deployed. During the day, or when a performance was going on, these narrow halls and cramped rooms were bustling with activity, but after hours a pall fell over them. They were gloomy as a dungeon, and though he'd been sorry to leave Lucinda there, it had seemed the safest and most reasonable harbor for the present.

As he approached the sewing room, he could see light spilling from the open doorway and hear Lucinda softly humming. It sounded like a lullaby. He stopped at the threshold and watched her fingers flying as she sewed a sleeve onto a jacket. He'd already been told, by Ellen Terry and others, that Lucinda's work was exemplary, and done quickly. She might prove a worthy, and permanent, addition to the theater's crew. Pulling a stitch through and biting off the excess, she saw him there, and startled, said, "You scared me half to death."

"Sorry, I didn't mean to."

"How long have you been there?"

"Only a few seconds."

She looked down at the jacket again, then held it up to the light to assess her work. It was a peacoat, but made of all sorts of scraps of fabric from the rag bin. And in a child's size.

Stoker could not think of what production it might be for.

"Is that a costume?"

"Oh no," she said. "I only used the cloth that wasn't good for anything else."

"A coat of many colors."

"You could call it that, I guess. I just wanted it to be warm."

"But for whom?"

"Davey, a' course." She turned it front ways and back, tugging on a button or two to make sure they were securely fastened.

Stoker did not know what to say. He had so hoped she was making progress, that she would be able, over time, to move forward in her life. But now . . . this.

"Don't you think Davey's in a place now where he no longer has to fear the cold, or hunger, or anything else?"

"Oh, I'm not complaining. What you've done for him is wonderful—that's a beautiful spot over in the cemetery. And he likes the ducks, the ones in that pond nearby."

"I'm glad."

"But he was always shiverin', as he was so thin. And there's no tellin' how long he'll be there."

"He will be there always, Lucinda. They will never move his grave."

A look of puzzlement crossed her face, and reaching into the basket at her feet, she picked out a pair of sharp scissors and snipped off a flap of velvet protruding from one shoulder of the jacket.

"If you don't mind my askin'," she said, "he did tell me something that's been tormenting my mind ever since."

"When was that?"

"Just t'other night, when I went to visit."

"And what was it he told you?" Stoker asked, patiently. Perhaps he could cut to the root of the problem, help her to vanquish this sad delusion, and bring her back to her wits.

"It was about the Matron. At the mission house."

"Yes?" He pictured her in her Eastern garb and garish face paint, fleeing the rats.

"He said . . . well, it didn't make much sense . . . but he said that she'd eaten his soul."

As she stared into his eyes, awaiting his reply like an earnest pupil, Stoker was immobilized. His hand instinctively went to the vest pocket in which the parchment lay.

"Could she do such a thing?" Lucinda asked.

And though he did his best to conceal his true thoughts, he did not doubt it for a moment.

CHAPTER TWENTY-NINE

"Waiter," Ludvig said, snapping his fingers.

"Sir?"

"Another pot of coffee, and make it hot this time."

"Yes sir," the waiter said, skulking off, but not before Ludvig had picked up the slightest scent of suspicion. He was good at detecting that; all his life he'd had to be. The operator in the lift had seemed less obsequious than when he had first checked in, and the desk clerk had appeared to follow his movements as he made his way into the Palm Court.

It was that damn mounting bill. Mina Harcourt had done nothing to address it.

Ludvig had chosen this hotel, the Langham, not only for its fine reputation, but for its sheer size; one of the largest in London, with hundreds of rooms, many of them, quite obligingly, filled with rich Americans (a couple of whom he had already fleeced for some ready cash, playing backgammon). He figured it would be easier to meld into the ebb and flow of the many guests. In his experience, if one had to check out, as it were, before settling one's bill, it was easier at a grand palace than at a smaller, and more vigilant, establishment.

Still, things were coming to a head.

He had already forged a modest check in Mina's name and tried to pass it at her bank, but he had been shocked when the clerk denied it, claiming the account was at present devoid of funds. Had she cleared it out in advance? Could she conceivably be one step ahead of him? It seemed highly unlikely. No one was ever a step ahead of Ludvig Gerhard.

The coffee arrived, so blazingly hot that he wondered for a moment if it was intended, as it did, to scald his lips. But he said nothing; no reason to call any more attention to himself. Besides, he had plans.

The shoeblack had informed him that Miss Harcourt had a man in her life—a burly gent of means, with an overheard Irish accent—who had taken her to a fancy party in Belgravia. This was valuable information, as it could be played in several ways. If the gentleman was merely keeping her (though not well), Ludvig could present himself as a rival for her affections, and grudgingly allow himself to be bought off. Better yet, if the gentleman was of the married kind, perhaps he could be persuaded to part with some hush money in return for his discretion. There were a number of angles, and Ludvig had, at one time or another, played them all.

Right now, he was awaiting word from his young confederate as to her whereabouts. After glancing at his pocket watch, he looked out the window just as the boy set up his blacking box beneath the lamppost across from the hotel entrance. At last. Thinking he might have to make some other plans for the evening's entertainment, he'd begun to size up the American dowager whose three ropes of pearls were dangling just above the plate of pastries she was plowing through.

Signing his bill to the room with a flourish, Ludvig went outside; there was a nip in the air, and he turned up the velvet collar of his coat. He crossed the busy street, put a boot on the stand, and said, "What have you got for me?"

Swiping a rag across the top of the shoe, the boy, sounding as winded as if he had run a marathon, said, "She took the omnibus."

"Where to?"

"The West End."

"And?"

"She went into that fancy theater."

"There are several fancy theaters. Which one?"

"The one on the corner of Wellington Street—starts with an *L*."

"The Lyceum?"

"That's it."

Strange that her gentleman had not called for her (all the more reason to believe he might be married), but at least he knew now where to find her. Flipping a coin to the boy, he hurried off to the theater.

"There was bus fare, too!" the boy protested, but Ludvig pretended not to hear.

By the time he arrived and bought a seat in the gods, the auditorium was almost full. From his perch on high, he scanned the audience, looking for Mina. She was not in the orchestra section, so far as he could tell, and it was only when she leaned forward, as if in eager anticipation of the play, that he saw she had been seated in a curtained box to the left of the stage.

Just where a lover might put her.

The house lights went down, and the curtain rose on the evening's entertainment—a production of *Macbeth*, featuring Henry Irving in the title role and Ellen Terry, of course, as Lady Macbeth. The three witches were seen on the stage, stirring a bubbling cauldron beneath the barren branches of a stunted tree.

"When shall we three meet again?" the first witch said. "In thunder, lightning, or in rain?"

"When the hurly-burly's done," the second replied. "When the battle's lost and won."

"That will be ere the set of sun," intoned the third.

With the play off and running, Ludvig trained his gaze on Mina in her box. A spindly young man seated next to Ludvig—undoubtedly one of the legion of young men enamored of the leading lady—had a pair of opera glasses with him, and Ludvig was allowed to borrow them, now and again, whenever she was not on stage. Though there were three extra chairs in Mina's box, they remained unoccupied, and it was only between the first and second acts that Ludvig saw her turn in her chair to welcome her lover—a broad-shouldered man with a neatly trimmed russet beard, who pulled a chair behind her, the better to lean close and whisper something in her ear. The shoeblack had done his work well. But who was this man?

Instead of staying put, the gent got up after a while and left, then returned only toward the end, when Macbeth had been informed of the queen's death and launched into the famous soliloquy that began, "To-morrow, and to-morrow, and to-morrow / Creeps in this petty pace from day to day." Irving rendered it in a Scottish burr, pacing the stage with his left leg dragging slightly behind. What was the world coming to when mere actors were knighted, while the third sons of European aristocrats, disinherited for youthful follies, were reduced to confidence schemes, cardsharping, and blackmail?

After the curtain fell and the last bows had been taken—when Ellen Terry had come out, the spindly young man had been riveted to his glasses, his mouth hanging open—Ludvig hurried down to the lobby to look for Mina and her gentleman leaving the theater. Whether or not he would accost them remained an open question in his mind, but soon became a moot one. Mina came down, on her own, and left the theater equally unescorted. He was torn between following her and remaining in wait for her lover.

Who never exited at all.

The ushers finally forced Ludvig out onto the street, and he stood there, watching the doors being locked and the lights extinguished. It was then that he put two and two together—the man's irregular appearances in the box, his absence now. He must be affiliated with the theater in some manner, which would also explain Mina's private box. Going around to the alley, Ludvig loitered in the shadows, watching the stage door, and after an hour or so, during which he felt the cold, damp pavement coming up through the soles of his shoes, he was rewarded by the sight of Henry Irving, wrapped in a warm coat and scarf, escorted down the rickety staircase by Ellen Terry on one side and the burly gent on the other. The two thespians were helped up into a waiting coach, and the lady leaned her head out the window.

"Are you sure you don't want to come with us?" she said, but the burly fellow shook his head and said, "I like the walk home. See you tomorrow for the matinee."

"Don't remind me," she said, with a trilling laugh.

"'Night, Bram," the man called out. "Don't forget to draw up my itinerary."

So he was some sort of assistant to the actor.

"You'll have it by noon," Bram replied, lifting a hand as the coach drove off.

If he worked for the actor, he might not be as rich or as influential as Ludvig had hoped, but there was still a chance he could be exploited. It would all depend. The man took off briskly, and Ludvig did not emerge until he had rounded the corner. Then he continued to follow him, staying a safe distance behind. Though this Bram was a heavyset fellow, he moved with the easy assurance of a former athlete. Ludvig had known such creatures at boarding school in Switzerland, and despised them one and all. Anyone could build his muscles, if he put his mind to it, but living by your wits, he had come to believe, was the true mark of a man.

It was immediately clear that the fellow wasn't heading for the East End, where Mina lived above the furniture shop, but was he going to some other place of assignation? Nor was it easy, keeping up and keeping unnoticed. Although his target had no idea he was being followed, and the streets of London were never completely unpopulated, still it required some deftness; once or twice, the man stopped to look at something in a shop window, or to light his cigar, and Ludvig had to duck into a doorway, or stop and pretend to lace his shoe.

More and more, it struck Ludvig that this Bram was not on his way to a romantic rendezvous; men on such a mission as that did not ramble or pause, as this one did, to read what turned out to be, when Ludvig passed it, a poster advertising an upcoming show at a Covent Garden theater. In his youth, when he had lived in London for several years, Ludvig had haunted the theaters; he had even courted one or two of the ladies of the stage, but they were always after bigger game. Actresses, he discovered, were as mercenary as bankers, and false as preachers.

They were moving toward Chelsea, the briny scent of the Thames in the air, and when they approached a stylish townhouse on the corner of Cheyne Walk, Bram took a key from his pants pocket, went up the short flight of steps, and then inside. By the time Ludvig approached, the porch light had been extinguished and only one remained on upstairs. Fortuitously, a blonde woman in a robe—no doubt the wife— was drawing the curtains closed, now that her husband was safely home. This was a favorable development, as far as Ludvig was concerned.

Looking up and down the street, and seeing no one else about, he went up the stairs to the brass postbox, handsomely engraved with the name "Stoker." Bram Stoker. The name rang a distant bell. A discreet inquiry or two, in the right quarters, and Ludvig would know everything else he needed to know.

CHAPTER THIRTY

Once inside the foyer, Stoker closed the door behind him with the back of his boot, as he shrugged off his overcoat and hat. He was inclined to hang them on the rack beside the mirror, but knew that Florence would chastise him in the morning if he did, and with Noel returning home for the school holiday, he wanted nothing but peace. So he went to the hall closet instead and hung them properly. Even when she was presumably asleep—he had seen her bedroom light on when he approached the house, but he knew by now that she would have extinguished it and gone to bed, lest he trouble her—her spirit reigned.

The house was as quiet as the grave, and his boot heels made the wooden floorboards creak as he went into the library and gently closed the double doors behind him. It was only then that he took a full breath, and after pouring himself a generous measure of Scotch, plopped into the wingback chair by the window. A notebook in which he had been jotting story ideas the night before lay where he had left it on the side table.

Exhausted as he was—it had been a long day, and a long night of revelry—he felt restless and at odds. It wasn't only about Lucinda Watts, whose sanity was plainly still imperiled. Something else was gnawing at him, and though he would have been ashamed to express it aloud, it had to do with Irving's knighthood. For years now, he had labored in the great man's shadow, making sure that everything having to do with the theater continued to function as it was meant to do, easing Irving's way through the vicissitudes of life, and shielding him from the thousand and one problems that cropped up daily. It wasn't that he begrudged him his success—the man was a genius on the stage and had well-earned this honor—it was more that he, Bram, had sacrificed so much and still could not see what mark of his own, if any, he would leave on the world. His short stories, almost always of a macabre nature, were occasionally published in some of the smaller magazines, as were his essays and various letters to the editors, but of such stuff no literary reputation was ever forged. What he needed was some singular idea, something that had not been done, something that would create a sensation.

He drained the glass, then poured himself another. Surely, he thought, the recent events in his life should have provided him with more than adequate material . . . the mummy ceremony overwhelmed by a tide of rats, the attack in the underground tunnel as he and Lucinda carried the corpse of young Davey back above ground, the séance at Lady Wilde's where he was warned that something was coming for him. He even had the makings of a cast of characters—from the multilingual Professor Vambéry to the soulless and rapacious Thornes, from the fraudulent medium to the pair of girls who had entered his life at nearly the same moment—the lost Lucinda and the fearless Minerva Harcourt. But the story failed to present itself, as yet, in any artistically organized or coherent manner. It was a tale still unfolding, and one that he did not dare to write, anyway, for fear of exposing dangerous secrets or damaging fragile relationships. How had Charles Dickens and Wilkie Collins, Trollope and Stevenson, done it—how had they gone to the well so many times and never failed to draw up a full bucket?

The wind was picking up outside, rattling the window frame, and though the warmth of the whiskey suffused his limbs, he drew the afghan off the back of the chair and wrapped it around his shoulders. Picking up the notebook, he reviewed his rough sketch of a locked-room mystery involving an Egyptologist and an ancient curse. But in trying to take just a taste of the elements introduced into his actual life and transmuting them into this distinct and separate tale, he had somehow robbed them of their energy. The notes, made only the night before, already failed to inspire him.

There were just a few drops left in the Scotch decanter, and as he watched them descend into his glass like drops of liquid honey, he thought he heard the front door latch turn. He waited, but there was no other sound but the wind off the river, now buffeting the shutters of the house. He drained the glass, then glanced back down at his notes—he had made a mysterious cat central to the action—and wondered where the story was meant to go next. Putting his head back on the antimacassar, he turned down the lamp to rest his eyes. He was so very tired. But perhaps if he let his thoughts roam, some inspiration might yet strike.

Wilkie Collins had his moonstone, Dickens had his Christmas carol, Stevenson—whom he had met at the Lyceum, and found to be quite a queer duck—had his Jekyll and Hyde. What would he, Bram, have? *Roam*, he told his thoughts, *roam . . .*

And that they did, though not in any fruitful fictional direction. They kept circling back to the bizarre events of recent days. A draft stirred in the room—the maid must not have closed the flue properly— and by the light of the streetlamp outside, he saw a figure seemingly materialize inside the dim confines of the library, closing the double doors, and then leaning back against them, her arms behind her.

Could it be . . . ?

"Your front door wasn't properly latched."

Had he failed to boot it fully shut?

"What are you doing here?"

She didn't reply, but it hardly mattered. He found he was not merely confounded to see her there . . . but happy. Happier than he deemed right, happier than he could ever let on. He was, after all, a married man, and one whose wife was asleep upstairs.

As she came closer, he thought he could smell the fresh scent of her young skin, thought he could make out the tawny complexion and jet-black hair. He felt he should rise from the chair—he must have made such an undignified spectacle, with the afghan wrapped around his shoulders and the empty Scotch glass still in his hand—but couldn't. It was as if he were transfixed, deprived of all volition.

So even as Mina knelt down before him, he remained immobilized.

"I needed to be with you."

"I'm glad."

"Can you forgive me?"

"Nothing to forgive." Could he not summon up something more compelling to say? It was as if his powers of speech were compromised, too.

"My mind," she said, her hands resting lightly on his knees, "has seemed so . . . unsettled."

"As has mine."

"That is comforting to hear."

One of her hands inched up his thigh, under the cover of the blanket.

"Even the wind tonight frightened me."

It wasn't like her, he thought, to be frightened, much less of something so ordinary. But his limbs felt electrified.

"At night," she murmured, taking the glass from his hand and placing it back on the table, "the shadows run free."

At night, he thought with some puzzlement, the only shadows were unnatural ones—created not by the sun, but by artificial illumination. But why was he dickering over such things? How many angels could dance on the head of a pin? Why couldn't he focus his mind? Why couldn't he say what was buried deep in his heart?

But what *was* it that lurked there? What *had* he been unable to acknowledge till now?

Slowly, as if she were a snake slinking up a tree, she slid up his body, and before he could speak, her lips had closed on his. At first, he did not respond; he was taken too much by surprise. But then, as she pressed them harder, he did.

Her hands traveled freely about his body, and his followed suit, clasping her hips and then inching up her sides, each rib another hurdle crossed on the way to her bosom. How could this be happening? How could he be thus engaged? But what was there to stop him? He felt his will had been entirely subsumed.

Her tongue darted at his mouth, wetting his lips, then burrowed in, parting them. He felt the very breath inside him being sucked out, and thought of the *ba* escaping the body of a dead man.

But he was alive, more alive than he had felt in years.

In the air, there was a strange aroma . . . salty.

Like the natron used to preserve mummified remains.

Her fingers were closed around the back of his neck, first caressing him, then holding him fast. His heart was beating a mile a minute. He opened his eyes, but her face, so close to his, was unrecognizable.

In a trick of the light, her hair took on a paler shade.

To catch his breath, he tried to pull away, but the fingers at his neck squeezed tighter. His hands, sculpting her breasts, went to her collarbone, and tried again to push away, but her body was too insistent . . . and more fleshless than he would have imaged. The bones felt brittle, and the skin, even through the fabric of her dress, seemed as desiccated as papyrus.

Her tongue wormed its way into the cavern of his mouth, probing, scouring, relentless, as if it were searching something out.

His heart skipped a beat, then two, and he squirmed in the chair.

Her body atop him was no longer welcome; it was a weight that seemed increasingly oppressive. How could he be having such trouble repelling it?

He twisted in the chair, the afghan snagging around his shoulders and sweeping the edge of the table, and heard a crash of glass shattering on the floor. With a sudden and concerted effort, he was able to shove her away and stagger to his feet. Swaying in place and gasping for breath, he fumbled at the lamp, but by the time its light had leavened the library gloom, all he could see were the shards of the broken whiskey glass and his open notebook, lying where Mina—and hadn't it been she?—had knelt.

But no one was there.

Where had she gone? She could not have evaporated into thin air.

He looked all around the room, even peering behind the curtains. On the street outside, a torn newspaper flew past on the gusting wind.

His heart was still racing from her embrace, but his ardor had been overcome by something more akin to terror. And doubt.

He left the library and went to the front door, which he found firmly locked, from the inside.

A dream. It had all been a dream, though the most vivid he had ever known. It could not be anything else. His lips were wet from the Scotch, and the twisted afghan still hung from one shoulder. At his core, he had a vague sense of depletion. Closing his eyes, he leaned his forehead against the hard, unyielding oak of the door. Somewhere outside, he could hear a plaintive wailing, some poor creature who could find no shelter from the cold wind blowing through the streets. He wished he could open his door to it, but he knew that it would not be wise. He remembered boyhood stories of banshees, howling around the windows of a house where a death was about to occur, and a shiver descended his spine.

No, it would not be wise to unlatch the door.

He returned to his library, picked up his notebook and pen, and began to write.

CHAPTER THIRTY-ONE

"And what's this?" Eli Strauss said, waving a letter at Mina as she entered the building, a basket filled with some meager provisions on her arm. It was a bright and sunny day, and even the East End looked a little less derelict than usual. "It came by private messenger, not an hour ago."

The monogram stamped on the flap—BT—told her whom it had come from, but she had no idea what it might contain. For a moment, she waited for Strauss to retire before she opened it, but then she realized he wasn't going anywhere. She opened it, anyway, and quickly scanned the few lines. Bartholomew Thorne was apologizing for having sprung the news of her father's death in such an inopportune fashion, and was inviting her to dinner that night for a more proper discussion of that, and other matters.

"Who's it from, and what's he want?" Strauss demanded.

"It's from a man who worked with my father."

"That doesn't tell me what he wants with you. My brother-in-law vouched for you, and I consider myself a pretty good judge of character, but who are all these fellows? The one you asked me to throw out if I ever saw him again? The one who showed up to carry you off to the theater? And now this one? I'm not one for English manners—hypocrites, all of these so-called aristocrats—but still it's not looking right, not at all, if you take my meaning."

"I take your meaning," she said, "and I assure you nothing untoward is happening." But her eyes were riveted to the postscript, where Thorne had written, "Professor Vambéry tells me you have a Carpathian box of some antiquity. I would very much like to see it. Please bring it with you."

Despite it seeming a casual afterthought, Mina had the strong intuition that it was the box Thorne was most interested in, not her. She, however, was vitally interested in Thorne—and in finding out more about his past dealings with her father. It would be a match of wits, and if showing the box was the price of admission, she was willing to pay it.

In her room, she dashed off a hasty reply, then removed the gold box from its hiding place behind the wallboard, and tucked it into her valise, resolving to go straight from her appointment with Mr. Cruikshank at the British Museum to Thorne's mansion. At worst, she would get a fine dinner there—*sans* rats this time—and at best, some answers. It was even possible that Thorne could shed some light on the mysteries of the gold box.

At the museum, she climbed several flights of stairs, and passed through a dozen galleries, before coming to the narrow staircase that led up under the eaves, as it were, where half a dozen curators worked in cubbyholes that looked out over the rooftops and chimney stacks behind the museum. Cruikshank's, she remembered, was the last one on the end, and she was surprised to see the door standing open and a flood of light spilling out into the otherwise gloomy corridor. Poking her head in, she was surprised again by the sight of Cruikshank himself, his frail shoulders hunched, his head buried in a book. A man of advanced years to begin with, he seemed to have aged another decade in a matter of days. His white hair was sparser than ever, his skin was sallow, and his expression moribund.

When she announced herself, he nearly jumped out of his seat.

"Oh, I did not hear you approach."

"I'm sorry if I startled you."

"Everything does these days," he said, gesturing to a dilapidated leather chair opposite his desk. "Be careful where you step—the mouse-traps." There were several scattered around the edges of the desk, and a few more she could see under the radiator. Was the museum undergoing a rodent infestation? The other hazard was the sheer accumulation of research materials—she had to navigate around teetering piles of books and papers everywhere, some of them appearing ready to topple over at any second. Reading her thoughts, he said, "Rest assured, there is a method to my madness."

"I don't doubt it."

As he reached for a teacup nestled among several heavy volumes, she could not help but notice a visible trembling in his hand that she had never noted before.

"Are you quite well?" she asked.

"Well enough," he said, with no conviction. "I have had some difficulty sleeping."

Mina was unused to Cruikshank taking such a personal tone, but appreciated his trust in her. "Have you seen a doctor? Perhaps he could prescribe a sleeping draught?"

"That might only make things worse."

"In what way?"

He looked at her with rheumy eyes. "Because then, instead of being able to awaken from bad dreams, I might be trapped inside them."

Mina was taken aback. "It sounds awful. How long have you been suffering from this?"

"Since the night of the unraveling at Thorne's." Shaking his head slowly, he said, "I am not one to believe in things I cannot see with my own eyes, or scientifically prove. I think you know that much about me."

"I do."

"But there was something about that ceremony that troubled me deeply, and not only in respect to its terrible denouement."

Was that why the mousetraps were everywhere? She spotted one on the windowsill. Was he expecting another onslaught?

"You cannot labor in the field of Middle Eastern antiquities for as long as I have without running into dozens of tales of curses and plagues and spirits, and I have never treated them as anything more than myth and legend. I have never before given them any credence, or felt in any way complicit in some sacrilege. Never."

"But now you have?"

"Now I am . . . not so sure." He passed a liver-spotted hand across his eyes. "Judging from the words of the papyrus clutched in her hands, the Chantress of Amun had some earthly business that still weighed heavily on her mind. She was not yet done with this world, and sometimes I fear that we are not yet done with her." He paused, turning in his chair to gaze out the dusty dormer window. "Do you ever hear . . . singing?"

"Singing?"

Cruikshank nodded. "It would take a linguist of Professor Vambéry's caliber to decipher it, but I hear ancient words, to an ancient tune, whispered in the dark. Is it any wonder I approach my bed as if it were the gibbet?"

No wonder at all, Mina thought.

Gathering himself together, Cruikshank sat up straighter in his chair, and said, "But that's not what I called you here for, to listen to an old man tell you about his troubles."

"I am always happy to lend an ear. I know my father always had the greatest respect for your knowledge and your opinions."

"As I had for his . . . and, for that matter, yours."

Mina blushed.

"Look around you," he said, rallying. "I am a man besieged. The number of books and monographs and essays, by everyone from Oxford dons to amateur Egyptologists, grows larger every day. There is seemingly no end to their fervor, and they all want my blessing or imprimatur. I can no longer keep up."

"It must keep you from attending to your own work."

"It does, though the days when I could conduct my own research are fast receding. I haven't the strength, or even the habits of mind, anymore. What I have finally come to accept is that I need an assistant."

His gaze remained level, and it dawned on Mina that he was not making a statement so much as he was posing a question.

"Are you asking me . . . ?"

"To be that assistant? Yes, I am."

Mina was thunderstruck. She hadn't expected anything like this, and the idea that such an august institution as the British Museum would employ a woman—a young woman, and of no special breeding—was almost unthinkable.

"Truly?" she blurted out. "Why me?"

"Why not? Is there anyone better versed in what this practice is all about? There could be no better teacher than your late father was. And who would I ever be able to find who has *been* to the places where these treasures originated? Who understands the processes of discovery and authentication? It would take me years simply to train someone to reach the corresponding level of expertise you have already acquired—and I do not have that long."

Although she hated to hear him referring in such a way to his mortality, she was overwhelmed by the offer.

"The salary, I'm afraid, would be low, but I can occasionally put you on to a private collector who will pay you for some particular commission. Your credential here, I assure you, will serve you in good stead."

Mina was still trying to take it all in. Her situation had, in the blink of an eye, utterly changed. She had gone from living on a shoestring— and a shoestring of no great length at that—to being a salaried employee of the most venerable museum in the world. She saw a future beyond a rented room in the depths of the East End. "Should I say that I need some time to consider it?" she said. "Or may I simply express my profound gratitude for your faith in me, and say yes, a hundred times over, yes?"

"One yes will suffice."

Before she could say another word, there was a snapping sound from under the radiator as one of the mousetraps sprang shut. In an instant, the expression on Cruikshank's face went from satisfaction to perturbation, from relief to dread.

"It looks like you haven't set your traps for naught," Mina said, hoping to pass over the moment.

"They follow me now," he said. "They follow me."

And just as quickly, her joy dissipated, as she wondered if the old man behind the desk, the one who had just thrown her a life preserver, had not gone further than she knew into that vale of unknowingness where so many had gone before.

CHAPTER THIRTY-TWO

"It's not too big for you, is it?"

"No, mother, it's just right."

Lucinda was pleased. Even though she had made the coat from scraps of fabric torn from old costumes, it looked quite respectable, especially in the moonlight. "And is it warm?"

"Oh, ever so." Standing beside his headstone, he hugged his skinny arms about him.

In the pond nearby, the ducks quacked.

"What else can I bring you, dear? Are you hungry?" She was annoyed with herself for not thinking of it sooner.

"Oh, I don't get very hungry anymore," he said absently, before amending it with some enthusiasm, "but a hot cross bun, with lots of butter and jam, would be nice."

"You shall have it. And what else? What more can I do?" She needed to know of anything that she could provide. It was the only joy she still had in life.

"There is one other thing."

"Tell me what it is—whatever it is, I'll find a way to get it for you."

"It's what the Matron took."

Her heart sank. How in the world would she ever get that back? "Oh, Davey, honey, I'm sure she's got that hidden where I'll never find it."

He pouted.

"And besides, it looks to me like you're not lacking it, or anything like it. Are you sure it's gone?"

His expression instantly altered, so much so that she hardly recognized him. "You asked me what I wanted, and I told you." He'd never spoken to her like that, either.

"Oh, Davey, let's not quarrel! I couldn't stand that. Not now. Not after everything that's happened."

He was fading in and out a bit, and she wasn't sure if it was the clouds scudding before the moon, or if he was losing strength. She was terribly afraid of tiring him.

"Let me think a bit," she said, "and see what I can do." She could never approach the Matron herself—she'd be shown the door, or worse, and that would be *before* she could even find a way to level an accusation.

"I have to go."

"Are you angry with me, darling?"

"I have to go."

"Why?"

His eyes seemed to glance behind her, and when she turned, she saw a short fat man with a lantern, weaving his way through the tombstones. He'd seen her, too, and he called out, "You there—didn't you hear the bells ring?"

She quickly turned back toward Davey to tell him to hide, but he was already gone.

"The graveyard closed an hour ago. You're not s'posed to be in here. Nobody is but me."

"I'm sorry. I lost track of the time."

"Did you lose track of the sun, too? It's dark out! Are you daft?"

"I said I was sorry. I'll go now."

"You can bet on it—and don't let me catch you out here again after closing time."

She started to go, but as she passed him, he grabbed her sleeve and said, "Ain't you forgettin' something?"

She looked back—the coat was neatly draped about the headstone. "No, that stays where it is."

There must have been something in her face—the set of her inflamed jaw, the obstinate gaze—that convinced him not to argue the point.

"Well, then, let's get going," he said, and like a border collie, he dogged her steps all the way to the gates of the cemetery. Once outside, Lucinda paused. Raising his lantern to the bars, the watchman said, "All right then, don't stop there neither. There must be someplace you can go."

And that was when it came to her. While she doubted she could make any headway with Winifred Thorne, she did have a certain amount of sway—or at least she once had—with her brother. He might still be irate about what had happened in the tunnel, but wouldn't he be relieved to learn she had no intention of exposing him . . . so long as he helped her now?

She had only been to his mansion once—she recalled that it made the Matron's sumptuous quarters in the mission house look paltry by comparison—but she was sure she could find it again. Turning away from the lantern light, she set off to recover her son's lost soul.

CHAPTER THIRTY-THREE

It was with mixed feelings that Mina heard several voices emanating from the drawing room as the butler showed her in. On the one hand, a tête-à-tête would have afforded her a better opportunity to bore in on the questions she most wanted answered, but on the other, she dreaded being alone with a man of such strange and ungovernable appetites.

Thorne, standing by the mantel, moved to greet her, as Vambéry, leaning on his cane, rose from his chair.

"Delighted you could come, Miss Harcourt," her host said, taking her hand and kissing the back of it. "I think you know the professor," he said, "and have at least met my sister, Winifred."

Seated in a wheelchair drawn close to the hearth, Winifred gave her a frosty smile and nod of the head. The last time Mina had seen her—in full Egyptian garb, in the greenhouse—she had moved freely about the stage. What had happened since to occasion this change?

Offered a glass of sherry, Mina took it, and seated herself on a silken divan. Around her neck she wore the carnelian ankh as a good-luck charm; in her lap, she held a clutch purse containing the Carpathian box. Unless she was mistaken, Thorne's eyes had flicked from one to the other already, though he studiously avoided any direct query about either. He turned the conversation instead to the recent parliamentary elections, but having lived so much abroad, she had little interest in the topic, and even less to contribute.

"There's all the usual caterwauling about the poor and downtrodden of Whitechapel and Bethnal Green," Thorne said, resting an elbow beside the marble clock on the mantelpiece, "but precious little suggested in the way of governmental reform or remedies."

"They would do well to emulate your success with the mission house," Vambéry said.

"Tell the politicians that," Winfred said, "or the queen, for that matter. My brother should have been recognized for his services to the nation long ago."

"And you, too," Vambéry added. "Are you not the presiding spirit there?"

"I am, and a more thankless job you cannot imagine."

Mina could immediately think of many.

"Ministering to the needs of so many indigent and lost souls," Winifred said, "takes the patience of an angel and the temperament of a saint."

Was she implying that she possessed both? It certainly seemed so.

"The match factory gives many of them necessary employment, yes?" Vambéry continued. "Surely that is a useful means of getting them back on their feet?"

Mina had seldom seen such a slavish display toward one's hosts. It made Cruikshank's acquiescence to the mummy's unraveling seem tepid. Did money, and the power it conferred, wield an even more outsized influence in society than she had previously conceived? Indifferent to material wealth herself, she was unaffected by its display; her father had taught her to think quite differently from most people on that score.

"Yes, but so many of them lack the most basic incentive to work or improve themselves," Winifred said. "It's all I can do to inspire them with the right attitude."

"We hope to spur them on," her brother put in, "to lives of hard work and individual betterment."

Mina could finally no longer restrain herself in the face of such self-aggrandizement and hypocrisy. "I live in the East End," she said, holding her sherry glass very still, "among the sort of people who no doubt wind up in the workhouses when all else has failed. What I see is no want of initiative or the willingness to do hard labor. Indeed, I see quite the opposite." She thought of Eli Strauss and the crew that worked in his furniture shop, from dawn to dusk, seven days a week. "I see people who lead the most desperate and hardscrabble lives, against almost insurmountable odds. They live in squalid tenements, for which they pay dearly, and work their fingers to the bone for wages that remain insufficient to supply anything but the most basic necessities of life—enough, merely, to go on for another day of living the same precarious hand-to-mouth existence."

"Really?" Winifred retorted. "Because from my vantage, I see them reeling from the pubs, or dandling babies they can ill-afford to have, one on each knee."

"If they drink—and Lord knows they do, many of them—it is because it's the only pleasurable refuge they've got, the only means they have of escape from the dreary lives they lead. Three ha'pence of gin and they can be transported, for even a short time, out of the filthy streets they inhabit and the noxious air they must breathe."

Vambéry was looking at her agog. A veteran diplomat, he must have been in shock at her contrariness.

As for Thorne, he seemed to be taking it all in good humor. The smile on his full, jowly face betrayed a grudging respect, even admiration, for her candor; it was as titillating as if she'd shown him a bit of bare ankle. Winifred, however, appeared to be seething, and was about to counter again when, as luck would have it, the butler announced that dinner was served.

Vambéry quickly offered Mina his arm to go in to dinner, while Thorne pushed his sister's chair, the rattan of the seat creaking, the wheels rattling, down the marble floor of the hall. As the table was long enough to easily accommodate twenty, their places had all been set at one end, with Thorne at the head, his sister to his right, and Vambéry to hers. Which left Mina alone on Thorne's left, feeling oddly exposed and vulnerable. She wished the comforting presence of Bram Stoker were seated beside her to provide a bulwark.

In what seemed an attempt to smooth things over, the professor launched into a review of Henry Irving's production of *Macbeth*, which he had just attended. "One can easily see why the man has been knighted," but if he was looking for agreement on that, he had again erred, as Winifred snorted, and Bartholomew devoted all his attention to his turtle soup. Trying again, he brought up the Constable sketches he had seen for sale in a fashionable gallery. "I can think of no artist with a greater capacity for capturing the English landscape and sky."

Again, the conversational gambit dropped like a stone. The only sounds in the room were the clinking of cutlery and the hushed rustling of the staff as they served one lavish course after another, from raw oysters to pheasant under glass. Vambéry, looking as uncomfortable as Mina felt, refused to give up hope, and on occasion he was able to kindle some brief flame of interest, on one topic or another, from Thorne or his disgruntled sister. "Oscar Wilde, I read in the papers, has been quite broken by his incarceration. He is a shadow of his former self."

"The man was too big to begin with," Winifred opined. "And for the crimes against nature that he and his confederates committed, he deserved no less punishment than he has received."

"All the same, the Marquess of Queensberry is a brute and a fool to have prosecuted the case," Thorne said. "He'd have been wiser to let the whole thing drop, especially as it is his son who's been cast in the unenviable role of catamite."

"Serves that silly Lady Wilde right," Winifred interjected. "You won't hear her going on about her brilliant boy anymore, now that he's a convicted felon and pederast. He'll be run out of the country if he lives out his sentence."

Mina was shocked, though she knew she should not have been, by the callous and cruel nature of Miss Thorne's remarks. When she wasn't congratulating herself for some imagined virtue, she was castigating someone else for his or her human failings. That she should be in charge of a mission house was an abomination.

Thorne, attempting to steer the table toward safer waters, asked Mina if she had had time to attend many lectures or exhibitions since coming back to London, and she demurred. "I have had too much to do."

"At the museum?"

"Yes, among other things." Under the flap of the damask tablecloth, her fingers clutched her little evening bag more tightly.

"If you ask me," Thorne said, "Mr. Cruikshank is overwhelmed these days. Wouldn't you say so, Professor?"

Predictably, Vambéry agreed, before returning to his dessert.

"I'd say he needs an assistant—some young blood to reinvigorate the department," Thorne went on, an open question in his eyes.

Did he know about the job offer she had received only hours before? How could he? And then an even more awful thought crossed her mind—had he engineered it in some way? Was he moving her about, now, like Vambéry and others, just another pawn on his chessboard? And if so, to what end? To gain greater leverage in the placement of his donations?

When the meal ended, Winifred announced that she was weary, and without so much as saying good-night to Mina, had Thorne wheel her to his carriage outside, where one of the servants was dispatched to escort her the rest of the way home.

Coming back, Thorne clapped his hands together and, unwilling to wait any longer, said, "Well now, shall we retire to the library, and have a look at that Carpathian relic you've been cradling all night?"

CHAPTER THIRTY-FOUR

"What say we have a toast," Stoker said, "to the return of the conquering hero?"

"With what?" Florence said, dabbing at the corner of her mouth as the maid cleared the plates from the table.

"Yes, Father," Noel said, still wearing his dark-blue Winchester school uniform. "What shall we toast with?"

Laying a finger slyly against his nose, Stoker said, "I've laid aside a certain bottle of champagne for just such an occasion as this."

"You know I don't encourage drinking for someone of Noel's age."

"I'm sixteen, Mother! And it won't be the first time I've had champagne."

"That is not an admission, I hope, that you would make to the headmaster."

Noel, a strapping lad back home for a school holiday, said, "All the boys have managed it one way or another." Turning to his father, where he was assured of success, he said, "Shall I go and get it?"

"It's been cooling in a bucket, just out of sight behind the scullery door."

Like a shot, Noel was up and out of his chair, his napkin flying onto the table. He had the energy Bram had had as a young man, too—eager, impetuous, athletic—but wedded to the more fragile features and complexion of his mother. Bram's hair had been a dark russet color at that age; Noel's was a sandy thatch, and his shoulders, though broad, were not as thick and muscular as his father's had been. He was more of a cricket player than a rugby boy.

But Bram was inordinately proud of him; Noel had done well on all his examinations, and carried an unblemished record of personal conduct. When he returned, the champagne was popped and the dessert was brought out—a strawberry trifle, always Noel's favorite—and as Bram looked down the table at his handsome son and elegant wife, he could not help but reflect on his good fortune. The scene was virtually perfect, even if it did hide some serious cracks. But what marriage did not have them, just as well concealed as their own were? Looking at Florence now, he could still see the tall, blonde debutante who had once been the belle of the ball, and he still yearned for her. It was no wonder, in retrospect, that he had had that powerfully erotic dream in the study the night before. But that was all it had been—a dream. Men of his age were wont to feel attraction toward younger women. It was only natural, just as it was natural that Mina should feel for him a certain fondness, even admiration, that went no further than that. To think otherwise, or to act upon some foolish impulse he might momentarily entertain, would be mad.

"Did I tell you that I've been made an editor of the *Trusty Servant*?" Noel remarked, hoping to distract them from the fact that he had just poured himself a second glass of the champagne. "The prefect said it was long overdue."

"That's marvelous, dear," his mother said, "but that's quite enough of the champagne for one night. And what is the *Trusty Servant*?"

"It's the college magazine—all the Old Wykehamists read it."

"Following in your old man's footsteps," Bram said. "When I was just a few years older than you are now, and just out of Trinity, I wrote my first reviews for the *Dublin Evening Mail*." He was about to expatiate on his days as a young journalist when a knocking was heard at the front door.

"Who could that be at this hour?" Florence remarked, but Stoker's only hope was that it not be a messenger from the Lyceum, there to tell him something had gone horribly awry. His son's visit was to be a short one, and he had looked forward to spending time with the boy.

"I'll get it," Noel said, finishing off his glass and bounding out of his chair in one swift motion. Intercepting the parlormaid in the vestibule, he opened the door while Stoker and Florence sat quietly, waiting to overhear the news.

"Yes, he is at home," Stoker, who was closer to the door, heard Noel say. "But whom should I say is calling?"

The answer was lost, and then Noel said, "And he will know what this is about?"

Again, Stoker could not make out the reply, but by now he was getting up and going to see for himself.

"A private matter, you say?" Noel was repeating. "Well, I can't say I much like the sound of that."

Looking over Noel's shoulder, Stoker saw a man in a dark overcoat, holding a hat in his hands, his longish brown hair parted in the center. He was no one he knew.

"May I help you?" Stoker said.

"Ludvig Gerhard," the man replied, extending his hand, which Stoker shook. "I'm very sorry if I have come at an inopportune time." His accent was Austrian.

"What's this about?" Stoker said, already wondering if this wasn't another importunate playwright, hoping to go through him to get his work to Henry Irving. It wouldn't be the first time.

"I am a friend of a friend," Gerhard said.

"What's his name?" Stoker was already tiring of this intrusion, and the man's opacity.

"It is a female friend," Gerhard answered in a low voice, his eyes flicking toward Florence, who had appeared in the hallway.

Stoker was momentarily taken aback. Given the man's skulking demeanor, his first thought was of Lucinda—had she done something, in her derangement, to warrant this visit?

"Well, out with it then."

"I would much prefer to speak with you in private."

When Stoker hesitated, he added, "It would be, I believe, in your own best interest, too."

Was that a threat of some kind? Both Noel and Florence had turned their eyes to him, and unsure of what was to come next, Stoker simply waved the man toward the study. "In there." To his wife and son, he said, "I shan't be long," and followed his unwelcome guest.

Once the doors were closed, Gerhard took a chair by the cold hearth, crossing his legs and settling in very comfortably, having altogether dropped any pretense of servility.

"It is a brisk night out there," he said, rubbing his hands together. "You wouldn't have anything to warm a wary traveler, would you?"

"*Weary* traveler," Stoker corrected him. "That's the expression."

"I thank you. I am always seeking to perfect my English."

Reluctantly, Stoker poured him a glass of brandy from the sideboard, handed it to him, and sat down opposite. Waiting.

Gerhard sipped the brandy, looking about the well-appointed room like an appraiser.

In any negotiation—and as manager of a commercial theater, Stoker had had to conduct many—it was always best to let the other person speak first, to force them to introduce their terms or demands before you committed yourself to anything. But as he was also in a hurry to get this man out of his house, he was growing more impatient by the second.

"The Lyceum, it is a going proposition," Gerhard finally said. "I have that expression right, yes?"

"Near enough."

"Full house, almost every night. Henry Irving, the greatest actor in the land. Ellen Terry, the greatest actress. I saw the performance of *Macbeth*. It was very good."

"The audiences like it."

"Exactly. Especially young women."

Where was this going? "I don't know that that's true."

"Well, I know of one at least." He took another sip and, glancing at a murky oil painting on the wall, said, "Is that a Corot?"

"No."

"Then it is the school of. And an excellent example."

"To what young lady are you referring?" Stoker said, though by now of course he knew, and it was not Lucinda.

"She is living in such a humble abode. Right again, yes? Humble abode? She should not be hidden away in such a place."

"Mina is not hiding from anyone."

"No?"

"Why should she?"

"You are right. She has nothing to be ashamed of. A lovely young woman, with no means of support, washed up on these English shores. It is no wonder that she allows herself to become a close . . . friend of a man, an older man, who is wealthy and well established. Nor am I," he said hastily, raising a hand in protest, "in a position to judge anyone. I know what it is like to have difficulties." He chuckled. "It can happen to anyone," he said, pressing a hand to his chest.

Stoker, no stranger to melodrama, didn't need to read another page of this script to know where it was headed. Still, he felt it was his job to recite the next line.

"And what do you want?"

Gerhard pretended to be taken aback. "It is what you want that concerns me."

"What *I* want?"

"Yes. Surely, you want to maintain everything you have here," he said, his glance taking in everything from the furnishings to the air of respectability. "A loving wife, a noble son, a place in society."

"And you are going to somehow take all of that from me?"

"Sir, you mistake my nature. Gravely."

"I doubt it."

"I am here to *protect* you from such a fate. No one need ever know that you have found happiness outside these walls. Nothing need change."

"Except some money needs to change hands."

Gerhard finished the brandy, and put the glass on the table—the very table that the glass had fallen from the night before, during Stoker's dream. He felt a sudden flush of guilt, as if he'd cheated in real life, and he had to remind himself once more that it had only been a dream.

"Forgive me," Gerhard said, "I am unused to this sort of thing." Stoker barked a laugh, and Gerhard looked offended.

"You are no more unaccustomed to this sort of thing," Stoker said dismissively, "than you are to cheating at cards or picking someone's pocket. I had taken your measure at the foyer."

"As a gentleman, I am offended by your words."

"That was their intent."

"So then, you are not going to listen to reason?" Gerhard said, suddenly adopting a sharper tone. "You are going to force me to make certain things public?"

"No, I'm not," Stoker said, rising abruptly and going to the study door. "I am going to do it for you." He threw open the doors and called out to Florence and Noel to come.

"What is it, Father?" Noel said, first on the scene.

"I need you to help me with some baggage."

"Baggage?"

"What is going on, Bram?" Florence said, coming down from upstairs.

"You see that?" Stoker said, gesturing at Gerhard, who had risen, perplexed, from his chair. "You need to help me throw that out."

It took a second for Noel to understand that his father was being serious, but then he said, "With pleasure."

Together, the two of them grabbed Gerhard, one by each arm, and hauled him from the study so rapidly his feet dragged on the carpets.

"You'll regret this!" Gerhard shouted, then looking at Florence, added, "Your husband is keeping a mistress!"

With one hand, Stoker threw the front door open, and then he and his son propelled Gerhard down the front steps so hard that he skidded on the pavement before banging up against the base of a lamppost.

A passing bobby, the one who walked this beat every night, said, "Here now—what's this about?"

"An intruder."

The policeman eyed the man lying on the sidewalk, who for once had nothing to say for himself, and said, "Do you want him to be charged with anything, Mr. Stoker?"

"No, just clear him out."

"That I'll do," he said, nudging the prostrate Gerhard with the toe of his boot. "You there, move along now."

Stoker closed the door, and looked at his wife and son. Noel was grinning at the sheer adventure of it, but Florence, whose face Stoker glimpsed as she turned to go back upstairs, had set her jaw in a most unhappy way. He did not relish the explanations and amends he would need to offer.

CHAPTER THIRTY-FIVE

Standing by the hearth, Thorne turned the little box over and over in his hands, plainly admiring the rough but sturdy construction, as Mina herself had done when it had first come into her possession. Its golden surface glimmered in the firelight.

Holding it to his eye, he attempted to peer into its aperture, no bigger than a keyhole, and asked, "Have you ever seen anything inside?"

"No, never."

"Nor did I when I first saw the box at Lady Wilde's," Vambéry said, sipping from his glass of port. Mina had barely touched her own.

"And this latch, you say it only opens and closes of its own accord?"

"At sunrise and sunset."

"Remarkable."

Thorne's acquisitive instincts were on full display; Mina could see that the more he learned of the box, the more intent he would be on keeping it in his own collection. It would be all she could do to reclaim it before leaving his house that night.

"But I cannot reconcile its Egyptian character with its Carpathian provenance," Thorne said, shaking his head.

"That is one of the reasons I was convinced you would wish to see it," Vambéry said. "It is a puzzle extraordinaire."

Thorne grunted, holding the box to his ear and giving it a gentle shake. He had already extracted from Mina the story of the monumental sphinx atop the mountain, the cave in which the box had been wrested from the hands of a skeleton, the subsequent recovery of it from the Gypsies. He had listened absorbedly to the entire narrative, urging her all the while to sample the port. "It's the best in the world, from the cellars laid down by the Abbot of Lamego in the Douro River valley of Portugal. You'll never taste its like."

Vambéry had certainly taken him at his word, and was already on his second glass. His eyelids were beginning to droop. Obligingly, Mina drank half a glass, but not being a connoisseur of these things, wasn't sure if she fully appreciated its unique character.

Chuckling, Thorne said, "I think, Professor, that you are ready for bed."

Vambéry, draining the second glass, mumbled something in his native Hungarian as his chin touched down on his chest. Thorne pulled a bell cord, and the butler came into the library so quickly, it was as if he had been standing sentinel right outside. "Help the professor to his room," Thorne said, and bidding them a slurred good-night, Vambéry was escorted out. Nervous at being left alone now in Thorne's company, Mina sipped from her glass again—there was some slightly pungent aftertaste, and she wondered if that was some special characteristic of rare port—and prepared to take the conversation in her preferred direction.

Alluding to the photograph above the fire, she said, "Surely, that picture wasn't taken on your first, and last, expedition with my father. How did you two become acquainted?"

Filling her glass from the crystal flask, Thorne said, "It was quite a story in itself. I had just finished excavating a tomb, and was piloting a barge down the Nile to Thebes. We were loaded with treasures, when a little skiff blew into our path. The collision was unavoidable, and the skiff collapsed like a bundle of twigs. The crocodiles weren't about to miss an opportunity like that, and in fact they got the boatman. I was able to pull your father from the water in the nick of time. He bore a scar on his heel as a memento of the snapping jaws that almost pulled him under."

Mina remembered the scar well. His left shoe had always had to be specially made to ease the pain in that foot.

"Didn't he ever tell you that story?"

"Yes, he did," she said, though in her father's telling, the barge had recklessly rammed his boat. And what's more, she remembered being brought to the hospital by her nanny; her father's foot was being patched up, and a big man with a brown moustache was clapping him on the back and leaving the ward just as she came in. *My God*, she thought—it must have been Thorne!

"Anyway, we got to talking, and the rest, as they say, is history. His expertise was crucial to many of our later discoveries. Here," he said, pouring her a bit more port, "drink up."

"No, thank you, I've had enough. You have it."

"I'm sticking to whiskey tonight. Otherwise, I'm going to wind up with the gout one day."

"But what of me?"

"You are far too young," he said, sitting beside her on the divan, "and far too healthy to worry about such things." Moving an inch or two closer, he said, "And far too beautiful."

"I don't know that anyone's physical appearance has ever had much to do with their susceptibility to disease." For some reason, it felt as if composing that sentence had required a more sustained effort than usual.

"Ah, but if it is, you will number among the immortals." A facetious smile twitched at the ends of his moustache, as if to signal that it was all in playful jest, but Mina suspected it was not.

"You say that you made other discoveries together," she went on, staring down into her glass and ignoring his close proximity. "I wonder why I never heard of you before, especially as I accompanied him on several expeditions."

"You were a mere child when we worked together. I won't say a word against Sebastian, particularly to his daughter. He was a fine man, but we had our different methodologies."

"How so?"

Thorne shrugged. "Your father was a man of great deliberation and painstaking scholarship. I was a man of more practical and expedient aims."

His arm had slunk, like a snake, around the back of the divan, until his fingertips lay close to her shoulder. On the portico outside, she could hear the rising wind rattling the French doors.

"You don't like the port?"

"I do."

"Then let's drink to your late father."

He clinked his whiskey glass against hers, and watched closely as she sipped from the wine.

"And these practical aims," Mina said, "were what?"

"What *were* they?" he replied, with a laugh. "Look around you. I wanted to live like a pharaoh, while Sebastian, may he rest in peace, was content to remain—"

He stopped short, but Mina knew he had been about to say "a peasant," or something akin to it.

"—a digger," Thorne concluded. "He wasn't really happy if his hands weren't dirty and his bed wasn't a mat of reeds under the stars."

He was right about that, too. Memories of her father were flooding her mind, bringing a wave of sadness and regret. She had held those rough hands on arduous treks; she had slept on those mats; she had lain beside him as he pointed out the constellations above the rolling dunes of the Sahara. She felt tears welling up in her eyes—oh God, the last thing she wanted to do at a time like this was cry—but some governor had been overruled in her. There was a lassitude in her limbs to match that in her wits. The gold box sat squarely on the table, not three feet away, but she wondered if she had the strength even to reach out and reclaim it.

"Even this," Thorne said, delicately lifting the back of the silver chain from which the carnelian ankh hung around her neck, "was from one of our ventures."

He pulled back on the chain, so that her head came to rest against the top of the divan. It felt so good to rest it there. She was being fast overwhelmed by a delicious sense of abandonment.

"And I must say, it looks far better on you than it ever could have looked on its original owner."

"And who would that be?"

"I thought you knew."

"Knew what?" She was becoming lost in the conversation.

"Where it came from."

"My father gave it to me."

"And I gave it to him."

She was more lost than ever. Was he deliberately trying to confuse her?

"I think I told him I bought it from a street beggar in exchange for two cans of tinned rations."

That sounded familiar. She closed her eyes in an attempt to better focus her thoughts.

"But I assumed he had figured out where it actually came from."

"Where?" His voice, so very close to her ear now, was becoming an annoyance—what she wanted to do was sleep.

"The tomb of Nebetia."

"Who?" she mumbled.

"You met her the other night."

She had met so many people since coming to London.

"The Chantress of Amun. . . . I knew that your father, with all his scruples about grave robbing, would have looked askance at it. But there it was, hanging around the wooden shell encasing the mummy, and, well, I was feeling bad about the sunken skiff and his injured foot, and I thought it was just the kind of thing his little girl might like. There was always one way back into your father's good graces—and that was through you."

The breath had caught in her throat—and before she could regain it, she felt his mouth pressing down on hers and his fingers fumbling at the buttons of her bodice. She tried to turn her head to one side, but he braided the necklace chain around her neck like a lariat and held it firm. The bitter taste of his whiskey overwhelmed the sickly sweetness of the port as his tongue forced her lips apart. His other hand slipped down, then up, under her dress, so deftly that by the time she clamped her legs shut, his hand was trapped between her thighs.

She put her hands to his chest, but he maneuvered his body so that the bulk of him—and it was considerable—was half-atop her. She could breathe just enough to huff in protest and alarm, but it was to no avail. Her mind, lulled into drowsy complacence only moments before, was struggling to reassert itself.

"Go ahead," he muttered, "fight me." As he kissed her neck, the bristles of his moustache scraped her cheek. "I like it." His hand gripped one thigh like a vise. "And you like it, too."

Twisting her body, and dropping her hands flat against the cushions, she tried to lever herself up, but he was too strong. She slumped back, exhausted, the port threatening to come up in her throat like a burning tide. His hands were everywhere at once, his body was crushing her; her mind raced for some new defense, as a cool breeze, out of nowhere, seemed to blow through the room.

His breathing was so hoarse and urgent it was all she could hear.

Until, and she was sure she had imagined it, she did hear something else. A voice—a woman's—over by the French doors that opened to the portico.

"Mr. Thorne," the voice said, in an everyday manner. "I need to talk to you, Mr. Thorne."

His brow furrowed, as if he, too, thought he must be imagining this, but then he leaned back enough to look over. Mina turned to look, too, and saw, framed by the billowing curtains, a young woman in a shabby overcoat, a pair of silver sewing scissors dangling loosely from one hand.

"It's about Davey."

Even if Mina had ever thought to meet her guardian angel, she would never have considered that she might look like this. But look like this she did—and Mina was so overcome that the tears she cried were of relief and joy.

CHAPTER THIRTY-SIX

"I rather enjoyed that," Noel said, slapping his hands together. "Good riddance to bad rubbish."

"Precisely," Stoker replied, though throwing Ludvig Gerhard down the steps was the easy part. The hard part would be going upstairs and convincing his wife that there was no truth to what the man had shouted on his ignominious way out.

"Who was he, anyway?"

"A scurrilous creature, the kind the theater world attracts in droves."

"And what was all that about . . . well . . ." The boy didn't even know how to say it.

"Nonsense. Utter and complete rot." Stoker refused to lend it any more credence than that, and his son was just as happy to dismiss it out of hand.

"I think you had better go up and talk to Mother, though."

"I think you are right."

Noel bounded off to his room—"I'm writing my first short story for the magazine," he said, "and when it's done, you can show me what I did wrong."—while Stoker trudged up the steps as if his feet were encased in cement. Perhaps what bothered him most was not the unfounded charge, but the fact that Gerhard had divined something so secret Stoker had trouble acknowledging it even to himself. The dream in the study was an enactment of a very real desire . . . but a dream, he knew quite well, was all it could ever be.

Her door, not surprisingly, was closed, and when he knocked, he got no answer. Trying the handle, he found it locked.

"Florence," he said softly, not wanting his son to hear, "let me in."

When there was still no reply, he repeated himself, adding, "We need to talk. Let's not have this become a row, not while Noel is home."

He waited, and he could hear the padding of her slippered feet, the swish of her dressing gown, and then the turning of the lock. She left it to him to open the door, and when he did, she was already returning to her dressing table to complete her nightly regimen.

"It's only because of Noel," she said, resuming her seat on the stool before the mirrored vanity. "Otherwise, I'd want to hear no more about it."

He shut the door behind him, and said, "Even if it is a denial?"

"What else could it be?"

For a moment, he wondered if she'd care if it were true. Had the marriage come to such a pass as that? "It could be a confession, I suppose. But it's not. The man is a bounder and a blackmailer."

"He must have thought he had some evidence on which to base his charge."

"He has none."

"Who is she?"

"Who is who?"

"The mistress, Bram. Don't be coy," she said, taking her hair down.

She was right—there was no point in professing greater ignorance than was warranted. "The woman in question is named Minerva Harcourt. She is the daughter of an archaeologist. If it comes to that, she is an archaeologist herself."

"That does not sound like someone who swims in your usual pool," Florence said, glancing at him only in the mirror. "Aren't you and Mr. Irving awash in actresses? That's how it was done in my day."

Her day, he reflected, had been very brief indeed; she liked to pretend that the performance or two that she had been in had constituted a career, and it was an illusion that he had never challenged. Nor would now be the time to start. "What Henry Irving does is his business."

"He does have a wife, you forget."

"In name only."

"And Ellen Terry is not that name."

As their affair was an open secret, Stoker saw no point in trying to defend his leading actress's honor.

"Are you emulating your boss then?" she said.

She knew he hated it when she referred to Irving as his boss—that was not the kind of relationship they shared—which was precisely why she had done it now.

"I'm not Henry Irving. And I'm not keeping a mistress."

"Exactly what role then does this Miss Harcourt fulfill in your life?" she asked, pulling the brush, with its mother-of-pearl backing, through her hair. "It's hard to see why the Lyceum would require the services of an archaeologist."

What role *did* she fill? It was a far more complex question than Florence might have known, and Stoker was momentarily stymied for an answer. His wife noticed the pause.

"Don't overthink it, Bram. Try honesty."

"I met her at Lady Wilde's, when I returned to fetch your fan."

"Ah, so this little affair—and it has been recent then—is somehow my fault."

"It's not an affair, and it's not your fault, and just let me finish. She came to the salon because she was researching an ancient box, similar to one which Lady Wilde's late husband possessed. Professor Vambéry was there, too—"

"Another man I do not entirely trust."

"—and we both marveled at its intricacy and mysterious origins," he said, letting her last remark pass. "I have since engaged with her, along with the curator of Middle Eastern antiquities at the British Museum, to learn more about it."

"Why would you care a whit?"

"Because it is *interesting*," he said, with asperity. "Because it is a riddle, because it is intellectually challenging, and because, in case you have forgotten, I write stories of a mysterious and occult cast. It is material. Grist for the mill. The stuff of which my tales are made."

"Not often enough. When was your last one bought or published anywhere?"

She had an unfailing instinct for his sore spot.

"And where is this magical box now?" she moved on.

"Wherever Miss Harcourt keeps it."

"And where does she keep herself? Or does the Lyceum pay for her flat somewhere? I know that Irving has done it for his consorts many times."

"She lives on her own, at her own expense," he said, treading cautiously. He did not want to say so much that it seemed he was overly familiar with her domestic arrangements. "Somewhere over in the East End."

"You have not seen it?"

"No." It was only a mild prevarication; true, he had picked her up in a carriage, but had he come upstairs and actually seen her rooms? No, he had not.

But Florence, he could tell, was losing interest in the tale, anyway. Truth be told, she knew that he was a man of boring rectitude, and, for that matter, he suspected she could not even imagine any self-respecting young woman feeling any attraction to him. It was both a relief and an insult.

"I'm tired now," she said, putting the brush aside and swiveling on her stool to face him.

Even with all that had just passed between them, he felt a surge of latent desire. Her long blonde hair, down like this, was appealingly wild and shining; the sprigs of gray had been artfully dyed. And her features were as fine and delicate as ever, though the line of her mouth had taken on a narrower, firmer, altogether less pliant cast.

"Then we are done with this topic?" he said, just to be sure.

"I for one have no more to say about it."

Whether that was because her doubts had been quelled, or au fond she did not really care, he could not tell. They remained facing each other, silent, until he took his cue and turned to the door.

"Good night," he said.

"Good night."

Once in the hallway, he could hear the clatter of Noel's typewriter keys; he was wedded to that new machine, which he'd been given on his sixteenth birthday. It took Stoker back to his school days in Dublin, when he had holed up in his room late at night, a sheaf of paper and a full inkwell before him, to scribble out wild stories. His head had been filled with dreams of literary fame and glory. And though, to all outward appearances, he had done well in life, he was conscious of the never-ending ticking of the clock, and the feeling that there were things—ideas, passions, masterpieces even—still locked inside him. Turning off the gas lamp in the hallway, he went back down the stairs to the comfort of his study—and his Scotch—where, try as he might, he could not shut out the indelible image of Mina Harcourt, her eyes shining, her lips parted, rising up his body like a tide. Leafing through the notebook in which he had scrawled some impressions after the visitation that night, he found mention of banshees and phantoms and, most tellingly, succubi. Food for thought, or a story, there . . .

CHAPTER THIRTY-SEVEN

It was as if they had all been frozen in a tableau vivant—Mina with her hand pressed to her throat on the sofa, Thorne flushed but on his feet, and the intruder, nervously clasping the glistening scissors, before the open French doors.

"What are you doing here, Lucinda? You know I told you never to come here again."

"I needed to talk to you," she repeated, in a strangely vacant tone.

"You could certainly have waited until a more convenient time, and place."

"It couldn't wait."

"Then out with it, before I have you thrown out."

So this Lucinda, with the raw jawline, was someone he knew, someone who had been to the house before. Mina was torn between taking this opportunity, while Thorne was otherwise engaged, to flee from the room or remain right where she was to see what this was all about.

"I think maybe we ought to be alone," Lucinda said, with a tilt of her head toward Mina. "It's private."

"Yes, fine," Thorne barked. "My coach will take you home, Miss Harcourt, as soon as it returns. You can wait in the vestibule."

Rubbing her neck where he had nearly strangled her with the necklace chain, Mina said, "With the young lady's permission, I'll stay." For one thing, the effect of the port, or whatever he might have added to it, was still exerting its influence; she wasn't sure if she could even make a quick escape. But for another, having just undergone an attack of her own, she was not about to leave this waif alone, exposed to the same risk or worse.

Thorne looked thunderstruck, but Lucinda shrugged. "Have it your way," she said, before addressing Thorne again, unfazed. "It's about your sister."

"You just missed her. She's gone."

"I know. I waited till I saw her leave, then came around the old way—the way you showed me."

"I'll take measures to have it secured in future," he said, stuffing his shirttails back into the top of his trousers. "But if you expect to be let back into the mission house yet again, you are sorely mistaken. Any privileges you've had there have been revoked. For good."

One of the Thorne match girls, Mina surmised. And, given that she had been to the mansion before, something more than that. It wasn't hard to guess what.

"My Davey—our Davey—told me she didn't treat him right."

Our Davey? Did they have someone—a child?—in common?

"Davey told you this?" he said, scornfully. "Really? When, pray tell, did he manage that?"

"Tonight."

"He told you this tonight?"

She nodded, absentmindedly batting the scissors against her leg.

"Dead and in his grave, and he's still talking to you, is he?"

"I made him a coat."

Thorne actually threw a complicit smile at Mina, as if to say, *You see what a lunatic we have on our hands here?* But she gave him nothing but a hard stare in return.

"And next time I'll bring him a warm bun," Lucinda added. "He asked for that."

"If you've come for a warm bun, I'll be sure you get a dozen on your way out the door," he said, casually moving toward the fireplace.

"Thank you, but that's all right. I've got a job now. At a theater." She glanced down at the scissors. "Sewin' costumes and such."

Before she went on, Mina guessed where.

"The Lyceum," the girl said, with a hint of pride.

"Ah, Stoker's place," Thorne said, as if it were all beginning to fall into place. "Interesting. What are you now, his ward?" He sneered, casually taking up a poker to poke at the dying embers in the hearth.

"Nothin' like what you're suggesting." She swung the scissors again. "He's not like that. He's not like you."

Mina, too, could attest to that. With every word that this woman spoke, she felt as if some greater bond were being formed between Lucinda and herself.

"Men are more alike than you know," Thorne scoffed. "You should have figured that much out by now."

"I haven't come here to quarrel with you. I've come here to ask for your help."

"Then ask and be done with it."

"Davey tells me your sister took something from him."

"What could Winifred possibly have taken from him? He had nothing."

"He had a soul."

Thorne paused, but not as if he were puzzled. To Mina, he looked like a child who had just been charged with an infraction he had plainly committed, but did not know how to refute it. He kept his head down and stirred the fire logs.

"A neat trick that would be," he said, but even Mina knew that that was an evasion.

"I know if I go to her," Lucinda said, "she'll lie to my face and say it never happened."

"Because she'll think you've gone mad."

"But you know better. If I'm to have any chance of getting it back—and Davey, he needs and wants it so—I'll need you to get it from her. You, she won't deny. No one ever does."

"All right then," he said, straightening and turning from the fire, "I think I've heard quite enough of this nonsense. It's time for you to go out the same way you came in. Otherwise, I shall have to call a constable, and you'll wind up in jail or the madhouse."

"I don't think so," Mina said, her mounting anger aiding in her recovery.

"You'd do best to stay out of it," Thorne said.

Which was precisely the wrong thing to say to her; her father had raised her to stay *in* it, whether the situation presented an intellectual challenge, or a physical one.

"Not until you give her a proper answer," Mina insisted.

"To a question so absurd?"

"To a question that has clearly cut you to the quick."

Lucinda, who had been following the exchange with widened eyes, appeared to be growing more agitated. The scissors were rhythmically banging against her thigh, the blades opening and closing. Having found an ally, she seemed to have gained strength.

"You can both get out," Thorne said. "Right now."

"Not till I have your promise," Lucinda said, actually advancing a step. "Not until you promise to get what I asked for from your sister."

"I'll do no such thing."

"Then I will go to her myself! And what's more, I'll go to the police and tell them all about your underground tunnel. I'll them what you do there, too. See if I don't!"

A flash of anger blazed in Thorne's eyes, and before Mina could stop him, he lashed out at Lucinda with the poker in his hand, knocking the scissors across the floor. Her bruised hand jerked up to her mouth, and a sob came from her lips as she staggered back toward the French doors.

The poker came up again, to deal another blow, and Mina instinctively leaped from the sofa and caught Thorne's arm as it was raised in the air. Off-balance now, he stumbled, and Mina took full advantage to push him hard. He wheeled backward, and with one more shove, she had toppled him all the way over. His bulky body crashed into the hearth, sparks and ashes flew, the fire screen collapsed, and the other pokers clattered down around him like iron bowling pins.

"Quick!" Mina said, snatching up her gold box and bag. "We have to go!" Grabbing Lucinda's hand, she dragged her out the doors and into the night air. Already, she could hear a footman rushing in and exclaiming, "Sir! What's happened here?"

Thorne was bellowing something incomprehensible, but Mina kept them moving, down the lamplit pathway, which had once been covered with a swarm of rats, and into the gloom of the glass hothouse.

But if she thought they had made their escape, she was wrong. Everywhere she looked, she was surrounded by towering ferns and flowering plants, a wall of greenery and waxy leaves. But where was the exit? There had to be another door at the far end.

"How dare you?" she heard Thorne shouting. "In my own house!"

Glancing back at the pathway, she could see him charging down the path with the poker still in hand, and a footman close behind. "I'll bash your bloody heads in!"

Ducking low, Mina led Lucinda down one row, and then another, deeper into the labyrinth. Thorne barged in, his black tie askew, his white shirtfront singed, swinging the poker at his precious plants willy-nilly, breaking branches, shredding leaves, bashing terra-cotta pots into a thousand pieces. In the moonlight filtering through the glass skylights, Mina could only dimly discern the passageways between the plants, but Lucinda seemed to know the way. Skulking along, it was she who now led Mina along a dark, circuitous trail.

"Both of you," Thorne shouted, "I'll grind you to mulch and feed you to the goddamned plants!"

"This way," Lucinda whispered, "it's how I came in." There was a wooden door, the latch hanging undone, at the farthest corner. A placard on it read, "Tradesmen Only. No Trespassing."

They scuttled through, and just beyond it, were confronted with yet another gate, this one fully locked—Mina yanked at it, but it didn't give an inch—set in a brick wall covered with ivy. "Like this," Lucinda exhorted her, gripping the ivy tendrils and hauling herself to the top of the wall. Mina would not have thought her strong enough. Tossing her purse up to her, Mina snatched a handful of the prickly vines and scaled the wall herself. As she hitched up her long skirt and threw one leg over the other side—Lucinda in the alleyway, urging her to "Jump! Jump!"—Thorne stormed out of the greenhouse, shouting, "Stop right there!"

Mina hopped down, just as the poker, flung in impotent fury, clanged against the brick. Landing on wobbly legs, she felt Lucinda slipping an arm around her waist and helping her hobble down the alley. A cat yowled, but by the time they had emerged again into a gaslit thoroughfare, Mina was walking much better, and in the shelter of a closed tobacconist's shop, they stopped to catch their breath and marvel that they had indeed made their escape.

"Mina Harcourt," she huffed, extending a hand coated with dirt and grit.

"Lucinda Watts."

"Pleased to meet you."

After several more seconds doubled over, hands on knees to gather themselves, Mina looked up into Lucinda's eyes, which had lost their earlier vacancy and now looked positively alive, and smiled.

"Your handbag," Lucinda said, giving it back.

"Thank you."

"I had to drop it down the wall. I hope no harm came to that pretty little box."

Glancing inside, Mina assured her no damage had been done. The gold box had come to seem impervious to her.

And then, pressing one palm against her ruined jaw, Lucinda managed to laugh, in relief and exultation.

Mina laughed, too—no laugh had ever felt so well-earned or so urgently needed—and soon they were both gasping for breath again, their foreheads bent to touch each other, their hands resting on the other's shoulders, with the Carpathian relic, unblemished, in the bag dangling from Mina's arm.

CHAPTER THIRTY-EIGHT

"You landed like a mackerel, you did," the shoeblack said, chuckling. "Never saw a man get throwed like that."

"You should not have seen it at all," Ludvig growled, wrapping the bandage once more around his sprained wrist. "What were you even doing there?"

"You pays me to follow people. It's what I do."

"Not me, you fool."

Owen scratched his head.

Perhaps, Ludvig thought, the job was becoming too complex for the boy. "Tell me more about the lady."

"No more I can tell you. She went to a fancy house in Belgravia last night, like I said, but I never seen her leave."

"But, plainly, you weren't there the whole time."

"Can't be in two places at once, can I?"

Maybe Stoker hadn't been entirely lying. Maybe this Mina Harcourt belonged to someone else, too, some other, and much richer, man. Pretty women, Ludvig thought, were a commodity like any other. They went to the highest bidder.

Having failed to persuade Stoker to pay up, Ludvig had one more angle to play. Stoker was a mere theater manager, after all, but his employer was Henry Irving, owner of the theater and as such, vitally concerned with the reputation of the Lyceum, not to mention his new status as a knight of the realm. He might not want some love scandal embroiling his right-hand man, especially if Ludvig was simultaneously dangling before him the prospect of a command performance for Kaiser Wilhelm himself. It was a long shot, but sometimes those were the ones most worth taking. It was that, or finding another dowager to cheat at cards that night. And so he hatched an alternative plan.

He knew he couldn't wear the suit he'd been thrown in—the knee had been torn and even with a patch would be unpresentable—so his next best resort was his evening wear. Upon consideration, he had decided that formal attire was a better idea, anyway; having determined to pass himself off as an emissary of the German theater, it would be wise to look as if he had just come from some gala entertainment. That afternoon, he had even gone to the trouble and expense of having a printshop on the next street make up a dozen calling cards with his name on them, along with a fashionable business address in Berlin, and designating him as a producer for a mythical theatrical enterprise. He would wait until the evening's performance was over, and then present himself at the stage door. The only danger? Stumbling into Stoker first. He would have to make it clear that he required a *private* audience with Mr. Irving.

In that respect, all went well. A short while after the curtain had fallen on that night's presentation of *Faust*—always a sold-out event— Ludvig went around to the stage door, explained to the ancient guardian who he was, and that he needed a word with Sir Henry, "If he is not too exhausted from his brilliant performance tonight." Cowed by Ludvig's attire and accent and commanding demeanor, the man said, "P'raps you should just go straight in then. He's at the Beefsteak."

"The Beefsteak?"

"The dinner, inside. He and the gents."

"Oh, well, I would be loath to intrude upon such a gathering unin-vited. Mr. Bram Stoker, I assume, is in attendance?"

"Not tonight. Left early, as his son's in town on holiday."

"Oh, what a pity." It was just as he had hoped.

"You know our Mr. Stoker?"

"Only in passing."

"Capital chap. But then you know that."

Much as he might have liked to take exception, Ludwig simply nodded and followed the stagehand's mumbled directions. But whether by accident, or simple good fortune, he quickly found himself at the dead end of a hallway, and when he turned back came upon the same rickety staircase he had already passed. The whole area reeked of greasepaint and sweat, musty costumes and dusty props. But at the bottom of the stairs, he saw light and heard the sound of voices. Women's voices. One of which was oddly familiar.

Descending, he found himself in a corridor lined with racks of old clothing, everything from ball gowns to bejeweled crowns, and at the end a room where he could hear two women in earnest conversation. He slowed his step and, when he got close, stopped just short of the door, which was ajar.

"But I must get it back," an unknown, and forlorn, voice said.

"Lucinda, listen to me," the familiar one replied. "Your dear, sweet boy is gone, and he is in heaven now. You can put your mind at ease."

Damned if he hadn't been right—it *was* Mina Harcourt who was offering the reassurance. This little detour had certainly been worth it.

"I'd thought Mr. Thorne would help me."

"He is no friend, to you or anyone."

"Then I must go straight to the Matron herself."

"That would not do any good either. Bram has found you a safe haven here, and I do believe that the management has taken notice of your hard work. It will be rewarded."

Safe haven? Good God, had he been wrong about Mina, but right about this Lucinda person? Or was Stoker keeping *two* mistresses—who knew about each other? He rubbed his sprained wrist and waited for more.

"Have you eaten tonight?"

"Yes," Lucinda replied. "Sam brought me a plate from the Beefsteak Club."

"That was good of him."

"And Mr. Stoker, he always looks in. Didn't see him tonight, though."

"He's not here."

"Then why are you?"

"To see you, silly."

"Me?"

"Yes, you. We've been through the fire together. Now we're stuck with each other." Mina's voice was as tender as Lucinda's was incredulous.

"Is your hand all right?"

"The poker broke the scissors, but not my hand. Glad your little golden box didn't get hit, too."

Golden box?

"Don't worry about that," Mina said. "It's as durable as it is ancient."

"What's it for? It's too small to be a sewing kit. Is it for coins?"

"No, just a keepsake," Mina said.

What was all this talk of a golden box? And how had he, and that idiot Owen, missed it when they'd rifled her bag and searched her room?

"Still, I think you should give your hand a rest," Mina said. "Enough sewing for one night."

Lest he be discovered lurking in the hall, Ludvig pressed his fingertips to the door to open it more widely, then stepped forward, and said to a stunned Mina, "Fancy meeting you here."

"How on earth . . ."

The other woman, perhaps taking her cue from Mina's reaction, drew a long knitting needle into her hand. A costume lay across her lap.

"No need to arm yourself," he said. "Miss Harcourt and I are well acquainted."

"What are you doing here?" Mina said from her seat on the sagging divan.

"I came to congratulate Sir Henry on his knighthood."

"*You* know Henry Irving?"

"I know everyone. It's time you understood that."

Lucinda was looking from one to the other, puzzled. Mina remained on her guard.

Even Ludvig was momentarily at a loss as to how best to proceed or, more to the point, profit from this fortuitous turn of events. Stoker had claimed no impropriety, and yet, here she was, the very woman, lodged, and dispensing advice, in the bowels of his theater.

"And are you the seamstress?" Ludvig asked Lucinda, still trying to get the lay of the land.

"I do some of it."

"And how did you and Miss Harcourt become acquainted?"

"That's none of your business," Mina broke in, rising and smoothing out her skirts. "You're not welcome here."

"And I thought the English were so well known for their manners."

"Gypsies are not."

"Your words," he said, with a sly smile, "not mine." Taking a step toward Lucinda, he said, "What's that you're making?"

She started to lift an edge of the costume to show him—women of her class instinctively acceded to a gentleman's request—but Mina interposed herself between them.

"I still don't know how you got here," she said, "but I do know that it's time you left."

"Or what? We're not in a boiler room here—there's no furnace to push me into." There was such a glint of fire in her eyes, he did not doubt that she'd have done so if she could.

"Cake?" came a voice from down the hall. "Would anyone care for a bit o' cake?"

There was the sound of shuffling feet, and the old man from the stage door appeared, holding a plate of cake in a trembling hand.

"Did you get lost?" he asked, confused at encountering Ludvig. "What are you doin' down here?"

"He was making a nuisance of himself, Sam. See that he leaves."

Handing the plate off to Lucinda, the old man reached to take Ludvig by the elbow, but he brushed him off.

"Don't you dare to touch me." It was astonishing, the indignities he'd had to suffer of late. He threaded his way past the wardrobe racks, the old man wheezing right behind, then back up the creaking stairs. At the top, he took another wrong turn, and the old man had the gall to touch him again—"This way!"—and a moment later he found himself engulfed among several of the Beefsteak gentlemen adjourning for the night. Irving himself, his hands on two of their shoulders, still sharing a joke, looked taken aback.

"And who is this, pray tell?"

"Just some kind of stage-door Johnny," Sam said. "He was down below, botherin' the ladies."

"Was he now?"

"Sir Henry," Ludvig interjected, "allow me to introduce myself. I represent the German theater and carry a special request from Kaiser Wilhelm himself."

"Oh you do, do you?" he said, taking the calling card Ludvig had proffered.

"If I could just have a private conference with you, I could lay out a quite lucrative business arrangement."

Rubbing the card and then examining his fingers, Irving said, "The ink's so fresh, it's smudged." Then he tore it in two, letting the pieces flutter to the floor. Snapping his fingers, he called out, "Charles!" and two of the waiters instantly came running.

"Do me the honor," he said, "of showing this great impresario to the exit."

Without a word, they grabbed Ludvig by the arms and hustled him toward the stage door. Sam was already holding it open.

This could not be happening, Ludvig thought. It simply could not be happening! Not again. Not to him.

But then there he was, getting one final shove down the wooden stairs and tumbling head over heels into the alleyway. The Beefsteakers were laughing—he must have provided them with quite a show—as he gathered himself up, dusted off his trousers (now these were torn, too) and without so much as turning around, marched away.

Go ahead and laugh, he thought, dodging between carriages as he crossed the street. *I'll be coming back for you—and Mina Harcourt—*and, while he was at it, that little golden box of which he'd just heard tell.

CHAPTER THIRTY-NINE

"But that is an outrage," Stoker said, feeling the blood quickening again in his veins, "an outrage."

Mina raised a hand to lower his voice, but he could not contain himself.

"He came to the theater, and accosted you and Lucinda?"

"As I said," she replied, getting up to close the door to the museum corridor, "no harm was done. Sam showed up in the nick of time, and Sir Henry had him summarily tossed into the street."

"Just as I did when he showed up at my house." The idea of Gerhard being ejected again, and in that same manner—something that he had told Mina about only minutes before—did give him satisfaction. Confidence men were only as good as their confidence, and this one's must have been shaken to the core.

"What troubles me more is Lucinda's fixation," Mina said, taking her seat again behind a desk covered with Cruikshank's excess correspondence. "She cannot let go of the notion that her son is still alive in some fashion, and that Winifred Thorne holds the key to his salvation."

It was, Stoker realized, a lunatic idea on the surface of it, but he had seen enough to know that there also might be some terrible truth to it. The papyrus he had prized from Davey's hands lay on the table before them, and Mina had been as puzzled by it as Vambéry had been. She agreed it appeared to be a modern document, a forgery of an ancient scroll.

"But by whose hand?" he asked, seeking confirmation of his suspicion.

"Thorne's, most likely."

"Which he'll never admit to."

"Of course not. What's important, though, are its directions."

"Or *mis*directions," he amended.

"Exactly. Telling the *ka* not to return to its rightful home, but to this illicit owner, as it were."

"Thorne, I presume?"

"Or, if Davey is to be believed, his sister, Winifred."

Now Mina, too, was talking as if the testimony of a child's ghost could be given credence—and from her new post at the British Museum yet. Stoker had been surprised at the appointment—young women were not normally accorded such honors—but knew that Cruikshank had chosen wisely. There could be no one, of either sex, better suited to the job.

"It sounds to me," Stoker said, "as if I have no recourse but to pay a visit to the Matron herself."

"*We* have no recourse but to pay a visit."

"I'm not sure that's a good idea. You've just secured this post; it wouldn't do to have you crossing swords, yet again, with museum benefactors like the Thornes."

"I think we're already well past that point. If Bartholomew Thorne wants my head, he'll have it. But what about Lucinda? Shouldn't she be brought along, too?"

Of that, Stoker was unsure. "As the aggrieved party, by all means. But would she be able to withstand the strain? Wouldn't we be doing her a disservice by bringing her into such a confrontation?" He didn't know which he feared most—Lucinda losing her mind altogether, or losing control of herself and physically assaulting the Matron.

"You may be right. If we learn anything of value, we can share it with her later."

Leaving a note for Mr. Cruikshank, who was off inspecting the new gallery, Mina took her coat from the hook on the wall and joined Stoker in the hallway. It was less an office than an alcove, but already it had her name on the door, and he was pleased beyond measure to think that she had secured a place for herself in the often-inhospitable environs of the city.

On the way to the mission house, he took the opportunity to inquire into the role of Professor Vambéry in all this. "You say he was in the library with you while Thorne was inspecting the gold box?"

"He was, though he was virtually carried out after his second glass of port."

"Doctored, as you believe yours was?"

"Possibly. I suspect Thorne had his grand seduction planned well in advance, and needed to be sure Vambéry was safely out of the way."

Stoker looked out the window of the cab. That such a man as Thorne could occupy a place of prominence, that he should stand tall in public opinion as a philanthropist and archaeological explorer, was criminal. But Vambéry was almost as puzzling.

"Whose side do you think he is on?" Stoker asked.

"There are sides?"

"Of course—good and evil. Light and dark. Thorne and common decency."

"I believe he is a diplomat. He lives under Thorne's roof at present, eats at his table, does the work Thorne asks him to do, but as for his scruples, I'm not so sure. Why do you ask?"

"Because if it ever comes down to it, I need to know who our allies are."

Mina was silent. The coach took a sharp turn, and they were jostled against each other before resuming their former positions. Stoker's arm felt surprisingly warm where it had brushed the sleeve of her coat.

"Speaking of allies," Mina said, "how are things at home?"

"Noel goes back to school tomorrow."

"I meant with your wife."

"I know you did."

"Have her suspicions been allayed? Does she know that there was nothing whatsoever to what Gerhard was saying?"

It was the "whatsoever" that smarted. "I think she does."

"That's a relief."

"But I also think that she doesn't much care either way."

"That can't be right."

"She cares only insofar as appearances are concerned. She would not want anything to interfere with the perfectly proper figure she cuts in what passes for society."

"Are you sure you're not doing her an injustice? She's your wife, the mother of your son, and she loves you."

He felt a wave of shame. Mina was right; he should not have spoken so bluntly about Florence. It wasn't a gentlemanly thing to do. "I apologize."

"No need," she said, reaching over to squeeze his hand.

His eyes lingered on the sight.

"I think we are there," she said, shifting away as the hansom pulled up to the porter's lodge of the mission house.

The gatekeeper opened the cab door, and Mina stepped down. Although he was an old man, he did not fail to give her an appraising look. When Stoker followed, he touched the brim of his cap and said, "And how may I help you, sir?"

"We're here to see Miss Thorne."

"Oh, then you'll want to cross the courtyard and go up them main stairs. She lives all the way up top."

But as they moved on, he called out, "But you won't find her there. Not this time o' the day."

"Oh, then where will we find her?"

"Makin' her rounds of the wards. You might try the infirmary right about now. She runs like clockwork."

"Thank you," Mina said, "I'm sure we'll find it."

There were a couple of forlorn women sweeping the bricks of the court, and off at one end some very young children, squatting around a mewling kitten, but rather than inquire of them, Stoker guided Mina into the gray fortress of the mission house. His first impression was of a vast mausoleum—echoing, dreary, and inescapable.

A woman on her knees, scrubbing the stairs with a bucket of dirty water, pointed them up a flight of stairs and to the left. Under a sign that said "*Mens Sana In Corpore Sano*," they found a low-ceiling corridor lined with straw-covered pallets, on which the mission house residents who'd fallen too desperately ill to be put to work were laid like fish on ice. Grim as the madhouse ward at St. Thomas's Hospital had been, this was ten times worse, with little light and no nurse, and barely any semblance of a therapeutic environment. It was a holding pen, no more.

There was no sign of Winifred Thorne.

As Stoker and Mina passed the patients, several looked up hopefully at them, and more than one stretched out a hand and asked for anything from water to another blanket—the ones that covered them were threadbare—or something to ease their pain. Stoker was aggrieved at his inability to help, but he could see that Mina was even more affected by such unrelieved misery. They found a woman kneeling by one of the pallets, a kerchief tied around her hair, tending to a feverish boy, and it was only when she turned her face to look at them that Stoker recognized Maude and her son Timmy, from Davey's graveside service.

"Oh, sir, you're the last person I 'spected to see in here."

"And I am sorry to see you here." He hastily introduced Mina—the woman bobbed her head in respect—then said, "What's wrong with Timmy?"

"No one rightly knows. He's been sickly, and always feelin' oh so cold, ever since that day we saw you at the cemetery." Lowering her voice so the boy wouldn't hear, she said, "I'm worried it's what laid poor little Davey low."

The boy did indeed look like he was at death's door. His eyes were open but unfocused, his brown hair was matted to his forehead, there was a hectic flush to his cheeks.

"What has he been doing?" Mina asked, bending down to tuck the worn blanket more tightly under his chin. "Was he caught out in the rain? Did he catch a chill?"

"No more than usual. He's been workin' close to me, in the match factory."

"Doing what?"

"I make the boxes. The little ones stir the phossy pot."

Stoker knew what those fumes could do. Lucinda's jaw showed the damage. But for children, with frail constitutions, hovering over the hot cauldron for hours on end could wreak all kinds of havoc.

"But what're you two doing here?" Maude asked. "The Matron, she'll be by any minute, and she won't like my bein' here, and you even worse."

"We have something we need to discuss with her," Stoker said.

"Better you than me," Maude said. "There's somethin' not right about that one."

"We need to take Timmy out of here," Mina said. "He needs proper nursing."

"Pardon miss, and I know your heart's in the right place, but the only thing keepin' him alive right now is his mother."

"Then you will have to come, too."

"What? And lose our place here? Matron'll never let us back in."

"Lucinda Watts managed it," Stoker said.

"Aye," she said, giving him a sidelong glance, "but that there was what you might call a special case."

"How so?" Mina asked.

Stoker was sorry he had brought it up.

"On account o' her and Mr. Thorne . . ." Maude said, trailing off.

"What's all this?" Stoker heard from the other end of the infirmary, at the same moment as the squeaking of the wheelchair. "What's going on in here?"

Winifred Thorne's hair, piled in a blonde funnel atop her head, swayed as she wheeled furiously toward them, narrowly missing the feet of the patients lying among the straw. "Who let you in here? What do you think you're doing?" A burly attendant trotted along behind her.

When she got close enough to confirm exactly who it was, she gasped in astonishment. "You!" she said to Mina. "As if you hadn't given enough offense at dinner." Then, taking in Stoker, "And you I recognize from the unraveling party."

"At your service," he said, dryly.

"Maude, you know the visiting hour—you've already been warned—and this isn't it. If you're not back at the factory in five minutes, you'll find yourself out on the street instead."

"Yes, ma'am, I'm leaving now," Maude said, scrambling up from her knees. "I'm on my way." Throwing a cautionary glance back at Mina and Stoker, she hurried around the attendant and disappeared down the corridor.

Timmy, somehow registering her departure, let out a low moan.

"This boy needs a doctor," Mina said.

"And so he shall have. But you didn't break in here to tell me that. Before I have Alfred escort you out, tell me what possible business you could have here."

"This," Stoker said, taking the papyrus scroll from the inside pocket of his coat and unfurling it.

Though she feigned ignorance, her eyes grew large at the sight of it.

"Did you write this, or did your brother?" Stoker said.

"So it was you then . . . in the tunnel that night."

"You took something from Davey Watts," Mina said, "and now you have to give it back."

"Pshaw," she said, "what could I have taken? I gave him the best of care, in my own chambers—just as I am going to do for this lad—and when he passed on, he did so in perfect peace."

"Without his soul," Mina said.

If she had shot an arrow, Stoker thought, it could not have more squarely hit its mark. Winifred's eyes went black with rage, and her lips pressed into a tight slit.

"How did you do it?" Stoker asked.

Tilting her head in Alfred's direction, she hissed, "Get them out of here."

"How?" Stoker repeated.

"You heard the lady," Alfred said, stepping forward, chin up. "Out you go!"

"Was it an ancient Egyptian incantation?"

Alfred rolled up a sleeve, and said, "You been asked nice. Now you're gonna be asked not so nice." He clenched his fist, but before he could throw the punch, Stoker put his head down, as if in a rugby scrimmage at Trinity, and butted him so hard with his shoulder that the man went reeling backward. There was a sudden screeching sound— Winifred was blowing on a tin whistle—and by the time Alfred had regained his breath and balance, Stoker could hear footsteps racing up the stairs.

Winifred blew the whistle again and again, the patients clamping their hands over their ears, and two more men, one armed with a mallet, the other holding a saw that he must have been working with, charged into the room, looking a bit bewildered.

The Matron simply pointed a bony finger at her unwelcome guests, and they needed no more instruction than that. Fanning out behind Alfred, they closed in, but Mina stepped in front of Stoker, who was prepared to do battle with the whole lot of them, and raising a hand, said, "We were just leaving."

Stoker's heart was pumping like a piston—he could see red—but Mina firmly clamped her arm through his and drew him along. She didn't even look back, though Stoker felt compelled to, after they had threaded their way through their opponents. Winifred had swiveled her chair around to watch them go, and the three men stood about, legs spread, arms flexed, waiting for further instruction. He found that the papyrus was still clutched, though crumpled, in his hand.

At least now, he knew beyond a shadow of a doubt that the little ghost in Tower Hamlets Cemetery had spoken true. The Thornes had mastered some arcane secret entombed since the time of pharaohs, and they were stealing the souls of the dead . . . but to what end he could not yet fathom.

CHAPTER FORTY

It was late afternoon, and Ludvig must have been up and down Raven Row a half dozen times already, waiting to see some sign of the activity slowing down in the furniture assembly store on the first floor of Mina's building. He did not want to bump into that fellow again—the landlord, he presumed—who had given him such a suspicious once-over before. But the place was a veritable hive, with laborers carting lumber in, or chairs and tables out, all day. What possessed people, he wondered, to work so hard for their daily bread? He had always looked for, and generally found, less taxing ways to keep the wolf from his door.

It wasn't until nearly dusk that most of the workers, probably for want of proper light, rolled down their shirtsleeves and trudged off toward their own bleak homes. The landlord took down a tattered poster for some union rally, and after tossing it in a trash bin, marched off toward the corner market.

Ludvig wasted no time slipping into the foyer—there was no telling when Mina Harcourt might return from the British Museum—and then, with a glance upward to make sure no one was on the stairs, bolted up them, skeleton key already in hand. Even on the dim landing, it was the work of no more than a minute to jimmy the lock. Inside, he went quickly to the window and surveyed the street. Directly below was the awning advertising the shop, and a broken-down delivery cart that some stray dog had made its bed in. He pulled the thin muslin curtain closed, then turned to the task at hand.

What had he overlooked? He had thoroughly rifled her drawers and closet the first time he had broken into the room, but just to be on the safe side, he did so again, lingering, though he knew he shouldn't waste any time, on the scent of her that clung to her dresses and undergarments. Under normal circumstances, if he and Mina had not been cast as natural adversaries, he would have considered seducing her; the disrespectable Gypsy blood only made her that much more alluring. Stuffing a pair of her stockings into his pocket as a souvenir, he continued his search, but the room was small and her belongings fairly meager. If this gold box was here, she must have used some ingenuity to conceal it. He lifted the mattress, felt it for lumps, shook out the pillow, checked under the dresser and the bed, and then stood in the center of the room, casting his eye about. He had nearly given up—maybe she had taken the box with her?—when he noticed a bit of sawdust, splinters really, on the floor by the washstand. Kneeling, he saw that the board there was loose, and prying it away from the wall, he saw a velvet pouch tucked into the crevice, and his heart skipped a beat. Taking the pouch out, he quickly went to the window and drew the curtain aside enough to catch the last light of day. The top of the gold box glinted, as if it were winking at him, and the human figure, with its vaguely canine head, was of a distinctly Egyptian cast. Though it fit neatly into the palm of his hand, the weight of the gold gave the box surprising heft. There was a slim latch of some kind, which he found immovable, and a quick shake gave no indication of any contents. So what was it for? Could that seamstress at the theater know? Unlike Mina, she would be someone he could pry open as easily as an oyster.

Either way, it was definitely gold—some collector of Egyptian artifacts would pay him a fortune for it . . . someone like that fellow Bartholomew Thorne, whose name had just again appeared in the paper announcing a donation to the British Museum. The writer was that famous muckraker, William Stead, and he made it sound like this Thorne was as rich as Croesus.

He was just about to drop the box into the pocket of his overcoat when he heard voices below. Someone said, "That lamp's been faulty." The gas lighter replied, "I've got it fixed. Right as rain now."

Ludvig peeked out the curtain, and saw that the sun had just disappeared below the rooftops across the street and night had descended on the East End. At precisely the same moment, he felt a twitch in his palm, and the latch moved, revealing a black slot. What in the world? He tried to peer inside, but the slot was so slim and tiny there was nothing to see. And yet, he had the distinct impression, growing every second, that something had just escaped. He felt the hair on the back of his neck prickle, and he looked hastily around the cramped quarters.

All was still, and he was as alone as ever . . . or was he? He'd be damned if he hadn't seen something move out of the corner of his eye, but every time he shifted his gaze, the movement seemed to come from a different corner. Shadows flitted on the walls, but their motions seemed somehow intentional. They moved with the ripple of black silk, unfurling, creeping, changing direction. It seemed to him that they were rapidly gaining momentum, and then it occurred to him that they were moving like a trapped animal, running from pillar to post in a frenzy to find some way out. In terror now, he stood with his back pressed against the wall, the glow from the gas lamp outside penetrating the worn muslin drape. The shadows appeared to coalesce above the iron bedstead, like a cobra rising to strike, and then with a sudden dash they shot in his direction, ripping through the curtain and smashing the window into a thousand pieces. Slivers of glass flew past his nose, and one embedded itself in his cheek. The cold night air flooded into the room as the shards of glass tinkled onto the floorboards or tumbled down onto the awning below.

Ludvig could finally take a breath, and when he glanced outside, he saw the landlord of the building standing, mouth agape, with a loaf of bread under one arm and a clump of carrots in the other.

There was no time to lose. He made for the door, but by the time he threw the bolt open, he could hear the vestibule door downstairs slamming closed and footsteps racing up the stairs. Throwing the bolt back into place, he ran to the window, and looked down. The awning was at least twenty feet below, but there was a drainpipe he could hang onto for part of the way down, then jump to the awning, and hope it could hold his weight enough to break the fall.

A hammering came at the door, and he could see the knob twisting. "Who's in there? Come out now!"

With a last backward glance, he climbed out the window, shimmied down the pipe, and plunged onto the awning—which gave way, tumbling him into the broken-down delivery cart and startling the mangy dog sleeping on the straw. Instead of running for cover, the mongrel bared its teeth, prepared to fight for its bed. "It is all yours," Ludvig said, holding up his hand as he rolled off the wagon, scrambled to his feet, and lurched down the street. From Mina's window, he could hear the landlord shouting, "I see you, you thieving bastard!"

Hansom cabs being scarce in this part of town, Ludvig made for the first entry to the Underground and stumbled down the steps. Passengers coming up registered surprise at the straw clinging to his clothes and the blood trickling from the splinter of glass stuck to his cheek. But what did he care? Once he slumped into a seat on the noisy, crowded train, he slipped a hand into the pocket of his coat and made sure the gold box hadn't been lost while he was making his escape. But it was there, as powerful as it was mysterious. The one question that remained was—would whatever had escaped from it attempt to return?

CHAPTER FORTY-ONE

"I know who stole it," Mina said, leaning forward at her cluttered desk. "Strauss even saw him running away from the building."

"Did you notify the police?" Stoker asked, moving his chair slightly so that the afternoon sun was not hitting him directly in the eyes.

"Yes, and they went to his hotel already."

"Was he put under arrest?"

"He was already gone."

"Checked out?"

"Hardly. He had run up a huge bill, and absconded without paying."

Stoker certainly could not say he was surprised by any of this, but Mina looked positively stricken. For her, the theft of the gold box was more than a material loss. The box had cost her dearly in other terms— she had sacrificed so much, and undergone so many trials, in procuring it and then transporting it all the way from the mountains of Carpathia to the drawing rooms of London. Worst of all, she had lost it without fully fathoming whatever secrets it might have contained.

"They have put out an alert," Mina said, "but something tells me that a man like Ludvig Gerhard is adept at evading the authorities."

"The only way to catch him," Stoker said, "is to try to think like him."

"Like a thief and a scoundrel, in other words."

"Like a man who tries to turn anything, from information to stolen goods, to his immediate profit. He's tried blackmail with me, and failed. He's tried imposture with Irving, and failed. But now he has an actual artifact in hand. If you were Gerhard, where would you go with it?"

"I'd leave England and take it to the Continent, and try to sell it there."

"But what if you were short on funds for first-class passage, and didn't want to hang on to incriminating items any longer than you needed to?"

"I'd look for a fence, someone to pawn it off on."

Stoker frowned. "No, not an object as rare as this. A fence would give him only a fraction of its true value."

"So who would?"

"A collector."

Mina looked deep in thought. "Are you talking about Thorne?"

"He has been in the papers lately, all about his donations to the Egyptian galleries here. His name is all over the city, not only on the mission house but on the matchbooks in every pub."

"But Thorne has already seen the box—he knows who it rightfully belongs to."

"I doubt that Gerhard knows that."

"Nor, come to think of it, would he care," she admitted. "In fact, I think he would relish the opportunity to wrest it from me in this way. But does this mean that I have no choice but to reenter the lion's den?"

"If you mean his mansion, no. I would never let you go in there again, and certainly not alone."

"But where else?"

"The mission house itself."

"Why would Gerhard have taken the box there?"

"It's always possible that he knows where Bartholomew lives—he's clever enough that way—but he's in a hurry right now, and one thing he would undoubtedly know is the location of the mission. It's where he might start."

"You're starting to sound like your friend Conan Doyle."

"I'll take that as a compliment."

"But we'd never get past the porter's lodge."

"As it happens, I know another way in, and I was planning to take it tonight, anyway."

"Ah," Mina said, "but it was not to retrieve the box."

"No, though that only makes the expedition more critical."

In a subdued voice, she said, "So you've been haunted by him, too."

"Yes. I can't let that boy die in the Matron's embrace. Whatever she did to Davey, she is about to do to Timmy. If I can rescue him, and then make the story public—with this young victim to prove it—I can bring the whole damn temple tumbling down around their ears. And I have just the man to make the scandal a cause célèbre."

"Who?"

"William Stead, the editor and writer and muckraker. He's a member of the Beefsteak Club, and this would be like serving him the reddest, rawest slab of meat that he has ever seen."

Mina, Stoker could see, was warming to the idea. "When do we go in?"

"*I*," he said pointedly, "plan to go in tonight. You will be waiting in a coach for me to emerge with the boy."

"Waiting? On the sidelines?"

"We will need to get him straight to hospital."

"Bram, do we really need to have this debate yet again?"

"What debate?"

"I am coming with you. All the way."

"It will be very dangerous," he said, remembering the hideous attack in the tunnel. "I can't allow it."

"Fine. Then I shall drop by your house, introduce myself to Florence, and alert her to the danger her husband is in."

"You wouldn't."

"Try me."

Their eyes met; each one waiting for the other to avert their gaze. He knew, in his heart, that she would never do such a thing to compromise his home life; she was bluffing. At the same time he had to acknowledge that it might indeed be useful, even necessary, to have someone along to watch his flank. He would be carrying the boy in his arms, after all, making it harder to fend off any attack that might come.

Nor was there a soul on earth whose bravery and resourcefulness he trusted more.

He realized that they could remain there at loggerheads indefinitely, or he could yield, accept her offer, and they could go about saving not just one life, but possibly countless others. How long, he had to wonder, had the Thornes been preying upon the unlucky inhabitants of the mission house? Men and women, young and old. How many victims had they quietly dispatched for their nefarious purposes, which even now remained unclear? The residents of the mission were the outcasts and castoffs of society, the lost souls and worn-out laborers who would never be missed, a grim fact that the Thornes had apparently been capitalizing upon for years. Saving Timmy was the immediate goal, but once he was safe, and he could speak out, along with his mother, Maude, perhaps Stoker could unmask the perpetrators and bring the whole murderous enterprise to a crashing halt.

Without another word, Stoker rose from his chair, Mina from hers, and they shook hands. The pact was made. Glancing at the clock on the wall, Stoker said, "I'll be at the museum gates in precisely eight hours."

Mina merely nodded, perhaps afraid that by uttering another syllable she might reignite the debate.

Stoker, feeling the same, turned on his heel and left. Crossing the forecourt of the museum, he stopped to have his boots blacked by a forlorn-looking redheaded boy stationed in his path. The sooner the scratches on his boot were erased, the better. He couldn't help but wonder, however, if new ones might not be added that very night.

CHAPTER FORTY-TWO

Ludvig had no sooner located the right house—it had to be the one with the gatepost lamps shaped like pyramids—than he saw a black coach, the monogram *T* etched in silver on its doors, exiting the premises.

There was no time to lose, not if he hoped to be rid of the damn box before another night had passed—another awful night of troubled sleep and disturbing dreams.

He ran to the side of the carriage and glanced inside, where he saw a burly man lighting a cigar, and jumped onto the running board. The coachman turned in his seat, whip at the ready, but Ludvig had already blurted out, "Mr. Thorne—I need only a minute of your time!"

"Bloody hell? Get off my carriage!"

"I have something you will want to see!"

"Who are you?"

The coach had slowed, and the driver shouted down eagerly, "Shall I whip him, sir?"

"It is a rare antique!"

"Bugger off, you," the coachman warned, brandishing the whip, "or you'll get a taste of this!"

But the gambit had paid off. Thorne hesitated, then unlatched the door handle, and Ludvig, much to the driver's disappointment, was able to scramble inside.

"Drive on!" Thorne called to the coachman, as Ludvig fell back, winded, against the seat opposite. The upholstery was a deep red leather, and the floor was warmed by a thick Persian rug. The rich aroma from the cigar—Jamaican, if Ludvig was not mistaken—permeated the close air.

Thorne inspected him as if he were some bug, and barely moved his outstretched legs to allow him any room. "So," he finally said, "this isn't a cab. Tell me what you really want and then you can get out."

"What I want," Ludvig said, trying to straighten himself up in the seat and regain some measure of respectability—not an easy thing to do after the indignity of his arrival—"is, as a fellow gentleman, to make your acquaintance." He extended a hand—which Thorne did not take—and introduced himself properly, adding a "von" before the Gerhard to make it seem a bit more illustrious.

Thorne grunted and blew a cloud of smoke out the half-open window.

"I have been a great admirer of your philanthropy," Ludvig went on, "especially to the British Museum. I look forward to the opening of the new galleries of Egyptian artifacts."

"Continue," Thorne said, though it wasn't clear if he was enjoying the praise, or just wanted to move things along.

"Something has come into my possession, which I felt might interest you."

"Go on."

"It is of great antiquity, and its composition alone makes it of enormous value."

Now he saw that he had piqued the man's interest. The cigar came down, and for the first time Thorne's dark eyes seemed to take him in with some seriousness.

"Show me."

Making as much of a presentation as he could, Ludvig drew the velvet pouch out of his pocket and removed the gold box. Beautiful as it was, Ludvig had developed a strong aversion to it. He had not seen the shadow again, but he had not been able to shake the feeling that he was forever being watched.

Thorne took the box from his hand, inspected it briefly, then cradled it in his lap. Proprietorially.

"So—how do you know Minerva Harcourt?"

Aha. So Owen had been right—it *had* been Thorne's house that Mina had gone to that night. But that she had already shown him the box *did* come as a surprise. An unwelcome one.

"We became friends on a crossing from Bremen." One thing Ludvig had learned about lying was to keep as much to the truth as possible; it made things so much easier to keep track of.

"For her to give you this," Thorne said, "you'd have had to be a good deal more than that."

"Professional colleagues, too, since that time."

Thorne looked highly skeptical. "And why would she have entrusted this box to you?"

It was getting harder to dissemble every second. "I would not claim that. Let us just say, it is presently mine to dispose of, as I see fit."

Skepticism plainly changed to outright disbelief, and for a moment Ludvig thought he might be chucked from the moving coach. Then, to his relief, he saw a look of pure cunning and greed come to Thorne's jowly face. "So any transaction between us . . ." he said.

"Would be kept in the strictest confidence," Ludvig said, completing his thought. "Of course."

The coach rattled along, past a row of fashionable shops. Ludvig spotted a handsome astrakhan coat in a window, and made a mental note of it. Appearances were important in his line of work.

"How much do you want for it?"

"You are the expert in these matters," Ludvig said, "and one who is widely known for his generosity." Whatever the offer was, Ludvig was determined to appear disappointed in it; first offers were only the starting point of any negotiation.

"A hundred pounds."

Ludvig's disappointment was genuine, and he let it show. "An *objet* as old as this, and made of gold yet, is worth considerably more than that."

"Then name your price."

"Five hundred pounds would be much closer to its true value."

"Wilson," Thorne shouted, thumping a fist on the roof of the carriage. "Bank of England."

The coach made a sharp turn at the next corner, nearly colliding with a crowded omnibus drawn by a team of sweating horses, and then navigated down a busy side street lined with pubs and costermongers. Ludvig kicked himself for not asking a thousand. When the coach emerged on Threadneedle Street, and the great looming bulk of the bank came into view, his heart lifted. Five hundred pounds was still a goodly sum for a day's work.

Making a wide turn, the coach stopped before the iron gates, and Thorne threw the door open before the driver could even think of coming down. "After you," he said, and Ludvig lowered his head and stepped down onto the pavement, straightening his coat. The one that would soon be replaced with astrakhan.

A second later, the door clapped shut again, and he heard Thorne shout, "The Athenaeum."

The coach was momentarily blocked by a constable directing traffic, and Ludvig, stunned, had time to shout, "Where is your honor, sir?"

"There is no honor," he heard from within the carriage as it jolted off under Wilson's cracking whip, "among thieves."

CHAPTER FORTY-THREE

Although the night sky was clear and the moon full, the wind was so strong it nearly knocked the hat off Stoker's head, and Mina's loose black skirt rippled around her legs. He waited until the hansom cab had moved off before he stepped into a doorway, removed the short-barreled shotgun from under his cloak—a mahogany-stocked Luigi Franchi, which he had used exactly twice in his life—and slung it across his back. Mina, holding the unlit, bull's-eye lantern—the same kind the constables carried—said, "Now where?"

"There," he said, pointing to a sidewalk grate that looked suspiciously askew. Had he left it that way on the night he had first ventured into the tunnel? He strongly doubted it. But the fireplace poker he had brought along to pry it up would still serve them well as a potential weapon.

Once a pair of drunken sailors had finished ambling past, raucously singing, and the street appeared deserted, he said, "Quickly now," and moving swiftly, he slid the grate to one side, and waited for Mina to descend the iron rungs into the underground. Lighting the lantern, he handed it down to her, along with the poker, then climbed only far enough down to slide the grate back into place, before joining her on the hard concrete floor. At his feet, he saw the crowbar and broken lantern he had dropped on his previous narrow escape from this netherworld.

She raised the lamp and swung it slowly from side to side, revealing the cavernous tunnel and rusted, unused tracks. Although he saw no sign of any shambling creatures best left to the hellish imagination of Hieronymus Bosch, Mina's face, in the amber glow, took on its own demonic cast. He wondered, yet again, if it was madness to be doing what he was doing, much less with a young woman in tow.

But a little boy's life hung in the balance, and that alone left little choice in the matter.

"It's this direction?" Mina said, taking a step toward the tracks, the lantern held in one hand, the poker in the other.

"Yes."

"Then lead on."

Stoker unslung the rifle and, keeping its barrel pointed down lest he trip and accidentally fire off one of the two rounds already chambered, led the way, stepping carefully between the rotted rail ties. Mina stuck close to his side, moving the lantern back and forth, back and forth, to guide them. Macabre shadows danced across the curved brick walls, and more than once Stoker was inclined to point the gun at one that suddenly looked more corporeal than not. The two of them were deep enough that almost no sounds could be heard, except when they passed one of the hooded vents, mounted in the wall, and the muffled clip-clop of a horse's hooves or the rattling wheels of a wagon on the street overhead penetrated the gloom. To Stoker, it felt as if he were moving in a dream—a bad one—but he had only to glance at Mina's determined features to remind himself that it was all too real.

They had gone several hundred yards before she gripped his arm and whispered, "I hear something." She pointed ahead and to their left, but outside the penumbra of light in which they traveled, it was impossible to see anything. They stopped, listening carefully, and this time he heard it, too. Was it just the scrambling of vermin? There was a slow bend in the tunnel, and from Stoker's recollection, the raised train platform, on which he had seen the mummies, was not far beyond.

He put out one hand to have Mina lower the lantern so as not to make their approach any more apparent, and as they rounded the curve, Mina silently touched his elbow and pointed to some broken-down wheelbarrows and machinery. He stopped, lifting the barrel of the gun slightly. She turned the lantern, so that its beam was concentrated on the detritus. The red eyes of several rats glittered in the light. But something larger loomed behind an abandoned barrow, something that hunched lower even as he watched it.

Stoker instinctively swept Mina behind him with one arm and raised the gun with the other. Before he could even think to get a bead on it, the creature bolted, out of the light and into the shadows.

"Stop!" he shouted, wondering if he was speaking to anything that might understand human speech, but he could hear its stumbling prog- ress. With Mina holding the lantern aloft, they gave pursuit, stumbling over the tracks and rubble. He heard an *oof*, and a fall, and when he got within a few yards, he could see that it was a woman, face down, her hands covering the back of her head. Only when she turned to meet her fate did he see who it was.

"Lucinda?"

"Mr. Stoker," she gasped, in evident relief. And then, "Mina?"

He dropped the barrel of the gun, and hunching down beside her, said, "What are you doing here?" Packets of Thorne matchsticks littered the ground where she'd fallen.

Looking from one of them to the other, she said, "I came to see the Matron."

Tucked into a belt beneath her open coat, Stoker could see a pair of glistening scissors, no doubt from the Lyceum's wardrobe closet, and he could easily surmise why she was carrying them.

"What are *you* doing here?" she asked.

Mina said, "We're here to rescue Timmy Conway," and Stoker added, "What happened to your Davey must not happen to him, too."

"What? He's in danger of that?"

"He's been sick," Mina said. "The Matron said she would look after him."

"We all know what that means," Lucinda said, her eyes narrowing and her inflamed jaw setting firm.

Although Stoker had known he might encounter all sorts of unexpected turns, this had not been one of them. Still, there was nothing he could do about it now but forge ahead. "Are you all right to walk on?"

She nodded vigorously and got to her feet. "Not much farther, as I remember it, to the platform and the stairway up."

Stoker thought so, too, but as for what would await them there, he had no clue. As he did when writing his stories, he hoped that as the obstacles presented themselves, the solutions would immediately follow. Even he knew that as strategies go, it was a weak one—which was why he had brought along the shotgun.

CHAPTER FORTY-FOUR

"Just pick him up, Alfred."

"He ain't got nothin' catching, does he?"

Winifred snorted in derision. "Would I have been his nurse if he had?"

"Pick him up already," Thorne said, glancing at the gold pocket watch in the pocket of his waistcoat. "We haven't got all night."

Wrapping the boy in his ragged sheet, Alfred hoisted him from the sofa and carried him toward the door of the Matron's rooms. She was happy to see him go—and would be even happier, and stronger, when she had taken from him the one thing he had left. It wouldn't be much—Davey hadn't offered much sustenance either—but still, any port in a storm. Whatever came to hand—a sickly child, a trusting young buck with a broken ankle, an old woman with a stubborn will to live—she would put to her own use. She allowed her brother to push her wheelchair all the way to the stairs, but then she said, "I can walk the rest."

"You're sure?"

"I wouldn't say it if I weren't," she said, rising unsteadily from the rattan seat and leaning on the cane she'd held in her lap.

"Have it your way."

"I always do."

They followed Alfred down the back staircase; this would be no time to bump into the boy's mother, or any of the other pathetic residents of her mission house. *Cattle* was how she thought of them. Dumb as beasts, and ready for the slaughter. In her view, she was doing them a favor. With her woeful, and deliberate, lack of care, she had brought this boy to the very brink of extinction, and now, tonight, was the time to reap the fruits of her labor. Ripeness was all, according, if she was not mistaken, to the Bard.

Once outside, she felt the wind cutting across the courtyard like a scythe, and she clutched the collar of her coat around her throat. Her brother, though he was wearing no overcoat, appeared not to feel it. He'd grown stout over the years, just as she had wasted away. Passing the match factory, she glimpsed through the one small window in the boxing room the faint sulfurous glow of the phossy pots, which were kept astir all night long to keep the chemicals from coagulating.

The boy, his head lolling over Alfred's thick shoulder, let out a soft moan, and she told Bartholomew to hurry. "I don't want it happening out here, for God's sake. Not after all the trouble I've taken."

There was a jangling as her brother unfastened the padlock on the entrance to the underground, flicked on the lights, and stepped to one side to allow Alfred down the stairs first. She'd forgotten just how vertiginous the flight of steps was, and she clung to the railing on one side and her brother on the other as she made her slow and careful descent. At each landing, she took a brief breather. She'd feel better, she knew, on the way back up, once she'd been restored by the completion of the ritual.

The lights suspended over the train platform were on, and in their harsh white glare she saw that everything had been prepared—the nemset jars and bone instruments were laid out on the tables, the bier was draped in fresh white linens topped with a fine sprinkling of the sacred red sand of Saqqara. Alfred, following Bartholomew's directions, laid the boy on his back atop the sand, facing south, then receded into the shadows, hands folded in front of him like an usher at the theater. The boy was dressed already in a white nightshirt.

"You want to do the painting, or shall I?" her brother asked. "I'm usually faster at it."

"I'll do it," she said. "You still show no artistic ability whatsoever."

Winifred rested her cane against the side of one of the worktables and pushed the sleeves of her coat up. Taking the lids off several of the jars, she surveyed her choices—red, yellow, blue, green. She took some pride in her handiwork and liked to make sure that each of her creations was unique. What was important, her brother had often reminded her, was not the color scheme so much as the delineation of the particular features. The mouth and eyes and nose had to be outlined and emphasized by the paint, as all of these were considered critical to sustaining life, in this world and the next. The ancient Egyptians had wanted to be certain their mummified remains retained all the requisite functions, and so, he had said more than once, theirs should, too.

Even if that life they preserved was, under the Thornes' guidance, directed elsewhere.

Bending over the boy, she took note of his low breathing and closed eyes. He was very near the end, but it would not do to simply extinguish the flame prematurely. Bartholomew had warned her that to do so might injure the *ka*, and it was the *ka*—the life force—she was after. Each time it flew from a pair of dying lips, on its sudden journey to reunite with the *ba*, or soul, she was there to inhale it, to absorb it, to incorporate its remaining vigor into her own consumptive frame. For years, these regular infusions had revived and sustained her.

"Well, get on with it," Bartholomew said. "You don't have to be a Rembrandt."

She took a small hand mirror from the table and held it under the boy's nose. When the glass fogged nicely, she put the mirror back, and lifted the lid from an alabaster vessel filled with a thick and sticky unguent. This, she applied to the closed lids of his eyes with a sliver of bamboo so that they'd stay that way while she went about her work.

Choosing her color carefully—blue, she thought, to match the eyes she had just sealed—she dipped a brush into the jar, then daubed a bright circle around each orbit, and a dot in the center of each one to represent the pupil. For good measure, she also used the blue to outline his nose. For the mouth, she turned to the red—an obvious choice, but ideal for someone so young—and used the green for accents here and there. The yellow she reserved for a crude outline of the sacred ibis, symbol of magic, on his forehead.

"Whenever you're ready," her brother said, impatiently. He was already preparing the water and natron and incense for the rest of the purification ceremony.

But she wasn't quite finished; something was lacking. And then, in a moment of inspiration, she thought to enclose the ibis in an ornamental cartouche. Leaning back, she studied the boy's face—he was as pale as the alabaster jar, and couldn't be more than a few minutes from death. Putting the brush back on the table, she declared, "Done."

CHAPTER FORTY-FIVE

Before he heard any sound, Stoker saw the light spilling onto the tracks, and motioned for Mina to shutter the aperture on the lantern. Just before she did, Lucinda pointed to some bulky shapes lying close to the platform, and Stoker nodded. As stealthily as they could, the three of them crept forward in the tunnel, all the while Thorne's voice becoming more distinct. He was chanting something in the Arabic tongue—an incantation of some kind, if Stoker didn't miss his guess.

Hunkering down behind the bound mummies that had fallen onto the tracks and been left there to be gnawed on by rats, Stoker saw a tableau he would never forget. In the glare of the lamps suspended overhead, Thorne and Winifred hovered over a raised bier silted with red sand. On it lay the body of a boy in a nightshirt, his face so horribly painted it was difficult to tell who it was.

"Is it Timmy?" he whispered to Lucinda.

She nodded solemnly.

"Then let's go," Mina murmured, but Stoker laid a hand on her arm. He wanted to take a few seconds to assess the situation. The Thornes were hardly likely to let them simply take the boy and leave.

Bartholomew was sprinkling water on the body, and muttering more of the magic spell—but was he uttering it over a living boy, or a corpse? Had they come too late, or in the nick of time?

"It's the purification ceremony," Mina whispered in his ear.

"What next?" he mouthed.

"Natron."

And lo and behold, a moment later Thorne put the water away and took what looked like clumps of salt from a jar and rubbed them over the boy's face and neck, paying special attention to the mouth and nose.

"Is he alive?" Lucinda whispered. "What are we waiting for?"

"Give me that censer," Thorne said, and someone suddenly emerged from the shadows. A brute Stoker remembered was named Alfred. He had not even seen him until now. Were there others?

Thorne took the censer and began to swing it slowly around the bier. A cloud of incense, smelling of sandalwood, drifted into the air and made its way into the tunnel. When the smoke settled on the boy, Timmy stirred, and Stoker heard the lowest, but most welcome, moan.

Mina gripped his elbow like a vise. But before he could feel another second of exultation, Winifred stepped forward with a strange, striated instrument that looked like a funnel, or a horn cut from the head of some exotic beast.

"It could be any moment now," she said.

"Or it could be an hour," Thorne replied.

"I'll be the judge of that."

Like a doctor about to listen to a patient's heart, she bent low, and over her shoulder said, "No, no, he's going," and then wedged the tip of the funnel between the boy's lips. To Stoker's astonishment, she stuck her face into the open end.

There could be no further delay.

"Step back!" Stoker shouted, standing up and loudly cocking the gun.

Thorne's jaw dropped, and Winifred jerked her head up in shock.

"I said, step back from the boy!"

"Christ Almighty, is that you, Stoker?"

"And Mina Harcourt!" Mina shouted.

"And Lucinda Watts!"

Stepping over the mummies, Stoker advanced, the gun raised, the two women flanking him on either side.

"Alfred, deal with this bastard!" Thorne ordered, handing him a long handled knife from the table.

"But he's got a bloody rifle."

"He won't shoot—he's a gentleman," Thorne said scornfully.

"I wouldn't bet on that," Stoker said, leaping up onto the platform. He had scarcely gained his balance before Alfred lunged at him with the blade. Stoker parried the blow with the barrel of the gun, as Mina ran toward the bier. Winifred dropped the funnel, turned, and staggered, as fast as her bad legs would carry her, toward the stairs, but Lucinda intercepted her, and said, "You'll answer for my Davey," and swiped the open scissors at her.

The Matron dodged the attack, and before another could be launched, Thorne had punched Lucinda in the belly so hard she doubled over and went flying backward, all the way down onto the tracks again.

Alfred, feinting left, then right, then left again, was backing Stoker toward the edge of the platform. He'd grown confident that his adversary would not use the gun after all—and Stoker was hard pressed to shoot a man in cold blood.

"One more step and I'll shoot!" he warned.

But Alfred gave him a broken-toothed grin and jabbed the long knife at him again. Stoker pointed the gun at his chest, and as his finger felt for the trigger, Alfred suddenly groaned and buckled to his knees, having been struck a stunning blow from behind by the censer on its chain, swung like a mace. Mina stood above him, the smoking censer still swaying back and forth at her side, deliberating over another blow, until Alfred sprawled forward in a heap, unconscious.

"Is Timmy alive?" Stoker asked.

"Yes, but barely."

"Where's Lucinda?"

He turned, just as she crawled to the edge of the platform holding her stomach, and saying, "Don't let them get away!"

But gone the Thornes were.

CHAPTER FORTY-SIX

Mina let the censer clatter to the floor. "We can't let them escape. Not this time."

"I can take care of Timmy," Lucinda said, wincing, but making her way to the bier. "Go!"

No further words needed to be exchanged. Mina looked at Stoker, and she knew they were in league. She raced to the stairs and began bounding up them three at a time, with Stoker close behind. She could hear the Thornes' footsteps far above, but wondered how Winifred was making such progress at all. Was her brother carrying her? Rounding the first landing, she still saw no sign of them up ahead. But what if they did catch up to them, then what? Bram could corral them with the shotgun, they could call in Scotland Yard, but the word of a Gypsy girl and a theater manager against two of London's richest and most reputable citizens?

First you have to catch them, a little voice in her head reiterated, and she decided to heed its advice.

It was only when they'd passed the next landing that she glimpsed Thorne at the top of the steps, winded and leaning one hand against the wall. Glancing down, he immediately fumbled for the light switch, and the staircase went dark.

"Damn him!" Stoker swore.

But clinging to the rail, Mina was able to haul herself up the rest of the stairs, with Stoker so close behind she could feel his breath on the back of her neck. Not surprisingly, when she got to the top, she found the door firmly shut.

"It's locked!"

"Stand back," Stoker said, fumbling for the handle to get his bearings. "Are you away from the door?"

"Yes!"

A second later, the shotgun went off, the blast blowing a hole clean through the faceplate. But still the lock held.

"Hold on!" he said.

Another shot blew the handle and lock clean off, and with a kick of his boot, Stoker knocked the door off its hinges, and it yawned wide. Mina was the first one through, and she saw the Matron, who had surely heard the shots, ducking for cover inside the match factory. Thorne was barreling across the narrow courtyard, his head down against the battering wind, heading for the mission house itself.

"You go after him!" Mina shouted to Stoker as he reloaded the gun. "I'll get her." If only she'd hung on to the poker, or the censer . . . but even unarmed, how hard could it be to prevail over Winifred Thorne?

The little window at the front of the match works shed an orange glow, like the inside of a furnace, and Mina was halfway through the door before she saw the startled face of an old man stirring a bubbling pot of phosphorous over a coal fire, and Winifred Thorne huddling behind him.

"You're done for!" Mina shouted.

The Matron shoved the man's shoulder and said, "Throw the phossy at her!"

But the old man clung to the long iron-handled stirrer, his hands in heavy mitts, frozen, until the Matron grabbed it away from him and instantly regretted it, dropping the heated rod and shrieking in pain. It splatted into the cauldron and a dollop of the white-hot liquid splashed onto her coat, the cloth sizzling. She whipped the coat off, but in attempting to throw it to one side, she only made things worse. The coat skimmed the pot and caught fire, sparks flying everywhere. Several landed on a crate, and the wood crackled at their touch. The old man, sensing the danger, made for the door, brushing Mina aside in his mad scramble. The curtains went up next, setting the shutters ablaze.

Mina backed toward the door, expecting the Matron to take the same escape route, but the woman went the other way instead, heading into what looked like a warren of manufacturing rooms beyond.

"You have to get out of here!" Mina shouted, "Now!"

But all she saw was the back of the Matron's dyed blonde hair as the woman tottered, as if blind, hands extended on either side, from one wall to the other.

The flames were racing across the floorboards, before suddenly coalescing and rising up like a crimson sheet, the intensity of their heat driving Mina out the door.

She was out in the courtyard, coughing as smoke and ash poured from the match works, when she saw through bleary eyes Lucinda stumbling out of the underground entry, with Timmy clutched in her arms.

A moment later, the roof caved in, and a river of burning phosphorus poured like lava out onto the cobblestones. Mina staggered away from the sizzling flood, waving Lucinda off. This fire, she could tell, had only just begun.

CHAPTER FORTY-SEVEN

Once inside the mission house, Stoker had stopped, looking in every direction for some sign of his quarry. But the man had successfully gone to ground.

"Thorne!" he shouted. "You won't get far!"

But all he succeeded in doing was to wake the sleeping residents, a few of whom had emerged from their barracks to ask what all the noise was about.

"Have you seen Bartholomew Thorne?"

"What?" one woman asked. "In here? In the dead of night? You must be mad."

"And why're you carrying a gun?" a man in a rumpled nightshirt said. "Get that out of here before somebody gets hurt."

"Who are you, anyway?" another woman, a blanket wrapped around her shoulders, inquired. "You got business with the Matron? She's all the way up top."

Which was probably where Thorne had gone to hide. Taking the stairs in great strides, Stoker charged up one flight, then another, then another, past huge rooms barren of ornament or comfort, but crammed with narrow pallets to accommodate the hundreds of exhausted and destitute souls lying upon them. When he could go no higher, he saw an oaken door with a brass plaque that read "Miss Winifred Thorne, Matron & Benefactress."

The door was ajar—a good sign.

Pushing it the rest of the way open with the barrel of the gun, Stoker entered cautiously, looking all around. A wheelchair was parked to one side. The gas lamps were lit, illuminating rooms filled with Egyptian antiquities. Oil paintings in gilded frames, also of ancient subject matter, hung from silver chains on the walls; Paul on the road to Damascus was the subject of one. In the next room stood a grand piano, its gleaming black lid raised, sheet music scattered on the floor. Had someone just passed through in such a rush as to disturb it?

Stoker advanced farther, toward what must be the bedroom, his footsteps muffled by the rich Oriental carpets. The Matron certainly lived differently than her wards, he reflected. The door was open, and peering in he saw no sign of Thorne. Was he wrong? Had Thorne eluded him completely?

The bed, a four-poster with a brocade canopy, was empty, but in a far corner of the spacious room he saw a leaded, casement window and beneath it a divan on which a girl lay sleeping.

This was the last thing he expected to find here.

He entered silently and advanced to her side. Who was she, and what was she doing here? An end table near her head was littered with medicinal vials, a dropper, and incense sticks that, even unlit, smelled of sandalwood.

Was she, he thought with horror, to be the next victim? Even with her back turned to him, he guessed she was no more than twelve or thirteen years of age.

Resting the rifle against the edge of the table, he reached down and touched her shoulder. "Wake up," he said softly. "Wake up."

The girl stirred, but remained asleep under a thin blanket. He wondered if she had been drugged, and glancing at the bottles, he saw one that looked suspiciously like laudanum.

"You need to leave here," he said. "And quickly." He did not want to end his pursuit of Thorne, but he couldn't abandon this girl in such imminent danger, either.

He shook her more forcefully, and murmuring unhappily, she rolled over to face him. Her pale eyes were unfocused, and like Lucinda, she had an inflamed jaw. She looked at him blankly, neither surprised nor alarmed.

"Can you get up and walk?"

She didn't reply.

"You need to get up," he said, gathering the blanket around her shoulders and attempting to help her sit up. Again, she neither resisted, nor cooperated.

"We have to hurry," he said, but it was then that he saw her eyes shift to something right behind him, and he abruptly let go of her shoulders and grabbed for the shotgun.

But it was too late. Thorne had already snatched it by the barrel, and swung it so that the stock caught Stoker under the chin. His jaw snapped shut and his head back. He fell onto the divan, the girl immune to this, too, as Thorne stepped away, leveling the gun. Stoker shook his head to regain his senses. Under his thick brown moustache, Thorne wore a grin.

"Did you use this on Alfred?" he said. "I never would have thought you capable."

Stoker didn't doubt that Thorne was.

"Just don't hurt the girl," Stoker said, "any more than you have already." There was the taste of blood in his mouth.

"Oh, that's more in Winifred's line. I would never hurt you, would I, Alice?"

The girl looked at him dreamily.

"The game is up," Stoker said. "You know that, don't you?"

"For you, perhaps. Alice, move to one side, please."

Only to get a cleaner shot at him, Stoker surmised, but in that instant an explosion, greater than anything he could ever have imagined, rocked the entire building. The casement windows shattered, the floor wobbled, and not wanting to miss his one chance, Stoker launched himself at Thorne. The gun went off, the bullet whizzing past his cheek, and then he managed to drag him to the ground. Thorne rolled onto all fours, trying to scramble for the door, but the thick carpets slid under his grasp, and Stoker held on tight. Thorne flailed, but Stoker wrapped an arm around his throat, choking the breath out of him. He tried to reach around and break the grip, but Stoker only squeezed harder, and harder again, until he felt Thorne's body go slack, all resistance stop . . . and he heard the girl crying.

Letting go, he looked behind him, and thought, at first, that she was crying because of his attack on Thorne.

Then he saw the bloody wound in her side, where the errant shot must have grazed her.

Outside the shattered windows, orange flames licked the sky, the acrid stench of phosphorous already burning in his nostrils.

Pray God Mina had been nowhere near the explosion.

"Press your hands to it," Stoker said, going to the girl and guiding her hands to the wound. "And keep them there."

With a blanket tightly wound around her, they stepped over Thorne's prostrate body and then through the rest of the Matron's rooms. In the stairwell, chaos reigned—the residents clambering over each other to get down, trampling the ends of blankets and sheets trailing after those who had just left their beds, screams echoing from the halls and barracks, and all of it bathed in an infernal glow coming through the broken windows.

Stoker was protecting the girl on the way down when a hysterical woman shouting, "Alice! Alice!" fought her way through the mob, and the girl fell into her arms, sobbing. "What have they done to you, my darling? What have they done to you?"

She saw the blood, and looked at Stoker, unsure whether to thank him or curse him.

But there was time for neither. "She'll be all right," he said. "It's just a flesh wound. Keep going!"

There was little choice in that either. They were carried down the steps and around each landing by a swelling tide of panic-stricken people, who spilled into the courtyard before surging toward the porter's lodge and, after demolishing the iron gates, onto the street beyond.

Stoker stopped, searching for Mina in all directions. The grounds of the mission house were aflame, smoke and ash billowing everywhere, sparks flying in the gusting winds and alighting on anything not yet ablaze. Yanking his shirt collar up around his mouth, he forged ahead, waving smoke away with his free hand, batting out the sparks that threatened to catch his clothes on fire. Outside the match factory—its roof gone, its walls collapsed—a river of white phosphorous smoldered like coals on the cobblestones.

Good God, please let Mina have been clear of that.

Turning around, he looked through eyes bleary from the smoke toward the gates. There seemed to be almost no air left in the compound; the oxygen he could inhale was hot and searing his lungs. He staggered away from the match works to avoid passing out, and by the time he reached the mangled gates, he was coughing uncontrollably. He tried to grab the bars to hold himself up, but the metal was red-hot, and he jerked his hand away, swiveling out onto the sidewalk already littered with the bodies of those who'd been overcome. The bells of fire wagons clanged in the distance. The wind roared in his ears, enveloping him in a maelstrom of black smoke, and he might have succumbed himself had he not felt an arm slip around his waist and pull him on.

He knew who it was without even being able to see her, and together they staggered across the street before tumbling down an escarpment. At the bottom, surrounded by dozens of others moaning and writhing like the condemned in Dante's vision of hell, they huddled close, gasping for fresh air and holding on to each other for dear life.

By the time the fire brigade arrived, alarms ringing, horses whinnying in fear, there was nothing of the mission house left to save.

CHAPTER FORTY-EIGHT

For the next several days, the newspapers were filled with nothing but breathless reports and anguished editorials on the great conflagration that had consumed the Thorne Mission House and a dozen other buildings in too-close proximity. The casualty figures stood at twenty-three, but according to printed comments from the city's fire marshal, "The exact number will never be known, as the incineration was so intense, and the devastation so thorough, any bodily remains we found were incomplete and unidentifiable."

All the workhouse records, too, had of course been destroyed.

Stoker read about it as best he could; his eyes still smarted from the smoke and ash, and when Florence found him in the study using a magnifying glass, she promptly took it away. "You know what the doctor said. No reading. You have to let your eyes rest."

On the one hand, he knew she was looking after his welfare; on the other, he felt that she was still punishing him for the suspicions she harbored. The charges that Ludvig Gerhard had leveled before being thrown out of the house had taken root, and they had been significantly abetted by this present calamity. Why, Florence had wanted to know, had he been anywhere near the Thorne Mission House, much less on its grounds? What possible business could he have had at such a place, and more to the point, what person—what woman—might he have been there to see? His explanations—that he was just a passerby who could not help but try to do what he could in an unfolding disaster—fell on deaf ears.

"I thought we had satisfied that reckless impulse," Florence said, "after you jumped into the Thames to save that suicidal girl."

"It is my nature."

"It is your excuse."

"Should I have simply walked on by?"

"Isn't that girl you saved—that Lucy something—a resident there?"

"No," he replied, splitting hairs; she wasn't a resident *now*.

But Florence, smelling a rat, had not let it go. "What ever did happen to her?"

"She found employment elsewhere."

"Where?"

"A theater." Forestalling the inevitable.

"Which one, pray tell?"

"The Lyceum," he admitted, knowing that he had just thrown fuel on the fire. But before his wife could respond, he added, "She is an able seamstress, and that is all she is. Abandoning her to the streets would only have brought her back to the brink of self-destruction."

Florence had let it drop there—perhaps because she did not want to know any more of the unseemly details—but he knew she had not stopped stewing about it. When she rapped on the study door that afternoon to announce that he had a visitor, she did it with all the warmth of a civil servant ushering in the next applicant to a job interview.

"Who is it?"

"William Stead."

Ah, that was a bit of a relief. Had Mina come by to look in on him—against his explicit instructions—his life would not have been worth a penny.

"How are you doing, old man?" Stead announced, entering the room with a copy of the *Pall Mall Gazette*, which he was now editing, in his hand. "The latest edition."

"I will leave him to you then," Florence said, excusing herself.

"Handsome woman, your wife," Stead said, once the doors had been closed. "You're a lucky man."

Appearances, Stoker reflected, were oft so deceiving.

Drawing a chair close to Stoker's, Stead said, "And are the eyes any better?"

"Yes, thanks."

"Can't imagine it myself. Reading and writing is all I do all day. How would I fill my time?"

"It's not easy," Stoker admitted. Without those two activities to distract him, his thoughts turned, inevitably, in the darkest direction. He had killed a man. Yes, there were extenuating circumstances—of that there was no doubt—but the fact remained that his hands had choked the life out of another human being.

"The Beefsteak's not the same without you. Irving dithers about, but the Guv'nor is plainly lost without you."

It was nice of him to say so. Stoker had gone into the theater each day, but only for a few hours. The chemicals in the smoke had singed his throat, and he found himself short of breath. He had even curtailed his long walks home, taking a coach or omnibus, on which he had happened to hear much discussion of the fire.

"I hear there were peculiar things going on there," one woman confided to another. "Things not right."

"It smelled of sulfur, it did, like somethin' of the devil himself," the other replied.

Even if he had shared the truth with them, they would never have believed him.

Stoker picked up the edition of the *Gazette*, and said, "I look forward to reading this, though it's against doctor's orders. Has anything new come to light?"

"Yes, as it happens, and we've got it first."

"What?" Stoker asked, holding his breath.

"They found his watch."

"Thorne's?"

"Gold, with his initials inscribed in it."

"And the remains?"

"No telling. The whole place fell in on itself, as you know, like the House of Usher." He stopped to make a mental note. "That's not a bad analogy. I must remember to use it in the next editorial."

"And his sister, Winifred?"

"Still missing, too, though they've got the twisted wreckage of her wheelchair. Some of the other newspapers are giving out that they died heroically, trying to save their occupants."

"I can assure you, that was not the case."

"So you've said," Stead replied, his penetrating gaze giving the lie to his casual affectation. "Anything else you can recall of them, from that night?"

Stoker recognized that this was more than a convalescent call. Stead, ever the journalist and promoter, was looking for new material.

"No. But as you know, I had met them socially, sometime before, and they did not strike me as a pair that would make any sacrifice at all, much less that of their lives, for others. Their reputation for charitable work was a sham, a masquerade for public consumption and social acceptance. And if they died in the fire, as it seems they did, the world is no worse off for it."

"A harsh judgment indeed."

"But merited."

"Still, I doubt I can use it. Speaking ill of the dead, you know . . . it would be considered bad form just now."

"I quite understand. But why don't you ask Professor Vambéry, Thorne's houseguest for lo these many months? He might be able to add a bit more complementary color."

"I would, but he has not made an appearance at the Beefsteak, nor has his sponsor Conan Doyle for that matter. For all I know, Doyle is at home in his study, working like a beaver on a Sherlock Holmes story revolving around a mysterious mission house." He snapped his fingers. "Another good idea—I should write one myself. Talking to you is a wonderful way of stimulating the mind, Stoker. Anyone ever tell you that?"

"Irving told me I was like a burr in his saddle."

Stead laughed. "That, too, of course. You kept the man on his toes." Correcting himself, he said, "You *keep* the man on his toes. When may we expect to see you at the club again?"

"I expect to be there this Friday."

"Capital! I'll let the others know—they'll be eager to welcome you back." Rising, he clapped Stoker on the shoulder and said, "I'll show myself out." Then, with a wink, "It'll give me a chance to be alone with the fetching Florence."

Stoker smiled, and raised a hand off the afghan draped across his lap. Truth was, even this much talking had strained his voice a bit. Retrieving the magnifying glass, he picked up the *Gazette* and went straight to the editor's letter to see what Stead had had to say. The man was always interesting and generally provocative, and even if editing the *Pall Mall Gazette* had temporarily required him to pull some punches, Stoker did not regret having gone on record regarding the Thornes. The one regret he did have was that they had not been exposed while alive . . . and suitably punished for their terrible crimes.

CHAPTER FORTY-NINE

The scene at Tower Hamlets Cemetery could not have been more dismal. The fog had been thick all day, with a strangely yellow cast to it, and seemed to wrap each funeral carriage—and there were many—in its jaundiced embrace. The horses, in black plumage, pawed the cold ground and snorted clouds of vapor. Open graves were everywhere, with tiny clutches of people around some of them, and no one at all around others. The priests, ministers, and other officiants scuttled from one plot to another, Bibles and prayer books in hand, looking like harried passengers trying to make their train connections.

Mina and Lucinda each held Timmy by one hand. Mina had not thought it was a good idea to come at all; the boy had only begun to recover from his fever, and the air was wickedly chill. But Lucinda had seemed intent on it.

"It's his mother being buried today," she said. "He'll never forgive me if I kept him away."

True enough, Mina thought, but not if it meant putting him at risk, too. She had personally wound a heavy scarf around his throat and bought him a warm woolen coat, matching mittens, and a stocking hat. She asked a caretaker where Maude Conway was to be buried, and after consulting a scrawled list, he pointed them to an open pit not far from a duck pond. A couple of dozen other mourners were already gathered around it, and Mina soon saw why. It was a mass grave, dug especially deep, the coffins to be laid into it one atop the other. Right now, they were stacked like cordwood under a bare-branched oak tree.

While some of the coffins contained only remnants of the deceased, Maude's held her entire body. She had been found under a pile of timbers and rubble, close to where the infirmary had once been; she had no doubt died from smoke inhalation in a desperate attempt to buck the tide of fleeing humanity and make her way to the ward to rescue her son. Mina had accompanied Lucinda to the morgue to identify the body.

"Don't you worry now," Lucinda had said, clutching the limp, pallid hand that hung from the table. "I've got your little Timmy now, and I'll treat him and love him like he was my own little Davey. See if I don't."

Mina had been touched—how could she not be?—and resolved to help in that endeavor, too, in whatever way she could. The misery in which so many of the city's inhabitants lived had surprised and appalled her in equal measure, and she wondered at how she could have been so oblivious to it when she was younger. Or how so many Londoners remained oblivious to it even now.

Once the minister had called everyone to gather close—"I've a sore and aching throat today, and this fog isn't helping matters."—Mina stepped nearer to the pit, feeling Timmy's hand squeezing hers. She squeezed back, and murmured, "It's all right. Everything will be all right."

"But is Mum in one of those?" he whispered, tilting his chin toward the stacked caskets.

"Yes."

"Does she know I'm here?"

"Yes," Lucinda put in, having overheard. "She's watching over us all right now."

His lower lip trembled, and a tear rolled down one cheek; he was doing his best to put up a brave front, but Mina wasn't sure how long the dam could hold. She prayed the minister would be brief.

For once, her prayer was answered. Stopping to cough every other sentence or two, he rushed through the words of his eulogy, offering many platitudes but little succor, barely raising his eyes above his spectacles to look at the grieving friends and family members, dressed in their best, clustered around the yawning pit. When he was done, and offering his last perfunctory benediction, the people gathered there turned to each other for the comfort and solace his words had failed to provide.

Several of the woman gravitated to Lucinda, not only to commiserate, but also to hear about how she had managed to escape the world of the workhouse for a paid position at a real place of business. A theater, yet—it was as if her victory had given them all hope. Mina was singled out by the minister, who had noticed she did not quite fit in with the others and asked her how she had come to be there.

"I knew Maude Conway."

"And she was one of those we buried just now?"

"Yes."

"She was in your employ at one time?"

"No. She was simply a social acquaintance." That, she knew, would confound him. And it did.

Hiding behind a cough for a moment, he said, "Well then, it was very kind of you to come and pay your respects."

"It was the least I could do."

"And the boy who was here? He's your son?"

It was only then that she realized he wasn't cowering behind her skirts. Where had he gone?

"No, he's the son—newly adopted—of Lucinda Watts, the woman over by the grave."

He threw a cursory glance that way—Lucinda was being embraced by an elderly man with a tear in his eye—and Mina could see that Timmy wasn't there, either.

"Did you see where he went?"

"In this fog," the minister said, "who can tell."

Turning all around, Mina failed to see Timmy anywhere. He could not have gone far, it had only been a matter of seconds, but she felt a sense of alarm nonetheless. He was far from fully recovered yet, and she had hoped to convey him and Lucinda out of the cemetery and into warmer precincts—a tea shop, perhaps, with hot buttered scones to restore them—as quickly as she could. Touching the elbow of a woman close by, she said, "Did you see the little boy I was with?"

"Maudie's boy?"

"Yes. Do you know where he went?"

Pointing a gnarled finger in the direction of the duck pond, she said, "Over that way."

Mina thanked her, and set off after him, threading her way through the gray mist that shrouded the headstones and barren trees. In the distance, she could hear the ducks squawking in the water.

And laughter.

Watching her step so as not to collide with a monument, or worse yet, plummet into an open grave, she followed the sounds until she saw a pond, glistening green, surrounded by drooping yews. On its shore, she saw the shadowy figures of two little boys skipping stones into the water.

"Three!" one of them exulted, and the other said, "Watch this," then shouted, "Four!"

One of them, she was relieved to see, was Timmy, though she was less than pleased that he had chosen to take off his warm stocking hat and give it to the other boy. She did not want him to relapse.

"Timmy," she said, "you shouldn't have gone off without telling me."

Timmy turned, and the other boy went silent. He was wearing a strange patchwork coat, and she did not remember seeing him at the gravesite ceremony. He was pale, with hollow eyes, and all the joy had instantly drained from his face, replaced by a vague apprehension.

"Who's this?" she said to Timmy as she moved down the slope toward the water.

"My friend."

"I can see that. But does he have a name?" she asked, smiling at the pale boy, determined already to take him with them to the tea shop. No one looked more like he could use some hot tea and scones.

"That's Davey."

But Davey, still holding a pebble, was slowly moving away from her. She stopped, so as not to spook him further.

"Davey, I'm Mina Harcourt. Please don't be afraid."

"I'm not."

"He's not," Timmy confirmed. "Davey's not afraid of nothing."

Hadn't that been the name of Lucinda's poor dead son?

"Not even Matron," the pale boy said.

And why would he say that? "Were people afraid of the Matron?" she said, though she could well imagine why.

The two boys exchanged a look.

"Because if they were, they don't have to be anymore. The Matron's gone, Davey. No one needs to be afraid of her anymore."

"I said I'm not."

"That's good."

"But she's not gone."

What an odd conversation they were having. "She is," Mina replied. "She was caught in the fire."

"No, she wasn't," the boy said, slipping even further into the mist. "I'd know."

"And how is that?"

"Because I'm gone."

A duck landed in the water, its wings splashing, and when Mina looked back, the boy had receded even farther into the fog. She was having trouble seeing him at all.

"Don't keep going that way," she warned. "You'll get lost."

And then he was swallowed up altogether. Mina looked at the crestfallen Timmy, whose arms hung limply by his sides. "I'm sorry. I didn't mean to scare him off. How will he get home?"

"He is home." Timmy dropped his stone on the ground, all the fun of the game lost, and trudged up the slope. "I want to leave now."

Could it be? Mina slipped an arm around Timmy's bony shoulders and turned back toward the others. Lucinda was just coming toward them.

"There you are."

Should she say something? Mina wondered. What?

"It's too cold to stay here anymore," Lucinda said. "Let's go home."

By which she meant Mina's room on Raven Row. It had been temporarily converted into a convalescent ward—a very crowded one—to which Strauss's wife brought bowls of steaming hot matzo ball soup.

Lucinda folded Timmy under her arm and walked back to the pathway, while Mina lingered behind, casting one last look at the duck pond. What frightened her more than the fact that she might have just had an encounter with a ghost—and shouldn't that have been enough to send shivers down the spine?—was what he had told her from beyond the grave.

The Matron was still alive.

CHAPTER FIFTY

The clamor of the Beefsteak Club was still hammering in his ears as Stoker pulled up the collar of his coat against the damp night wind and stepped out of the Lyceum's alleyway. Again, he had been celebrated as the man of the hour, racing to the aid of those trapped in the mission house fire, just as he had once saved a girl from leaping into the Thames, but this time he felt like a fraud. Had he not broken into the workhouse in the first place, the fight—and the conflagration that sprang from it—would never have occurred. In an attempt to rescue one little boy, he had wound up costing dozens of others their own lives.

And it was a secret of which he could never unburden himself.

What he needed, after several days of being cooped up in his study, was another of his nocturnal walks, and it felt good now to stretch his sturdy legs. Lighting a cigar—which he would never have dared to do in front of Florence given the damage to his lungs from the fire—he set out for the Thames Embankment. There was something about the river, and watching the boats bobbing at anchor, or slowly wending their way along the dark concourse, that never failed to distract him and calm his mind.

As it happened, the show tonight had been the very play that had pushed Lucinda to the brink of suicide—*Faust*. And he soon found himself walking along the pavement where he had first spotted her, leaning with suspicious intent over the railing. What a cascade of events had emanated from that one encounter! Even now, he could hardly grasp the enormity of it all. His had always been a busy life, what with arranging the production schedules and travel itineraries of London's most successful theatrical enterprise, but it had been in its own way prosaic. It was all about soliloquies and set designs, train timetables and hotel bookings, copyrights and costumes. It was all in a day's work.

But life of late had become séances and psychics, gold boxes and sinister shakedown artists, underground tunnels and mummification rituals, forged papyri and brutal fights. He could still barely believe that the hand now holding a cigar had strangled a man . . . a man with a public reputation as unsoiled as his soul was black. Even if he were to share the stories at the Beefsteak, the members would undoubtedly write them off as just more of his familiar flights of fancy. The grim stuff of his stories.

In honor of Stoker's return to the club, Thorne's houseguest, Professor Vambéry, had put in an appearance—his last, as he confided.

"With the apparent demise of my host, I think it is unseemly for me to stay on in the house," he had told Stoker. "I have made my plans to return to the Continent."

"Where will you be going?"

"To Transylvania first, to see some old friends. But then," he said, glancing down at his walking stick, "if I am able, I am going to attempt one more great adventure."

"And what is that?"

"I am going to follow that young woman's lead."

"Mina's?"

Nodding, he said, "I am going to scale the Bucegi Massif, and see for myself, on All Hallows' Eve, the face of the Carpathian Sphinx. I am going to see, with these old failing eyes, whether or not the face changes with the dying sun."

For a moment, Stoker felt a rush of blood in his veins. What a marvelous adventure that would be! What a spectacular scene for the opening of a novel for that matter!

When they had parted at the door of the club, Vambéry had crooked a finger at Stoker and, bending his head to speak sotto voce, shared one final confidence. "I am older than you and have lived many places, among many different peoples. So allow me to echo the words of your poet, and say, 'There are more things in heaven and earth, Horatio, than are dreamt of in your philosophy.'"

Why, Stoker had wondered, had he chosen to share that admonition? The puzzlement must have shown on his face because Vambéry resumed.

"I think you are an exceptional man, Stoker, but perhaps too rational. I, too, used to be that way. But if experience has taught me anything, it is that reason can carry you only so far. Beyond that, there is a world that can only be understood by something deeper, and older, embedded within us. Do not be afraid to open your mind to the impossible."

No sentiment could have struck him more forcibly.

Had he not witnessed bizarre rituals in secret tunnels? Had he not escaped a swarm of vermin summoned as if by Beelzebub himself? Had he not been told by Mina, an unimpeachable source, that a ghost had informed her of the Matron's miraculous survival?

He had opened his mind to the impossible in life. But now it was a matter of doing so in his art. What he had been looking for was the kind of idea that would grab him by his throat—and in like manner his readers—and shake him like a terrier savaging a rat. His entanglement with the Thornes and Mina, and Lucinda and her dead son, were certainly grist for the mill, but it would all need to be transmuted somehow. Egyptomania, for one thing, was already done to death, and for another, he had never been able to take actual events and personages and render them convincingly on the page. Other writers—his friend Hall Caine, for instance—could do that, but for Stoker real people and real occur-rences needed to be passed through some kind of imaginative filter, but without—and this was the maddeningly hard part of it—losing their inherent, and oddly ineffable, power.

Down below, a tugboat churned upstream, a yellow lantern swing-ing slowly, back and forth, on its bow. For how many centuries, Stoker wondered, had vessels of all sorts, from Roman galleys to clipper ships, navigated this serpentine waterway? And for how many more to come would they do the same? Long, long after he had passed on, that was for sure. It was a banal thought—that life would go on without one being there to witness, much less participate in, it. But what if one *could* live forever? What if there *were* a way to go on and on? The Egyptians believed that if all the right ceremonies were performed, and in precisely the right way, the soul, if that was the correct word for it, could persist. But—and here was the rub for Stoker—at no cost. In his view, that was too easy. There had to be a price to pay for eternal life. It was a deal with the devil—and the devil always got his due.

There he was again, his thoughts taking a turn toward the dark side. An Irish upbringing, that could account for part of it. His boy-hood infirmity, that was another. But in his soul, there was a longing for immortality. Maybe that was what motivated every artist. Having a child was supposedly one way of satisfying it; in your offspring you saw your blood being carried on, into an indefinite future. But when he looked at Noel, whom he loved with every fiber of his being, he did not feel that that urge had been met. Was he defective, as a parent, in that regard? It was a secret he could never have shared with anyone; he was ashamed even to admit it to himself. It simply wasn't enough that his son, or his grandchildren, go on. Stoker wanted it for himself. *He* wanted to go on.

A constable ambled past, giving him an appraising glance, before deciding that he posed no problem. Stoker nodded, and the policeman said, "A fine cigar, that. I could smell it a hundred yards off."

"May I offer you one?" Stoker said, reaching for the case in his breast pocket.

"Oh, no, sir, that's quite all right." He started to move on, but stopped and said, "Aren't you the gentleman who helped me with that poor girl who had jumped into the river?"

Now that he said it, Stoker recognized him, too. "Yes, I am."

"And what became of her? Do you know?"

"I do. She is presently employed as a seamstress at the Lyceum Theatre."

"Well, I'll be. Stories like that don't often have such a happy ending. I'm glad that one of 'em did."

"You *must* have a cigar. It's the least I can do in recognition of our common bond." Stoker opened the case and held it out to him.

"Well, seeing as we do have something to celebrate . . ." the constable replied, looking about as if he were being caught taking a bribe.

"Mum's the word," Stoker said, snapping the case shut once the man had selected a cigar. "Smoke it in good health."

"That I'll do."

When his footsteps had died off, Stoker resumed his walk toward home. He had, in Lucinda and in Mina, an unlikely pair—two women, both of whom were simultaneously victims and heroines, assaulted by various forces but strong in their resistance, constrained by social mores but capable of defying them in the search for justice and answers. What could he make of the two of them in a fictional context? *"Open your mind,"* Vambéry had advised him. For that matter, what could he make of the professor himself—an itinerant linguist and erstwhile adventurer, a cosmopolitan but mysterious figure steeped in, among other things, occult wisdom and ancient superstition? The Wandering Jew of legend and lore? Could a story be concocted in which all these elements were fused and explored, along with his own fixation on the idea of eternal life? He felt something stirring inside him, something that was already quickening his pace. He wanted to get to his study and his desk. There was a creative storm brewing, and it was important at such moments to catch it at its full tide. His fingers itched with the urge to hold his pen, while his brain teemed with words and ideas rushing by like foaming rapids. But of all those words—and he could not have guessed why—one word, recently spoken to him—came to the fore. In its foreign aspect and in its literal meaning—the land beyond the forests—it rang in his ears like the pealing of a church bell, holding in its tone the promise, and the premise, of an entire universe. One word.

Transylvania.

1912

"Death be all that we can rightly depend on . . .
    Maybe it's in that wind
out over the sea that's bringin' with it loss and
    wreck, and sore distress, and
sad hearts. Look! Look!" he cried suddenly.
    "There's something in that wind
and in the hoast beyont that sounds, and looks,
    and tastes, and smells like
death. It's in the air; I feel it comin'."

—From *Dracula*, published 1897

CHAPTER FIFTY-ONE

Knowing that his friend Bram arose rather late in the morning, William T. Stead sat on a wooden bench outside the little house at 26 St. George's Square until he heard the church bells ring ten o'clock. As usual, he had a sheaf of the daily newspapers to keep him busy, including one that he edited himself. Having finished reading his own editorial for the day—another earnest appeal for peace among nations—he folded up the papers under his arm and crossed the street. He could barely wait to impart the shocking news he had acquired.

The house itself, he noted, was a definite comedown from Stoker's prior residence on Cheyne Walk. Since Sir Henry Irving's death seven years earlier—a sad and sudden event in the lobby of the Midland Hotel—and the subsequent collapse of the Lyceum, Stoker's fortunes, like his health, had precipitously declined. He had done his best to make up for the losses with his pen, writing novels and stories and even polemics—anything that might catch the attention of the public, or bring in a bit of ready cash—but it was a constant struggle. One such screed that had struck Stead as particularly out of keeping with his previous character was an attack on so-called unwholesome or suggestive works; to Stead's mind, the piece carried a peculiar, self-incriminating streak. Was he the only one who found certain passages in Stoker's *Dracula*, published by Constable in 1897 and his only real success to date, rather more scandalous than what was found in most supernatural tales? He thought especially of the three seductive vampire maids, succubi, who descended en masse upon the prostrate Jonathan Harker, held prisoner in the Carpathian castle. Or the scene in which the character of Mina Murray and her mate are simultaneously drained of their blood and made to drink of the evil count's, their lips pressed firmly to an open wound in his chest. You did not have to be a subscriber to Carrington's scurrilous *Catalogue of Erotica* to know a bit of sublimation and indirection when you saw it; substitute one fluid for another and you had a fix on at least a portion of the strange fascination the book had exerted on its audience ever since its publication fifteen years before. In Stead's view, the novel should have done much better than it did—it was miles beyond any other book of its sort, in both its conception and its madly original execution—and had been not unfavorably compared to such notable works as *Frankenstein* and *Wuthering Heights*; Stoker's friend, Conan Doyle, had even proclaimed it "the very best story of diablerie I have read for many years." But the subject matter had relegated it to a lower tier of critical interest and acceptance, and Stoker's royalty had been a mere two shillings on each copy sold.

Banging the brass knocker, he was surprised to have Florence herself, rather than a housemaid, answer the door. Another economy? But she lit up when she saw him.

"Bram is just up, but still in his robe and slippers."

"Who said I came to see Bram?"

She blushed. Her hair was still tinted gold, and the cornflower-blue dress set off her blue-gray eyes. If there was one thing that Stead felt he knew about women, it was that no matter how old they were, at heart they were still girls, and as pleased as ever—no, come to think of it, more so—by a compliment. For him as a journalist, flattery had greased the way in many an interview, with everyone from barmaids to the Queen of England.

Not that he didn't mean it. Florence still cut a lovely figure, though he could tell, as most of their friends could, that the marriage had not been an ideal one. She had wanted more of a man of the world, wealthier, more successful, more respectable in every way; and Stoker had wanted a more affectionate and supportive spouse, one who admired his fidelity, his unflagging industry, and his work. Never once had Stead heard her utter a favorable word about her husband's oeuvre—at a party he had even overheard her confess to being vaguely embarrassed at the notoriety of *Dracula*—and as a writer himself, he knew that had to sting.

"He's just having his breakfast. What can I get you? Some tea? Toast? Would you like some eggs and bacon?"

"No need, no need," he assured her. "The pleasure of his company is all I seek."

"Is that you I hear, Stead?" came a voice from the dining room. "Come in already!"

The dining room, too, was smaller than their old one, the table barely fitting into it, the curtains hanging lower than the windows warranted. Stoker himself looked diminished; his once burly shoulders hunched in his dressing gown, his brown hair thinner across the pate, his reading glasses snugly perched on the bridge of his nose. The *Daily Telegram* was spread on the table before him.

"What brings you out at this ungodly hour?"

"It's past ten, Bram—time for all good men to be about their business."

"Not if they were at it until the dead of night."

"So you are at work on a new novel?"

"Not quite sure what it is yet. Started out as a short story, but it's taking great strides. Might be the best thing I've done since *The Lair of the White Worm*."

"That's marvelous news," Stead said, though he felt a falling in his heart. Though it had created something of a brief sensation, that most recent novel, published the year before, had been largely incoherent and overstuffed, filled with nearly hallucinatory imagery and lurid symbolism. Talk about unwholesome and suggestive literature!

Florence came in with a pot of hot tea and poured Stead a cup. "And what are you up to?" she asked, offering a plate with milk and sugar and a lemon wedge artfully arranged on it.

"I've been off on a speaking tour."

"On topics of a supernatural bent?" she asked. "I've kept every issue of your magazine *Borderland*."

"They're collector's items now," he said, as it had closed down in 1897. "No, it has had to do with my war against war. I've been trying to promote the formation of an international union to combat militarism."

"That's quite a good idea," Florence said. "Those Germans and French and Russians are forever stirring things up, looking for a fight."

"As are we."

She paused, the teapot in midair.

"We had no business going to war in the Transvaal, for instance, and I did all that I could to stop it at the time. But that hasn't stopped the imperial adventuring in which we still engage."

Florence looked quite flustered now, as were most Britons he addressed on this topic. The notion that other countries were transgressors was accepted as an indisputable fact, but any suggestion that the British were equally at fault was met with consternation, and even cries of treason. He had been hung in effigy more than once, though he always took issue with his likeness: "My beard is much fuller and whiter now—they should really strive for accuracy."

"If you're looking for a solicitation to the cause," Stoker said, "you've come to the wrong place. My royalties came to a grand total of nineteen pounds last month."

Stead hastily waved the suggestion away. "No, no, I've come to bid you adieu, for now. I'm traveling to America, at the invitation of their President Taft. I'm going to be taking part in a peace conference at Carnegie Hall, in New York, on the twenty-first of this month."

Florence mumbled some words of congratulation, but still in shock, retired from the room—which was what Stead had been hoping for. His private business with Bram could hardly wait much longer.

"It's not the only honor I have heard you are being proposed for," Stoker said.

"That is only a rumor, though a persistent one, and highly unlikely."

"Not so, my friend. The committee behind the Nobel Peace Prize keeps you firmly in its sights—I have it on the best of authority."

"We shall see, we shall see. But that isn't what I've come to tell you about," he said, leaning closer and lowering his voice. "The most extraordinary thing has happened, and before I left London, I simply had to share it with you."

Stoker removed the reading glasses from his nose.

"When I went to the booking office to buy my ticket, there was quite a long line ahead of me. It's a maiden voyage, from Southampton, and quite a grand ship. Many of the people in line were plainly servants of their very wealthy masters. But there was one who was not, and he clearly stood out."

"Why?"

"Because he is, by all accounts, dead."

Stoker sat back in his chair, looking like a man braced to receive a terrible diagnosis.

"Although he had altered his appearance—he is clean-shaven now, and his skin has taken on a ruddier tone, perhaps from living in some tropical clime?—it was the spitting image of Bartholomew Thorne."

"But he died in the fire."

"If he did, then he has certainly been reborn, a phoenix if you will."

Stead sat back, too, giving his friend a moment to absorb this revelation.

"And his sister?"

"I sidled close enough to hear that he was purchasing two tickets, first class."

"Surely not in his own name."

"A close facsimile. North."

"A simple anagram," Stoker said, rubbing his chin contemplatively, "if not for the final *e*. Don't tell me—his first name is now Ernest?"

"Edgar," Stead said, thumping the table in triumph.

"And you're *sure* you recognized him, even after all these years?"

"Ah, there you have put your very finger on the nub of it. My knees have gotten arthritic, your eyes have gotten weaker, but Thorne? He looked, if anything, *younger* than he had when I saw him unraveling that mummy in his hothouse. It's a pity that I'm not still publishing that damned magazine." He shook his head ruefully, taking a hasty slurp from his teacup. "It looks like I've stumbled on a real-life Dorian Gray," he added, referring to Oscar Wilde's creation—the scoundrel whose corruption was reflected not on his face, but in a magical painting. "Well, I've a good deal of planning and packing to do, so I will take my leave and allow you to mull over all this—food for thought, eh?—while you finish your breakfast. Or is it an early lunch?"

Stoker looked so deep in thought, he barely acknowledged Stead's departure, and even Florence was nowhere to be seen. Letting himself out, Stead felt a sense of relief. At least he had shared this astonishing tale with someone who might put it to good use. There was a damn good story, however unbelievable, in there somewhere.

Stoker heard the front door close, but as if it were a million miles away. In the pit of his stomach, he felt a cold stone.

If what Stead had told him was true—and there was no cause, other than simple reason, to doubt it—then Thorne had continued his old and unnatural practices, maintaining and restoring his own, and his sister's, health with the vitality of their victims. It was a terrible technique, one that he, Stoker, had artfully transmuted in his most famous novel: the *ka*, in his telling, had become blood. But now, like his own undying count, Thorne was preparing to take his vile show on the road. Just as the fictional Dracula, in search of fresh blood, had departed Transylvania for the teeming city of London, so, now, the real Bartholomew Thorne—or Edgar North, as he now styled himself—was leaving London to descend like a plague upon the American continent. Hadn't Oscar Wilde written about just that sort of inversion, too? Hadn't he argued in one of his most provocative essays that life imitated art, not the other way around? At the time, Stoker had been amused at the absurd contention, taking it as simply another of that late author's controversial tongue-in-cheek positions, but now . . . now he saw it in another light altogether. Hadn't he, the author of *Dracula*, displayed an uncanny sort of prescience, anticipating in fiction the flight of a monster from one depleted killing ground to another? What else, he wondered, might he have imagined that was still to come true?

For years, he had carried—and needlessly, it appeared—the guilt over having taken a man's life—even a man like Thorne, who had ruthlessly preyed upon so many. He remembered sitting by Lucinda's bedside, holding her brittle hand as she finally succumbed to the ravages of the cancerous phossy jaw; though it came too late to save her, an act of Parliament outlawed the deadly white phosphorus matches in 1908. He remembered, too, the bodies in the underground, lined up like nine pins, and the bodies of those caught in the inferno of the mission house. The funeral for little Davey. But how many more had Thorne killed in these past years while living free and unfettered? Now, any vestige of that guilt was utterly and forever expunged, replaced by a sense of duty. Many lives were still at stake, and regardless of the toll it would take on his own withered frame—his eye inadvertently dropped to his unsteady legs and his fingers, gnarled from a stroke the year before—he had no choice but to take up the gauntlet. He could not sit idle and allow such malevolence to continue, unabated and unchallenged. On this journey, which might well be his last, he would need the one and only able-bodied ally in whom he could place his perfect trust.

CHAPTER FIFTY-TWO

When Stoker came through the jailhouse door, Mina didn't know whether to hang her head against the bars in shame or relief. She had not known who else to turn to for the bail money; Eli Strauss was already overextended, bailing out members of the Hebrew Union, and she did not want to have to put any additional strain upon the precarious finances of the WSPU—Women's Social and Political Union—of which she was one of the leading firebrands.

"Fancy meeting you here," Stoker said to lighten the awkward situation.

"I'm so sorry to have importuned you, Bram."

"I'm pleased that you did. I was planning to call upon you, anyway, as it happened." Looking around at the cells, he said, "But I never imagined these surroundings."

"I will pay you back, of course."

He scoffed at the suggestion. "But just what did you get up to? The sergeant at the front desk seemed to think you were a danger to the empire. He even warned me to stay well-clear of the bars."

Mina smiled, though wearily. She hadn't slept a wink—the other miscreants in the neighboring cells had snored, sworn, and bellowed all night—and she felt rank and disheveled in the clothes she'd worn to the rally. Even the beribboned WSPU badge she wore—purple for the royal blood that flowed in the veins of every suffragette, white for purity, and green for the hope of spring—looked forlorn and askew.

"You're quite safe," she replied. "They've knocked the stuffing out of me for the time being. I just want to get back to the Barnardo Home, clean myself up, and get some rest."

"They are vetting my check and credentials," Stoker explained, "and will release you just as soon as they are assured that you are leaving under the positive recognizance of an upright citizen like myself."

"Upright citizen?" she said, with a chuckle. "Do they know they're talking to the author of *Dracula*?"

"Let us hope not."

But when he asked what she had done to warrant imprisonment, she could hardly say herself. It had all happened so fast. The stage had been set up in its usual spot in Hyde Park, but the crowd had been somewhat unruly from the start. Several of the women who had spoken before her had been heckled by a gang of drunken louts, whom even the police could not keep in line, and more than once a projectile—a rotten tomato or a spoiled spud—had narrowly missed the head of a speaker bent over the microphone, reading a speech. That was one more advantage to her own, more freewheeling oratorical method—with only some notes to guide her, she was able to keep her head up and see what, if anything, might be coming. The subject of her remarks was not only the need to enact women's suffrage, but also the salubrious effects it would have on the problem of child welfare, which she dealt with every day in the Barnardo Home where she was employed. At the microphone, she was recounting her most recent foray into the streets, gathering homeless children, when a brute in a costermonger's smock shouted something inane, and she had, as usual, ignored it.

Which only incensed him more.

"Come to my street sometime, and I'll show you somethin' you ain't seen!" he hollered, to the amusement of his pals. "And it won't be no beggars nor brats!"

Focusing her thoughts, she had continued to describe the privations and abuse suffered by these innocents, until, happening to glance in the costermonger's direction, she saw him pretending to shake a tambourine and heard him cry, "Ain't you a gyppo? I got a fortune needs tellin'!"

The next speaker touched her elbow and said, "Maybe you'd better stop before it gets worse!" But at that moment, a clump of dried horse dung flew into their faces, spattering them both and igniting such a riot of laughter from the hooligans that Mina saw nothing but red. She had leaped from the stage and into the melee, clawing her way to the costermonger with nothing but her nails and her fury to cut a path. Two constables were converging on the same spot from other directions, but before they could intervene, Mina had fetched the man such a swat to the side of his head that he had tumbled into the arms of his fellow hecklers, slack jawed with amazement. The moment the police arrived, he saw his advantage and complained loudly about the attack.

"For no reason!" he insisted. "Hit me, she did, for no reason at all! Arrest the Gypsy bitch!"

"That's enough outta you," the senior constable said, "or we'll be arresting you, too!"

"You're arresting *me*?" Mina protested. "I've been under attack for the last ten minutes, and you didn't do a thing!"

"And now you're tellin' us how to do our job?" the constable said, nodding to the other policeman as he drew her arms behind her to put on the handcuffs.

A lady at the podium loudly objected, but she, too, was drowned out by the jeering mob, and Mina soon found herself jolting along in the back of a police wagon, and then—after she'd been allowed a few minutes in the lavatory to clean herself off—summarily deposited in the jail cell of the Marylebone Police Station. Allowed to send word to one person, Bram had immediately come to mind.

"You can go now," the sergeant said, though it sounded more like a threat than a deliverance, as he came to unlock the cell. "You'll be notified of any further proceedings."

"What further proceedings?" Stoker asked.

"Depends on Mr. Jenkins, the gentleman that got hit."

"Gentleman!" Mina objected, but Stoker put a hand on her arm to quiet her down and escorted her out of the police station. He seemed to regard the whole thing as vaguely amusing, which at first she resented, but by the time they had made their way through the now-dark streets and settled into a booth in the restaurant of a nearby hotel, she, too, had begun to see it with some detachment.

"Good God, I must look a mess," she said.

"I would recommend removing the rally badge."

"Why?" she said, a trifle defensively.

"Let's just say it is no longer unsullied."

Glancing down, she saw what he was referring to and quickly unfastened it from her bodice. "I'm so sorry I dragged you into any of this. What must you think of me?"

"I think the world of you—you know that."

She did, but there was many a night when she lay awake wondering how her life had taken the turns it had. The day Cruikshank had made her his assistant in the Middle Eastern antiquities department at the British Museum, she had foreseen a bright future, working in a field for which her whole life had prepared her. But what it had not prepared her for was his retirement. Within weeks of his departure, the son of a minor aristocrat, with his Cambridge degree clutched tight in his fist, had been appointed in his place, and Mina had found herself relegated to the most menial tasks that could be devised. Sent clear across town to pick up a riding habit, she had returned with a pair of boots, a whip, and her letter of resignation, which had been accepted on the spot.

It was Eli Strauss, of all people, who had set her on the path that had landed her in jail. Although she had moved out of his tenement on

Raven Row, she had not lost touch with him, or the issues with which he was involved. When the Jewish garment workers of the East End joined the strike that was begun by the Jewish garment workers of the West End, she had marched with them in the streets, and when the suffragettes, 300,000 strong, had come together on Women's Sunday in June of 1908, to demand the right to vote, she had been among them, too. She wasn't scaling the Carpathian Mountains anymore, but she was using her energy and indignation to fight for causes worth fighting for, and for people who could not necessarily do so themselves.

"And who are the most vulnerable of all?" Strauss had said to her in a conversation they held after a riotous union meeting one night. "The children, that's who."

It had struck an immediate chord. Ever since the events at the mission house, she had been haunted by the fate of those children who had died, and the ones who even now roamed the streets as orphans and outcasts, starved and neglected in every manner. Imperial England ruled the globe, but in Mina's view it had much to answer for right here at home. The Barnardo Homes, a charitable organization founded by a philanthropist named Dr. Thomas Barnardo in 1866, took in these poor and unfortunate children, and for Mina, it was a cause worth devoting her life to.

Even if it did lead to the occasional arrest.

"I hate to ask, but will this brief incarceration affect your employment?" Stoker said, and Mina smiled.

"It's not the first time. I'll be back this evening."

"But how do they feel about somewhat longer leaves of absence?"

Mina cocked her head.

"I was thinking, an ocean cruise. To New York. All expenses paid."

The waitress took their order for tea and sandwiches, and when she left, Mina said, "What are you talking about? I hardly need to leave the country on charges like these."

"You might consider it, when I tell you who else will be aboard this particular ship."

"You're serious."

"As can be."

She had known Bram for many years now, and she knew when he was being jocular and when he was not. The look on his face, already haggard from his bad health, was particularly telling. But when he began the story of Stead's visit to his home, and the news that the man had conveyed, she was thunderstruck. "It cannot be."

But Stoker, his eyes bloodshot and weary, held her gaze, and said, "Can you say, with any conviction, that the likes of Bartholomew Thorne and his sister would be incapable of such a feat?"

"But the fire . . ."

"Left no trace of either one of their bodies. Just the twisted wreckage of her wheelchair, and his pocket watch."

"But didn't you say that you had choked the life out of him, up in the Matron's flat?"

"And didn't you say that Davey's ghost had told you the spirit of the Matron had not moved on?"

Stoker shrugged, and drained the last of the tea from his cup. The tremor in his hand, she noticed, had grown worse. "This would not be the first time they had tricked people into believing an untruth. Did your father die of a contagion, as was first claimed, or from an accidental fall? They say whatever is expeditious and advantageous at the time."

Mina found herself struggling to accept the shocking news, at the same time that a part of her found it utterly plausible. If any two people could carry off such an escape and resurrection, it was the Thornes. Their evil knew no bounds.

"According to Stead," Stoker said, "their ship sails in two days, from Southampton. I have already taken the last available stateroom in first class."

"What exactly are you suggesting?"

Stoker looked down, swirling the dregs in his teacup. "First, you have to understand one thing. For all intents and purposes, my life is over."

The moment she started to protest, he put up a hand to stop her.

"I've written my books, I've done my best, but there's not much left in me. What there is, I would like to expend on some truly useful, even noble, purpose. Preventing Bartholomew and Winifred Thorne from exporting their murderous rituals to another continent, where they can practice them anew on other unwitting victims, seems tailor-made for that."

She could not disagree.

"But given my present infirmities, I may require some assistance. That, of course, is where you come in."

Before he could even put the question, she knew the answer she would give. It wasn't even a hard decision. Taking the last of the cucumber sandwiches from the plate, she said, "I'll need to alert the Barnardo Home to my temporary absence."

CHAPTER FIFTY-THREE

"Mind the ruts," the man said, as the porter pushed the wheelchair along the wooden planks of the crowded quay. The man's sister was clutching the chair's metal arms for dear life.

"That I am, Mr. North, that I am, but there's plenty of 'em."

"I can see that." What he could also see just ahead was a mighty throng of passengers, easily two thousand strong, all clutching tickets and handbags, or trailed by stewards and servants pushing barrows and carts of luggage in a veritable maelstrom of wild activity. Several of the ladies cradled in their arms small, yapping dogs. Life aboard the ship had better be a good deal more tranquil than the scene of its departure, or he would regret having made this decision.

It hadn't been easy. For seventeen years now, he had been plotting one move or the next. Having worn out their welcome, as it were, in London, he and his sister had absconded first to Edinburgh, where the weather was even worse than it had been in London; then the South of France, where Winifred found herself increasingly annoyed by the people, the language, the sunshine, and the occasional scorpion in the flower beds. Switzerland had been a calamity. "Why do people put up with so many mountains?" she had complained.

The difficulty of arranging what they had come to call their "reinvigorations," in such a disparate number of locales, had become intolerable, too. In New York, or its immediate environs—he had heard good things about a place called the Hudson River Valley—he hoped to find new and fresh terrain, a region where the erstwhile Bartholomew and Winifred Thorne had never been seen or heard of, and the Norths—Edgar and Augusta—would be readily accepted and left to their own devices.

To that end, he carried the most crucial items of their trade—the Canopic jars, the papyri, the book of incantations—in a leather satchel that he would not relinquish to anyone for even a moment. And nestled beneath all the rest, in a black velvet pouch, was the most treasured possession of all—the gold box he had rescued from that laughably incompetent Austrian swindler. A short time after their encounter, he'd seen a small item in the paper, mentioning that collection men from the Langham Hotel had caught up to him, and he'd been summarily deported to the Continent, where even now he was undoubtedly cheating some old baroness out of her last pfennig.

"This way to the first-class gangway," the porter said, using the chair as a sort of battering ram as he led them through the surging crowd of boarding passengers and well-wishers there to see their friends and family off. The white and black ship, even by the grand standards of the day, was massive—almost nine hundred feet long and eleven stories high—with four immense black-topped funnels rising above its ten decks, and gleaming as only a ship on its maiden voyage can do. There was a special sense of excitement in the crowd, that only grew louder as the funnels blew preliminary clouds of steam, or clanking anchor chains were raised. Thorne and his sister bumped their laborious way up the long ramp, the porter huffing and puffing, and eventually were shown down an endless, plushly carpeted corridor, to their stateroom on B deck, the premier location.

"They'll be pushing off in about ten more minutes," the porter said, "if you'd like to take a place on the promenade deck and wave goodbye."

For now, Thorne was content to look about the suite, and find that it met with his highest expectations. The company brochures had done it justice. The walls were polished mahogany, the beds were covered with satin bedspreads, the artwork on the wall—a vaguely Flemish landscape—was tasteful. The private bath, when he poked his head in, was tight, but clean and utilitarian, with a marble sink, and a button to call for immediate service of any kind.

Finally, and most important of all, was the wall safe, into which he placed the contents of his leather satchel, spinning the dial twice and firmly shaking the handle to make sure the lock was secured.

"Shall we go outside for the departure?" he asked.

"I've had enough of those to last a lifetime," Winifred said, slowly and unsteadily rising from her chair. "You go, I'll unpack."

Thorne was like a wolf that way—as soon as he arrived anywhere, he needed to survey his surroundings and mark off his territory. The staterooms on this level were the most coveted, as they had their own exclusive deck, and he found a couple of hundred other first-class passengers, all well-dressed and accoutered, standing at the railing, some waving handkerchiefs, others smoking cigars in the cool but bright April day. Wherever he went, however, he kept a close eye out for anyone who might have known his former self. The assumption of his death had, of course, put a stop to most such suspicions that might arise—but he had taken additional precautions, nonetheless. He couldn't very well disguise the imposing figure he cut, but he had exchanged his full beard for a neat little Vandyke that still concealed his square chin, and wore his brown hair in a longer fashion—a habit he'd adopted in France. He dressed in a slightly more bohemian way; his ties had been replaced by cravats, and his Savile Row suits had been retired in favor of more trimly tailored waistcoats from Italian tailors.

After a series of shrieking whistles, and three sustained blasts from the ship's deafening horn, the boat slipped away from the dock and was drawn toward the sea by tugboats. The people on the wharves below, who looked small to begin with, became tiny; the customs buildings and warehouses took on the aspect of matchboxes; the other boats in their berths looked like mere cockleshells. Green water rolled away in white billows from the sides of the ship as the cries of those on shore faded away, replaced by the cawing of the gulls swooping around the masts and funnels.

"They say we'll make the crossing in seven days," he overheard an elderly gentleman say to his wife. "Plenty of time to make the rehearsal dinner."

"Provided they haven't come to their senses and broken it off," she said, and they both laughed.

They were almost out of the harbor, passing the last and most extended of the piers when Thorne saw something strange. Another large ship, with *New York* emblazoned on its side, was bobbing on the swell created by their ship's passing—but bobbing so uncontrollably that, with a report as sharp as a gunshot, it suddenly snapped its hawsers, the thick ropes lashing into the air like snakes from the head of a monstrous Medusa. He saw people on the pier running to escape, and one woman, too slow on her feet, lashed flat to the ground.

There were murmured exclamations from the others lingering on the promenade deck who had witnessed it, and even more when they saw the *New York*, drifting slowly, inexorably, toward them.

"What are they doing?" one man declared. "We're going to collide!"

But Thorne could see that the other boat was simply caught in the overwhelming suction created by the passing of the gigantic steamer, incapable of mustering enough power to withstand its irresistible pull.

There was a juddering under his feet, and a tilting of the deck, as the liner turned hard astern to avoid the imminent collision with the *New York*. One of the tugs, meanwhile, had managed to come around from behind, throw a chain to the overpowered boat, and was now pouring on all engines to drag it away. At best, the effort seemed to have stopped its forward progress, holding it in place just long enough for the bigger ship to sail serenely past, a giant brushing a gnat from its sleeve, and out into the channel, bound first for Cherbourg and Queensland, then on to its final destination in the United States.

The crisis averted, Thorne observed the other passengers heading inside to their cabins or the main saloons—"That was a close call," one declared, while another said, "This calls for a drink!"—but among the few deckhands he could see, there was an expression of dark foreboding. Sailors were a notoriously superstitious lot, and this was a less than auspicious launching for a ship so grandly titled the RMS *Titanic*.

CHAPTER FIFTY-FOUR

"How ever did you afford something like this?" Mina said, whirling around in the sitting room that separated the bedrooms on either side. There was even a little fireplace with a cozy electric glow emanating from behind an iron grate.

"It took a bit of improvising," Stoker said, keeping to himself the gory details, which included pawning his best cufflinks, cashing in an insurance policy, and begging a loan off William Stead, the man who had put him on to the scent in the first place.

"I was sure you would like to know about the Thornes," Stead had said, "but not to the point of booking passage on the same ship. Why would you want to do that?"

"I have my reasons."

"That you must. Then I shall see you en route!"

Stoker had figured that if the Thornes were traveling on this ship, they would be traveling in the style to which they were accustomed. If he hoped to get within striking distance, he had to have access to all the private salons and other amenities to which only the first-class passengers would be admitted. Aboard an ocean liner, he knew from experience, the social hierarchy was strictly observed.

But he had not seen Thorne, or his sister, yet. The boat train from Waterloo Station had been uncharacteristically delayed, which had given him all the more time to reflect on what he had so impulsively done. By now, his wife had surely found the letter he had left propped against his bedside lamp. In it, he had tried to express the gratitude he felt to her for having become his wife, and mother to their son, while acknowledging the difficulties they had encountered in their marriage. "For that, I assume more than my share of the blame; in some ways we were ill-suited," he had written. But he was embarking now on a journey from which, he confessed, he might not return—it was a journey as important as anything he had ever done in his life and, as he hastily assured her, if he returned safely from it, this would be their last separation. "The summer of our life may be past, but I wish for nothing more fervently than to spend the winter of it beside a glowing hearth, with you." He had signed it, "Your Loving Bram."

Arriving behind their time, he and Mina had had to scurry up the gangway as smoke billowed from the stacks and horns blasted. The second officer, his dark-blue cap tightly perched on his head, cautioned them, "Nary a second to spare, but welcome aboard," as he strode past on his way to the bridge.

Glancing out the porthole now, Stoker could see a great expanse of gray sea and frothy white waves. When Mina had gone into her chamber to unpack her things, he went into his own, taking pains to conceal in a drawer of the bureau the veritable pharmacopeia he needed to ease his pains, clear his mind, control the shaking in his hands or his legs. Once a giant on the rugby field, he now felt himself to be a bundle of twigs barely held together with string and glue. Thomas Hardy, who had once attended a Beefsteak dinner, had observed that every man knows and marks his birthday each year, but can take no notice of his deathday, though it comes round with the same regularity. What was his, Stoker wondered? He guessed it could not be terribly far off, and though he had lost the common dread of it any man feels, it had been ages since he felt what he felt now—and that was a sense of purpose.

It was brought home to him by the Webley revolver he removed from the shoulder holster he had worn under his coat. He was wondering what to do with it when his eye fell on the wall safe. Of course.

But he had just opened it when Mina rapped on the open door and said, "What are you planning to do with that? Shoot him?"

Without turning around, he placed the gun and coiled holster in the safe. There was just enough room.

Perching on the edge of his bed, she said, "In all the haste of this excursion, that's the one thing we haven't really discussed."

He locked the safe.

"What is our plan, Bram? Even if we find Thorne and his sister, what do we do next? Do we simply shadow them, and make sure they have no victim in their sights? Or do we unmask them on the spot, call them out for their crimes and arrest them?"

"We have no authority to do something like that."

"I was speaking in hyperbole. Do we follow them off the boat in New York and alert the local constabulary? And if so, to what? There's no record of their crimes, no proof, and they don't even bear the names they once had. Whatever their nefarious plans might be, how can we stop them?"

He sat beside her on the edge of the bed, took off his glasses, and passed his hand across his eyes. He was suddenly bone-tired; all the activity of the day—racing for the train, and thence to the ship, climbing the gangway—while taking away nothing of his determination, had all but drained him of energy. "We can deprive them of the tools of their practice, for a start. Whatever scrolls or incantations, sacred sands or jars, they possess, we can consign to the vast ocean around us."

"But they can replace them."

"Maybe so, maybe not. It might not be so easy, especially from the States. Those items are rare, perhaps even unique. And while aboard ship, we can keep an eye on them. If we see them making any design upon a passenger, among first class or steerage—it makes no difference at all—we can step in."

"But that's only for the next seven days. Then we land."

Here, his own thoughts, too, came to an abrupt halt. It was as if he were gazing into a crystal ball that had suddenly become occluded; he could not see beyond it. What *would* he do? The prospect of the Thornes entering a new continent with their savage schemes intact, their evil objectives unhindered, was beyond contemplation. He pictured the revolver lying in the safe. Could he do it? Would he?

Perhaps sensing that she had pushed him too far, Mina put a hand on his and said, "I'm tired."

He knew she was saying this for his benefit.

"I think I'll take a nap before getting all dressed up for dinner. Why don't you take one, too?"

"I think you're right," he said, "though with one caveat."

"What is that?"

"On the first night of a cruise, it is the custom to dress informally. Tomorrow night, you may wear your diamond tiara and sable stole. That's when full dress becomes en règle."

She laughed. "Thanks for keeping me from committing a faux pas."

"We live to serve."

She laughed again, and rising, kissed him on the top of his head, and went into her bedroom, closing the door behind her.

The impression of her lips, even on the crown of his head, stayed with him for several seconds more.

CHAPTER FIFTY-FIVE

While one hand held to the wheel, Second Officer Charles Lightoller—who should have been first officer, he thought with some annoyance still—raised the other to shield his eyes from the last rays of the setting sun. The sky had turned a fiery red, then blazing orange, and now a pale pink. The sea that lay before him, seen from the bridge, was as smooth and reflective as glass.

"A beautiful sunset, wasn't it, Mr. Lightoller?" he heard the captain say. "They can't ask for a better one than that."

"No, sir, they cannot."

Captain Edward J. Smith stepped beside him, stroking his bristly white beard. "Although I wouldn't bruit about it, I suspect we'll make New York by Tuesday night, rather than Wednesday morning."

"It all depends on the pack ice and the bergs."

"Yes, there's that, of course. We'll have to keep a careful eye out, particularly in the Devil's Hole," referring to an especially hazardous region of the North Atlantic route. Glancing at Lightoller's chest, he said, "Where are your binoculars?"

"I'm afraid they've gone missing."

"Missing?"

"When the new chief officer was installed yesterday, and the roster was adjusted accordingly"—and there was the sore point—"Mr. Blair was dismissed, and he took with him, quite by accident I'm sure, the only pair available."

"That is rum luck," Captain Smith harrumphed.

"Yes, sir."

"Well, then, make extra sure to keep Frederick Fleet in the crow's nest, on night watch. He's got the sharpest eyes on board."

"Aye aye, sir."

The sky was turning an inky indigo by the time Captain Smith continued his rounds, and there wasn't much of a moon. The ship's wheel stood on a brass pedestal, with the most advanced hydraulic control system, or telemotor, built into its base; beneath the soles of his shoes, Lightoller could feel its effects in the powerful thrumming of the two triple-expansion engines down below. Among the most powerful ever installed in the liner of any fleet, he could see the white froth at the bow as the ship sliced its way through the water as easily as a knife might cut a wedding cake. They were keeping to a steady nineteen knots, though he knew that, if pushed to it, the engines could easily muster twenty-three. He was riding a prize stallion—and as someone who had done his share of ranching, too, he knew what he was talking about. Born and raised in Chorley, Lancashire, to a family that ran cotton-spinning mills, the one thing he knew for sure was that he had had no interest in being tied down to a factory job. He wanted to travel, to see the world, and at thirteen he had gone on a four-year apprenticeship at sea. In the wildly checkered career that followed, he had not only sailed all over the globe, but wound up doing everything from cattle wrangling in Alberta, Canada, to mining for gold in the Yukon. But always, he had returned to the life of a sailor, and now, at thirty-eight, here he was, at the wheel of the greatest ocean liner that had ever been built. So far, it had all been a grand, and successful, adventure, but what, he wondered as he gazed out to sea, could ever cap this?

CHAPTER FIFTY-SIX

The scale of the ship was so grand, Mina could barely take it all in. There were dining saloons and cafés, smoking rooms and libraries, palm courts and card rooms, a gymnasium and a Turkish bath, a squash court and a saltwater swimming pool, kennels for the many dogs brought aboard, and three elevators to take the guests from the lower depths of the ship to the sunnier climes of the A and B decks. Everything was spanking new—indeed, the smell of the white paint and linseed oil still lingered in the air—lending the ship the ambiance, not so much of a newly christened royal mail steamer (thus the initials RMS before its name), but of an opulent hotel in a bustling city. Contributing to that impression was the *Titanic*'s strange imperturbability: the deck was as even and unswaying as the pavement in Mayfair. There was barely any suggestion of movement, and yet, if she looked out to sea, Mina could see the white foam churning along the sides of the hull as the ship plowed steadily across the cold Atlantic waters.

Even Bram, whose health she had watched steadily decline over the past few years, seemed newly invigorated by the salt breeze and the sheer adventure of being at sea. Although they'd spent the late afternoon and evening trekking up and down, climbing grand staircases inside, or strolling along the wide and open decks, his cane—a blackthorn stick that looked more like a shillelagh—helped to keep him steady and marching along at a robust pace. His eyes, which had been blood-shot and lackluster for years, had their old twinkle in them again—and they were certainly alert, searching among the hordes of passengers aboard, and in all the many public areas of the boat, for any sign of Bartholomew Thorne and his sister.

But so far, to no avail. Once, Mina had spotted a wheelchair being pushed along the far end of the promenade deck and had grabbed Bram's elbow, but on closer inspection, it had turned out to be a per-ambulator holding both a baby and a Pomeranian. Mina had dutifully smiled, and introduced herself, as she and Bram had previously agreed upon, as a niece accompanying her dear uncle to New York on business.

The woman, perhaps accustomed to hearing such stories among the cosmopolitan set, said to Bram, "How fortunate that you have such a lovely young niece to help you with your business." And then sailed on.

Mina and Bram shared a glance, and once she was out of earshot, shared laughter, too.

"Perhaps we need a better cover story," Bram said.

"Such as what? We are colleagues chasing down a pair of villains intent on stealing the souls of children and the infirm?"

"That might be a bit much."

"At least she said I was young and lovely. At my age, I don't hear that so often anymore."

"You should. You should."

It was no secret to Mina that Bram nursed a long-standing passion for her. But she also knew that, out of a fundamental sense of propriety coupled with his respect for her and her sensibilities, he would never have acted upon it, not back when he was hale and hearty, and certainly not now. She loved him, too, but in the way of that uncle they were pretending him to be. Ever since her return to England, seventeen years before, he had been her Rock of Gibraltar, the one person she could count on, no matter what life threw at her, to be available for comfort, counsel, or assistance of any kind.

And life had thrown plenty at her.

Not only had she lost her position at the museum, but she had also lost at the game of love. Oh, there had been plenty of overtures at first, but once she had entered her thirties—well past her prime, in the view of most men—she had begun to be treated as if she should have already resigned herself to spinsterhood. Nor was there a suitable spot for her in the rigid class and social structure of the city. She was at once too exotic (and that was the *kind* word for it) to be an acceptable match for a gentleman, and far too cultivated and intelligent to be a partner to anyone who wasn't. For a time, she had been courted by a Harley Street physician, but of a decidedly too feminine nature himself; and later by a roguish viscount, who had had the temerity to bring her to a weekend party at the family seat, where his mother had frozen her at the door with a stare worthy of a gorgon.

"Don't let her frighten you," the viscount had whispered in her ear. "Give it right back to her."

But that was not a match Mina wanted to engage in. Worse, she felt that she had been brought there deliberately to bait the woman.

More and more, she had retreated into her work, both at the Barnardo Home and on behalf of those causes in which she believed. The right of workers to unionize. The improvement of the living quarters in the East End. The right of women to cast a vote in parliamentary elections. It was, all things considered, a full life, and a rewarding one . . . but lonely.

"Do you think it's possible that we have made a mistake?" Bram said, with a heavy sigh as he eased himself onto one of the chaise longues that lined the deck. "Is it possible that Stead was wrong, and they are not on this boat at all?"

The thought had occurred to her, too. But what a monumental miscalculation it would have been. "We could ask the chief steward about them."

"No, no. I don't want any chance of their getting wind of an inquiry."

"Then we shall keep an eye out all day tomorrow, and if worse comes to worst, we shall undoubtedly find them at the first formal dinner. You said it yourself—that's the grand occasion on these voyages."

"True," he mumbled, settling back in the chair, "true." The cane propped against the armrest, he folded his hands across his chest, and in less than a minute, he had fallen asleep. The night was cool, but not cold, and she unrolled the blue wool blanket—every chaise had one, with a white star emblazoned on it—and draped it across the top of his overcoat. Then she took another, threw it across her legs, and reclined on the neighboring chaise, sheltered in the shadows of the boat deck, listening to the steady susurration of the waves and the rippling of the night wind in the rigging. It had been an exhausting day, and a short rest before heading back to the confines of their stateroom might do them both good.

How long she dozed that way, she couldn't tell, but when she awoke, her feet were numb, her cheeks were cold, and something was making a creaking noise as it moved along the deck. She glanced at Bram, who was still as a stone, the ruff of his brown beard protruding above the top of the blanket. Then she looked the other way, and saw an indistinct shape coming toward them. It was a wheelchair, with its occupant wearing what looked like a raised black mantilla. A tall man in a camel's hair coat was pushing it. Her heart froze in her chest, but she lay perfectly still, barely breathing under the blanket. When they drew virtually abreast of her, the woman said, "Enough. I'm getting up."

"Now's a time as good as any," he said, pushing the chair to a stop at the railing. "Everyone's in bed."

Mina recognized their voices, and pulled the blanket up to just below her eyes.

Wobbling a bit, the woman stood, then leaned on the iron rail.

"Still weak?" the man said.

"No, it's just from sitting in that damn chair so long."

"I don't want you getting over confident."

"No fear of that in your company."

He drew a silver case from his breast pocket, snapped it open, and a few seconds later Mina saw an orange flame cupped in his hands as he lit a cigar. Even the smell of it, a tobacco tinged with rum, she remembered.

"So far, so good," he said, between puffs. "Not a soul we ever knew on board."

"It's only the first night. Give it time."

"The Thornes are dead, no matter what anyone might conjecture. Only the Norths live on."

"And on, and on, and on."

He chuckled, spitting a bit of tobacco from his lip.

Other words were exchanged, but she couldn't hear them in the stiffening wind. The tarps on the lifeboats crackled, the ropes on the davits strained and creaked. When the smoke from the cigar drifted their way, she sensed Bram stirring. His head rolled on the chaise, and she put out a hand and gently laid it atop his own. His eyes opened, and she put a finger to her lips, slowly shaking her head and glancing at the rail. He looked that way and immediately took her meaning.

"The wind's picking up," Thorne said, and his sister plopped back down in the chair. "Time to call it a night."

"Time for a cup of hot bouillon," she said.

"Whatever you wish."

"I wish we were there already."

He turned the chair around, still oblivious to his witnesses.

"By the way, did you let it out tonight?" she asked.

"No, perhaps tomorrow."

Let what out? Mina wondered. Had they brought a dog on board?

Thorne pushed his sister back the way they had come, and only when they were well out of sight and earshot did Mina let the blanket drop from her face, her fingers stiff from the cold. Stoker audibly exhaled.

"Stead was not mistaken," Mina said. "We are on the right boat."

"Most assuredly," Stoker concurred. *But those two,* he thought, *must never get off it.*

CHAPTER FIFTY-SEVEN

The next night, when the bugle sounded at 7 p.m. sharp—playing, appropriately enough, "The Roast Beef of Old England"—Stoker was already dressed in his formal attire. With a lifetime of dinner parties and theatrical events behind him, he could tie his bow tie, put in his shirt studs, and fasten his cufflinks in the dark, if need be. And in this instance he was champing at the bit to get to dinner—not from hunger, but from the desire to see his quarry in the full light of the first-class dining saloon. Although he had been on the lookout again all day, the Thornes had either eluded him or remained holed up in their cabin.

When he stepped into the small sitting room of his suite, he had to wait only seconds before he heard a rustling behind the opposite door, saw the handle turn, and watched Mina appear, her jet-black hair swept back from her shoulders, wearing a long lavender gown with delicate silver lace passementerie on the sleeves and bodice. He had never seen her look so lovely, and she must have registered his reaction. Blushing, she lowered her eyes, and said, "A gift from the viscount, for our weekend in the country."

"And the earrings?"

"From the physician," she said, self-consciously touching one of the dangling pearls. "God, you're starting to make me feel like Madame de Pompadour."

Offering her his arm, he said, "And you make me feel like Louis Quinze."

Up and down the corridors, like butterflies escaping their cocoons, women were emerging in elegant evening dresses, the billowing silks and satins swishing and rustling, as they made their way toward the grand staircase leading to the dining room. The men accompanying them were in black tuxedos, or white tie and tails, some twisting the ends of their moustaches into neat points, others shooting their cuffs. Stoker jauntily wielded his blackthorn stick as he and Mina sauntered past the ornate clock—set into a carved relief of Honor and Glory crowning Time—at the top of the steps; then down through the Palm Court, past the trio playing Puccini on piano, violin, and cello; and into the dining room, where the tables gleamed with crisp white napery, sparkling crystal and silver, and upright menu cards, all under an elaborately plastered white ceiling. The maître d's and waiters, also in white shirts and black jackets, stood at attention along the peripheries, hands folded, nodding and smiling as the guests entered and took their seats for the first formal evening of the voyage. There was room for five hundred of them at a time.

"Stoker!" he heard from a table to his far right, and turned to see Stead gesturing at a pair of empty chairs at his table. "We've saved these for you."

Already seated beside Stead was a middle-aged woman with a broad, open face under a large hat. Stoker, a keen judge of these things, took her for a wealthy American at first sight. His suspicions were confirmed the moment she introduced herself—"Margaret Brown, Denver, Colorado."—and shook his hand firmly, twice, as if it were a pump handle. Looking Mina over approvingly, she declared, "And you take the cake, my dear. Just stunning. Any chance you've got some Indian blood in you? I have."

Stoker was momentarily nonplussed. Coming from an Englishwoman, the remark would have been considered unspeakably rude, but offered as it was, so frankly and openly, he could only laugh, as did Mina.

"My mother was Romany."

"That's another name for Gypsy?"

"Yes."

"Good. Then you and Stead are going to get along fine, as he's already promised to give me a tarot card reading tomorrow night."

For Stoker, the only problem was that his chair did not face out into the room, but he couldn't very well ask everyone to switch seats. He'd have to rely on Mina, who had a partial view of the entry, through which dozens of the other first-class travelers were still passing. But what, he wondered, would he do? Would the very sight of Thorne bring his blood to a boil? If they saw each other, would Thorne even recognize him? The years had not been kind to him, Bram knew that much; it was, he thought ruefully, the only advantage to his disintegration.

The musical trio struck up a German waltz as the waiters poured wine, took dining orders, made notes of any special requests. These were guests accustomed to getting exactly what they wanted, and the fact that they were at sea made no difference; if anything, it heightened their expectations, as the culinary experience aboard these grand ocean liners was a matter of great pride. The most important choice, for the shipping line, whether it was Cunard or White Star or Hamburg-Amerika, was the captain of the ship, but the second was the master chef, whose reputation could actually influence bookings. And on that score, again, the *Titanic* excelled, for in addition to the main dining saloons for each class of passenger, the famous London restaurateur Luigi Gatti presided over separate establishments, the Café Parisien and the adjoining À La Carte, for passengers who wanted an even more intimate and extravagantly priced meal, served among ivy-covered trellises emulating a boîte you might find on the Left Bank. Stoker hoped the Thornes had not chosen to dine there tonight.

"Have you been checking Captain Smith's postings so far?" Stead asked him, and Stoker had to confess that he had not. He'd had other things on his mind.

"Each day outside the purser's office, he posts a notice of the miles traveled so far. Yesterday, we made 484 miles, at an average speed of twenty knots, and if the weather holds fair, and the sea stays as calm as it has, we should beat the record set by the *Olympic*."

The sea had indeed been calm, calmer than Stoker, who had made many crossings, had ever before seen it.

"If you ask me," Mrs. Brown interjected, "what's the rush?" Flicking her napkin and taking in the elegant room and exquisitely attired clientele, she said, "It doesn't get much better than this."

A waiter placed before her a dozen pepper-dusted oysters a la Russe on a bed of shaved ice, and after glancing around to make sure that everyone else had also been served their first course, she dug in with gusto. "Aren't oysters the best?" she confided to Mina, leaning over so far the brim of her hat brushed Mina's hair. "The Rocky Mountain variety can't hold a candle to them," she said with a hearty laugh.

Again, it was the sort of remark an English lady would never make, but Mina went along with it, smiling and unruffled. The woman was so guileless, it was impossible to take offense at anything she said. And by the third course—roasted saddle of lamb with mint sauce—Mina had discovered that Mrs. Brown was as ardent an advocate of women's suffrage in America, as Mina was in the United Kingdom. Stoker was happy to see that she had struck up an incipient friendship, especially on a trip whose main burden was so dreadful.

Stead, the inveterate reporter, had apparently been taking copious notes for an account of the great ship's maiden voyage, and was even now jotting down the bill of fare on a tiny notepad. Many publications, on both sides of the Atlantic, featured his every word, even those that he claimed came to him through the spirit of a girl named Julia. She communicated with him through automatic writing and the occasional séance, and he had compiled her messages in a popular book called *After Death*. The reviewers, Stoker recalled, had been as befuddled as he was, that this world-renowned journalist and social crusader should also be so credulous when it came to the spirit world. And hadn't Mrs. Brown already mentioned something about a tarot reading?

Stoker had about given up hope—once more, it seemed that the Thornes had managed to escape him—when he saw Stead looking over at the vestibule and then nodding discreetly at him. The voluble Mrs. Brown was in the middle of another Wild West story, and Mina was paying close attention, but Stoker swiveled in his seat just enough to see the maître d' welcoming their quarry. Thorne, remarkably enough, looked more fit than he had seventeen years before, his hair as thick and deeply brown as ever; he was wearing it longer, along with a close-cropped Vandyke beard, which gave him a positively Mephistophelian air. His sister, though still in her wheelchair, had also withstood the ravages of time; her skin was unwrinkled, and her blonde hair was still piled high atop her head. It wasn't just that they had been unaffected by the passage of the years—it was as if they had been able to turn the clock back altogether.

But at what terrible cost, and to how many, had that unnatural feat been accomplished?

They were being shown to a table in the main concourse, but Thorne shook his head and pointed instead to an empty table for two at the most remote corner of the room; the maître d' gestured for the second chair to be whisked away so that the wheelchair could be drawn up in its place. They took their seats, bent their heads to study the menu, and dispatched their server, presumably to fill their wine order.

By now, Mina had noticed them, too, and she looked at Stoker not only to confirm his sighting, but as if to reassure him that he hadn't lost his wits; she shared his shock and horror.

"Friends of yours?" Mrs. Brown said, having realized that she'd lost her audience.

"I believe I knew them in a previous life," Stoker replied, and she laughed, smacking the table with an open palm.

"Well, then, Stead here is your man. Either he'll know all about it, or he'll dispatch his spirit girl, Julia, to go find out."

The next course arrived—calvados-glazed duck breast—as Stead launched into an explanation of reincarnation theory and the transmigration of souls. Stoker listened with half an ear, his thoughts focused instead on the couple he had just seen. Although he had come across them on deck the night before, that sighting had been in the dark, and somehow it had seemed unreal to him, like a bad dream. It was not until this minute, when he had watched them traverse the dining room in the full glare of the electric chandeliers, that it had been brought fully home to him that Bartholomew Thorne and his sister were no phantoms or figments of his imagination. Though traveling under assumed names, they were alive and well, dining under the same roof he was, listening to the same strains of the same trio.

He was reminded, strangely, of a scene from his novel, when Professor Van Helsing first confronts the evil Count Dracula. It had been so simple to write. But now, in real life, could Stoker display the same bravery and unswerving purpose as his vampire hunter had?

CHAPTER FIFTY-EIGHT

Clear sailing, Thorne thought. They had made it to their table expeditiously, without anyone recognizing them, and without his recognizing anyone else, either. He had noticed a few of the more famous personages on board—the richest man in America, John Jacob Astor, the fashion designer Lucy Duff Gordon, the artist Frank Millet—but only from having seen their pictures in the press. They didn't know him from Adam, and he would not have to field any awkward questions or lingering, puzzled looks. Once, in the Casbah, he had briefly encountered a man who asked him if he might have had a much older brother named Bartholomew Thorne—"Died in a fire, poor chap, along with his maiden sister, years ago."—but he had of course denied it. "Remarkable likeness," the fellow said, wandering off behind his already overburdened dragoman, "remarkable."

As the meal progressed—and the cuisine, he discovered, was unquestionably first rate—he relaxed a bit. He could feel his shoulders falling, his guard going down, too, and he ordered a double cognac with his dessert.

"You'll sleep like the dead tonight," Winifred said.

"Bite your tongue."

Once she had retired for the evening, he put on his overcoat, turned up the collar, and went out onto the promenade deck for a smoke.

The sea was calm. There was almost no wind; it was as if the ship were on some enchanted voyage, impervious to the usual elements. In one pocket of his overcoat, he carried a silver brandy flask, and in the other the gold box—the box that its previous thief had utterly failed to comprehend. But Thorne had understood its import at first glance. Whether it contained the shadow of a pharaoh, or merely that of a ruler of some long-forgotten sect, he couldn't at first say, but he knew it carried a latent charge—even a possible curse. Hadn't his carefully constructed life in London collapsed in short order after acquiring it? Hadn't he almost died at the hands of that theater manager? No, he had suspected its power, and diligently studied the more arcane passages from the ancient Egyptian text, *The Book of Going Forth by Day*, in order to become, as it were, his own Prospero. He could conjure the spirit, and compel it to do his bidding, and in the nocturnal hours free it to roam at will. It was his slave, as he sometimes denigrated it, kept on an invisible chain.

"And how are you enjoying your voyage so far?" he heard, and turned from the rail to see a ship's officer—Charles Lightoller was the name on his badge—making his rounds.

"Everything has been capital, thank you. And we seem to be making great progress."

"That we are. Have you traveled this route before?"

"Yes, but never under such perfect conditions. Not a wave, not a wind. I haven't even seen a speck of ice."

Lightoller nodded. "There is some, ahead, but we are altering our route slightly to the south in order to stay on the safe side."

"A wise decision."

"The captain thinks so."

"And you?"

"Oh, of course, sir. I didn't mean to suggest anything to the contrary. Captain Smith is the best commander in the fleet." Touching the brim of his blue cap, he bade him good-night, and continued his tour of inspection.

Thorne watched him greet a young couple holding a baby, and then bound up the stairs to the bridge. The baby was crying, and the father was gently bouncing him in his arms as they approached. Thorne, whose antenna was well attuned to such things, could hear in the baby's cry a note of some deeper distress; he wasn't just fidgety. He was unwell. The life force in him was weak, the *ka* would be departing soon. As they passed, Thorne gave the worried parents an indulgent smile—*ah, babies, they will have their way, won't they?*—but his nostrils flared as if at the scent of a bloody, raw steak. What short work he and his sister could make of such a creature.

When the family had gone on, he removed the gold box from his pocket, and saw that the latch was open. His slave was out and about, somewhere on the boat. Strictly to reinforce his authority, he recited by heart the ancient spell, calling it home to its sanctuary. When there was no immediate response, he recited it again, and like a dog that did not want to return from the open fields, it dallied again, before bending to his will. Thorne felt a tiny shudder in the box, and the latch clicked shut.

"Good dog," he said.

CHAPTER FIFTY-NINE

Stoker was rapidly becoming his own Hamlet—a would-be man of action, paralyzed by doubt and indecision. Not about the righteousness of his cause—no, never that. But about how to put it into effect, and in such a way that there were as few repercussions as possible to his friends—most notably, Mina—and his family back home. It would not do to have himself caught in, or just after, the act, arrested aboard ship, and then returned, in manacles and disgrace, to face murder charges at the Old Bailey.

And what could his defense in court be? "These two were impostors, Your Honor, villains who, through secret rituals, have long sucked the souls out of innocents in order to prolong their own unspeakably corrupt and contemptible lives. Someone had to put a stop to it." If it weren't for the fact that he knew better—that he knew these preposterous charges were absolutely true—he'd have laughed at them himself. Nor did it help his cause that he was most famous for grisly tales of just such occult practices, and for creating in Count Dracula an indelible monster that still lurked in booksellers' stalls and stalked the floorboards of various stages.

"Your fertile imagination," he could all but hear the magistrate in his fuzzy white wig declaiming, "has, with tragic results, o'ertaken your senses, Mr. Stoker."

Mina, he feared, was even more gravely divided about what to do than he was. It had even occurred to him that she had come along on this voyage less to prosecute the malefactors than to protect him from doing something that would cost him his life, or his freedom.

Which left both of them hobbled in different, but equally deleterious, ways. Hardly an ideal team.

"More and more, I think we should confront them—tell them we are onto their awful game, and that they will be publicly unmasked at the first sign of their continuing in their practices," Mina said, returning to the topic they had repeatedly debated; it was like a bad tooth that they could not stop probing. As they took a turn, arm in arm, around the deck overlooking the stern, they observed the third-class passengers playing games below in the glare of the noonday sun. "We should warn them that we are prepared to take our charges straight to the local police."

"We've been over that. What good would it do? The charges would only make us appear insane."

"I know," she conceded, in frustration. "And once they discovered I'm not your niece, we'd be lucky not to be locked up on a morals charge."

Once more, his thoughts circled around to the one solution they both recognized, but were so reluctant to articulate. Saying it aloud would bring them one big step closer to its inception.

A rubber ball soared up from the open deck below, followed by laughter and cries for help, in several languages, as it rolled close to their feet.

"You may do the honors," Bram said.

Mina retrieved the ball and tossed it down to a curly-haired young man with bare arms and a red kerchief tied around his neck.

"Bellissima!" he cried, kissing his fingertips and grinning up at her.

She smiled, though Bram could see she was trying to conceal it.

"You have an admirer."

"Yes, it is a deep and profound connection we have made."

The man kicked the ball back into play, but not without casting one more longing look at the restricted upper deck.

"How many of them are there aboard?"

"Admirers?" he joked.

"Third class."

"I believe it is well over a thousand."

"And all of them down below decks, in the steerage compartments?"

"I'm told the quarters are nicer than most."

"But still . . ."

He saw that she was looking at a family—father, mother, and four small children, all with their pale, pinched faces tilted toward the welcome rays of the sun. Mediterranean by the looks of them, their clothes were old and patched, their meager lunch of bread and cheese spread on a rag.

"What a strange and terrifying voyage this must be for them," Mina said. "Leaving everything and everyone they know behind, and emigrating to a new world where they have nothing, may know no one, and can't even speak the language."

"I admire their courage."

"And I pity them for their desperation. What privations, what starvation, what atrocities have driven them from their homes and goaded them into the hold of this ship?"

She was right, of course, about most of them, but Stoker also saw something else, particularly among the younger travelers. He saw hope on their faces, a sense of adventure, and great expectations. He saw the young men kicking the ball about, and the girls watching them from the bulwarks, occasionally cheering one or another on. He saw Jews in yarmulkes bent over books, studying as intently as he had once done for his first job in the petty court. He saw a red-haired, freckled girl—a daughter of Eire, if ever he saw one—learning needlework under the guidance of an older woman, who kept correcting her work. And then he saw something else, something unexpected . . . a thin woman in a fur coat and wide-brimmed hat, closely tailed by a steward with a basket over each arm. She was moving slowly among the dozens of third-class passengers enjoying the cool air and bright sun. At each group, she stopped, and often turned to the steward, who then dispensed what looked like napkins filled with sandwiches or scones. She seemed especially attentive to the children or the elderly.

"A good Samaritan," he remarked, and Mina, moving closer to the railing, agreed.

"What a good idea. I wish that I had thought of it."

Stoker had no doubt that she would be doing the same by the next afternoon. As he watched, the woman approached the family with their scraps of bread and cheese, and after a few moments of conversation—did she speak their language?—knelt and handed each delighted child a treat. As their mother looked on with gratitude, the woman picked up the youngest—an infant, in a tattered blue blanket—and cradled it in her arms. She nuzzled its little face and held it close, rocking back and forth. Her face was buried in the folds of its blanket, breathing its very exhalations.

"*Mi potete aiutare?*" he heard, as the ball, picked up by the breeze, once again soared to the upper deck. Below, the same young man, who had probably kicked it there deliberately, waited with hands outstretched and a big smile on his face.

But the woman's eyes had been drawn to the ball, too, and she raised her head, the brim of her hat snapping back in the wind, to see where it went.

The baby in her arms was as still as a stone—it looked narcotized—and her eyes, far from being filled with kindness, were the cold and greedy eyes of a basilisk.

"My God," Mina said, her hands clenching the rail.

Stoker had grasped the metal, too.

"It's Winifred Thorne."

It was too late, Stoker realized, to duck out of sight. Instead, for several seconds they merely held each other's gaze, a cobra confronting a mongoose, until the mother, perhaps sensing something amiss, rose up and snatched her baby back, juggling it in her arms until a wail arose.

The steward leaned forward and said something in Winifred's ear. She hesitated, then nodded. He placed the baskets beside a capstan, made some announcement to those within range, and guided her toward the stairs leading back to the first-class accommodations. She disappeared from Stoker's purview, as the young Italian in the kerchief called again for some help with the ball. This time Stoker retrieved it and threw it down to the plainly disappointed fellow.

Mina had already turned away. "Do you think she recognized us?"

"I do."

"That changes everything, doesn't it?"

"It was inevitable."

But even if the battle was joined, how would it be fought, he wondered. Much less won?

CHAPTER SIXTY

"I tell you, they recognized me."

"From such a distance?" Thorne replied. "The sun in their eyes?"

"They recognized me."

He had warned her to keep a low profile, to stay in the cabin whenever possible. Much as he had wanted, for instance, to take a steam bath, he had avoided doing so, as the close confines encouraged all kinds of conversations. And he had expressly forbidden his sister from mingling with the third-class passengers; no one from first, or even second, class could do that without drawing undue attention. But when had she ever heeded his advice, much less his orders?

And now, the damage was done.

"Is it conceivable that they are simply on board by chance?" she said, slumped back in her wheelchair in the sitting room of their suite. "Could it all be no more than an unlucky coincidence?"

It was, he thought, possible. But he remembered well the violent struggle he had endured with Stoker, the mission house burning down around their very ears; he had played dead just long enough, and convincingly enough, to escape. Had the man picked up his trail again, all these years later, and followed him onto the ship? And with the Gypsy girl in tow?

"What should we do?"

He knew what he would have liked to do. With the recollection of their last encounter firmly in mind, he'd have liked to find Stoker on deck some night, brain him with a grappling hook, and hurl him over the side of the ship. And if the opportunity presented itself, he had no doubt he would do just that.

"We could brazen it out," Winifred continued. "Go about our business, and wait and see if he tries to arrange a confrontation. What could he do, actually? Make an accusation—and of what? No one is going to believe anything that he, or that tart he's traveling with, has to say."

"Or we can simply lie low," he said. The voyage would soon be over, and they'd have a whole new continent on which to lose themselves and start over.

"What, like children afraid of the dark? We've paid a great deal for this trip, and I'm not about to be confined to my cabin by some old prig and his inamorata."

"Do you think that's what she is?" The girl had been devilishly good looking, he remembered that. But had he misjudged Stoker? He had struck him as just the kind of proper gentleman—or fool—who would fail to make the most of what Providence had laid in his path. "Was she still attractive?"

"Oh, good God, Bartholomew, is that all you ever think of? She's not some fetching young thing anymore. It's been almost two decades."

He stroked the neat little beard on his chin meditatively.

"The only woman who looks younger after all this time is sitting right in front of you."

He should have seen that coming.

"And you could show her some respect."

Nothing new there. But he could not quite move past the notion that this Stoker might indeed have made Mina Harcourt his mistress; the very thought was repugnant—as was the aging male body in every particular. The sagging shoulders, the sunken chest. The knobby knees and spindly arms. The balding pate, the cataract-dimmed eyes, the foul breath, pendulous ears, and liver-spotted hands. The prospect of one day becoming so himself had horrified him as long as he could remember; when some of the older masters had come swimming with the boys at boarding school, he had felt a visceral revulsion at the sight of them. Life, he had concluded, was a horror show, and how everyone else was able to endure it was beyond him. He could only thank God—though who knew which one that might be?—that he had discovered the secret of eternal rejuvenation. No, he could not return to the halcyon days of his youth, but he could keep the ongoing sea of troubles at bay. The ravages of time would make no further inroads on him, or on Winifred. Her legs, too badly damaged by a bone cancer before he had found the cure, could never be lastingly restored—a fault for which she often chided him—but in all other respects, she, too, would neither wither nor die. Not so long as there were ancient rites to perform and human sheep to be shorn.

"Well, what'll it be?" Winifred said. "Cower in our room, or go out among the multitudes? Hunt, or be hunted?"

Shaken from his grim reverie, he said he agreed.

"With what?"

"Let's go out." She was right. Why should he be the prey, and Stoker the predator? Why not reverse it? After all, the man had tried to kill him once, and very nearly done it. But where Stoker had failed, perhaps he could succeed. He felt a quickening in his blood. What sweet revenge it would be, to rise from the grave, as it were, and choke the life out of his pursuer. And then, claim an even greater, and unprotected, prize. She'd put up a fight—she wasn't her father's child for nothing—but in the end he'd get what he wanted. He always did.

CHAPTER SIXTY-ONE

"This should do fine," Stead said, commandeering, as was his wont, the round table in the center of the Palm Court. "After that dinner, I don't think I can go any farther, anyway."

Margaret Brown laughed, and said, "If I eat one more meal like that, I'll sink this boat myself!"

Mina did not disagree; she couldn't remember ever dining on such rich fare, and in such a regal manner, so many nights in a row. Although she had never needed to wear a corset, she noticed Mrs. Brown tugging at hers as she took the seat Bram was holding out for her.

Despite that, a waiter immediately appeared to take their order for more food or drink; Mrs. Brown asked for a glass of seltzer, and the others opted for coffee and nothing more.

"It's best to keep the senses clear—especially mine," Stead said, "before doing a reading. It's a very sensitive process."

Mina had seen readings done before—Gypsies were reputedly the originators of the tarot, and supposedly possessed the one true deck of cards encompassing all the wisdom of the ages—but it had been years, and every reader interpreted things differently. Most of them had, in fact, their own deck, which varied in many small details and depictions.

Stead proved to be no exception, drawing from his breast pocket a stiff leather case and unsnapping it to reveal a pack of dog-eared cards, whose bright colors had long since faded.

"These once belonged to Jean-Baptiste Alliette himself," he said, and when Mrs. Brown asked who that was—"Sounds French to me."— he explained that Alliette was the eighteenth-century mystic who had first exploited the cards for occult purposes. "He believed that they contained, in their symbolism, the hermetic wisdom of the ancient Egyptian *Book of Thoth*, and he wrote quite a bit about that. This particular set, he designed at the end of his life expressly for purposes of divination. He incorporated into them the older forms of French and Romany cartomancy, along with the existing iconography from the Middle East."

"Whew," Mrs. Brown said, taking the seltzer glass from the tray being proffered, "anybody else able to follow all that? I just wanted to have my fortune told."

"And that you shall," Stead said, clearing a space atop the green baize tabletop. "That you shall."

Once the coffee had been served, Stead handed the deck to Mrs. Brown, and asked her to shuffle them. "Though gently. They are rather fragile, as you can see." She did as she was told, and when she had returned them to him, he fanned them out on the table, face down, in a broad arc, and asked her to pick six of them at random.

"With poker, we usually play five," she joked.

"If you bet enough while playing poker," Stead said, "it may well determine your future, but these will serve to predict it." After the six cards had been turned over, he placed them in a circle, with a seventh— the Fool, depicted as a young man with a dog, blithely whistling along the edge of a cliff—in the center.

"That's your version of the Joker?" Mrs. Brown said.

"Yes, but he's no joke. If the Fool comes into play, it signals the end of the world."

Mina was having trouble focusing on the cards. She heard Stead explicating the meaning of each of them, but her mind was still back in the dining saloon, where only hours before, Bartholomew and Winifred Thorne—she refused to engage in the ruse involving their names—had entered as if they were royalty. For the occasion, Winifred was even on her feet—moving slowly, clutching her brother's arm, but walking, nonetheless, with her head held high and her blonde hair higher. When the maître d' had tried to show them to the same obscure table as the night before, she saw Thorne refuse and stride instead to a table squarely in the middle of the restaurant. As his sister was being seated, Thorne turned his head slowly, surveying the entire room, until he spotted her and Bram. Thorne held Mina's gaze, nodding almost imperceptibly. It said all she needed to know: *I know who you are, and you know who I am.* Then he flipped the tails of his dinner jacket aside, and sat down, snapping his fingers for the wine list.

It was as if he had thrown down the gauntlet.

"The major arcana, as certain cards are called, embody the Wheel of Life," Stead was saying, "and by your selection of these, you have revealed your own pathway forward."

"Hope it includes finding another gold mine or two," Mrs. Brown said.

"It is seldom so specific," Stead said, already studying the cards laid out before him. "But they also tell me something about your basic nature; for instance, you have chosen the Strength card"—a picture of a young girl closing the mouth of a lion—"and that indicates you will need to call upon all your reserves, physical and mental, in the near future."

"What's that insignia above her head?" Mrs. Brown said, indicating what looked like a figure eight lying on its side.

"That is called the lemniscate, and it connotes universal and eternal life."

"Am I going to live forever then?"

"Unlikely," Stead said, though his brow, Mina could not help but notice, had furrowed.

"I don't much like the look of that one," Mrs. Brown said, pointing to the Hanged Man.

"Yes, that is a problematic card. In the Hebrew alphabet, the letter *mem* accompanies this figure on the tree of life, and *mem* is one of the three letters that stands for water. Water itself signifies a change to another plane or level of consciousness."

"What if I like the one I'm on?"

Stead did not respond to her jest, but studied the four other cards. Some were right-side up, some were upside down, but Mina noted that Stead had left them exactly as Mrs. Brown had placed them.

"So . . . what's the verdict?" Mrs. Brown chirped. "Am I going to live a long and happy life, or not?"

"You are going to . . . undergo great trials, I'm afraid."

She looked taken aback.

"But from which you will emerge even stronger and more resolute than ever, as the position of your Strength and Sun cards would indicate."

"Well, that much at least sounds like me," Mrs. Brown said, trying to look on the bright side. "Who's next? How about you, Bram?"

"Oh no, ladies first," he said, yielding to Mina, who took the cards reluctantly, shuffled them and drew six.

Stead laid them out, and after a minute or two of concentrated study, looked no more relieved than he had before. Even Mina, who knew something of the game—the very name tarot was thought to derive from the Hungarian Gypsy word, *tar*, for a pack of cards—could see trouble ahead. In addition to the Devil, whose right hand held the burning torch of destruction, and the powerful High Priestess, whose veil must never be raised by the profane, the Hanged Man appeared among her cards, too.

"Maybe we needed a better shuffle," Mrs. Brown said.

"It can't be all bad," Stoker said. "I see a card with a beautiful woman on a throne, wearing a headdress with horns and many points."

"That's the High Priestess, and the twelve points signify the signs of the zodiac, which together comprise reality. Even in the face of what seems impossible, Mina retains a firm grasp on what is real and what is not. She will follow her own intuition, wherever it leads."

"I can vouch for that," Stoker said.

"But how come she's got that hangin' fella again?" Mrs. Brown asked.

"Because she, too, will undergo a terrible ordeal, a trial by some elemental force—air or fire or water—and prevail, though barely, after absolute submission to the Will Divine."

The table grew silent, and Stead's piercing blue-gray eyes, even behind his bifocals, looked as if they were seeing much more than he could tell. Shuffling the deck again and then passing it to Stoker, who declined, Stead said, "No, I wish you to fan them out for me. I will select six, and you must place them out just as I have done, in a circle around the Fool."

"But I won't know how to interpret them."

"I will."

Stoker did as he was told, and arranged the chosen cards on the table. It was plain to Mina that Stead was conducting a kind of test, running his own tarot reading to see if something was going awry. The images on the cards he had drawn were uniformly dire, including a depiction of a tower struck by lightning, a gaunt hermit in rags, and death itself, a knight in black armor wielding a scythe. She waited as he assessed the cards and their relative positions.

"What do you see for yourself?" Mrs. Brown asked.

But before he could answer, the waiter, coming to their table with a fresh pot of coffee, stumbled over the bottom of Stoker's cane, propped against the arm of his chair, and splashed coffee onto the table.

Mortified, he whisked a napkin at the spot, and in the process blew the Fool card into Stead's lap. Stead leaped up as if he had been scalded and tried to brush the card away, but already damp from the coffee, it stuck to his trousers for an instant. The look in his eyes was one of extreme dismay.

Mrs. Brown, making light of the whole business, said, "What's all the fuss about? It's not like it's the end of the world."

But Mina knew that, in Stead's view, it was. He used his napkin to blot the ancient card, which spelled doom to any true believer, and silently returned it to the deck, which he then replaced in its leather case. On his face, he wore the faraway expression of someone who has just received a terminal diagnosis.

CHAPTER SIXTY-TWO

"Getting cold out, sir," seaman Hemming said, stepping into the wheel-house and handing Second Officer Lightoller another message from the telegraph room.

"Hit freezing yet?"

"Almost there—thirty-six degrees, and still dropping steadily."

Lightoller studied the telegram, this one from a ship called the *Mesaba*, reporting pack ice and bergs ahead. There had been simi-lar warnings from other ships—the SS *Caronia*, the *Californian*, the *Amerika*—since late in the afternoon, but so far Captain Smith had not elected to reduce speed. "If it begins to become hazy," he'd said, "then let me know, and we shall reconsider." They were traveling at a steady twenty-two and a half knots, and had taken the precaution of traveling ten miles to the south of the regular route. But the night was clear, the sea as placid as it had been for nearly the entire voyage, and the stars were shining so brightly they reflected off the water.

"Not a breath of wind out, either," the sailor said.

Lightoller wished that there were. Wind was a great aid in spotting bergs and the smaller floating chunks of ice called growlers; the breeze made waves that in turn created a white froth around the base of loose ice, allowing the debris to be seen and thus avoided. Under conditions like these, with no wind and no moon, the two men in the crow's nest would have to rely upon the starlight to help them pick out the blue-black outline of an iceberg looming ahead; and as any seaman knew, the bulk of the damn things lay deep below the surface. What you saw, however large, was just a tip of their hat as they drifted by.

Looking out now, however, Lightoller saw nothing but clear sea and the prospect of an early arrival in New York. That was probably what had motivated the captain to light the last boiler and keep the pace up, despite the ice warnings. Rumor had it that J. Bruce Ismay himself, the director of the White Star Line, was on board for this maiden voyage, and he had no doubt made it known to the captain that he wanted to set a transatlantic record. To Lightoller, it seemed ridiculous—what was the difference of a few hours, or even a day? The *Titanic* was the most technologically advanced ship in history—virtually unsinkable, due to its series of automatic, watertight compartments—and also its most luxuriously appointed; to sail aboard her was a privilege to be savored, not hurried along.

"Is there anything else I can do for you, sir?" Hemming asked, before leaving the bridge.

Lightoller started to dismiss him, then said, "Yes. The navigation lights."

"All turned on, sir."

That was what was troubling Lightoller. Too much ambient light could interfere not only with the lookouts' ability to peer into the darkness, but with the view from the bridge, as well.

"On the forecastle deck, there's a glow coming from the fore scuttle hatch. Shut it."

"Aye aye, sir."

"And make sure to put this up," he said, handing him the telegram from the *Mesaba*, "on the board in the chart room."

A blast of cold air blew through the bridge with Hemming's departure. The icy damp reminded him of a night he'd once spent in a cave in the Eiger Glacier, sheltering from a blizzard. All through that long and frigid night, he'd wondered if that would be where he would wind up leaving his bones.

"I'd say we could all use a round of very hot tea," he said, and Fourth Officer Joseph Boxhall immediately got on the horn to the galley to have some sent up.

"Make sure the lads up top get theirs, too," Lightoller added, glancing up at the crow's nest, where Lee and Fleet were huddled together one hundred feet atop the mast. "They're going to need it tonight."

CHAPTER SIXTY-THREE

There was a knock, but before Stoker could answer it, an envelope had been slipped under the stateroom door. It was addressed to him, and he opened it. On a cream-colored card emblazoned with the White Star insignia, he read, "Care to join me in the smoking room?" It was unsigned, but he knew that Thorne had sent it.

He glanced at Mina's door, which was shut, and could hear her undressing and getting ready for bed. He could also hear the hum of her room heater, which she'd hurried to put on: "I've never felt it so cold on this ship," she'd said the moment they'd come in from the Palm Court.

He folded the note and left it on the table, and then, after a moment's deliberation, opened the safe, removed the Webley revolver, still in its holster, and put it on under his dinner jacket. Over that, he donned his overcoat. Would this be the night he settled the issue once and for all?

The corridors had a chill they had never had before, and the floors were vibrating with the thrum of the engines as he had never known them to do. The ship must be traveling faster than it had for the entire voyage so far.

Even in the mahogany-paneled smoking room, normally crowded with men—and men only—smoking cigars and playing cards, there were only two occupied tables; at one, a quartet was playing auction bridge, and at the other, nestled beneath one of the stained-glass windows, sat Thorne, tamping his cigar into a silver ashtray beside a crystal sherry decanter. The room was not as warm as usual, and the lights seemed lower. When Stoker had stopped in the night before, the smoking lounge, with its mother-of-pearl inlays and red leather club chairs, had seemed the most congenial spot on board, but tonight it struck him as strangely forlorn.

"May I pour you a glass?" Thorne said, lifting the decanter as Stoker sat down, but he put this hand over the top of the second glass and said no. He remembered too well the story Mina had told him, of being drugged at the Thorne mansion. Signaling the waiter by raising his blackthorn cane, he ordered a brandy instead.

Thorne smiled, knowingly, and remained silent until the brandy had been brought.

"To your health," Thorne said, raising his glass.

Stoker did not return the toast.

"So," Thorne continued, "I see that you and Mina Harcourt are sharing one of the more commodious suites on board. Also one of the most expensive. Did *Dracula* really sell all that well?"

"It was a success."

"D'estime or monetary?"

Stoker did not take the bait.

"Winifred and I read it, you know. She is more devoted to fiction than I am. She had this crazy notion about it. Thought that you were writing about us. She thinks you modeled Dracula on me, and his three evil brides on her."

"She flatters herself."

"Does she? The corollaries seem inescapable after a while. Mina *Harker* in place of Harcourt? Lucy Westenra instead of Lucinda Watts? Why, one might even think that our mutual friend Professor Arminius Vambéry was the precursor of the vampire-hunter Professor Van

Helsing. Was it to throw us off the track that you had Van Helsing mention Vambéry, by name, in a casual reference?"

It was, but Stoker was not about to give him the satisfaction of his admitting it.

"Personally, I found the whole story rather overblown and in parts downright tedious, if you don't mind my saying so."

"Say whatever you like."

"But the conceit was ingenious. I'll give you that. People are always fascinated by the idea of eternal life, even if it has to be acquired by the most dreadful means."

On that score, he was right again. Looking into Thorne's face now, no older than it was when he had first seen it in London, Stoker was still astonished. If anything, the man appeared younger and more vigorous than he had at the unraveling of the mummy. Could he go on in such a way indefinitely, continually revivified by an endless string of victims?

"But what, I wonder," Thorne said, relighting his cigar and blowing out a cloud of rum-scented smoke, "is your plan now? Have you come as some avenging angel? Are you Inspector Javert to my Jean Valjean, determined to send me back to finish my sentence? I was never prosecuted for anything, as you well know."

"I'm well aware of that."

"And could hardly be prosecuted now. After all, the man you'd be accusing of unspeakable crimes—Bartholomew Thorne—was a pillar of rectitude. You'd be roundly vilified just for trying to sully his name."

"Probably."

"Oh, undoubtedly! And with apologies for paraphrasing Christopher Marlowe, it was in another country and besides, the *wretch* is dead."

"I know that, too."

"Ah, so does that explain why you are carrying that then?" Thorne said, gesturing with his cigar at the telltale bulge of the revolver.

Stoker had noticed a bit of a bulge, though of a more squarish nature, in the pocket of Thorne's coat, too. It was about the dimensions of the gold box Mina had once owned, before it was stolen by Ludvig Gerhard, all those years ago. But could it have wound up in Thorne's possession, after all?

The clock in the corner rang eleven times, and the steward quietly notified the gentlemen playing cards that the smoking room would close as soon as they had finished their hand. It was growing uncomfortably chilly, as it was.

"That's our cue, too," Thorne said, swigging down the last of his sherry. Stoker drained his brandy glass, and lifted his cane from the arm of the chair.

"If you're going to shoot me," Thorne said, "let's do it outside where it won't make such a mess."

Stoker was oddly confounded. The man was taunting him, but what could he do? Was he prepared, even now, to step out onto the deck and shoot him in cold blood? Did Thorne know him even better than he knew himself?

Outside, the air had turned positively arctic, and as a result the promenade was deserted, apart from a lone sailor trotting past with a rope looped over one shoulder. Thorne strolled on, smoking his cigar, his back to Stoker. When he had reached the forward well deck, close to the mighty bow of the ship, he stopped, and tossed the glowing butt of the cigar into the black ocean below.

"As good a place as any," he said, stuffing his hands into the deep pockets of his overcoat.

Steadying himself on his cane, Stoker reached into his jacket, and removed the revolver from its holster. His hand was shaking as he took the gun out.

"Is that a Webley?" Thorne said, his own hand moving in his pocket. He was fiddling with something. A pistol of his own?

"Damn fine weapon," he added, before muttering something else, under his breath. It didn't sound like English.

Stoker raised the gun and pointed the barrel at Thorne. He made a perfectly good target . . . at first. He didn't flinch or duck for cover. But something—perhaps it was simply his nerves coming over him—clouded Stoker's vision. He blinked hard to clear it, but that only seemed to make it worse. Was it the near-freezing air? Was it—he prayed not—the premonitory effects of another oncoming stroke?

"Something wrong?" Thorne smirked, and even his voice seemed further removed.

The deck was dark, but the starlight had been enough to see him by a few moments ago. Now a shadow seemed to stand between them, an amorphous black vapor that swam back and forth across Stoker's field of vision. With one hand still holding his cane for support, he had only the gun arm to quickly swipe at his eyes, the rough wool of his coat sleeve scratching his face, but when he looked again, he could barely see Thorne at all.

"I knew you couldn't do it," he heard.

There was something in Thorne's hands, though not a gun. It glinted a dull gold.

And then Stoker felt himself wrapped, as if in a cocoon, by that same black shadow. It was almost soothing in its way, until he felt its gentle embrace becoming tighter and more constricting . . . a hug becoming a python's coils. The cane was eased from his hand, clattering to the deck, as the arm holding the gun was drawn down. He felt himself nudged, then moved, and finally dragged toward the gunwale. He was going to be thrown over, he was sure of it, and tried to dig in his heels on the slippery wooden boards. But he could get no traction, and there was nothing corporeal about the shadow that he could grapple with and fight.

He tried to squeeze the trigger of the gun, also to no avail, and in a last effort to stop his own deadly progress, he willfully slumped to the ground, a dead weight. In his nostrils, he smelled the damp rot of a forest floor, cold stone, and deep green lichen.

"Safe journey," he heard Thorne say at precisely the same moment that a bell, high atop the forward mast, rang three times, and a sailor's voice urgently called out, "Iceberg straight ahead!"

The shadow seemed to sweep beneath him, as if scooping him up in an invisible hand, and Thorne was shouting, "Do it!"

But Stoker hunched down, as he'd once done in rugby scrimmages, his shoulders squared, his body as tense and as dense as he could make it, and on the bridge above he could hear voices raised in alarm, bells clanging, whistles shrieking. The engines, thrown into reverse, screamed as the ship attempted to turn its bow to port, and then there was a jolt, not a major one. Stoker's first impression was that the boat had sustained only a glancing blow. But then the shadow he had been wrestling with was overwhelmed by a far greater one—a towering mountain of ice, purple and silver, looming over the side of the ship.

From deep below he could hear, however muffled by the ocean, a gnashing, grinding sound, like a bored child dragging a metal pipe along a concrete wall. Sharp slivers and jagged chunks of ice rained down on the deck as the berg passed by, slamming the docking bridge to one side, jostling the lifeboats suspended from their davits. Thorne scurried for cover toward the wheelhouse, but a slab of ice sent him sprawling, arms and legs spread wide, the flaps of his coat flying open, and the gold box skittering across the slick wooden deck. Stoker felt the grip of his unseen assailant loosen.

As he crawled under a lifeboat, three sailors, holding deck chairs above their heads to ward off the hailstorm, ran past to gauge the damage. The air was colder than it had ever been, smelling now of fresh ice, calved from some primeval glacier, and dispatched, all this way, to spell his immediate salvation . . . or imminent doom.

CHAPTER SIXTY-FOUR

Captain Smith, roused from his bed by the impact, hurried from his cabin behind the wheelhouse, and still buttoning his jacket, said, "What did we hit?"

"An iceberg, sir," Lightoller reported. "I put her hard a' starboard and ran the engines full astern, but it was too close. I intended to port around it, but she hit before I could do anymore."

Indeed, less than a minute had passed between the time Fleet had bellowed his warning into the telephone from the crow's nest and the ship had struck the floating ice.

"Close the watertight doors," Smith commanded, fastening the top button of his tunic, but Lightoller told him that it had already been done.

"Was the warning bell rung?" Smith asked, and again he was told that it had been. "Cut the engines to half-speed ahead, and Boxhall, go and inspect for damages. Rouse Hutchinson and get him to sound the ship, too."

Hutchinson was the chief carpenter aboard, and knew as much, if not more, about the design of the ship as the director J. Bruce Ismay himself. Until those reports came back, there was little that Lightoller, or his captain, could do but pray.

Going out to the starboard side of the bridge, Lightoller looked along the flank of the ship but could see little damage other than perhaps a scrape or two from the paint. What he could see were the heads of several passengers on the A and B decks, poking out of their portholes to see what strange object had just blocked their view. The berg itself was fast receding, a bluish hulk of craggy ice serenely sailing away from the scene of the accident as if nothing at all had happened. He'd have liked to blow his whistle and order the damn thing to be put under arrest.

Down on the forward well deck, he saw a man emerge from under a lifeboat and scramble to pick up his walking stick and something gold that looked like a cigarette case. What the hell had he been doing out there, anyway, and on such a frigid night as this?

By the time he went back inside to report that he had seen no significant damage above the waterline, the reports were coming back from all quarters of the ship. And they were not good. Fourth Officer Boxhall had returned with word from the carpenter that there was a long gash in the hull and the ship was making water; the first six compartments toward the forward bulkhead had all been breached, and some of the boiler room workers had barely made it out before the flashing red lights had alerted them that the watertight doors were going to be automatically sealed. A geyser of freezing ocean water was exploding into the interior, the mailroom on G deck was already flooded, the forepeak tank was hissing like a gigantic teakettle as the air was forced out by the incoming tide. Captain Smith was taking it all in silently, stoically, but Lightoller knew what he was thinking because he was thinking the same thing himself. Although Chief Engineer Joseph Bell opined that the pumps might be able to keep her afloat long enough to limp into some port, Lightoller knew better. The pumps could never keep up with damage this great, and the unsinkable ship—no matter how you looked at it—was going to sink.

With only enough lifeboats to carry less than half of the 2,223 souls on board.

"Give the telegraph room our present coordinates," the captain said, "and tell them to send out an SOS."

The newly designated international distress call.

"We are going down at the head, and if some other ship does not come at once," Smith added, "it will be too late."

CHAPTER SIXTY-FIVE

Mina had fallen into a sort of stupor, brought on by the many courses of the heavy meal, the troubling tarot reading that followed, the sheer nervous toll of tracking Thorne and his sister. At night she had grown used to the vibrations of the mattress from the enormous power of the churning engines far below, but tonight it was more pronounced than ever—so pronounced that she barely registered the bump in the night. Even with the electric heater casting a pale orange glow, her cabin had a clammy and oppressive feel to it . . . a feel made worse by a growing sensation of pressure on her chest. It was as if a broad, cold hand was splayed flat against her bosom.

When she wriggled to remove it, the hand only seemed to press down harder, and she moaned in protest. The pressure increased. Opening her eyes just enough to peer up, she saw, close enough that had it been breathing she'd have felt its breath, something peering down at her.

She stiffened in the bed, her eyes opening wide.

Hovering in the ruddy gloom was a face like none she'd ever seen before—human and not human, flesh and not flesh, at once sentient and inanimate. The nose was as wide as the lips were thin, the eyes were sunken into deep hollows, the brow protruding like an overhanging cliff. Around its neck was a tattered strip of leather, adorned with colored beads and the tiniest flecks of gold, glinting like sparks in the electric glow.

For several seconds, they simply stared at each other, as Mina's mind fled back to another time and another place, to a windswept peak, and a cave in the Romanian mountains.

The specter's lips parted, but its words were in no immediately identifiable language. Yet Mina understood them—it was a sibilant exhalation, blending the cadence of the Romany tongue with an even more ancient Semitic-sounding vocabulary. Was this the language of the creators of the Carpathian Sphinx? It reminded her of her barely remembered mother's voice, crooning a lullaby above her bed. But this was no lullaby—this, she knew, was an imperative.

"But how . . ." Mina murmured, and the voice repeated the same order.

And then the cabin went dark.

And quiet.

The mattress stopped vibrating, the comforting rumble of the engines ceased. She felt as if the ship were a skater slowly, gracefully, skidding to a halt.

She bolted upright at the sound of the door to their suite banging open and Stoker shouting from the parlor, "Mina, wake up!" The bedroom door flew open, and a white light, flickering on and off, penetrated the darkness.

"Get up!" Bram was shouting. "We've hit an iceberg!"

Her bewildered eyes swept the tiny space—she was quite alone—and Bram, leaning hard on his cane, looked winded and alarmed.

"What of it?" she blurted. "The ship is unsinkable."

"Get dressed," he said, and going to the bureau, pulled down the life jacket nestled on top of it. "And put this on over your coat!"

Then he bustled out as she tried to gather her thoughts. What was going on? Had she conjured up that awful phantom on her own? Why did the ship feel so silent and adrift?

She could hear Bram unlocking the wall safe, presumably removing their money and small valuables. As she dressed, she called out, "Where were you?"

"The smoking room."

"With Stead?"

"No."

There was something about the way he said it. "Were you there with Thorne?"

He didn't answer, but that was answer enough. She quickly finished putting on her clothes, and when she came into the sitting room, Bram was waiting for her, his life jacket looped over one arm.

"You were, weren't you?" she said.

"I was."

"What happened?"

She could hear commotion in the hallway outside. It wasn't frantic, but there were doors opening and closing, voices inquiring, footsteps thudding on the thick carpets. A little dog barking.

"I failed."

"To do what, exactly?" She couldn't say *kill him*.

"We need to go up top. We can talk there."

The moment he opened the door, Mina saw a matronly woman in a fur stole lumbering by, followed by one of the elevator operators—a boy no more than seventeen or eighteen—carrying a toy poodle that was squirming in his arms.

"What is this all about?" Mina asked a passing steward, and he said, "Just a precaution, ma'am."

"Against what?"

"Just a precaution," he said, quickly moving on. "Captain's orders!"

Bram leaned in closer, so as not to be heard by anyone else. "I was out on the deck when it happened," he said, "under one of the lifeboats toward the bow."

"What were you doing under—"

"I heard it," he said, as he guided her up the stairs, which were growing more crowded by the minute, toward the outer deck.

"Heard what?"

"The crash. And the aftermath from the bridge. They don't want to create a panic, but it's bad. Very bad."

The fear that she had been holding at bay suddenly settled in.

"The ship has been mortally wounded by a glacier."

"And it's going down?" she asked.

"There are lifeboats," he said, as they emerged from the warm and lighted interior of the boat, "and you'll get into one. You'll be fine."

Hundreds of people from the first-class cabins, in all states of dress, were already milling about, looking confused or worried or, in the case of some young society bucks, feigning amusement, as if they were not about to take this drill quite seriously. Some of the gentlemen were still in their evening clothes, some of the ladies were in coats thrown over the trailing ends of silk nightgowns. Sleepy children were in pajamas, bundled in blankets and caps, their nannies shivering in shawls and unlaced boots.

"Oh, there you two are," Mrs. Brown said, forging her way through the crowd in a sable coat and another of her wide-brimmed hats. "They're saying we'll be able to return to our cabins later, but I'm not so sure about that. I'm thinking that this is the real thing." She scanned their faces eagerly, but apparently gained little reassurance. "I'd hoped that I'd find Stead with you."

"Have you seen him?" Bram asked.

"Yes, on the way up. He said he had something to do, and headed off toward the grand staircase, but that one doesn't lead out to the deck. It only goes down."

"Can I leave you two ladies for a few minutes?" Stoker said. Before turning away, he added sotto voce to Mina, "Perhaps it's best if you carry this now."

He dug into his pocket, then handed her the gold box she had long since despaired of ever seeing again. As her jaw dropped open in surprise, he said with a wry smile, "Take care not to lose it again. I went to considerable trouble to retrieve it."

CHAPTER SIXTY-SIX

Stoker knew enough about Stead to understand what was going on in the man's mind. As quickly as he could hobble with his cane, he fought against the rising tide of humanity coming up the stairs, and entered a corridor where he found two stewards smashing down a stuck stateroom door—a man's voice was bellowing in frustration from inside—then past a dozen other doors flung wide open, belongings of all sorts strewn about. The hallway floor, he noticed, was beginning to tilt, noticeably, toward the bow. At the grand staircase, the clock was tolling midnight. Quickly, he surveyed the Palm Court, where broken dishes already littered the floor, then the smoking room—now deserted entirely—and from there went into the first-class lounge where he spotted a lone figure, still in a black dinner jacket, sitting at a table facing the bar.

"Stead!"

The man didn't turn, but raised a glass of whiskey in salutation.

"For god's sake, man, we've got to get out of here while there's time!" Stoker said. He was close enough to see that Stead had helped himself to the whole bottle from the bar, and had laid out between the bottle and the glass the ancient deck of tarot cards. Death, a skeleton on a white horse, was squarely in front of him.

"They're just cards!" Stoker exclaimed. "It's a game."

Stead said, "Can I offer you a drink?"

His expression was one of total acceptance, even resignation.

"You don't have to die."

"Did you know that I once wrote an article, 'How the Mail Steamer Went Down in Mid-Atlantic,'" over twenty years ago, about just such a tragedy as this?"

Stoker racked his brain, and yes, he did remember it; it had caused a bit of a sensation at the time, as most of Stead's work did. "Fine, yes, of course. Let's discuss it on deck."

Languidly, Stead refilled his glass, and said, "Given the vagaries of my career, I always said I'd wind up lynched or drowned."

"Come on!" Stoker said, slipping a hand under one of Stead's arms, but the man was immoveable.

"The cards," he observed, "they're always right. You saw how that last one clung to me."

"It was wet from the coffee."

"That's when I knew." Looking straight into Stoker's eyes, he said, "But you have a chance. So do the others. Don't squander it down here."

There was a crash as the nautical painting above the bar slid from the wall and toppled a row of crystal decanters.

"You want to do one last good deed?" Stead asked.

"Yes!"

"Find Thorne and his sister. Put an end to that evil."

Stoker had never told Stead all that he knew, but it seemed he didn't need to. Throughout his life, the man had known, instinctively, how to identify the darkness in men's souls.

"I knew there was something irredeemable about them on the night of the unraveling," Stead added, "when the rats came. I should have done something then. Now, I fear, it's up to you."

Stoker knew there was no more that he could do here. He squeezed Stead's shoulder, and said, "Goodbye, old man." Stead patted the back of his hand in acknowledgment.

Going back up the stairs was considerably more difficult than having come down them. The slant was greater, and he had to cling tightly to the gilded balustrade to haul himself up each step. At the top, he was disoriented, and started down one corridor only to hit a dead end. Turning, he heard the gruff barking of big dogs, and then several more adding to the chorus. Was he near the kennels? The floor was dipping again, and as he approached the door that the stewards had smashed open, he heard the barking getting louder by the second. An Irish setter suddenly sprinted around the corner ahead, and on its heels was a pack of other dogs, beagles and Airedales and one Saint Bernard, loping along at the back of the pack. They were terrified and hysterical, racing along helter-skelter, and nearly knocking him over as the first of them got close. A Labrador retriever leaped up at his chest, and as he tried to extricate himself, he saw, coming around the bend, first a swirling green puddle, and then rising halfway to the ceiling, a wall of dark water. It rushed down the hallway like an angry fist, sweeping from side to side, and he had just enough time to duck into the room with the broken door before the water slammed past, snatching up several of the dogs and tumbling them like rag dolls. But the water wasn't about to spare him either and channeled into the room, rising rapidly, and he knew that if he didn't get out fast, he'd never get out at all.

CHAPTER SIXTY-SEVEN

"Christ Almighty, Winifred, forget the bloody tiara!"

"Easy for you to say," she threw back at him as she tried again to open the safe. "I'm not the fool that you are!"

He knew she would never forgive him for losing the gold box. But he couldn't very well scour the deck for it now—the damn ship was sinking beneath them.

"We're not leaving this boat empty-handed!" she said, exulting as the safe opened and she retrieved the diamond tiara and a raft of other jewels, stuffing them into a velvet pouch. "Can I trust you to carry these, or will you lose them, too?"

He snatched the pouch out of her hand, stuffed it into the pocket of his wet coat, and dragged her toward the door.

A thin rivulet of water was streaming down the side of the corridor, but at least the lights were still on and holding steady. He dreaded getting lost in the bowels of the ship with the lights out; it'd be even darker there than in the tunnel under the old mission house.

"Come on!" he urged, though he was not much better on his feet than she was at this point. When the hunk of ice had sent him flying, he'd bruised his shoulder and twisted his ankle. By the time he'd been able to raise his head to look around, Stoker was long gone, and the alarms had been raised.

Leaning on the rails and sometimes the walls, they crawled up one set of stairs after another, the ship heaving and groaning all around them, before finally emerging on deck, where a kind of bedlam reigned, and no wonder. Here, some of the richest and most privileged people in the world were being urged, by frantic sailors and officers—one of whom was wielding a gun!—to climb into lifeboats swinging precariously from their davits, and descend in them to a black ocean at least sixty or seventy feet below. Many were balking, reluctant to leave what they still perceived to be the relative safety of the ship. Wasn't this the mighty and unsinkable *Titanic*, after all?

Thorne knew better, and he pushed his way through the mob and toward the nearest lifeboat.

"Hold on there!" the armed officer declared, as Thorne dragged his sister after him.

"Get out of my way!"

"It's women and children only!"

"It's what?"

"You heard me," the officer said, reaching back to take Winifred by the arm and guide her toward the boat.

"I'll have your name and report you!"

"It's Lightoller, and you're welcome to it! Now get out of the way!" Winifred looked back at him. "What should I do?"

"Get into the damn boat. I'll find another."

"But what if you don't?"

"Then you'll get to New York without me."

"Madame," Lightoller interrupted "we do not have time for this!"

"But you know I'm no good without you!"

That much Thorne did know. Without him, she could never sustain the life—the *borrowed* life—that only he knew the spells and procedures to maintain.

And then she was being lifted into the boat like a sack of laundry, and his first thought, turning back toward the surging crowd around him, was how to disguise himself as a woman. He could throw a shawl over his head, and swap his pants for a long skirt, but there was nothing he could do about his size; he was simply too big a man to carry it off.

To his astonishment, a band started playing. He saw them now, arranged in a semicircle, their music stands teetering, as they launched into some ragtime number.

A sailor was sawing away with a penknife at the tangled lines holding the boat his sister was in. There was nothing to be done here, not with that bastard waving the gun.

His only hope, he realized, lay on the port side.

CHAPTER SIXTY-EIGHT

"Bram! Bram!"

Mina had broken away from Mrs. Brown's grasp—"Honey, you can't go back in there!"—only to find herself stymied at every turn. When she wasn't being run over by passengers or crew still emerging from the lower depths of the ship, she was stopped by floors too steep to navigate, stairs blocked by fallen debris, or corridors too far submerged to do anything but swim in. Wherever he had gone in search of Stead, he was now impossible to follow.

Still hoping against hope, and searching in every direction, she raced back out onto the deck, where Mrs. Brown grabbed her again, so powerfully this time that there was no escaping, and dragged her toward a lifeboat that was only now being freed from a tangled line.

"No, I won't go without Bram!" she said, digging in her heels, but the deck was as slick as ice, and before she knew it, a sailor had grabbed the straps of her lifejacket and used them to hoist her over the side, still protesting, and drop her into the boat. She landed on top of a lady in pearls, clutching a child to her bosom.

"Watch out!" the lady cried. "You'll kill us all."

But Mrs. Brown, who'd clambered in after her, retorted, "That's enough out of you. We're all in this together!"

"Lower away!" the sailor cried, and with a lurch that sent Mina tumbling again, the boat fell a few feet, one end higher than the other, then fell again, righting itself. In fits and starts, it descended the side of the ship, the women holding fast to their children, the children crying or screaming in terror. To Mina's horror, she could see inside the portholes of the ship, where all manner of things—clothes, furniture, bedding—were sloshing about in a rising tide of water glowing a sickly green in the cabin lights. Could Bram be imprisoned somewhere in there, too? Her heart was sick with fear for him.

Below them, the ocean was so calm it looked like a slab of polished onyx, but already several lifeboats had rowed away, their yellow lanterns bobbing in the night. The sailor manning the helm of their own boat was standing with legs spread wide, shouting orders and reprimands to anyone who threatened to tilt the boat or get themselves caught in the lines.

Overhead, an emergency flare rocketed up into the sky, blazing a trail of white light that arced and sputtered like a holiday firework. Some of the frightened children were momentarily distracted by the brilliant display, but Mina wondered if there was any ship close enough to see it and come to the rescue.

"He'll be all right," Mrs. Brown tried to console her, gripping her cold hands in hers. "He's the kind of fellow who will always find a way. You'll see."

The flare burned out just as the boat touched down into the sea, bobbing gently as the lines were let loose.

"Is there anybody here who knows how to use an oar?" the helmsman cried, and of the twenty or thirty souls on board only Mrs. Brown shouted, "I can!"

"Then do it! If we don't get good and clear, we'll get pulled down by the suction when she sinks!"

The bow of the ship was already settled below the waterline; the stern was rising slowly. Mrs. Brown wrested an oar from the gunwales, locked it into place, and then nodded at the one on the other side. "There's nothing to it," she said to Mina. "Just do what I'm doing."

And Mina, as numb inside as when she had first learned of her father's death, did.

CHAPTER SIXTY-NINE

With the water already to his waist, Stoker knew it was only a matter of seconds before the cabin became his tomb. Atop the bureau, he saw that one of the room's occupants had left a life jacket along with a silver-plated portrait of a young woman, and he threw the preserver over his shoulders, yanking and pulling it down as best he could over his overcoat. There wasn't time to fasten the straps. Wading against the current, he plunged into the hallway—only a few feet of air remained at the top—and half-slogged, half-swam around the bend, holding his head high, until he could grapple a stair rail. Water was spilling down, but he was able to pull himself up step by step, hand over hand, as if he were scaling a mountain peak. He was shocked at his own endurance—since the stroke, he had limited his range of activities—but in a fight for survival, the body could summon up reserves it did not know it had.

Reserves, however, that would not prove infinite.

The lights flickered, but again came on. There was a horrendous and unceasing howl from above, and once he had crawled out onto the deck, which was listing so sharply the lounge chairs were sliding down it like toboggans, he saw that the noise was coming from the four immense black funnels of the ship. They were venting the steam building up in the boilers far below, sending huge plumes of gray smoke up toward the starlit sky, and creating such a deafening roar it was enough to split an eardrum. Everywhere he looked chaos reigned.

He had come up on the port side, where the last of the lifeboats was being lowered away so hastily that many of its seats were still unfilled. A couple of men in bakers' uniforms shimmied out onto the crane, and tried to leap down into it. One missed and splashed into the sea, the other landed with such a thud Stoker was sure he'd broken his back. Farther below, toward the stern, he could see a shockingly great mass of people, the steerage passengers who had either been deliberately blocked, or otherwise impeded, from coming up in time to find a place in the meager supply of boats. With kerchiefs and caps on their heads, bundles clutched under their arms, children wrapped tight around their parents' legs, they huddled close, some of them gathered around what he now could see was a white-haired man in a clerical collar, reading aloud from an upheld Bible.

Incongruously, he could swear he heard the strains of the ship's band, playing a hymn he remembered from his childhood. "Nearer, My God, to Thee."

But of Mina there was no sign. He was glad of that; he prayed she had been taken off the ship on one of the earlier boats. He hoped that she was with the American woman Mrs. Brown, who struck him as the soul of capability.

It was then that he saw one figure standing rather taller and broader than the rest, balanced on a railing and clinging to a slack rope from an empty davit; he was kicking at a man standing on the railing below him who was desperately attempting to cling to the same line. To the last, Thorne was the same ruthless creature.

A sudden convulsion caught Stoker by surprise, his body shaking from the cold and the accumulating strains. It was highly unlikely that he would survive this night—or, for that matter, even another hour—and he felt himself overwhelmed not by a sense of fear, but a kind of acceptance. If this was to be his final resting place, then so be it. The journey of his life could end here as well as anywhere. But if these were to be his final hours, how best could he make use of them?

And that much was painfully clear.

He could do what he had come all this way to do, and rid the world, forever after, of a noxious force. He could swap his melancholy Dane for the bloody-minded Scotsman, Macbeth.

Whether Thorne would see him coming was unlikely. In the seething mob of panicked people, with his hair and beard dripping wet, the straps of his life jacket hanging loose, Stoker was no doubt indistinguishable from the rest of the doomed souls who had fled to the stern of the boat. It was only when he came within reach, and Thorne instinctively kicked out at him as he had at the other man, that Stoker saw recognition dawn on his face . . . followed by a hideous leer.

"Come to kill me again?" he shouted over the din.

Stoker, barely able to keep his footing, didn't want to waste a breath in reply.

"Can't be done! I'll survive this, too!"

Stoker reached toward the cuff of Thorne's trousers, but he was able to swing away from his grasp, and on the return deliver a swift kick to Stoker's ribs. Had it not been for the padding of the life jacket, it might have been enough to do him in.

Another flare zoomed into the sky, announced by a loud bang and a crackling crescendo of white sparks and stars. To Stoker, it was like a stage effect he might have managed from the wings of the Lyceum.

He lunged, grappling his adversary at the waist and clinging tight. Holding on to the rope, Thorne had no hand free to fight him off, but jerked his knees up, over and over again, to knock him loose. They were locked in an aerial embrace, like acrobats, though Stoker could feel his arthritic fingers, locked together, losing their grip.

Far below, there was an explosion, the rumble rippling up all the way to the deck, shaking the entire frame of the ship . . . and slowly, but relentlessly, lifting the stern of the boat even higher into the air, as the bow plunged deeper. Hundreds of screaming people who had been precariously clinging to rails and ropes, lines and hatchways and each other, lost their holds and tumbled, like loose scree on a mountain slope, down the tilting deck. Inside the ship, chairs and tables, dishes and crockery, bottles and bedsteads, statues and stained-glass windows, gilded clocks and oil paintings, kennel cages and cast-iron stoves, all crashed together in what Stoker could only imagine was the deafening sound of Pandemonium itself.

Thorne's hands slid off the rope, and with Stoker still hanging on, they were propelled over the side of the boat, only disengaging as they plummeted, like Icarus, toward the sea. The impact of hitting the water was nothing compared to the shock from its freezing temperature. To Stoker, it felt like a million little razors cutting his skin wherever it was exposed. He was sinking fast, before the buoyancy of his life jacket counteracted the plunge and shot him back to the surface.

He came up, sputtering, arms flailing, surrounded by others shrieking in pain and shock, but there was only one head he was looking for. And though he twisted this way and that, still gasping for air, he did not see it.

CHAPTER SEVENTY

Although Quartermaster Robert Hichens, manning the tiller of lifeboat six, shouted to the ladies to keep on rowing—"Row for your lives, or she'll drag us all down!"—Mina stopped pulling on her oar, as did Mrs. Brown and the others who had been subsequently dragooned into service.

The sight was too appalling.

The three massive bronze propellers of the ship, each blade the size of a boxcar, and its equally immense rudder were rising up as the bow disappeared. Miraculously, the lights on the ship were still burning, outlining its black funnels and teetering masts in a reddish glow. An anguished cry—sounding at once like a single voice and that of all humanity—echoed across the water, subsumed only in the unearthly roar of the ship being rent asunder, the gigantic boilers and engines loosed from their moorings, the rigging ripping and the masts snapping, the hull corkscrewing under the strain.

"My God . . . my God . . ." was all Mrs. Brown could say, as others wept openly or screamed the names of their missing loved ones. "This is really it."

The ship was almost perpendicular to the water now, suspended as if by some invisible force.

Is Bram aboard it? That was all Mina could think. Was he one of those drowning souls, whose voices were skittering across the sea? Or had he by the grace of God found his way into one of the lifeboats?

The lights went out in the ship.

It was now just a black silhouette, a cutout discernible only by the light of the stars—more than she had ever seen in a single sky—shining on the water, their reflections doubling their already countless multitude.

"Row away, I said!" Hichens shouted, tiller in one hand, and Mrs. Brown replied, "We'll row all right—but we'll row *toward* those poor souls drowning all around us!"

"Not in my boat you won't!"

Whipping around on her seat, Mina shouted, "This isn't your boat, and you're not in command!"

Mrs. Brown gave her a firm nod of approval.

"Now let's put our backs into it!" Mina shouted to the other rowers. "They can't last long in this freezing water!"

CHAPTER SEVENTY-ONE

Stoker could barely stay above the turbulent froth generated by the sinking ship and the thousand struggling souls frantically fighting for their lives in the frigid sea. The dripping stern, and one black funnel, still rose above him, neither plummeting to the bottom of the ocean nor slapping back down and crushing everyone below them. People were clutching at every kind of flotsam and jetsam bobbing on the water—barrels, doors, window frames, wooden lounge chairs—anything to keep their heads above water. A mother holding her baby aloft churned past, her desperate breaths fogging in the air; an elderly man, plainly dead, still neatly dressed in white tie, drifted by, eyes shut, mouth open. A panting bulldog, tongue hanging out, paddled past, no doubt looking for its master one last time. Stoker knew that when the rest of the ship took its final plunge, it would create a deadly whirlpool, but as he tried to swim away from it now, he felt a tug on a loose strap of his life jacket.

Was he snagged on something?

Turning, he saw Thorne—not grinning now, but deadly serious. "I'll be needing this," he said through gritted teeth, and Stoker realized that he was actually trying to rip the life jacket off him. Stoker squirmed in his grip, but Thorne had him fast, trying to wrest it from his shoulders. Stoker shoved him away, but found oddly enough that he was only being drawn closer. So was Thorne, however. They were caught in an eddy that was pulling them, inexorably, toward the massive broken hull.

"We'll both be sucked under!" he shouted, but Thorne was having none of it, and had managed to drag the life jacket off one of his shoulders.

There was a groan from the ship, the sound of metal giving way, and as it sank another few yards, the current grew stronger. *This is the end,* Stoker thought; he was about to be dragged all the way to the bottom of the sea. Instead, he was pinioned, like a butterfly on a mat, against a huge ventilator screen for the engines. Thorne was flattened against it, too, as water rushed through the chain-link grating and down a wide pitch-black shaft to the boiler rooms, from which hot air still wafted up.

If the time had come to die, Stoker resolved, he would at least make sure to take his enemy down with him.

Thorne scrabbled with freezing fingers at the rest of the life jacket, and rather than fight him, Stoker let it slide from his shoulders. As Thorne struggled to claim his prize, pulling it on over his head and shrugging it down his body, Stoker saw that the screen they were pinned against was giving way, bending under the strain. It was just a matter of seconds before they were both sucked down the shaft. First one corner sprang loose, then another, and even Thorne suddenly realized the mounting peril. But not before Stoker had grabbed a loose end of the lifebelt and with fingers almost too numb to feel anything, looped the strip of canvas cloth through the grate and yanked the knot tight.

"What the bloody hell!" Thorne shouted.

"Exactly," Stoker replied, as the only corner of the screen still holding tight crumpled.

In a jumble of twisted metal, his face filled with malice, and his arms reaching out to grab Stoker one last time, Thorne went spinning down the shaft, secured to the mangled grate, under a cascade of onrushing water.

Stoker fully expected to join him there, but something stopped him—the sleeve of his coat was hooked on a jagged bolt that had held the screen. The sleeve was ripping, and the shirt beneath it, too, and once the tear was complete, there'd be nothing to keep him from descending into the same maw. He didn't know whether to try to stop the ripping, or let it finish, and hope he could find the strength to swim free once it was done.

The decision was taken out of his hands a moment later when there was a concussive blast from below as the last boiler, flooded by the freezing water, exploded, demolishing the few remaining bulkheads, and belching a cloud of blazing steam and smoke up the vent like a geyser. Stoker was shot up and out of the water on a magic carpet of scalding hot air and must have been thrown fifty feet, because when he splashed down, and then fought his way to the surface again, he was near one of the few lifeboats that had stuck close enough to pick up survivors. His coat was gone, his shirt was in shreds, and one side of his face felt singed and raw. But he was still alive! An oar was extended to him, and after he had grappled it, several hands reached out to him from the bobbing bow of the boat.

"Come on then!" a man with a Scottish accent urged him. "Almost there!"

With his last ounce of strength, Stoker put out his arm and felt someone grab his wrist.

Like a gaffed fish, he was hauled over the gunwale and plopped into the bottom of the boat, already six inches deep in water.

"Good show," the Scotsman said. Someone tossed a blanket over him. He was shivering so hard he thought his bones would break.

And then, as one of the nearby boats sent up a flare—a long luminescent trail of light, exploding in a loud burst of shimmering white stars—Stoker lifted his head. He watched as the gargantuan stern of the *Titanic* executed a slow and graceful pirouette—a final curtain call—before sliding below the water; it left no vast whirlpool after all, barely a ripple even, to mark its passing. In stunned silence, everyone in the lifeboat either stared, or in some cases covered their eyes and turned away, until it had completely submerged. This monumental vessel, which only a minute before had still loomed large above the sea, was altogether gone. Someone muttered a prayer, others stifled sobs. The greatest ocean liner in the world, the mighty and unsinkable *Titanic*, was destined now to be nothing but a memory . . . one of the most ghastly in human history.

CHAPTER SEVENTY-TWO

"Keep your eyes peeled and your ears open," Mrs. Brown announced, "there might still be someone we can save!"

But even though Mina had no idea what time of night it was, she knew that at least two or three hours had passed, and the cries of those floundering in the water had all but ceased. Quartermaster Hichens, though nominally in charge of the boat, no longer dared defy Mrs. Brown, Mina, and a pair of suffragettes who had also voted to countermand his orders. Their boat—number six of the twenty on board—rowed slowly over the phosphorescent sea, the oars, to Mina's surprise, creating a greenish-yellow glow as the water dripped from their blades. Though there were dead bodies aplenty, most of them bobbing like apples in their white life jackets, frost on their blue and upturned faces, there was far less debris than she would have expected from the destruction of such an immense ship. Steamer chairs and a striped barber pole—she remembered seeing it on the C deck, where souvenirs of the voyage could be bought—floated by, but to think that this hallowed spot could already be so erased by the lapping waves was yet more reason for despair. Though this was a watery grave and not a desert waste, the poem "Ozymandias," and the magnitude of human hubris, inevitably came again to mind.

There were other boats—maybe a dozen that she could make out in the dark, some of them lashed together for greater safety—spread out widely around the site. Occasionally, some seaman would blow a whistle, or an argument would break out in her own boat—someone was sitting on someone else's foot, or a flask of brandy was not being shared—but otherwise, it was silent except for the sloshing of the water against the wooden hull and the rhythmic creaking of the oars. Her shoulders ached, but the exertion, she knew, was keeping her warm.

All she could think of was Bram. Was he alive, sitting in one of those other boats, even now wondering if she had survived? How she wished she could know. How she wished she could know *anything*. Were they destined to die at sea, adrift in a leaky boat? Had some other ship been notified of their catastrophe in time? Was help on the way, or were they on their own? The air was freezing, but thank God the sea had remained placid, no storm had threatened. The stars shone brightly, unobscured by clouds.

When Mrs. Brown said, "Look!" and pointed toward the southeast horizon, Mina wiped the salt spray from her eyes and saw what appeared, for a vanishing instant, to be a white signal flare.

"That's nothing," Hichens said dismissively. "Just a shooting star."

But when a minute later, the rumble of a distant cannon shot reverberated across the water, even Hichens couldn't discount it.

"There lies our salvation!" one of the other ladies at an oar crowed. "Let's row toward it!"

Still, there was nothing Mina could see of a ship. Dawn was only beginning to break, the palest pink light suffusing the sky. But as the sun rose, it revealed the most astonishing sight, a veritable field of icebergs all around them, some of them lying low like crocodiles in the Nile, others towering a hundred feet or more, with sharp peaks and deep blue crevices.

"Oh look, Mummy," the child in the arms of the woman Mina had landed on, cried. "It's like the North Pole without Santa!"

One of the neighboring lifeboats sent up its own flare—a green one that zigzagged a fizzling trajectory over the ice field and up into the rosy sky. The bergs did indeed look like some magical kingdom, gleaming in every color of the rainbow, from richest purple to lustrous gold. They were magnificent and so seemingly benign . . . though she could hardly forget that one of them had proved to be as deadly as any force on earth. Which one was it? Mina wondered, as she bent to her oar. Was it the one shaped like a minaret? Or the one more like an onion dome? Or had the perpetrator passed on hours ago?

Even now, their little boat had to steer a path through this deadly obstacle course, as did the ship coming to their aid, with the utmost care, and at a maddeningly slow pace. After much maneuvering, the rescue ship was able to approach the lifeboat from one side and cut its engine to reduce its wake. The name on its prow, though Mina at first couldn't believe that she had read it right, was *Carpathia*.

"We've only one seaman aboard!" Hichens shouted up, and the captain, leaning over the rail, signaled that he understood. Rope ladders were flung over the side, as well as a pulley system with a canvas ash bag big enough to hold an infant or small child; a bosun's chair was also lowered for any adult unable to climb the rungs. One by one, the passengers in the lifeboat were gotten on board, Mrs. Brown urging them on, while Mina rested over her heavy oar and Hichens held to the tiller. Finally, there was only one other passenger left, a woman who had been silent the whole trip, huddled under a black shawl that had been drawn over her head. From the back, she had appeared to Mina to be one of the Italian or even Lebanese women from third class, but when she went to her now, and drew the shawl back, a froth of dyed blonde hair spilled out. Her face was slack, her eyes were closed, and her skin was as cold and white as porcelain. Mina took in a quick breath.

"Do you know her?" Mrs. Brown asked.

"Yes."

"Is she alive?"

Mina had to bend close to see, and put the back of her hand under Winifred's nose. There was the faintest exhalation.

"Barely."

"What's the hold up?" Hichens complained from the stern. "I don't care if she's dead or alive! Get her out of the boat!"

Mrs. Brown put a hand under one of her arms, and Mina took the other, and together they lifted her into the swinging bosun's chair and lashed her tight. She went up the side of the *Carpathia*, both arms hanging limply from the conveyance, as Mina stepped to the ladder and with hands raw and bleeding from rowing, took hold of the bottom rungs and began her ascent.

CHAPTER SEVENTY-THREE

By the time the ocean liner got around to unloading the lifeboat that Stoker was in, it was already close to eight in the morning, and there wasn't a moment to lose. Under Second Officer Lightoller's direction, the boat contained seventy-five people—far beyond its expected capacity—and its gunwales were only inches above the now-choppy seas. While others had tried to bail the vessel out, Stoker had used the freezing water to repeatedly bathe the side of his face that had been scorched by the steam.

The bosun's chair was sent down, and others took advantage of it, but as a point of pride Stoker was not about to do so. Like a snail crawling up a drain spout, he slowly but surely made his way, rung by rung, up the swinging rope ladder, and nearly fell into the arms of the seaman at the top. The man took one look at him, and said, "We've set up a hospital in the dining lounge. Let me take you to the doctor there."

"First," Stoker croaked, through lips cracked from cold and salt, "can you tell me if a passenger named Mina Harcourt has been brought aboard?"

"A list is being made, sir, but let me get you to the doctor first."

Perhaps he looked worse than he thought. All around him he could see forlorn women, and some men, walking, as if in a stupor, on the open deck; many had been hovering by the rail, wrapped in blankets, scanning each person who had come up from the last lifeboat, searching desperately for their loved ones or friends, though now even that last hope was being extinguished.

Leaning hard on the sailor, Stoker was taken into a large and handsomely appointed lounge, though nothing compared to the *Titanic*'s, where makeshift screens had been set up to create small but private bays for each patient. A woman, so composed and well groomed that she could only have been a passenger on the *Carpathia*, gave him a glass of hot brandy, but the moment he touched it to his lips, it felt like fire, and he had to pull it away.

"Oh, I'm sorry," she said, "is there something else I can get you instead?"

"Just some water," he said, in a hoarse whisper. "Not cold."

She had no sooner ducked out than a harried doctor, his sleeves rolled up to his elbows, his bow tie askew, ducked into the bay, introduced himself—"Ship's physician, Townsend."—and asked, while gently turning his face to one side, what had caused this.

"Steam . . . from the boilers."

"Right. Well, it looks bad, but I don't think there's any serious damage to the bones. Can you move your jaw?"

Stoker nodded.

"Lose any teeth?"

"Not to this."

Townsend smiled. "I'll send my nurse in to treat it."

Before Stoker could ask him about Mina, he shot out to the next bay, and was quickly replaced by a nurse who told him she had simply been accompanying a *Carpathia* passenger on her vacation, "and then this happened." She had wheeled in a converted bar cart, on which a variety of medical supplies were arrayed. After cleaning the wounded area with an antiseptic that stung like a thousand bee stings, she coated it with a soothing unguent that smelled of cloves. "This ought to numb it a bit," she said, "but it's going to smart for weeks, I'm afraid." She wound a clean bandage under his chin and over the top of his head. Like a mummy, he reflected.

"Worse things can happen," Stoker said softly, and she put a consoling hand on the ripped shoulder of his shirt.

Recovered enough now to reconnoiter on his own, he poked his head out of the bay. There must have been another thirty or forty little enclosures, and he was determined to inspect each one before, if need be, searching the rest of the ship.

In some, a chaise longue had been deployed, and women were splayed across them under blankets, some moaning, some not so much asleep as utterly unconscious. In others, people sat speechless, staring at the floor, unable no doubt to stop reliving the horrors of the night. An elderly man in a torn tailcoat, someone Stoker had last seen dining in the Café Parisien, was sitting with his frostbitten feet in a tub of warm water, a cigarette dangling from his fingers. He did not even raise his weary eyes.

Stoker had nearly given up when he passed an alcove where a brittle old woman, a poultice on her forehead, lay beneath a pile of blankets, and another woman, whom he momentarily mistook for a servant, was seated by the bed with her back to him. Her hands, lying flat in her lap, were bandaged.

He tried to say her name, but his throat was still so parched nothing came out at first. He touched her sleeve, and she said, assuming he must be the nurse come to relieve her, "I have to go now. Someone else will have to attend to this woman."

But then she turned her ashen face up toward him. "Bram."

"Mina," he whispered, and she rose, throwing her arms around his neck. He wrapped his own arms around her, and felt her hot tears streaming down his undamaged cheek.

"I had given up hope," she said, between sobs.

"Never do that," he murmured in her ear. "Never do that."

How long they stood that way, he could not say. From his point of view, forever would have been just fine. The woman on the bed did not stir . . . but something about the sharp cut of her jawline and the wisps of dyed blonde hair, darker from the water, straggling from under the poultice, alerted him to who she was.

"My God, she made it?"

Mina nodded, and they separated enough to look at her.

"Did *he*?" she suddenly asked, fearfully.

"No."

"Small blessings."

"Is she expected to revive?"

"The doctor said the exposure was probably too much. He gave her a shot of morphine."

Stoker went to the bedside, still holding Mina by one hand.

Although Winifred's lids were shut, her eyeballs were jerking about beneath them; it was the only sign of life. The sockets had taken on an ochre cast. Fitting, he thought, as he hovered over her.

Perhaps sensing his presence, Winifred's eyes fluttered open, looking straight up in terror before realizing she was off the boat, and safe. Then, she turned her head enough to take in Stoker and Mina . . . and her expression changed again. The jawline firmed, the eyes took on that basilisk stare.

"Bartholomew?" she mouthed.

"Drowned," Stoker answered.

"You . . . lie."

He didn't reply. *A viper to the end,* he thought.

Which came suddenly. It looked as if she were mustering the strength to issue some last imprecation, even managing to raise her head from the pillow, when the effort proved too much. Her mouth went slack and her head fell back. Her angry eyes stayed stubbornly open, but whatever they were envisioning—some concocted glimpse of paradise, or the hell she so richly deserved—he could never have guessed.

Nor cared.

CHAPTER SEVENTY-FOUR

LONDON

Stoker told the coachman to stop across the street from his house on St. George's Square.

"It's pouring out," Mina said, "at least let him turn around at the corner and leave you off in front."

"No, this is fine," he said, as the carriage came to a halt. Looking out the little window, he could see the rain splashing on his front steps and gusts of wind battering the white shutters. It was only afternoon, but the lights were on inside. Florence was sure to be at home; Wednesday afternoon was when she received visitors.

How, he wondered, would she receive him? Meticulous as he had always been when planning anything for the stage of the Lyceum, this was one scene he had not properly rehearsed, or envisioned.

"Don't forget to apply the salve to your face," Mina said, "morning and night. Otherwise it will never heal."

"And you? Are you going to take care of those hands?" he said, taking them in his own. Her palms were still rough from the wounds the oars had inflicted.

"I will if you will."

He looked down at their hands entwined, then out the window again. Had someone just parted the lace curtains in the parlor?

"I wish you weren't going there," he said. "Are you determined?"

"Have you ever known me not to be?"

"No."

"It's the only way to end it all. To close the circle, as it were."

Much as he would have liked to dispute the point, he couldn't. There was a logic to her plan, as unequivocal as it was mysterious.

"I'll be back in the fall at the latest."

Fall. It seemed so very far away, and in his heart, as much as in his weary limbs, he was not sure he'd be there to welcome her home. Ever since that night at sea, he'd had a cold spot in his lungs and an unremitting ache in his bones that no amount of brandy or blankets could assuage.

But there it was again, an unmistakable parting of the curtain lace.

"She's seen us," he said.

Mina instinctively slumped back in her seat and out of sight. "Just the coach maybe."

"I must be going," he said, taking hold of the walking stick that he had bought in New York to replace the one that now lay miles deep in the north Atlantic . . . resting with the souls of over fifteen hundred of his fellow passengers.

"Yes, you must. But how I am going to miss you."

He squeezed her hands in acknowledgment, but when she unthinkingly went to kiss his cheek, he winced, and she apologized.

"Oh, how could I?" she said, with a laugh. "When I come back to London, it will be smooth again, and your beard will have completely returned to its former glory."

"That should prove to be a mighty incentive."

"I don't need any more than I already have."

The horse whinnied, unhappy at standing still in the pelting rain.

"Here's for the driver," Stoker said, abruptly handing her some money and cracking open the rear door. He could not bear to prolong this parting for another second. Putting out his cane first, he descended to the street.

The front door of his house opened, and framed in the golden light, he saw Florence with one hand still on the knob, the wind rustling her skirts. In his breast, he felt such a maelstrom of emotions—grief at parting from Mina, gratitude that he had lived long enough to return home to die in his own bed (for he knew the end could not be far off), and, beneath it all, a sense that he had truly achieved a great and noble deed. At last. In his *Dracula*, it had been the professor, Van Helsing, who finally unmasked and destroyed the monster. But in real life it was he, Bram Stoker, who had been the hero of the tale . . . even if it would never be known, or believed, by anyone but the woman from whom he had just parted.

Picking his way across the wet cobblestones, he heard the wheels creak and the horse's hooves splashing through a puddle as the carriage rolled off down the street. He resisted the urge to watch it go.

And then, one by one, he was climbing the steps to his house and its open door.

CHAPTER SEVENTY-FIVE

When it came to climbing, the younger Cezar was no match for his late father. More than once, Mina found herself leading the way up the vertiginous mountain slopes, with Cezar stumbling behind. Nor did he share his father's temperament. If there had been anyone else willing to make the trek, she'd have hired him first.

"Camp," he said now, for the tenth time that day. "We should make camp here for the night."

"No, we don't need to. There's still another hour or two of daylight, and we can make it to where we're going."

But could they? There were a dozen different routes, all of them difficult, up the mountainside, and it wasn't easy to recall which one had taken her to the cave. Seventeen years had passed since her first ascent, and though she could still handle the climb, it came at a much higher cost. Her backpack seemed to weigh twice what it used to, her knees complained at every step, and her arms ached from clinging to one rock or ledge after another.

Not to mention the trouble she had encountered at the village of Sinaia where the townsfolk had not forgotten the misfortunes of her last arrival there.

The moment she had shown up a few days before, she could hear her name flitting from one mouth to another like a hummingbird in a honeysuckle patch. When she walked down the one dirt road in the center of the town, dark glances were thrown her way, and hands went up in various signs to ward off the evil eye. At the inn, she was told they had no rooms available, even though she knew not a single guest was registered there. She had to bribe a blacksmith to let her share a straw-filled stall with his dray horse, and when he'd returned late at night, in a drunken haze, she had had to fend off his advances with the hunting knife that never left her side.

"Gypsy witch," he'd spat at her, reeling out the stable doors. "Find someplace else to sleep tomorrow."

She'd opted for the woods, on the outskirts of the town. In the hard-packed earth she could still discern the ruts made by the wagon wheels of the caravans that had used this spot for time immemorial . . . the same Gypsies, no doubt, who had swindled Radu out of the gold box, and then lived to regret their perfidy. Now, it nestled in a velvet pouch at the bottom of her coat pocket.

Stopping to catch her breath and look out over the craggy Carpathian landscape, she was taken back to those days when she had been filled with such a sense of purpose and inexhaustible stores of energy. She had learned so much since then, about the limits of life, the compromises and concessions one had to make, the unavoidable obstacles and, yes, the hard-won victories. Her journey had been unimaginably strange—who would ever have thought she'd battle soul-stealing monsters in the tunnels under London, or nearly perish in one of the young century's greatest calamities? But in some ways it was the path her father had set her on. He had always believed in her abilities, and to him, like her, convention meant conformity—both of which were to be spurned.

"What about that?" Cezar said, pointing with his staff to yet another cave under a barren precipice. "What's wrong with that one?"

"It's not the right one."

"You think you'll know it when you see it?" he countered. "They're all the same."

It wasn't a point worth arguing about, though she could tell he wanted to. She wondered, and not for the first time, if he would abandon her in the night.

They climbed higher, the sun descending behind the neighboring peaks—the Old Women of local lore—whose jagged and forbidding outlines took on an ominous purple cast. It was only when she had reached the height from which she attained the same perspective on the Old Women as before that she looked at each cavern with special interest. The hailstorm had driven them—old Cezar, Anton, Radu, and herself—into a black hole in the mountainside, where they had made a fire close to the entrance. The first four or five caves showed no such signs, but just as she was about to concede defeat for the night, she found it.

A few yards inside: charred sticks—the remains of old Cezar's walking staff—and ashes from the pages torn from her journal.

"Here," she said, and Cezar all but collapsed on the spot. He threw down his pack and slumped against a rocky wall, slurping from his metal canteen, but with such a surly look in his eye that she built the fire herself and made the hot stew. He ate it without a word of thanks, then scrunched himself up in a ball against a wall of the cave, a woolen blanket pulled up over his head.

With nightfall came the mountain wind, howling around the mouth of the cave.

Mina, meanwhile, waited. Cezar had asked her, repeatedly, what the point of this climb was—"Radu used to claim he found a treasure, but he was cheated out of it. Is there a treasure up here?"—and she had told him she was simply looking to record some geological and historical observations. Her real purpose had to remain concealed. If she had learned anything in life, it was that avarice could overrule reason.

When she was satisfied that Cezar's snoring indicated he was fast asleep, she got up and removed from her backpack one of the new electric torches. If only she'd had this on her first expedition, she thought. A fiber tube with a brass cap on one end and a bull's-eye lens at the other, it contained two batteries that, when it was switched on, provided an intermittent light. Some called it a "flashlight" for that reason. It was a most useful device, and as she crept toward the back of the cave, she used it to illuminate the ancient paintings on the walls. Here were the bats with outspread wings, the crocodiles and snarling hyenas, and finally, the robed figure in the helmet with protruding horns. But this time the figure looked different to her. This time, it strongly recalled an image she had seen on the tarot cards displayed by William Stead. The peculiar helmet, the nicks, a dozen of them now that she counted, chiseled into the rock around her head to simulate radiance . . . it was, unmistakably, the High Priestess, the first card he had drawn for her reading. The card he claimed represented who she was.

Which meant that these bones lying below it, adorned with colored beads and flecks of gold, were not the bones of a pharaoh or a king or even a priest—they were a woman's bones, and this shadow, secreted in the gold box, belonged to the priestess, too. Mina had to squat down on her haunches just to assimilate it all. A rush of thoughts and images went through her mind—from the old Gypsy's funeral pyre to the sight of János Szabó sliding down the coal chute and into the *Demeter*'s furnace—and for the first time she thought she understood something that had puzzled her all along. The gold box that had brought such misfortune to others had never harmed her. Indeed, it had acted at times as her protector. The High Priestess had recognized in her a kindred soul, perhaps even a direct descendant of the ancient race to which she had once ministered.

The flashlight went out, and while she let it recharge, she took from the pocket of her coat the velvet pouch containing the gold box. Now, more than ever, she knew that what she was doing was the only way to right the wrong that had been committed, and restore the natural order.

"I'm sorry we ever disturbed your rest," she said softly, and feeling for the skeletal fingers in the dark, she placed the box beneath them.

She switched the light back on, and in its sudden glare, she saw, standing silently above her, Cezar clutching the canteen in his fist. The flash startled him, enough so that when he swung his arm down, he struck her only a glancing blow to the head. She toppled to one side, and lay there, stunned, while he reached across her to pry the box free.

Mina heard the tiniest little sound, the snap of the latch opening, and then, in the time it took her to clear her head, a scream. She groped for the electric torch, turned its beam up and, in its white light, saw Cezar flailing about, fighting off an invisible assailant. All she could see was a shadow, swiftly wrapping round him like a winding sheet. Everything but his head was engulfed. His eyes were bulging, his mouth was open wide, as if the very breath was being squeezed out of him. Only a gurgle emerged from his throat, and then that, too, stopped, as he crumpled in a heap to the ground. The shadow released its embrace, swirling away like smoke from a chimney, and a second later, she heard another tiny snap.

She sat up and put her fingers to the side of her head. There was blood on them, but she'd only been grazed. Nothing was broken but her skin.

Cezar lay still. She crawled to his side, but he was as dead as the dented canteen still somehow clutched in his hand.

The box lay on the rocky floor of the cave, and she picked it up and once more put it where it belonged, lacing the disarticulated fingers across it.

The flashlight went out again, and in the dark Mina lay down, wearily, beside the ragged skeleton, feeling not fear, but the strangest and most comforting sort of safety she had ever known. She fell into a deep sleep, and during the night, Bram came to her in a dream; in the morning, when she awoke, she had accepted the fact that he would not be there to welcome her when she returned to London. He had gone on already, to a place, sadly, where she could not follow him.

She packed her kit, and before leaving the cave, offered a brief benediction over the stiffened body of Cezar, which she covered with his blanket. He would have to keep company there, perhaps forever, with the bones he had hoped to pillage.

Then she stepped outside, shielding her eyes from the brilliant sunlight glinting off the mountain peaks all around her. Her head still smarted from the blow, but the air was bracing, the sky was blue, and the wind was at her back. The journey would be long and dangerous; she would have to forge a path through the dark forests of Transylvania in order to avoid Sinaia entirely, but she would never feel entirely alone—not so long as she carried in her heart the two most beloved companions of all. Her father, and Bram.

POSTSCRIPT

A short time after the sinking of the *Titanic*, Bram Stoker died in his bed at 26 St. George's Square, London. He was sixty-four years old, and the cause of death was listed as exhaustion. His body was cremated four days later at Golders Green (where, coincidentally, Sir Henry Irving had been cremated seven years before), and his ashes were interred in a columbarium there in late April 1912.

His wife, Florence, lived until May 25, 1937, largely supported by the income from the renewed interest in *Dracula* and Stoker's other writings. She died at her home in Knightsbridge, and two days later she, too, was cremated, her ashes scattered in the garden outside the columbarium that housed her late husband's remains.

In 1961, Noel Stoker's ashes were added to the urn, which is kept under close supervision to this day.

AUTHOR'S NOTE

In writing historical fiction—much less *supernatural* historical fiction— there's always the question of what ground rules to set. What's fact, what's not, and where are the lines drawn?

In this novel, like most of my previous books, I have tried to keep my departures from the historical record to a minimum. Bram Stoker was indeed the manager of the Lyceum Theatre, he did indeed work for Henry Irving, the first actor ever to be knighted. He wrote his most famous book, *Dracula*, in 1897. He did enjoy evenings at the very real Beefsteak Club; he did marry the Dublin beauty Oscar Wilde had once courted; he was in fact a burly fellow who'd excelled in sports at Trinity College. The Hungarian linguist Arminius Vambéry was also real, and he has often been cited as a possible inspiration for the character of Professor Van Helsing, who hunts down and destroys the vampire Count. In fact, his name actually appears, as a kind of shout-out, in the text of *Dracula*.

In the one big departure from the historical record, Stoker did not sail on the *Titanic*. But he died shortly after it sank, and it was the nearness of those dates that first planted the notion of joining them in my head—that, and the epochal nature of the sinking. Historians have often looked back on that maritime tragedy as the end of an era, and the harbinger of the even greater cataclysm of the First World War. The contemporaneous demise of my protagonist and the last gasp of the previous century's Gilded Age resonated to my mind.

As for the *Titanic* material, the names of the officers and crew are all authentic, as are some of the incidental facts such as its launching, but the price of Stoker and Mina Harcourt's stateroom would have been more than even a generous loan from a friend could probably have covered. The crusading journalist and paranormal enthusiast, William T. Stead, was indeed a passenger on the boat, on his way to attend a peace conference in New York, and was one of the sinking's most famous casualties. The American mining millionaire, Margaret Brown, who came to be known as the Unsinkable Molly Brown thereafter, was a heroine of the doomed voyage, and did much to help the third-class survivors who arrived in New York with nothing at all to their name.

Oh, and about the missing binoculars? It's true—the two men in the crow's nest on that fateful night—Reginald Lee and Frederick Fleet—did not have any, nor were binoculars considered mandatory equipment at the time, anyway. As it would happen, the liner that rescued the survivors of the wreck was in fact called the *Carpathia*, after the region where this story began. That little coincidence, I considered a gift from the gods of fiction.

The immense Carpathian Sphinx, which appears in the opening chapters of this book, is real and still broods atop a mountain in Romania; it remains among the world's most mysterious monoliths.

In regard to the supernatural elements of this book, well . . . they're supernatural. That said, a mania for all things Egyptian really did sweep England at the time, and the accounts of various mummification rituals and ancient Egyptian belief systems, though somewhat simplified here, are true.

For anyone inspired to read more about Bram Stoker and his world, I can heartily recommend the nonfiction book, *Something in the Blood: The Untold Story of Bram Stoker, the Man Who Wrote Dracula*, by David J. Skal. For those interested in the *Titanic*, there are a thousand books on the subject, but one that I found especially readable and useful in my research was entitled *Gilded Lives, Fatal Voyage* by Hugh Brewster.

ABOUT THE AUTHOR

Robert Masello is an award-winning journalist, television writer, and bestselling author of many novels and nonfiction books. His supernatural thrillers have been published in seventeen languages and include *The Jekyll Revelation*, *The Einstein Prophecy*, *The Romanov Cross*, *The Medusa Amulet*, and *Blood and Ice*. His articles and essays have appeared in such prominent publications as the *Los Angeles Times*, the *Washington Post*, *New York* magazine, *People*, *Newsday*, *Parade*, *Glamour*, *Town and Country*, *Travel and Leisure*, and the *Wilson Quarterly*. An honors graduate of Princeton University, Masello has also taught and lectured nationwide, from the Columbia University Graduate School of Journalism to Claremont McKenna College, where he served as Visiting Lecturer in Literature for six years. A long-standing member of the Writers Guild of America, he now lives in Santa Monica, California. Visit him at www.robertmasello.com.